<u>Pigeons from</u> <u>Hell</u>
<u>and other tales of</u> <u>Horror and</u> <u>Mystery</u>

by

Robert E. Howard

British Library Cataloguing-in-Publication Data
A catalogue record for this book is available from
the British Library

Contents

Introduction

to

Pigeons from Hell and other tales of

Horror and Mystery

By

Robert E. Howard

"Hither came Conan, the Cimmerian, black-haired, sullen-eyed, sword in hand, a thief, a reaver, a slayer, with gigantic melancholies and gigantic mirth, to tread the jeweled thrones of the Earth under his sandaled feet."

Conan the Cimmerian, better known as Conan the Barbarian, is to Robert E. Howard what James Bond is to Ian Fleming – so synonymous with his creator that he threatens to overshadow him. Conan's popular imprint rivals that of Edgar Rice Burroughs' Tarzan – another civilization-shunning adventurer of the wild – and the barbarian has spawned almost countless adaptations since his first appearance in the pages of *Weird Tales* more than seventy years ago. As recently as 2011, there have been new cinematic and novelistic adaptations of the now-archetypal sword-and-sorcery fantasy.

However, over the course of his tragically short life – Howard published his first story in 1924, but committed suicide twelve years later, aged just thirty – Howard penned a vast amount of stories that had nothing to do with the rightful King of Aquilonia. Indeed, most of the Conan tales were not even published during his lifetime, and constituted only a small part of his earnings. Howard wrote in a range of genres, creating almost countless characters, and to many of his fans it is a great shame that his diverse oeuvre has been so overshadowed by his most famous creation.

Pigeons from Hell and other tales of Horror and Mystery aims, in some small part, to redress this balance. The twenty-one contained within this collection represent a brief cross-section of Howard's best tales outside of the Conan series – while still avoiding his more out-of-character work, such as his erotic 'spicy tales' and straight comedy. The publication dates stretch from 1925, when he had barely been writing professionally for a year, to the sixties, three decades after after his death. The tales themselves range greatly in style, from weirdly hard-boiled detective trails to flights of Lovecraftian horror.

'In the Forest of Villefore' and 'Wolfshead' form the first two parts of a trilogy starring de Montour, an unwilling werewolf hailing from Normandy. The first tale essentially acts as prologue for the second, and the switch in first-person narration across the tales – from de Montour himself, to a separate observer in the unwitting presence of a full moon — serves to give our freshly turned werewolf an air of distance and terror. Early on in 'Wolfshead', we are served a tantalising slice of dramatic irony, as de Montour tells our ignorant narrator "The moon is almost full, is it not, Monsieur?... Monsieur, whatever you do, be sure you bar and bolt your door tonight!"

However, in a testament to the skill and subtlety of Howard's pen, the werewolf de Montour is gradually and effectively cast as a sympathetic, even tragic character: "My hands are red," he laments, "my soul doomed to everlasting flames, my mind is torn with remorse for my crimes. And yet I can do nothing to help myself." 'Wolfshead' is truly an excellent, perfectly pitched tale; little wonder that it gained Howard his first *Weird Tales* front-cover illustration, in April of 1926.

'The Dream Snake', published in the February 1928 edition of *Weird Tales,* is the first of many Howard tales set in the Southwest United States. Just as writers such as Flannery O'Connor and William Faulkner self-consciously utilised the tools and tropes of the Gothic within a Deep South setting, over a number of years Howard tried (almost single-handedly) to conjure a 'Weird Southwest' out of his native Texas and the 'Arklatexoma' region. Essentially a pure horror story in the told-beside-the-campire vein, 'The Dream Snake' is notable for its excellent portrayal of a man in the grip of a "hellish" and recurring dream that has haunted him "since babyhood" (Howard himself suffered from a crippling phobia of snakes). The power and potential of dreams to either corrupt or inspire was a common theme in pulp tales of the late twenties, due in large part to the popularization of Freudian psychoanalysis occurring at the time.

'The Hyena', which appeared in the March 1928 edition of *Weird Tales,* is a story which draws on African mythology and folklore (a lifelong interest of Howard's) in presenting a shapeshifting and "horribly human" 'werehyena'. 'Sea Curse', which appeared two months later, is notable as one of Howard's standalone naval stories. Its gloomy depiction of sea life — "heaving grey" ships "stained with the memory of horrid crimes" brave the "restless grey ocean" — and its use of the *Flying Dutchman*-inspired vanishing vessel, render it reminiscent of the Gothic sea fiction in vogue during the nineteenth century.

'Rattle of Bones', which first appeared in the June 1929 edition of *Weird Tales,* features the wandering hero Solomon Kane — arguably Howard's most famous character creation to have never been played by Arnold Schwarzenegger. Over the course of his author's writing life, Kane appeared in nine (somewhat disjointed) short stories, as well as a number of poems and fragments. A turn-of-the-17th century puritan, he is one part sword-and-sorcery, à la Conan, but his adventures are far more horror-tinged, echoing the classical Gothic with their windswept European locations. 'Rattle of Bones', for example, opens with Kane and a mysterious Frenchman entering tavern with a "forbidding aspect," to which, we are told by its host, "few [guests] come twice."

'The Fearsome Touch of Death', which appeared in the February 1930 edition of *Weird Tales*, owes a great debt to Edgar Allen Poe. A pure tale of psychological terror, the story plays heavily on the hallucinogenic power of "a vivid imagination," and the potential power "lurking back in the dark corners of the brain." Its setting – a man sitting alongside a corpse, with the darkness of night exhibiting its "eerie domination over the human mind" – is a classically Poe-esque device, allowing for an unsettling, nervous meditation on mortality with in amusingly unlikely set of circumstances.

'The Children of the Night' is the first of several of Howard's stories to incorporate references to Lovecraft's famous Cthulhu Mythos. It appeared in the May 1931 edition of *Weird Tales*, not long after Howard had initiated a written correspondence with the legendary weird fiction writer which would stretch for many years. By this time, Howard had become a well-known and well-paid author – in 1931, he earned from his fiction alone the equivalent of $20,000. 'The Children of the Night' features a race of beasts with "hideously slanted eyes," "yellow fangs" and "hissing reptilian speech" who are stamped out by an Aryan tribe – in this regard it is one of those Howard tales which, even as it reads brilliantly, dwells on on genealogical anxieties and racist notions which by today's standards are more than a little discomforting.

'The Black Stone' and its sequel of sorts, 'The Thing on the Roof', are the most overtly Lovecraftian of Howard's stories. Howard himself told fellow author August Derleth in a letter that they "were written more as experiments than anything else," and admitted to Lovecraft that 'The Black Stone' "sounds as if I were trying, in my feeble and blunderingly crude way, to deliberately copy your style." Appearing in *Weird Tales* in November 1931 and February 1932 respectively, both stories are nonetheless enjoyable yarns, with playfully intertextual plots reminiscent of a less dense, more action-packed Borges.

'The Horror from the Mound', published in the May 1932 edition of *Weird Tales,* follows on from 'The Dream Snake' in being part of Howard's 'Weird Southwest' series. As the protagonist, a foolhardy cowboy named Steve Brill remarks to himself early on in the tale, "Of all the continent of North America there is no section so haunted by tales of lost or hidden treasure as is the Southwest." ('Treasure' here meaning both literary and monetary riches.) 'The Horror from the Mound' is also, by Howard's standards, highly autobiographical; Brill is,described as a "true son of the iron-bodied pioneers who wrenched West Texas from the wilderness" – something Howard undoubtedly (somewhat aspirationally) envisioned himself as being. A masterful story, 'The Horror from the Mound' predicts the explosions of 'Weird Westerns' that arrived towards the end of the 20th century, with their ubiquitous ghost towns, haunted mines and Native American myths.

In something of a break with tradition, Howard's 'People of the Dark' appeared not in *Weird Tales,* but in similarly themed *Strange Tales,* in June of 1932. Often regarded as his greatest 'past-life' tale, it again draws again on Howard's lifelong fascination with ancient myths and legends, this time of the Celtic variety. The reader may be surprised to encounter a central character with a "square-cut black mane," "massive naked limbs" and powerful torso" named Conan; indeed, 'People of the Dark' divides opinion between Howard scholars as to whether it is a forerunner to his famous series, or merely a standalone tale with an identically named protagonist. Despite slightly counteracting the ethos of this anthology, the story is included here so that informed readers may make up their own mind, and also because it is a good example of an instance in which Howard mixes an early brand of sword-and-sorcery with his more Lovecraftian horror streak. 'The Cairn on the Headland' (again published in *Strange Tales,* in January of 1933), meanwhile, is another example of the 'past-life' genre which Howard experimented with. Best read in sequence with the preceding 'The Grey God Passes', it is notable for its intermingling of Celtic and Scandinavian mythology, and for its oddly passive protagonist.

'Worms of the Earth', which appeared in the November 1932 edition of *Weird Tales,* features another of Howard's recurring protagonists, Bran Mak Morn – the last king of the ancient Celtic tribe of Picts. Having Scottish ancestry, Howard was fascinated with the country's history, and though his Bran Mak Morn tales are heavily imagined, they do bear some resemblance to real accounts of the country's past. The series as a whole plays heavily on Howard's interest in social Darwinism – the Picts are a "savage," untameable" race being gradually wiped out by the Romans – and also flirts once more with Lovecraft's Cthulhu Mythos. 'Worms of the Earth' is notable for being the only Bran Mak Morn story actually told from the King of the Pict's point of view. As an aside, it is of note that *Cerebus the Aardvark* – the longest-running English-language comic ever by a single creative team – features a character named Bran Mac Mufin, a parodic homage to Howard's character.

In the spring of 1933, Otis Adelbert Kline – another pulp author, most famous for his supposed literary feud with Tarzan creator Edgar Rice Burroughs – became Howard's agent. A shrewd businessman, Kline encouraged Howard to attempt some stories for the detective fiction magazines, which were hugely popular at the time thanks to the previous success of authors such as Dashiell Hammett. Although sceptical, Howard took his agent's advice, and went on to produce more than twenty detective stories.

In much the same way that he wrote extensively within the conventional Western mould, yet also spun an idiosyncratic version of the genre with his 'Weird West' series, Howard penned both fairly 'straight' detective fiction ,and his own brand of 'weird menace' tales. 'Black Talons', which appeared in the December 1933 edition of *Strange Detective Stories,* is an excellent version of the latter. Within the tale, the fairly one-dimensional *whodunnit* element of the plot takes a back-seat to Howard's imaginatively gruesome violence, swirling "Oriental mythologies," and the presence of an unknown creature with "a misshapen head" and "vague, monstrous shoulders." The appearance of a pair of detectives who, rather than being an unshakeable duo, harbour internal suspicions about each other's guilt, is also an unusual and refreshing device — one could even see it as lightly prefiguring the shadier, more cynical tone that would overcome detective fiction towards the end of the 20th century.

'Fangs of Gold', published in the February 1934 edition of *Strange Detective Stories,* is the second of Howard's ten-part series starring Steve Harrison, and is a good example of his more conventional detective fiction. Harrison is a fairly typical detective in the hardboiled mode — he is tough, short-spoken, and has "an almost obsessional preference for working alone." The plot, meanwhile, is highly clue-driven, and loaded with red herrings. However, even in this instance, Howard can't resist infusing the tale with voodoo, human sacrifice, and Haitian worshippers of the "Great Serpent." 'Graveyard Rats', first published in the February 1936 edition of *Thrilling Mystery,* is another Steve Harrison tale, notable mainly for its intense psychological horror, and its foreshadowing (with rats in place of pigeons) of Howard's famous tale, 'Pigeons from Hell'.

'The Fire of Asshurbanipal' is the first of twenty-one stories contained in the collection to have been published posthumously, following Howard's suicide in June of 1936. Submitted by his father, Isaac, and published in the December 1936 edition of *Weird Tales,* 'The Fire of Asshurbanipal' again has a Lovecraftian tone, and features, in typical Howard a style, a "lost desert city" and band of marauding Bedouin. Howard was an enthusiast of Assyrian history, and this story is a good example of his skill at maintaining a level of exposition that doesn't detract from the tension of the narrative.

The penultimate tale in the collection, 'Pigeons from Hell', is arguably Howard's single best-known story outside of his Conan series. Published posthumously by *Weird Tales* in May of 1938, it is a masterwork of Southern Gothic fiction, with an infectious, unsettling air of decay, madness and gore which represents Howard at the peak of his powers. Early on in the tale, the protagonist, Griswell, senses "a presence of fear and lunacy crouching in a dark corner"; a description which fits the tale itself perfectly. Stephen King once called 'Pigeons from Hell' "one of the finest horror stories of our century," and in its intensely psychological, needling terror, it is, in fact, quite King-esque. Within his entire body of work, Conan stories included, 'Pigeons from Hell' is one of Howard's finest works.

The final story, 'Delenda Est', is a good example of the standalone fantasy tales which continued to appear long after Howard's passing. First published in *Worlds of Fantasy* magazine in 1968, its title alludes to the Latin phrase *Carthago delenda est* ("Carthage must be destroyed"), and the tale itself reveals its author's deep interest in yet another period of ancient history. This time our protagonist – in typical Howard fashion, "the strongest man in the known world" – was born leads his mythical tribe South to surreptitiously attack a wilting Rome. However, the tale is given a weird twist when Howard presents us with the ghostly, reincarnated form of a famous Carthaginian military-man who remains extremely bitter about "Roman greed and treachery," and who Howard waits until the very last line of the tale to name. 'Delenda Est' is an excellent illustration of Howard's penchant for mixing hard historical fact with narrative flights of fancy.

Hopefully, then, the stories contained herein will help broaden readers' appreciation of Robert Ervin Howard's fiction. Ultimately, *Pigeons from Hell and other tales of Horror and Mystery* can never do anything but scratch the very top surface of his work; it can, however, act as an effective introduction to a body of work which can initially seem impenetrably vast and varied.

Howard was by all accounts a complex and

tragic man: In 1925, at the age of just nineteen, he declared to fellow author Tevis Clyde Smith that he had "no fear of the Hereafter" because "an orthodox hell could hardly be more torture than my life has been." In a letter to Lovecraft eight years later, he wrote "I hardly think life in this age is worth effort of living," and the circumstances of his suicide would suggest it was highly premeditated. However, tragic as Howard's ultimately losing battle with crippling depression and woe was – and many of his personal writings do make for painful reading – it is possible to also see it as the wellspring for much of his best work. Even at its most pulpish, Howard's fiction draws strongly on its author's lifelong existential angst. The doomed loneliness of so many of his protagonists, and the abiding atmosphere of lunacy and terror infecting so many of his tales, is rooted firmly in the real. Behind the lurid *Weird Tales* covers and larger-than-life characters, Howard was a writer who dealt very directly with the pains and perils of being human.

As a final point, readers should be wary of viewing Howard's themes of civilization, primitivism and bloody conquer too simply. Although Howard existed at a time when imperial benevolence and the validity of eugenics were accepted facts – and reading his work can at times feel like a celebration of "strong races" subjugating what he describes in 'People of the Dark' as "loathsome survivors of an outworn age" – his views weren't quite so straightforward as they might first seem. As an illustration, it is worth quoting a large section of a letter he wrote to Lovecraft, shortly after the 1935 invasion of Ethiopia by the Kingdom of Italy:

> You express amazement at my statement that 'civilized' men try to justify their looting, butchering and plundering by claiming that these things are done in the interests of art, progress and culture. That this simple statement of fact should cause surprise, amazes me in return. People claiming to possess superior civilization have always veneered their rapaciousness by such claims... Your friend Mussolini is a striking modern-day example. In that speech of his I heard translated he spoke feelingly of the expansion of civilization. From time to time he has announced; 'The sword and civilization go hand in hand!... Africa must be brought into civilization!' It is not, of course, because of any selfish motive that he has invaded a helpless country, bombing, burning and gassing both combatants and non-combatants by the thousands. Oh, no, according to his own assertions it is all in the interests of art, culture and progress, just as the German war- lords were determined to confer the advantages of Teutonic Kultur on a benighted world, by fire and lead and steel. Civilized nations never, never have selfish

motives for butchering, raping and looting; only horrid barbarians have those.

A complex and troubled man, then, but above all an important writer. As a master of the spectral and macabre, not to mention the founder of an entire genre, Howard absolutely deserves the ongoing expansion of what his legions of fans have dubbed the 'Second Howard Boom' of the early 21st century.

Aside from his tens of thousands of words of prose, Howard also found time to pen hundreds of poems. In a small effort to revive yet another neglected section of his oeuvre, and also perhaps to end on something of a lighter note, the following is a short Howard poem, taken from a letter to Tevis Clyde Smith dated 23rd June, 1926:

> My soul is a blaze
> Of passionate desire;
> My soul is a blaze
> That sets my pen on fire.

In the Forest of Villefore

The sun had set. The great shadows came striding over the forest. In the weird twilight of a late summer day, I saw the path ahead glide on among the mighty trees and disappear. And I shuddered and glanced fearfully over my shoulder. Miles behind lay the nearest village . . . miles ahead the next.

I looked to left and to right as I strode on, and anon I looked behind me. And anon I stopped short, grasping my rapier, as a breaking twig betokened the going of some small beast. Or was it a beast?

But the path led on and I followed, because, forsooth, I had naught else to do.

As I went I bethought me, 'My own thoughts will rout me, if I be not aware. What is there in this forest, except perhaps the creatures that roam it, deer and the like? Tush, the foolish legends of those villagers!'

And so I went and the twilight faded into dusk. Stars began to blink and the leaves of the trees murmured in the faint breeze. And then I stopped short, my sword leaping to my hand, for just ahead, around a curve of the path, someone was singing. The words I could not distinguish, but the accent was strange, almost barbaric.

I stepped behind a great tree, and the cold sweat beaded my forehead. Then the singer came in sight, a tall, thin man, vague in the twilight. I shrugged my shoulders. A *man* I did not fear. I sprang out, my point raised.

'Stand!'

He showed no surprise. 'I prithee, handle thy blade with care, friend,' he said.

Somewhat ashamed, I lowered my sword.

'I am new to this forest,' I quoth, apologetically. 'I heard talk of bandits. I crave pardon. Where lies the road to Villefore?'

'*Corbleu*, you've missed it,' he answered. 'You should have branched off to the right some distance back. I am going there myself. If you may abide my company, I will direct you.'

I hesitated. Yet why should I hesitate?

'Why, certainly. My name is de Montour, of Normandy.'

'And I am Carolus le Loup.'

'No!' I started back.

He looked at me in astonishment.

'Pardon,' said I; 'the name is strange. Does not *loup* mean wolf?'

'My family were always great hunters,' he answered. He did not offer his hand.

'You will pardon my staring,' said I as we walked down the path, 'but I can hardly see your face in the dusk.'

I sensed that he was laughing, though he made no sound.

'It is little to look upon,' he answered.

I stepped closer and then leaped away, my hair bristling.

'A mask!' I exclaimed. 'Why do you wear a mask, *m'sieu?*'

'It is a vow,' he exclaimed. 'In fleeing a pack of hounds I vowed that if I escaped I would wear a mask for a certain time.'

'Hounds, *m'sieu?*'

'Wolves,' he answered quickly; 'I said wolves.'

We walked in silence for awhile and then my companion said, 'I am surprised that you walk these woods by night. Few people come these ways even in the day.'

'I am in haste to reach the border,' I answered. 'A treaty has been signed with the English, and the Duke of Burgundy should know of it. The people at the village sought to dissuade me. They spoke of . . . a wolf that was purported to roam these woods.'

'Here the path branches to Villefore,' said he, and I saw a narrow, crooked path that I had not seen when I passed it before. It led in amid the darkness of the trees. I shuddered.

'You wish to return to the village?'

'No!' I exclaimed. 'No, no! Lead on.'

So narrow was the path that we walked single file, he leading. I looked well at him. He was taller, much taller than I, and thin, wiry. He was dressed in a costume that smacked of Spain. A long rapier swung at his hip. He walked with long easy strides, noiselessly.

Then he began to talk of travel and adventure. He spoke of many lands and seas he had seen and many strange things. So we talked and went farther and farther into the forest.

I presumed that he was French, and yet he had a very strange accent, that was neither French nor Spanish nor English, not like any language I had ever heard. Some words he slurred strangely and some he could not pronounce at all.

'This path is often used, is it?' I asked.

'Not by many,' he answered and laughed silently. I shuddered. It was very dark and the leaves whispered together among the branches.

'A fiend haunts this forest,' I said.

'So the peasants say,' he answered, 'but I have roamed it oft and have never seen his face.'

Then he began to speak of strange creatures of darkness, and the moon rose and shadows glided among the trees. He looked up at the moon.

'Haste!' said he. 'We must reach our destination before the moon reaches her zenith.'

We hurried along the trail.

'They say,' said I, 'that a werewolf haunts these woodlands.'

'It might be,' said he, and we argued much upon the subject.

'The old women say,' said he, 'that if a werewolf is slain while a wolf, then he is slain, but if he is slain as a man, then his half-soul will haunt his slayer forever. But haste thee, the moon nears her zenith.'

We came into a small moonlit glade and the stranger stopped.

'Let us pause a while,' said he.

'Nay, let us be gone,' I urged; 'I like not this place.'

He laughed without sound. 'Why,' said he, 'this is a fair glade. As good as a banquet hall it is, and many times have I feasted here. Ha, ha, ha! Look ye, I will show you a dance.' And he began bounding here and there, anon flinging back his head and laughing silently. Thought I, the man is mad.

As he danced his weird dance I looked about me. *The trail went not on but stopped in the glade.*

'Come,' said I, 'we must on. Do you not smell the rank, hairy scent that hovers about the glade? Wolves den here. Perhaps they are about us and are gliding upon us even now.'

He dropped upon all fours, bounded higher than my head, and came toward me with a strange slinking motion.

'That dance is called the Dance of the Wolf,' said he, and my hair bristled.

'Keep off!' I stepped back, and with a screech that set the echoes shuddering he leaped for me, and though a sword hung at his belt he did not draw it. My rapier was half out when he grasped my arm and flung me headlong. I dragged him with me and we struck the ground together. Wrenching a hand free I jerked off the mask. A shriek of horror broke from my lips. Beast eyes glittered beneath that mask, white fangs flashed in the moonlight. *The face was that of a wolf.*

In an instant those fangs were at my throat. Taloned hands tore the sword from my grasp. I beat at that horrible face with my clenched fists, but his jaws were fastened on my shoulders, his talons tore at my throat. Then I was on my back. The world was fading. Blindly I struck out. My hand dropped, then closed automatically about the hilt of my dagger, which I had been unable to get at. I drew and stabbed. A terrible, half-bestial bellowing screech. Then I reeled to my feet, free. At my feet lay the werewolf.

I stooped, raised the dagger, then paused, looked up. The moon hovered close to her zenith. *If I slew the thing as a man its frightful spirit would haunt me for ever.* I sat down waiting. The *thing* watched me with flaming wolf eyes. The long wiry limbs seemed to shrink, to crook; hair seemed to grow upon them. Fearing madness, I snatched up the *thing*'s own sword and hacked it to pieces. Then I flung the sword away and fled.

Wolfshead

Fear? Your pardon, Messieurs, but the meaning of fear you do not know. No, I hold to my statement. You are soldiers, adventurers. You have known the charges of regiments of dragoons, the frenzy of wind-lashed seas. But fear, real hair-raising, horror-crawling fear, you have not known. I myself have known such fear; but until the legions of darkness swirl from hell's gate and the world flames to ruin, will never such fear again be known to men.

Hark, I will tell you the tale; for it was many years ago and half across the world; and none of you will ever see the man of whom I tell you, or seeing, know.

Return, then, with me across the years to a day when I, a reckless young cavalier, stepped from the small boat that had landed me from the ship floating in the harbour, cursed the mud that littered the crude wharf, and strode up the landing toward the castle, in answer to the invitation of an old friend, Dom Vincente da Lusto.

Dom Vincente was a strange, far-sighted man – a strong man, one who saw visions beyond the ken of his time. In his veins, perhaps, ran the blood of those old Phoenicians who, the priests tell us, ruled the seas and built cities in far lands, in the dim ages. His plan of fortune was strange and yet successful; few men would have thought of it; fewer could have succeeded. For his estate was upon the western coast of that dark, mystic continent, that baffler of explorers . . . Africa.

There by a small bay had he cleared away the sullen jungle, built his castle and his storehouses, and with ruthless hand had he wrested the riches of the land. Four ships he had: three smaller craft and one great galleon. These plied between his domains and the cities of Spain, Portugal, France, and even England, laden with rare woods, ivory, slaves; the thousand strange riches that Dom Vincente had gained by trade and by conquest.

Aye, a wild venture, a wilder commerce. And yet might he have shaped an empire from the dark land, had it not been for the rat-faced Carlos, his nephew – but I run ahead of my tale.

Look, Messieurs, I draw a map on the table, thus, with finger dipped in wine. Here lay the small, shallow harbour, and here the wide wharves: a landing ran thus, up the slight slope with hut-like warehouses on each side, and here it stopped at a wide, shallow moat. Over it went a narrow drawbridge, and then one was confronted with a high palisade of logs set in the ground. This extended entirely around the castle. The castle itself was built on the model of another, earlier age; being more for strength than beauty. Built of stone brought from a great distance, years of labour and a thousand Negroes toiling beneath the lash had reared its walls, and now, completely, it offered an almost impregnable appearance. Such was the intention of its builders, for Barbary pirates ranged the coasts, and the horror of a native uprising lurked ever near.

A space of about a half-mile on every side of the castle was kept cleared away and roads had been built through the marshy land. All this had required an immense amount of labour, but manpower was plentiful. A present to a chief, and he furnished all that was needed. And Portuguese know how to make men work!

Less than three hundred yards to the east of the castle ran a wide, shallow river, which emptied into the harbour. The name has entirely slipt my mind. It was a heathenish title and I could never lay my tongue to it.

I found that I was not the only friend invited to the castle. It seems that once a year or some such matter, Dom Vincente brought a host of jolly companions to his lonely estate and made merry for some weeks, to make up for the work and solitude of the rest of the year.

In fact, it was nearly night, and a great banquet was in progress when I entered. I was acclaimed with great delight, greeted boisterously by friends and introduced to such strangers as were there.

Entirely too weary to take much part in the revelry, I ate, drank quietly, listened to the toasts and songs, and studied the feasters.

Dom Vincente, of course, I knew, as I had been intimate with him for years; also his pretty niece, Ysabel, who was one reason I had accepted his invitation to come to that stinking wilderness. Her second cousin, Carlos, I knew and disliked – a sly, mincing fellow with a face like a mink's. Then there was my old friend, Luigi Verenza, an Italian; and his flirt of a sister, Marcita, making eyes at the men as usual. Then there was a short, stocky German who called himself Baron von Schiller; and Jean Desmarte, an out-at-the-elbows nobleman of Gascony; and Don Florenzo de Seville, a lean, dark, silent man, who called himself a Spaniard and wore a rapier nearly as long as himself.

·There were others, men and women, but it was long ago and all their names and faces I do not remember. But there was one man whose face somehow drew my gaze as an alchemist's magnet draws steel. He was a leanly-built man of slightly more than medium height, dressed plainly, almost austerely, and he wore a sword almost as long as the Spaniard's.

But it was neither his clothes nor his sword which attracted my attention. It was his face. A refined, high-bred face, it was furrowed deep with lines that gave it a weary, haggard expression. Tiny scars flecked jaw and forehead as if torn by savage claws; I could have sworn the narrow grey eyes had a fleeting, haunted look in their expression at times.

I leaned over to that flirt, Marcita, and asked the name of the man, as it had slipt my mind that we had been introduced.

'De Montour, from Normandy,' she answered. 'A strange man. I don't think I like him.'

'Then he resists your snares, my little enchantress?' I murmured, long friendship making me as immune from her anger as from her wiles. But she chose not to be angry and answered coyly, glancing from under demurely lowered lashes.

I watched de Montour much, feeling somehow a strange fascination. He ate lightly, drank much, seldom spoke, and then only to answer questions.

Presently, toasts making the rounds, I noticed his companions urging him to rise and give a health. At first he refused, then rose, upon their repeated urgings, and stood silent for a moment, goblet raised. He seemed to dominate, to overawe the group of revellers. Then with a mocking, savage laugh, he lifted the goblet above his head.

'To Solomon,' he exclaimed, 'who bound all devils! And thrice cursed be he for that some escaped!'

A toast and a curse in one! It was drunk silently, and with many sidelong, doubting glances.

That night I retired early, weary of the long sea voyage and my head spinning from the strength of the wine, of which Dom Vincente kept such great stores.

My room was near the top of the castle and looked out toward the forests of the south and the river. The room was furnished in crude, barbaric splendour, as was all the rest of the castle.

Going to the window, I gazed out at the arquebusier pacing the castle grounds just inside the palisade; at the cleared space lying unsightly and barren in the moonlight; at the forest beyond; at the silent river.

From the native quarters close to the river bank came the weird twanging of some rude lute, sounding a barbaric melody.

In the dark shadows of the forest some uncanny nightbird lifted a mocking voice. A thousand minor notes sounded – birds, and beasts, and the devil knows what else! Some great jungle cat began a hair-lifting yowling. I shrugged my shoulders and turned from the windows. Surely devils lurked in those sombre depths.

There came a knock at my door and I opened it, to admit de Montour. He strode to the window and gazed at the moon, which rode resplendent and glorious.

'The moon is almost full, is it not, Monsieur?' he remarked, turning to me. I nodded, and I could have sworn that he shuddered.

'Your pardon, Monsieur. I will not annoy you further.' He turned to go, but at the door turned and retraced his steps.

'Monsieur,' he almost whispered, with a fierce intensity, 'whatever you do, be sure you bar and bolt your door tonight!'

Then he was gone, leaving me to stare after him bewilderedly.

I dozed off to sleep, the distant shouts of the revellers in my ears, and though I was weary, or perhaps because of it, I slept lightly. While I never really awoke until morning, sounds and noises seemed to drift to me through my veil of slumber, and once it seemed that something was prying and shoving against the bolted door.

As is to be supposed, most of the guests were in a beastly humour the following day and remained in their rooms most of the morning or else straggled down late. Besides Dom Vincente there were really only three of the masculine members sober: de Montour, the Spaniard, de Seville (as he called himself), and myself. The Spaniard never touched wine, and though de Montour consumed incredible quantities of it, it never affected him in any way.

The ladies greeted us most graciously.

'S'truth, Signor,' remarked that minx Marcita, giving me her hand with a gracious air that was like to make me snicker, 'I am glad to see there are gentlemen among us who care more for our company than for the wine cup; for most of them are most surprisingly befuddled this morning.'

Then with a most outrageous turning of her wondrous eyes, 'Methinks someone was too drunk to be discreet last night . . . or not

drunk enough. For unless my poor senses deceive me much, some-
one came fumbling at my door late in the night.'

'Ha!' I exclaimed in quick anger, 'some – !'

'No. Hush.' She glanced about as if to see that we were alone, then:
'Is it not strange that Signor de Montour, before he retired last
night, instructed me to fasten my door firmly?'

'Strange,' I murmured, but did not tell her that he had told me the
same thing.

'And is it not strange, Pierre, that though Signor de Montour left
the banquet hall even before you did, yet he has the appearance of
one who has been up all night?' I shrugged. A woman's fancies are
often strange.

'Tonight,' she said roguishly, 'I will leave my door unbolted and
see whom I catch.'

'You will do no such thing.'

She showed her little teeth in a contemptuous smile and displayed
a small, wicked dagger.

'Listen, imp. De Montour gave me the same warning he did
you. Whatever he knew, whoever prowled the halls last night, the
object was more apt murder than amorous adventure. Keep
you your doors bolted. The lady Ysabel shares your room, does
she not?'

'Not she. And I send my woman to the slave quarters at night,'
she murmured, gazing mischievously at me from beneath drooping
eyelids.

'One would think you a girl of no character from your talk,' I told
her, with the frankness of youth and of long friendship. 'Walk with
care, young lady, else I tell your brother to spank you.'

And I walked away to pay my respects to Ysabel. The Portuguese
girl was the very opposite of Marcita, being a shy, modest young
thing, not so beautiful as the Italian, but exquisitely pretty in an
appealing, almost childish air. I once had thoughts – Hi ho! to be
young and foolish!

Your pardon, Messieurs. An old man's mind wanders. It was of de
Montour that I meant to tell you . . . de Montour and Dom Vin-
cente's mink-faced cousin.

A band of armed natives were thronged about the gates, kept at a
distance by the Portuguese soldiers. Among them were some score
of young men and women all naked, chained neck to neck. Slaves
they were, captured by some warlike tribe and brought for sale. Dom
Vincente looked them over personally.

Followed a long haggling and bartering, of which I quickly wearied and turned away, wondering that a man of Dom Vincente's rank could so demean himself as to stoop to trade.

But I strolled back when one of the natives of the village nearby came up and interrupted the sale with a long harangue to Dom Vincente.

While they talked de Montour came up, and presently Dom Vincente turned to us and said, 'One of the woodcutters of the village was torn to pieces by a leopard or some such beast last night. A strong young man and unmarried.'

'A leopard? Did they, see it?' suddenly asked de Montour, and when Dom Vincente said no, that it came and went in the night, de Montour lifted a trembling hand and drew it across his forehead, as if to brush away cold sweat.

'Look you, Pierre,' quoth Dom Vincente, 'I have here a slave who, wonder of wonders, desires to be your man. Though the devil only knows why.'

He led up a slim young Jakri, a mere youth, whose main asset seemed a merry grin.

'He is yours,' said Dom Vincente. 'He is goodly trained and will make a fine servant. And look ye, a slave is of an advantage over a servant, for all he requires is food and a loincloth or so with a touch of the whip to keep him in his place.'

It was not long before I learned why Gola wished to be 'my man', choosing me among all the rest. It was because of my hair. Like many dandies of that day, I wore it long and curled, the strands falling to my shoulders. As it happened, I was the only man of the party who so wore my hair, and Gola would sit and gaze at it in silent admiration for hours at a time, or until, growing nervous under his unblinking scrutiny, I would boot him forth.

It was that night that a brooding animosity, hardly apparent, between Baron von Schiller and Jean Desmarie broke out into a flame.

As usual, woman was the cause. Marcita carried on a most outrageous flirtation with both of them.

That was not wise. Desmarte was a wild young fool. Von Schiller was a lustful beast. But when, Messieurs, did woman ever use wisdom?

Their hate flamed to a murderous fury when the German sought to kiss Marcita.

Swords were clashing in an instant. But before Dom Vincente could thunder a command to halt, Luigi was between the combatants, and had beaten their swords down, hurling them back viciously.

'Signori,' said he softly, but with a fierce intensity, 'is it the part of high-bred signori to fight over my sister? Ha, by the toenails of Satan, for the toss of a coin I would call you both out! You, Marcita, go to your chamber, instantly, nor leave until I give you permission.'

And she went, for, independent though she was, none cared to face the slim, effeminate-appearing youth when a tigerish snarl curled his lips, a murderous gleam lightened his dark eyes.

Apologies were made, but from the glances the two rivals threw at each other, we knew that the quarrel was not forgotten and would blaze forth again at the slightest pretext.

Late that night I woke suddenly with a strange, eerie feeling of horror. Why, I could not say. I rose, saw that the door was firmly bolted, and seeing Gola asleep on the floor, kicked him awake irritably.

And just as he got up, hastily, rubbing himself, the silence was broken by a wild scream, a scream that rang through the castle and brought a startled shout from the arquebusier pacing the palisade; a scream from the mouth of a girl, frenzied with terror.

Gola squawked and dived behind the divan. I jerked the door open and raced down the dark corridor. Dashing down a winding stair, I cannoned into someone at the bottom and we tumbled headlong.

He rasped something and I recognised the voice of Jean Desmarte. I hauled him to his feet, and raced along, he following; the screams had ceased, but the whole castle was in an uproar, voices shouting, the clank of weapons, lights flashing up, Dom Vincente's voice shouting for the soldiers, the noise of armed men rushing through the rooms and falling over each other. With all the confusion, Desmarte, the Spaniard, and I reached Marcita's room just as Luigi darted inside and snatched his sister into his arms.

Others rushed in, carrying lights and weapons, shouting, demanding to know what was occurring.

The girl lay quietly in her brother's arms, her dark hair loose and rippling over her shoulders, her dainty night-garments torn to shreds and exposing her lovely body. Long scratches showed upon her arms, breasts and shoulders.

Presently, she opened her eyes, shuddered, then shrieked wildly and clung frantically to Luigi, begging him not to let something take her.

'The door!' she whimpered. 'I left it unbarred. And something crept into my room through the darkness. I struck at it with my dagger and it hurled me to the floor, tearing, tearing at me. Then I fainted.'

'Where is von Schiller?' asked the Spaniard, a fierce glint in his dark eyes. Every man glanced at his neighbour. All the guests were there except the German. I noted de Montour gazing at the terrified girl, his face more haggard than usual. And I thought it strange that he wore no weapon.

'Aye, von Schiller!' exclaimed Desmarte fiercely. And half of us followed Dom Vincente out into the corridor. We began a vengeful search through the castle, and in a small, dark hallway we found von Schiller. On his face he lay, in a crimson, ever-widening stain.

'This is the work of some native!' exclaimed Desmarte, face aghast.

'Nonsense,' bellowed Dom Vincente. 'No native from the outside could pass the soldiers. All slaves, von Schiller's among them, were barred and bolted in the slave quarters, except Cola, who sleeps in Pierre's room, and Ysabel's woman.'

'But who else could have done this deed?' exclaimed Desmarte in a fury.

'You!' I said abruptly; 'else why ran you so swiftly away from the room of Marcita?'

'Curse you, you lie!' he shouted, and his swift-drawn sword leaped for my breast; but quick as he was, the Spaniard was quicker. Desmarte's rapier clattered against the wall and Desmarte stood like a statue, the Spaniard's motionless point just touching his throat.

'Bind him,' said the Spaniard without passion. 'Put down your blade, Don Florenzo,' commanded Dom Vincente, striding forward and dominating the scene. 'Signor Desmarte, you are one of my best friends, but I am the only law here and duty must be done. Give your word that you will not seek to escape.'

'I give it,' replied the Gascon calmly. 'I acted hastily. I apologise. I was not intentionally running away, but the halls and corridors of this cursed castle confuse me.' Of us all, probably but one man believed him.

'Messieurs!' De Montour stepped forward. 'This youth is not guilty. Turn the German over.'

Two soldiers did as he asked. De Montour shuddered, pointing. The rest of us glanced once, then recoiled in horror.

'Could man have done that thing?'

'With a dagger . . . ' began someone.

'No dagger makes wounds like that,' said the Spaniard: 'The German was torn to pieces by the talons of some frightful beast.'

We glanced about us, half expecting some hideous monster to leap upon us from the shadows.

We searched that castle; every foot, every inch of it. And we found no trace of any beast.

Dawn was breaking when I returned to my room, to find that Gola had barred himself in; and it took me nearly a half-hour to convince him to let me in. Having smacked him soundly and berated him for his cowardice, I told him what had taken place, as he could understand French and could speak a weird mixture which he proudly called French.

His mouth gaped and only the whites of his eyes showed as the tale reached its climax.

'Ju ju!' he whispered fearsomely. 'Fetish man!' Suddenly an idea came to me. I had heard vague tales, little more than hints of legends, of the devilish leopard cult that existed on the West Coast. No white man had ever seen one of its votaries, but Dom Vincente had told us tales of beast-men, disguised in skins of leopards, who stole through the midnight jungle and slew and devoured. A ghastly thrill travelled up and down my spine, and in an instant I had Gola in a grasp which made him veil.

'Was that a leopard-man?' I hissed, shaking him viciously.

'Me good boy! Ju ju man get! More besser no tell!'

'You'll tell me!' I gritted, renewing my endeavours, until, his hands waving feeble protests, he promised to tell me what he knew.

'No leopard-man!' he whispered. 'Moon, he full, woodcutter find, him heap clawed. Find 'nother woodcutter. Big Massa (Dom Vincente) say "leopard". No leopard. But leopard-man, he come to kill. Something kill leopard-man! Heap claw! Hai, hai! Moon full again. Something come in, lonely hut; claw um woman, claw um pick'nin. I am find um claw up. Big Massa say "leopard". Full moon again, and woodcutter find, heap clawed. Now come in castle. No leopard. But always footmarks of a man.'

I gave a startled, incredulous exclamation.

It was true, Gola averred. Always the footprints of a man led away from the scene of the murder. Then why did the natives not tell the Big Massa, that he might hunt down the fiend? Here Gola assumed a crafty expression and whispered in my ear, the footprints were of a man who wore shoes!

Even assuming that Gola was lying, I felt a thrill of unexplainable horror. Who, then, did the natives believe was doing these frightful murders?

And he answered: Dom Vincente!

By this time, Messieurs, my mind was in a whirl. What was the meaning of all this? Who slew the German and sought to ravish Marcita? And as I reviewed the crime, it appeared to me that murder rather than rape was the object of the attack.

Why did de Montour warn us, and then appear to have knowledge of the crime, telling us that Desmarte was innocent and then proving it?

It was all beyond me.

The tale of the slaughter got among the natives, in spite of all we could do, and they appeared restless and nervous. A brooding atmosphere pervaded the castle.

I considered going to Dom Vincente with Gola's tale, but decided to wait awhile.

The women kept their chambers that day, the men were restless and moody. Dom Vincente announced that the sentries would be doubled and some would patrol the corridors of the castle itself. I found myself musing cynically that if Gola's suspicions were true, sentries would be of little good.

I am not, Messieurs, a man to brook such a situation with patience. And I was young then. So as we drank before retiring, I flung my goblet on the table and angrily announced that in spite of man, beast or devil, I slept that night with doors flung wide. And I tramped angrily to my chamber.

Again, as on the first night, de Montour came. And his face was as a man who has looked into the gaping gates of hell.

'I have come,' he said, 'to ask you . . . nay, Monsieur, to implore you – to reconsider your rash determination.' I shook my head impatiently..

'You are resolved? Yes? Then I ask you do to this for me, that after I enter my chamber, you will bolt my doors from the outside.'

I did as he asked, and then made my way back to my chamber, my mind in a maze of wonderment. I had sent Gola to the slave quarters, and I laid rapier and dagger close at hand. Nor did I go to bed, but crouched in a great chair, in the darkness. Then I had much ado to keep from sleeping. To keep myself awake, I fell to musing on the strange words of de Montour. He seemed to be labouring under great excitement; his eyes hinted of ghastly mysteries known to him alone. And yet his face was not that of a wicked man.

Suddenly the notion took me to go to his chamber and talk with him.

Walking those dark passages was a shuddersome task, but eventually I stood before de Montour's door. I called softly. Silence. I reached out a hand and felt splintered fragments of wood. Hastily I struck flint and steel which I carried, and the flaming tinder showed the great oaken door sagging on its mighty hinges; showed a door smashed and splintered from the inside: And the chamber of de Montour was unoccupied.

Some instinct prompted me to hurry back to my room, swiftly but silently, shoeless feet treading softly. And as I neared the door, I was aware of something in the darkness before me. Something which crept in from a side corridor and glided stealthily along.

In a wild panic of fear I leaped, striking wildly and aimlessly in the darkness. All my clenched fist encountered a human head, and something went down with a crash. Again I struck a light; a man lay senseless on the floor, and he was de Montour.

I thrust a candle into a niche in the Wall, and just then de Montour's eyes opened and he rose uncertainly. 'You!' I exclaimed, hardly knowing what I said. 'You, of all men!'

He merely nodded.

'You killed von Schiller?'

'Yes.'

I recoiled with a gasp of horror.

'Listen.' He raised his hand. 'Take your rapier and run me through. No man will touch you.'

'No,' I exclaimed. 'I can not.'

'Then, quick,' he said hurriedly, 'get into your chamber and bolt the door. Haste! It will return!'

'What will return?' I asked, with a thrill of horror. 'If it will harm me, it will harm you. Come into the chamber with me.'

'No, no!' he fairly shrieked, springing back from my outstretched arm. 'Haste, haste! It left me for an instant, but it will return.' Then in a low-pitched voice of indescribable horror: 'It is returning. It is here now!'

And I felt a something, a formless, shapeless presence near. A thing of frightfulness.

De Montour was standing, legs braced, arms thrown back, fists clenched. The muscles bulged beneath his skin, his eyes widened and narrowed, the veins stood out upon his forehead as if in great physical effort. As I looked, to my horror, out of nothing, a shapeless, nameless something took vague form! Like a shadow it moved upon de Montour.

It was hovering about him! Good God, it was merging, becoming one with the man!

De Montour swayed; a great gasp escaped him. The dim thing vanished. De Montour wavered. Then he turned toward me, and may God grant that I never look on a face like that again!

It was a hideous, a bestial face. The eyes gleamed with a frightful ferocity; the snarling lips were drawn back from gleaming teeth, which to my startled gaze appeared more like bestial fangs than human teeth.

Silently the thing (I can not call it a human) slunk toward me. Gasping with horror I sprang back and through the door, just as the thing launched itself through the air, with a sinuous motion which even then made me think of a leaping wolf. I slammed the door, holding it against the frightful thing which hurled itself again and again against it.

Finally it desisted and I heard it slink stealthily off down the corridor. Faint and exhausted I sat down, waiting, listening. Through the open window wafted the breeze, bearing all the scents of Africa, the spicy and the foul. From the native village came the sound of a native drum. Other drums answered farther up the river and back in the bush. Then from somewhere in the jungle, horridly incongruous, sounded the long, high-pitched call of a timber wolf. My soul revolted.

Dawn brought a tale of terrified villagers, of a woman torn by some fiend of the night, barely escaping. And to de Montour I went.

On the way I met Dom Vincente. He was perplexed and angry.

'Some hellish thing is at work in this castle,' he said. 'Last night, though I have said naught of it to anyone, something leaped upon the back of one of the arquebusiers, tore the leather jerkin from his shoulders and pursued him to the barbican. More, someone locked de Montour into his room last night, and he was forced to smash the door to get out.'

He strode on, muttering to himself, and I proceeded down the stairs, more puzzled than ever.

De Montour sat upon a stool, gazing out the window. An indescribable air of weariness was about him.

His long hair was uncombed and tousled, his garments were tattered. With a shudder I saw faint crimson stains upon his hands, and noted that the nails were torn and broken.

He looked up as I came in, and waved me to a seat. His face was worn and haggard, but was that of a man.

After a moment's silence, he spoke.

'I will tell you my strange tale. Never before has it passed my lips, and why I tell you, knowing that you will not believe me, I can not say.'

And then I listened to what was surely the wildest, the most fantastic, the weirdest tale ever heard by man.

'Years ago,' said de Montour, 'I was upon a military mission in northern France. Alone, I was forced to pass through the fiend-haunted woodlands of Villefere. In those frightful forests I was beset by an inhuman, a ghastly thing – a werewolf. Beneath a midnight moon we fought, and I slew it. Now this is the truth: that if a werewolf is slain in the half-form of a man, its ghost will haunt its slayer through eternity. But if it is slain as a wolf, hell gapes to receive it. The true werewolf is not (as many think) a man who may take the form of a wolf, but a wolf who takes the form of a man!

'Now listen, my friend, and I will tell you of the wisdom, the hellish knowledge that is mine, gained through many a frightful deed, imparted to me amid the ghastly shadows of midnight forests where fiends and half-beasts roamed.

'In the beginning, the world was strange, misshapen. Grotesque beasts wandered through its jungles. Driven from another world, ancient demons and fiends came in great numbers and settled upon this newer, younger world. Long the forces of good and evil warred.

'A strange beast, known as man, wandered among the other beasts, and since good or bad must have a concrete form ere either accomplishes its desire, the spirits of good entered man. The fiends entered other beasts, reptiles and birds; and long and fiercely waged the age-old battle. But man conquered. The great dragons and serpents were slain and with them the demons. Finally, Solomon, wise beyond the ken of man, made great war upon them, and by virtue of his wisdom, slew, seized and bound. But there were some which were the fiercest, the boldest, and though Solomon drove them out he could not conquer them. Those had taken the form of wolves. As the ages passed, wolf and demon became merged. No longer could the fiend leave the body of the wolf at will. In many instances, the savagery of the wolf overcame the subtlety of the demon and enslaved him, so the wolf became again only a beast, a fierce, cunning beast, but merely a beast. But of the werewolves, there are many, even yet.

'And during the time of the full moon, the wolf may take the form, or the half-form, of a man. When the moon hovers at her zenith, however, the wolf-spirit again takes ascendancy and the werewolf becomes a true wolf once more. But if it is slain in the form of a man, then the spirit is free to haunt its slayer through the ages.

'Hearken now. I had thought to have slain the thing after it had changed to its true shape. But I slew it an instant too soon. The moon, though it approached the zenith, had not yet reached it, nor had the thing taken on fully the wolf-form.

'Of this I knew nothing and went my way. But when the next time approached for the full moon, I began to be aware of a strange, malicious influence. An atmosphere of horror hovered in the air and I was aware of inexplicable, uncanny impulses.

'One night in a small village in the centre of a great forest, the influence came upon me with full power. It was night, and the moon, nearly full, was rising over the forest. And between the moon and me, I saw, floating in the upper air, ghostly and barely discernible, the outline of a wolf's head!

'I remember little of what happened thereafter. I remember, dimly, clambering into the silent street, remember struggling, resisting briefly, vainly, and the rest is a crimson haze, until I came to myself the next morning and found my garments and hands caked and stained crimson; and heard the horrified chattering of the villagers, telling of a pair of clandestine lovers, slaughtered in a ghastly manner, scarcely outside the village, torn to pieces as if by wild beasts, as if by wolves.

'From that village I fled aghast, but I fled not alone. In the day I could not feel the drive of my fearful captor, but when night fell and the moon rose, I ranged the silent forest, a frightful thing, a slayer of humans, a fiend in a man's body.

'God, the battles I have fought! But always it overcame me and drove me ravening after some new victim. But after the moon had passed its fullness, the thing's power over me ceased suddenly. Nor did it return until three nights before the moon was full again.

'Since then I have roamed the world – fleeing, fleeing, seeking to escape. Always the thing follows, taking possession of my body when the moon is full. Gods, the frightful deeds I have done!

'I would have slain myself long ago, but I dare not. For the soul of a suicide is accursed, and my soul would be forever hunted through the flames of hell. And hearken, most frightful of all, my slain body would for ever roam the earth, moved and inhabited by the soul of the werewolf! Can any thought be more ghastly?

'And I seem immune to the weapons of man. Swords have pierced me, daggers have hacked me. I am covered with scars. Yet never have they struck me down. In Germany they bound and led me to the block. There would I have willingly placed my head, but the thing came upon me, and breaking my bonds, I slew and fled. Up and down the world I have wandered, leaving horror and slaughter in my trail. Chains, cells, cannot hold me. The thing is fastened to me through all eternity.

'In desperation I accepted Dom Vincente's invitation, for look you, none knows of my frightful double life, since no one could recognise me in the clutch of the demon; and few, seeing me, live to tell of it.

'My hands are red, my soul doomed to everlasting flames, my mind is torn with remorse for my crimes. And yet I can do nothing to help myself. Surely, Pierre, no man ever knew the hell that I have known.

'Yes, I slew von Schiller, and I sought to destroy the girl Marcita. Why I did not, I can not say, for I have slain both women and men.

'Now, if you will, take your sword and slay me, and with my last breath I will give you the good God's blessing. No?

'You know now my tale and you see before you a man, fiend-haunted for all eternity.'

My mind was spinning with wonderment as I left the room of de Montour. What to do, I knew not. It seemed likely that he would yet murder us all, and yet I could not bring myself to tell Dom Vincente all. From the bottom of my soul I pitied de Montour.

So I kept my peace, and in the days that followed I made occasion to seek him out and converse with him. A real friendship sprang up between us.

About this time that black devil, Gola, began to wear an air of suppressed excitement, as if he knew something he wished desperately to tell, but would not or else dared not.

So the days passed in feasting, drinking and hunting, until one night de Montour came to my chamber and pointed silently at the moon which was just rising.

'Look ye,' he said, 'I have a plan. I will give it out that I am going into the jungle for hunting and will go forth, apparently for several days. But at night I will return to the castle, and you must lock me into the dungeon which is used as a storeroom.'

This we did, and I managed to slip down twice a day and carry food and drink to my friend. He insisted on remaining in the dungeon even in the day, for though the fiend had never exerted its influence over him in the daytime, and he believed it powerless then, yet he would take no chances.

It was during this time that I began to notice that Dom Vincente's mink-faced cousin, Carlos, was forcing his attentions upon

Ysabel, who was his second cousin, and who seemed to resent those attentions.

Myself, I would have challenged him for a duel for the toss of a coin, for I despised him, but it was really none of my affair. However, it seemed that Ysabel feared him.

My friend Luigi, by the way, had become enamoured of the dainty Portuguese girl, and was making swift love to her daily.

And de Montour sat in his cell and reviewed his ghastly deeds until he battered the bars with his bare hands.

And Don Florenzo wandered about the castle grounds like a dour Mephistopheles.

And the other guests rode and quarrelled and drank.

And Gola slithered about, eyeing me as if always on the point of imparting momentous information. What wonder if my nerves became rasped to the shrieking point?

Each day the natives grew surlier and more and more sullen and intractable.

One night, not long before the full of the moon, I entered the dungeon where de Montour sat.

He looked up quickly.

'You dare much, coming to me in the night.'

I shrugged my shoulders, seating myself.

A small barred window let in the night scents and sounds of Africa.

'Hark to the native drums,' I said. 'For the past week they have sounded almost incessantly.'

De Montour assented.

'The natives are restless. Methinks 'tis deviltry they are planning. Have you noticed that Carlos is much among them?'

'No,' I answered, 'but 'tis like there will be a break between him and Luigi. Luigi is paying court to Ysabel.'

So we talked, when suddenly de Montour became silent and moody, answering only in monosyllables.

The moon rose and peered in at the barred windows. De Montour's face was illuminated by its beams.

And then the hand of horror grasped me. On the wall behind de Montour appeared a shadow, a shadow clearly defined of a wolf's head!

At the same instant de Montour felt its influence. With a shriek he bounded from his stool.

He pointed fiercely, and as with trembling hands I slammed and bolted the door behind me, I felt him hurl his weight against it.

As I fled up the stairway I heard a wild raving and battering at the iron-bound door. But with all the werewolf's might the great door held.

As I entered my room, Gola dashed in and gasped out the tale he had been keeping for days.

I listened, incredulously, and then dashed forth to find Dom Vincente.

I was told that Carlos had asked him to accompany him to the village to arrange a sale of slaves.

My informer was Don Florenzo of Seville, and when I gave him a brief outline of Gola's tale, he accompanied me.

Together we dashed through the castle gate, flinging a word to the guards, and down the landing toward the village.

Dom Vincente, Dom Vincente, walk with care, keep sword loosened in its sheath! Fool, fool, to walk in the night with Carlos, the traitor!

They were nearing the village when we caught up with them. 'Dom Vincente!' I exclaimed; 'return instantly to the castle. Carlos is selling you into the hands of the natives! Gola has told me that he lusts for your wealth and for Ysabel! A terrified native babbled to him of booted footprints near the places where the woodcutters were murdered, and Carlos has made the blacks believe that the slayer was you! Tonight the natives were to rise and slay every man in the castle except Carlos! Do you not believe me, Dom Vincente?'

'Is this the truth, Carlos?' asked Dom Vincente, in amaze.

Carlos laughed mockingly. 'The fool speaks truth,' he said, 'but it accomplishes you nothing. Ho!'

He shouted as he leaped for Dom Vincente. Steel flashed in the moonlight and the Spaniard's sword was through Carlos ere he could move.

And the shadows rose about us. Then it was back to back, sword and dagger, three men against a hundred. Spears flashed, and a fiendish yell went up from savage throats. I spitted three natives in as many thrusts and then went down from a stunning swing from a war-club, and an instant later Dom Vincente fell upon me, with a spear in one arm and another through the leg. Don Florenzo was standing above us, sword leaping like a live thing, when a charge of the arquebusiers swept the river bank clear and we were borne into the castle.

The hordes came with a rush, spears flashing like a wave of steel, a thunderous roar of savagery going up to the skies.

Time and again they swept up the slopes bounding the moat, until
they were swarming over the palisades. And time and again the fire
of the hundred-odd defenders hurled them back.

They had set fire to the plundered warehouses, and their light vied
with the light of the moon. Just across the river there was a larger
storehouse, and about this hordes of the natives gathered, tearing it
apart for plunder.

'Would that they would drop a torch upon it,' said Dom Vincente,
'for naught is stored therein save some thousand pounds of gun-
powder. I dared not store the treacherous stuff this side of the river.
All the tribes of the river and coast have gathered for our slaughter
and all my ships are upon the seas. We may hold out awhile, but
eventually they will swarm the palisade and put us to the slaughter.'

I hastened to the dungeon wherein de Montour sat. Outside the
door I called to him and he bade me enter in voice which told me the
fiend had left him for an instant.

'How goes the battle?'

I gave him the details of the betrayal and the fight, and mentioned
the powder-house across the river. He sprang to his feet.

'Now by my hag-ridden soul!' he exclaimed. 'I will fling the dice
once more with hell! Swift, let me out of the castle! I will essay to
swim the river and set off yon powder!'

'It is insanity!' I exclaimed. 'A thousand lurk between the palis-
ades and the river, and thrice that number beyond! The river itself
swarms with crocodiles!'

'I will attempt it!' he answered, a great light in his face. 'If I can
reach it, some thousand natives will lighten the siege; if I am slain,
then my soul is free and mayhap will gain some forgiveness for that I
gave my life to atone for my crimes.'

Then, 'Haste,' he exclaimed, 'for the demon is returning! Already I
feel his influence! Haste ye!'

For the castle gates we sped, and as de Montour ran he gasped as a
man in a terrific battle.

At the gate he pitched headlong, then rose, to spring through it.
Wild yells greeted him from the natives.

The arquebusiers shouted curses at him and at me. Peering down
from the top of the palisades I saw him turn from side to side uncert-
ainly. A score of natives were rushing recklessly forward, spears raised.

Then the eerie wolf-yell rose to the skies, and de Montour bounded
forward. Aghast, the natives paused, and before a man of them could
move he was among them. Wild shrieks, not of rage, but of terror.

In amazement the arquebusiers held their fire.

Straight through the group de Montour charged, and when they broke and fled, three of them fled not.

A dozen steps de Montour took in pursuit; then stopped stock-still. A moment he stood so while spears flew about him, then turned and ran swiftly in the direction of the river.

A few steps from the river another band barred his way. In the fading light of the burning houses the scene was clearly illuminated. A thrown spear tore through de Montour's shoulder. Without pausing in his stride he tore it forth and drove it through a native, leaping over his body to get among the others. They could not face the fiend-driven white man. With shrieks they fled, and de Montour, bounding upon the back of one, brought him down.

Then he rose, staggered and sprang to the river bank. An instant he paused there and then vanished in the shadows.

'Name of the devil!' gasped Dom Vincente at my shoulder. 'What manner of man is that? Was that de Montour?'

I nodded. The wild yells of the natives rose above the crackle of the arquebus fire. They were massed thick about the great warehouse across the river.

'They plan a great rush,' said Dom Vincente. 'They will swarm clear over the palisade, methinks. Ha!'

A crash that seemed to rip the skies apart! A burst of flame that mounted to the stars! The castle rocked with the explosion. Then silence, as the smoke, drifting away, showed only a great crater where the warehouse had stood.

I could tell of how Dom Vincente led a charge, crippled as he was, out of the castle gate and, down the slope, to fall upon the terrified blacks who had escaped the explosion. I could tell of the slaughter, of the victory and the pursuit of the fleeing natives.

I could tell, too, Messieurs, of how I became separated from the band and of how I wandered far into the jungle, unable to find my way back to the coast.

I could tell how I was captured by a wandering band of slave raiders, and of how I escaped. But such is not my intention. In itself it would make a long tale; and it is of de Montour that I am speaking.

I thought much of the things that had passed and wondered if indeed de Montour reached the storehouse to blow it to the skies or whether it was but the deed of chance.

That a man could swim that reptile-swarming river, fiend-driven though he was, seemed impossible. And if he blew up the storehouse, he must have gone up with it.

So one night I pushed my way wearily through the jungle and sighted the coast, and close to the shore a small, tumbledown hut of thatch. To it I went, thinking to sleep therein if insects and reptiles would allow.

I entered the doorway and then stopped short. Upon a makeshift stool sat a man. He looked up as I entered and the rays of the moon fell across his face.

I started back with a ghastly thrill of horror. It was de Montour, and the moon was full!

Then as I stood, unable to flee, he rose and came toward me. And his face, though haggard as of a man who has looked into hell, was the face of a sane man.

'Come in, my friend,' he said, and there was a great peace in his voice. 'Come in and fear me not. The fiend has left me forever.'

'But tell me, how conquered you?' I exclaimed as I grasped his hand.

'I fought a frightful battle, as I ran to the river,' he answered, 'for the fiend had me in its grasp and drove me to fall upon the natives. But for the first time my soul and mind gained ascendancy for an instant, an instant just long enough to hold me to my purpose. And I believe the good saints came to my aid, for I was giving my life to save life.

'I leaped into the river and swam, and in an instant the crocodiles were swarming about me. Again in the clutch of the fiend I fought them, there in the river. Then suddenly the thing left me. I climbed from the river and fired the warehouse. The explosion hurled me hundreds of feet, and for days I wandered witless through the jungle. But the full moon came, and came again, and I felt not the influence of the fiend. I am free, free!' And a wondrous note of exultation, nay, exaltation, thrilled his words.

'My soul is free. Incredible as it seems, the demon lies drowned upon the bed of the river, or else inhabits the body of one of the savage reptiles that swim the ways of the Niger.'

The Dream Snake

The night was strangely still. As we sat upon the wide veranda, gazing out over the broad, shadowy lawns, the silence of the hour entered our spirits and for a long while no one spoke.

Then far across the dim mountains that fringed the eastern sky-line, a faint haze began to glow, and presently a great golden moon came up, making a ghostly radiance over the land and etching boldly the dark clumps of shadows that were trees. A light breeze came whispering out of the east, and the unmowed grass swayed before it in long, sinuous waves, dimly visible in the moonlight; and from among the group upon the veranda there came a swift gasp, a sharp intake of breath that caused us all to turn and gaze.

Faming was leaning forward, clutching the arms of his chair, his face strange and pallid in the spectral light; a thin trickle of blood seeping from the lip in which he had set his teeth. Amazed, we looked at him, and suddenly he jerked about with a short, snarling laugh.

'There's no need of gawking at me like a flock of sheep!' he said irritably and stopped short. We sat bewildered, scarcely knowing what sort of reply to make, and suddenly he burst out again.

'Now I guess I'd better tell the whole thing or you'll be going off and putting me down as a lunatic. Don't interrupt me, any of you! I want to get this thing off my mind. You all know that I'm not a very imaginative man; but there's a thing, purely a figment of imagin-ation, that has haunted me since babyhood. A dream!' He fairly cringed back in his chair as he muttered, 'A dream! And God, what a dream! The first time . . . no, I can't remember the first time I ever dreamed it . . . I've been dreaming the hellish thing ever since I can remember. Now it's this way: there is a sort of bungalow, set upon a hill in the midst of wide grasslands – not unlike this estate; but this scene is in Africa. And I am living there with a sort of servant, a Hindu. Just why I am there is never clear to my waking mind, though I am always aware of the reason in my dreams. As a man of a dream,

I remember my past life (a life which in no way corresponds with my waking life), but when I am awake my subconscious mind fails to transmit these impressions. However, I think that I am a fugitive from justice and the Hindu is also a fugitive. How the bungalow came to be there I can never remember, nor do I know in what part of Africa it is, though all these things are known to my dream self. But the bungalow is a small one of a very few rooms, and is situated upon the top of the hill, as I said. There are no other hills about and the grasslands stretch to the horizon in every direction; knee-high in some places, waist-high in others.

'Now the dream always opens as I am coming up the hill, just as the sun is beginning to set. I am carrying a broken rifle and I have been on a hunting trip; how the rifle was broken, and the full details of the trip, I clearly remember . . . dreaming. But never upon waking. It is just as if a curtain were suddenly raised and a drama began; or just as if I were suddenly transferred to another man's body and life, remembering past years of that life, and not cognisant of any other existence. And that is the hellish part of it! As you know, most of us, dreaming, are, at the back of our consciousness, aware that we are dreaming. No matter how horrible the dream may become, we know that it is a dream, and thus insanity or possible death is staved off. But in this particular dream, there is no such knowledge. I tell you it is so vivid, so complete in every detail, that I wonder sometimes if that is not my real existence and this a dream! But no; for then I should have been dead years ago.

'As I was saying, I come up the hill and the first thing I am cognisant of that it is out of the ordinary is a sort of track leading up the hill in an irregular way; that is, the grass is mashed down as if something heavy had been dragged over it. But I pay no especial attention to it, for I am thinking, with some irritation, that the broken rifle I carry is my only arm and that now I must forgo hunting until I can send for another.

'You see, I remember thoughts and impressions of the dream itself, of the occurrences of the dream; it is the memories that the dream "I" had, of that other dream existence that I can not remember. So. I come up the hill and enter the bungalow. The doors are open and the Hindu is not there. But the main room is in confusion; chairs are broken, a table is overturned. The Hindu's dagger is lying upon the floor, but there is no blood anywhere.

'Now, in my dreams, I never remember the other dreams, as sometimes one does. Always it is the first dream, the first time. I always experience the same sensations, in my dreams, with as vivid a force as the first time I ever dreamed. So. I am not able to understand this. The Hindu is gone, but (thus I ruminate, standing in the centre of the disordered room) what did away with him? Had it been a raiding party they would have looted the bungalow and probably burned it. Had it been a lion, the place would have been smeared with blood. Then suddenly I remember the track I saw going up the hill, and a cold hand touches my spine; for instantly the whole thing is clear: the thing that came up from the grasslands and wrought havoc in the little bungalow could be naught else except a giant serpent. And as I think or the size of the spoor, cold sweat beads my forehead and the broken rifle shakes in my hand.

'Then I rush to the door in a wild panic, my only thought to make a dash for the coast. But the sun has set and dusk is stealing across the grasslands. And out there somewhere, lurking in the tall grass is that grisly thing . . . that horror. God!' The ejaculation broke from his lips with such feeling that all of us started, not realising the tension we had reached. There was a second's silence, then he continued.

'So I bolt the doors and windows, light the lamp I have and take my stand in the middle of the room. And I stand like a statue . . . waiting . . . listening. After a while the moon comes up and her haggard light drifts though the windows. And I stand still in the centre of the room; the night is very still . . . something like this night; the breeze occasionally whispers through the grass, and each time I start and clench my hands until the nails bite into the flesh and the blood trickles down my wrists . . . and I stand there and wait and listen but it does not come that night!' The sentence came suddenly and explosively, and an involuntary sigh came from the rest; a relaxing of tension.

'I am determined, if I live the night through, to start for the coast early the next morning, taking my chance out there in the grim grasslands with it. But with morning, I dare not. I do not know in which direction the monster went; and I dare not risk coming upon him in the open, unarmed as I am. So, as in a maze, I remain at the bungalow, and ever my eyes turn toward the sun, lurching relentless down the sky toward the horizon. Ah, God! if I could but halt the sun in the sky!'

The man was in the clutch of some terrific power; his words fairly leaped at us.

'Then the sun rides down the sky and the long grey shadows come stalking across the grasslands. Dizzy with fear, I have bolted the doors and windows and lighted the lamp long before the last faint glow of twilight fades. The light from the windows may attract the monster, but I dare not stay in the dark. And again I take my stand in the centre of the room . . . waiting.'

There was a shuddersome halt. Then he continued, barely above a whisper, moistening his lips: 'There is no knowing how long I stand there. Time has ceased to be and each second is an aeon; each minute is an eternity, stretching into endless eternities. Then, God! but what is that?' He leaned forward, the moonlight etching his face into such a mask of horrified listening that each of us shivered and flung a hasty glance over our shoulders.

'Not the night breeze this time,' he whispered. 'Something makes the grasses swish-swish . . . as if a great, long, pliant weight were being dragged through them. Above the bungalow it swishes and then ceases in front of the door; then the hinges creak . . . creak! The door begins to bulge inward . . . a small bit . . . then some more!' The man's arms were held in front of him, as if braced strongly against something, and his breath came in quick gasps. 'And I know I should lean against the door and hold it shut, but I do not, I cannot move. I stand there, like a sheep waiting to be slaughtered . . . but the door holds!' Again that sigh expressive of pent-up feeling.

He drew a shaky hand across his brow. 'And all night I stand in the centre of that room, as motionless as an image, except to turn slowly, as the swish-swish of the grass marks the fiend's course about the house. Ever I keep my eyes in the direction of the soft, sinister sound. Sometimes it ceases for an instant, or for several minutes, and then I stand scarcely breathing, for a horrible obsession has it that the serpent has in some way made entrance into the bungalow, and I start and whirl this way and that, frightfully fearful of making a noise, though I know not why, but ever with the feeling that the thing is at my back. Then the sounds commence again and I freeze motionless.

'Now here is the only time that my consciousness, which guides my waking hours, ever in any way pierces the veil of dreams. I am, in the dream, in no way conscious that it is a dream, but, in a detached sort of way, my other mind recognises certain facts and passes them on to my sleeping . . . shall I say "ego"? That is to say, my personality is for an instant truly dual and separate to an extent, as the right and left arms are separate, while making up parts in the same entity. My dreaming mind has no cognisance of my higher mind; for the time being the other mind is subordinated and the subconscious mind is in full control, to such an extent that it does not even recognise the existence of the other. But the conscious mind, now sleeping, is cognisant of dim thought-waves emanating from the dream mind. I know that I have not made this entirely clear, but the fact remains that I know that my mind, conscious and subconscious, is near to ruin. My obsession of fear, as I stand there in my dream, is that the serpent will raise itself and peer into the window at me. And I know, in my dream, that if this occurs I shall go insane. And so vivid is the impression imparted to my conscious, now sleeping mind that the thought-waves stir the dim seas of sleep, and somehow I can feel my sanity rocking as my sanity rocks in my dream. Back and forth it totters and sways until the motion takes on a physical aspect and I in my dream am swaying from side to side. Not always is the sensation the same, but I tell you, if that horror ever raises its terrible shape and leers at me, if I ever see the fearful thing in my dream, I shall become stark, wild insane.' There was a restless movement among the rest.

'God! but what a prospect!' he muttered. 'To be insane and forever dreaming that same dream, night and day! But there I stand, and centuries go by, but at last a dim grey light begins to steal through the windows, the swishing dies away in the distance and presently a red, haggard sun climbs the eastern sky. Then I turn about and gaze into a mirror . . . and my hair has become perfectly white. I stagger to the door and fling it wide. There is nothing in sight but a wide track leading away down the hill through the grasslands . . . in the opposite direction from that which I would take toward the coast. And with a shriek of maniacal laughter, I dash down the hill and race across the grasslands. I race until I drop from exhaustion, then I lie until I can stagger up and go on.

'All day I keep this up, with superhuman effort, spurred on by the horror behind me. And ever as I hurl myself forward on weakening legs, ever as I lie gasping for breath, I watch the sun with a terrible eagerness. How swiftly the sun travels when a man races it for life! A losing race it is, as I know when I watch the sun sinking toward the skyline, and the hills which I had to gain ere sundown seemingly as far away as ever.'

His voice was lowered and instinctively we leaned toward him; he was gripping the chair arms and the blood was seeping from his lip.

'Then the sun sets and the shadows come and I stagger on and fall and rise and reel on again. And I laugh, laugh, laugh! Then I cease, for the moon comes up and throws the grasslands in ghostly and silvery relief. The light is white across the land, though the moon itself is like blood. And I look back the way I have come . . . and far back . . . ' All of us leaned farther toward him, our hair a-prickle; his voice came like a ghostly whisper . . . 'far back . . . I . . . see . . . the . . . grass . . . waving. There is no breeze, but the tall grass parts and sways in the moonlight, in a narrow, sinuous line . . . far away, but nearing every instant.' His voice died away.

Somebody broke the ensuing stillness: 'And then . . . ?'

'Then I awake. Never yet have I seen the foul monster. But that is the dream that haunts me, and from which I have wakened, in my childhood screaming, in my manhood in cold sweat. At irregular intervals I dream it, and each time, lately' . . . he hesitated and then went on . . . 'each time lately, the thing has been getting closer . . . closer . . . the waving of the grass marks his progress and he nears me with each dream; and when he reaches me, then . . . '

He stopped short, then without a word rose abruptly and entered the house. The rest of us sat silent for awhile, then followed him, for it was late.

How long I slept I do not know, but I woke suddenly with the impression that somewhere in the house someone had laughed long, loud and hideously, as a maniac laughs. Starting up, wondering if I had been dreaming, I rushed from my room, just as a truly horrible shriek echoed through the house. The place was now alive with other people who had been awakened, and all of us rushed to Famings's room, whence the sounds had seemed to come.

Faming lay dead upon the floor, where it seemed he had fallen in some terrific struggle. There was no mark upon him, but his face was terribly distorted; as the face of a man who had been crushed by some superhuman force . . . such as some gigantic snake.

The Hyena

From the time when I first saw Senecoza, the fetish-man, I distrusted him, and from vague distrust the idea eventually grew into hatred.

I was but newly come to the East Coast, new to African ways, somewhat inclined to follow my impulses, and possessed of a large amount of curiosity.

Because I came from Virginia, race instinct and prejudice were strong in me, and doubtless the feeling of inferiority which Senecoza constantly inspired in me had a great deal to do with my antipathy for him.

He was surprisingly tall, and leanly built. Six inches above six feet he stood, and so muscular was his spare frame that he weighed a good two hundred pounds. His weight seemed incredible when one looked at his lanky build, but he was all muscle . . . a lean giant. His features more resembled Berber than Bantu, with the high, bulging forehead, thin nose and thin, straight lips. But his hair was as kinky as a Bushman's and his colour was blacker even than the Masai. In fact, his glossy hide had a different hue from those of the native tribesmen, and I believe that he was of a different tribe.

It was seldom that we of the ranch saw him. Then without warning he would be among us, or we would see him striding through the shoulder-high grass of the veldt, sometimes alone, sometimes followed at a respectful distance by several of the wilder Masai, who bunched up at a distance from the buildings, grasping their spears nervously and eyeing everyone suspiciously. He would make his greetings with a courtly grace; his manner was deferentially courteous, but somehow it 'rubbed me the wrong way', so to speak. He would stand before us, a naked bronze giant; make trade for a few simple articles, such as a copper kettle, beads or a trade musket; repeat words of some chief, and take his departure.

I did not like him. And being young and impetuous, I spoke my opinion to Ludtvik Strolvaus, a very distant relative, tenth cousin or suchlike, on whose trading-post ranch I was staying.

But Ludtvik chuckled in his blond beard and said that the fetish-man was all right.

'A power he is among the natives, true. They all fear him. But a friend he is to the whites. *Ja*.'

Ludtvik was long a resident on the East Coast; he knew natives and he knew the fat Australian cattle he raised, but he had little imagination.

The ranch buildings were in the midst of a stockade, on a kind of slope, overlooking countless miles on miles of the finest grazing land in Africa. The stockade was large, well suited for defence. Most of the thousand cattle could be driven inside in case of an uprising of the Masai. Ludtvik was inordinately proud of his cattle.

'One thousand now,' he would tell me; his round face beaming, 'one thousand now. But later, ah! Ten thousand and another ten thousand. This is a good beginning, but only a beginning. *Ja*.'

I must confess that I got little thrill out of the cattle. Natives herded and corralled them; all Ludtvik and I had to do was to ride about and give orders. That was the work he liked best, and I left it mostly to him.

My chief sport was in riding away across the veldt, alone or attended by a gun-bearer, with a rifle. Not that I ever bagged much game. In the first place I was an execrable marksman; I could hardly have hit an elephant at close range. In the second place, it seemed to me a shame to shoot so many things. A bush-antelope would bound up in front of me and race away, and I would sit watching him, admiring the slim, lithe figure, thrilled with the graceful beauty of the creature, my rifle lying idle across my saddle horn.

The native boy who served as my gun-bearer began to suspect that I was deliberately refraining from shooting, and he began in a covert way to throw sneering hints about my womanishness. I was young and valued even the opinion of a native; which is very foolish. His remarks stung my pride, and one day I hauled him off his horse and pounded him until he yelled for mercy. Thereafter my doings were not questioned.

But still I felt inferior when in the presence of the fetish-man. I could not get the other natives to talk about him. All I could get out of them was a gesticulation indicative of fear, and vague information that the fetish-man dwelt among the tribes some distance in the interior. General opinion seemed to be that Senecoza was a good man to let alone.

One incident made the mystery about the fetish-man take on, it seemed, a rather sinister form.

In the mysterious way that news travels in Africa, and which white men so seldom hear of, we learned that Senecoza and a minor chief had had a falling out of some kind. It was vague and seemed to have no especial basis of fact. But shortly afterward that chief was found half-devoured by hyenas. That, in itself, was not unusual, but the fright with which the natives heard the news was. The chief was nothing to them; in fact he was something of a villain, but his killing seemed to inspire them with a fright that was little short of homicidal. The next time Senecoza called, they rose and fled en masse and did not return until he had taken his departure.

Between the fear of the blacks, the tearing to pieces of the chief by the hyenas, and the fetish-man, I seemed to sense vaguely a connection of some kind. But I could not grasp the intangible thought.

Not long thereafter, that thought was intensified by another incident. I had ridden far out on the veldt, accompanied by my servant. As we paused to rest our horses close to a kopje, I saw, upon the top, a hyena eying us. Rather surprised, for the beasts are not in the habit of thus boldly approaching man in the daytime, I raised my rifle and was taking a steady aim, for I always hated the things, when my servant caught my arm.

'No shoot, *bwana*! No shoot!' he exclaimed hastily, jabbering a great deal in his own language, with which I was not familiar.

'What's up?' I asked impatiently.

He kept on jabbering and pulling my arm, until I gathered that the hyena was a fetish-beast of some kind.

'Oh, all right,' I conceded, lowering my rifle just as the hyena turned and sauntered out of sight.

Something about the lank, repulsive beast and his shambling yet gracefully lithe walk struck my sense of humour with a ludicrous comparison.

Laughing, I pointed toward the beast and said, 'That fellow looks like a hyena-imitation of Senecoza, the fetish-man.' My simple statement seemed to throw the native into a more abject fear than ever.

He turned his pony and dashed off in the general direction of the ranch, looking back at me with a scared face.

I followed, annoyed. And as I rode I pondered. Hyenas, a fetish-man, a chief torn to pieces, a countryside of natives in fear; what was the connection? I puzzled and puzzled, but I was new to Africa; I was young and impatient, and presently with a shrug of annoyance I discarded the whole problem.

The next time Senecoza came to the ranch, he managed to stop directly in front of me. For a fleeting instant his glittering eyes looked into mine. And in spite of myself, I shuddered and stepped back, involuntarily, feeling much as a man feels who looks unaware into the eyes of a serpent. There was nothing tangible, nothing on which I could base a quarrel, but there was a distinct threat. Before my Nordic pugnacity could reassert itself, he was gone. I said nothing. But I knew that Senecoza hated me for some reason and that he plotted my killing. Why, I did not know.

As for me, my distrust grew into bewildered rage, which in turn became hate.

And then Ellen Farel came to the ranch. Why she should choose a trading-ranch in East Africa for a place to rest from the society life of New York, I do not know. Africa is no place for a woman. That is what Ludtvik, also a cousin of hers, told her, but he was overjoyed to see her. As for me, girls never interested me much; usually I felt like a fool in their presence and was glad to be out. But there were few whites in the vicinity and I tired of the company of Ludtvik.

Ellen was standing on the wide veranda when I first saw her, a slim, pretty young thing, with rosy cheeks and hair like gold and large grey eyes. She was surprisingly winsome in her costume of riding-breeches, puttees, jacket and light helmet.

I felt extremely awkward, dusty and stupid as I sat on my wiry African pony and stared at her.

She saw a stocky youth of medium height, with sandy hair, eyes in which a kind of grey predominated; an ordinary, unhandsome youth, clad in dusty riding-clothes and a cartridge belt on one side of which was slung an ancient Colt of big calibre, and on the other a long, wicked hunting-knife.

I dismounted, and she came forward, hand outstretched.

'I'm Ellen,' she said, 'and I know you're Steve. Cousin Ludtvik has been telling me about you.'

I shook hands, surprised at the thrill the mere touch of her hand gave me.

She was enthusiastic about the ranch. She was enthusiastic about everything. Seldom have I seen anyone who had more vigour and vim, more enjoyment of everything done. She fairly scintillated with mirth and gaiety.

Ludtvik gave her the best horse on the place, and we rode much about the ranch and over the veldt.

She couldn't understand why she should treat the black people as dust beneath her feet. We had long arguments about it. I could not convince her, so I told her bluntly that she didn't know anything about it and she must do as I told her.

She pouted her pretty lips and called me a tyrant, and then was off over the veldt like an antelope, laughing at me over her shoulder, her hair blowing free in the breeze.

Tyrant! I was her slave from the first. Somehow the idea of becoming a lover never enter my mind. It was not the fact that she was several years older than I, or that she had a sweetheart (several of them, I think) back in New York. Simply, I worshipped her; her presence intoxicated me, and I could think of no more enjoyable existence than serving her as a devoted slave.

I was mending a saddle one day when she came running in.

'Oh, Steve!' she called; 'there's the most romantic-looking savage! Come quick and tell me what his name is.'

She led me out of the veranda.

'There he is,' she said, naively pointing. Arms folded, haughty head thrown back, stood Senecoza.

Ludtvik who was talking to him, paid no attention to the girl until he had completed his business with the fetish-man; and then, turning, he took her arm and they went into the house together.

Again I was face to face with the savage; but this time he was not looking at me. With a rage amounting almost to madness, I saw that he was gazing after the girl. There was an expression in his serpent-like eyes . . .

On the instant my gun was out and levelled. My hand shook like a leaf with the intensity of my fury. Surely I must shoot Senecoza down like the snake he was, shoot him down and riddle him, shoot him into a shredded heap!

The fleeting expression left his eyes and they were fixed on me. Detached they seemed, inhuman in their sardonic calm. And I could not pull the trigger.

For a moment we stood, and then he turned and strode away, a magnificent figure, while I glared after him and snarled with helpless fury.

I sat down on the veranda. What a man of mystery was that savage! What strange power did he possess? Was I right, I wondered, in interpreting the fleeting expression as he gazed after the girl? It seemed to me, in my youth and folly, incredible that a black man, no matter what his rank, should look at a white woman as he did. Most astonishing of all, why could I not shoot him down?

I started as a hand touched my arm.

'What are thinking about, Steve?' asked Ellen, laughing. Then before I could say anything, 'Wasn't that chief, or whatever he was, a fine specimen of a savage? He invited us to come to his kraal; is that what you call it? It's away off in the veldt somewhere, and we're going.'

'No!' I exclaimed violently, springing up.

'Why Steve,' she gasped recoiling, 'how rude! He's a perfect gentleman, isn't he, Cousin Ludtvik?'

'*Ja*,' nodded Ludtvik, placidly, 'we go to his kraal sometime soon, maybe. A strong chief, that savage. His chief has perhaps good trade.'

'No!' I repeated furiously. '*I'll* go if somebody has to! Ellen's not going near that beast!'

'Well, that's nice!' remarked Ellen, somewhat indignantly. 'I guess you're my boss, mister man?'

With all her sweetness, she had a mind of her own. In spite of all I could do, they arranged to go to the fetish-man's village the next day.

That night the girl came out to me, where I sat on the veranda in the moonlight, and she sat down on the arm of my chair.

'You're not angry at me, are you, Steve?' she said, wistfully, putting her arm around my shoulders. 'Not mad, are you?'

Mad? Yes, maddened by the touch of her soft body – such mad devotion as a slave feels. I wanted to grovel in the dust at her feet and kiss her dainty shoes. Will women never learn the effect they have on men?

I took her hand hesitantly and pressed it to my lips. I think she must have sensed some of my devotion.

'Dear Steve,' she murmured, and the words were like a caress, 'come, let's walk in the moonlight.'

We walked outside the stockade. I should have known better, for I had no weapon but the big Turkish dagger I carried and used for a hunting-knife, but she wished to.

'Tell me about this Senecoza,' she asked, and I welcomed the opportunity. And then I thought: what could I tell her? That hyenas had eaten a small chief of the Masai? That the natives feared the fetish-man? That he had looked at her?

And then the girl screamed as out of the tall grass leaped a vague shape, half-seen in the moonlight.

I felt a heavy, hairy form crash against my shoulders; keen fangs ripped my upflung arm. I went to the earth, fighting with frenzied horror. My jacket was slit to ribbons and the fangs were at my throat before I found and drew my knife and stabbed, blindly and savagely. I felt my blade rip into my foe, and then, like a shadow, it was gone. I staggered to my feet, somewhat shaken. The girl caught and steadied me.

'What was it?' she gasped, leading me toward the stockade.

'A hyena,' I answered. 'I could tell by the scent. But I never heard of one attacking like that.'

She shuddered. Later on, after my torn arm had been bandaged, she came close to me and said in a wondrously subdued voice, 'Steve, I've decided not to go to the village, if you don't want me to.'

After the wounds on my arm had become scars Ellen and I resumed our rides, as might be expected. One day we had wandered rather far out on the veldt, and she challenged me to a race. Her horse easily distanced mine, and she stopped and waited for me, laughing.

She had stopped on a sort of kopje, and she pointed to a clump of trees some distance away.

'Trees!' she said gleefully. 'Let's ride down there. There are so few trees on the veldt.'

And she dashed away. I followed some instinctive caution, loosening my pistol in its holster, and, drawing my knife, I thrust it down in my boot so that it was entirely concealed.

We were perhaps halfway to the trees when from the tall grass about us leaped Senecoza and some twenty warriors.

One seized the girl's bridle and the others rushed me. The one who caught at Ellen went down with a bullet between his eyes, and another crumpled at my second shot. Then a thrown war-club hurled me from the saddle, half-senseless, and as the blacks closed in on me I saw Ellen's horse, driven frantic by the prick of a carelessly handled spear, scream and rear, scattering the blacks who held her, and dash away at headlong speed, the bit in her teeth.

I saw Senecoza leap on my horse and give chase, flinging a savage command over his shoulder; and both vanished over the kopje.

The warriors bound me hand and foot and carried me into the trees. A hut stood among them – a native hut of thatch and bark. Somehow the sight of it set me shuddering. It seemed to lurk, repellent and indescribably malevolent amongst the trees; to hint of horrid and obscene rites; of voodoo.

I know not why it is, but the sight of a native hut, alone and hidden, far from a village or tribe, always has to me a suggestion of nameless horror.

In front of the hut they threw me down.

'When Senecoza returns with the girl,' said they, 'you will enter.' And they laughed like fiends. Then, leaving one to see that I did not escape, they left.

The black who remained kicked me viciously; he was armed with a trade-musket.

'They go to kill, fool!' he mocked me. 'They go to the ranches and trading-posts, first to that fool of an Englishman.' Meaning Smith, the owner of a neighbouring ranch.

And he went on giving details. Senecoza had made the plot, he boasted. They would chase all the white men to the coast.

'Senecoza is more than a man,' he boasted. 'You shall see, white man,' lowering his voice and glancing about him, from beneath his low, beetling brows; 'you shall see the magic of Senecoza.'

And meantime Ellen was riding like mad, gaining on the fetish-man, but unable to ride toward the ranch, for he had gotten between and was forcing her steadily out upon the veldt.

The black unfastened my bonds. His line of reasoning was easy to see; absurdly easy. He could not kill a prisoner of the fetish-man, but he could kill him to prevent his escape. And he was maddened with the blood-lust. Stepping back, he half-raised his trade-musket, watching me as a snake watches a rabbit.

It must have been about that time, as she afterward told me, that Ellen's horse stumbled and threw her. Before she could rise, the black had leaped from his horse and seized her in his arms. She screamed and fought, but he gripped her, held her helpless and laughed at her. Tearing her jacket to pieces, he bound her arms and legs, remounted and started back, carrying the half-fainting girl in front of him.

Back in front of the hut I rose slowly. I rubbed my arms where the ropes had been, moved a little closer, stretched, stooped and rubbed my legs; then with a catlike bound I was on him, my knife flashing from my boot. The trade-musket crashed and the charge whizzed above my head as I knocked up the barrel and closed with him. Hand to hand, I would have been no match for the giant; but I had the knife. Clinched close together we were too close for him to use the trade-musket for a club. He wasted time trying to do that, and with a desperate effort I threw him off his balance and drove the dagger to the hilt in his chest.

I wrenched it out again; I had no other weapon, for I could find no more ammunition for the trade-musket.

I had no idea which way Ellen had fled. I assumed she had gone toward the ranch, and in that direction I took my way. Smith must be warned. The warriors were far ahead of me. Even then they might be creeping up about the unsuspecting ranch.

I had not covered a fourth of the distance, when a drumming of hoofs behind me caused me to turn my head. Ellen's horse was thundering toward me, riderless. I caught her as she raced past me, and managed to stop her. The story was plain. The girl had either reached a place of safety and had turned the horse loose, or what was much more likely, had been captured, the horse escaping and fleeing toward the ranch, as a horse will do. I gripped the saddle, torn with indecision. Finally I leaped on the horse and sent her flying toward Smith's ranch. It was not many miles; Smith must not be massacred by those devils, and I must find a gun if I escaped to rescue the girl from Senecoza.

A half-mile from Smith's I overtook the raiders and went through them like drifting smoke. The workers at Smith's place were startled by a wild-riding horseman charging headlong into the stockade, shouting, 'Masai! Masai! A raid, you fools!' snatching a gun and flying out again.

So when the savages arrived they found everybody ready for them, and they got such a warm reception that after one attempt they turned tail and fled back across the veldt.

And I was riding as I never rode before. The mare was almost exhausted, but I pushed her mercilessly. On, on!

I aimed for the only place I knew likely. The hut among the trees. I assumed that the fetish-man would return there.

And long before the hut came into sight, a horseman dashed from the grass, going at right angles to my course, and our horses, colliding, sent both tired animals to the ground.

'Steve!' It was a cry of joy mingled with fear. Ellen lay, tied hand and foot, gazing up at me wildly as I regained my feet.

Senecoza came with a rush, his long knife flashing in the sunlight. Back and forth we fought – slash, ward and parry, my ferocity and agility matching his savagery and skill.

A terrific lunge which he aimed at me, I caught on my point, laying his arm open, and then with a quick engage and wrench, disarmed him. But before I could use my advantage, he sprang away into the grass and vanished.

I caught up the girl, slashing her bonds, and she clung to me, poor child, until I lifted her and carried her toward the horses. But we were not yet through with Senecoza. He must have had a rifle cached away somewhere in the bush, for the first I knew of him was when a bullet spat within a foot above my head.

I caught at the bridles, and then I saw that the mare had done all she could, temporarily. She was exhausted. I swung Ellen up on the horse.

'Ride for our ranch,' I ordered her. 'The raiders are out, but you can get through. Ride low and ride fast!'

'But you, Steve!'

'Go, go!' I ordered, swinging her horse around and starting it. She dashed away, looking at me wistfully over her shoulder. Then I snatched the rifle and a handful of cartridges I had gotten at Smith's, and took to the bush. And through the hot African day, Senecoza and I played a game of hide-and-seek. Crawling, slipping in and out of the scanty veldt-bushes, crouching in the tall grass, we traded shots back and forth. A movement of the grass, a snapping twig, the rasp of grass-blades, and a bullet came questing, another answering it.

I had but a few cartridges and I fired carefully, but presently I pushed my one remaining cartridge into the rifle – a big, six-bore, single-barrel breech-loader, for I had not had time to pick when I snatched it up.

I crouched in my covert and watched. Not a sound, not a whisper among the grasses. Away off over the veldt a hyena sounded his fiendish laugh and another answered, closer at hand. The cold sweat broke out on my brow.

What was that? A drumming of many horses' hoofs! Raiders returning? I ventured a look and could have shouted for joy. At least twenty men were sweeping toward me, and ahead of them all rode Ellen! They were still some distance away. I darted behind a tall bush and rose, waving my hand to attract their attention.

They shouted and pointed to something beyond me. I whirled and saw, some thirty yards away, a huge hyena slinking toward me, rapidly. I glanced carefully across the veldt. Somewhere out there, hidden by the billowing grasses, lurked Senecoza. A shot would betray to him my position – and I had but one cartridge. The rescue party was still out of range.

I looked again at the hyena. He was still rushing toward me. There was no doubt as to his intentions. His eyes glittered like a fiend's from Hell, and a scar on his shoulder showed him to be the same beast that had once before attacked me. Then a kind of horror took hold of me, and resting the old elephant rifle over my elbow, I sent my last bullet crashing through the bestial thing. With a scream that seemed to have a horribly human note in it, the hyena turned and fled back into the bush, reeling as it ran.

And the rescue party swept up around me.

A fusillade of bullets crashed through the bush from which Senecoza had sent his last shot. There was no reply.

'Ve hunt ter snake down,' quoth Cousin Ludtvik, his Boer accent increasing with his excitement. And we scattered through the veldt in a skirmish line, combing every inch of it warily.

Not a trace of the fetish-man did we find. A rifle we found, empty, with empty shells scattered about, and (which was very strange) *hyena tracks leading away from the rifle.*

I felt the short hairs of my neck bristle with intangible horror. We looked at each other, and said not a word, as with a tacit agreement we took up the trail of the hyena.

We followed it as it wound in and out in the shoulder-high grass, showing how it had slipped up on me, stalking me as a tiger stalks its victim. We struck the trail the thing had made, returning to the bush after I had shot it. Splashes of blood marked the way it had taken. We followed.

'It leads toward the fetish-hut,' muttered an Englishman. 'Here, sirs, is a damnable mystery.'

And Cousin Ludtvik ordered Ellen to stay back, leaving two men with her.

We followed the trail over the kopje and into the clump of trees. Straight to the door of the hut it led. We circled the hut cautiously, but no tracks led away. It was inside the hut. Rifles ready, we forced the rude door.

No tracks led away from the hut and no tracks led to it except the tracks of the hyena. Yet there was no hyena within that hut; and on the dirt floor, a bullet through his breast, lay Senecoza, the fetish-man.

Rattle of Bones

"Landlord, ho!" The shout broke the lowering silence and reverberated through the black forest with sinister echoing.

"This place hath a forbidding aspect, meseemeth."

Two men stood in front of the forest tavern. The building was low, long and rambling, built of heavy logs. Its small windows were heavily barred and the door was closed. Above the door its sinister sign showed faintly--a cleft skull.

This door swung slowly open and a bearded face peered out. The owner of the face stepped back and motioned his guests to enter—with a grudging gesture it seemed. A candle gleamed on a table; a flame smoldered in the fireplace.

"Your names?"

"Solomon Kane," said the taller man briefly.

"Gaston l'Armon," the other spoke curtly. "But what is that to you?"

"Strangers are few in the Black Forest," grunted the host, "bandits many. Sit at yonder table and I will bring food."

The two men sat down, with the bearing of

men who have traveled far. One was a tall gaunt man, clad in a featherless hat and somber black garments, which set off the dark pallor of his forbidding face. The other was of a different type entirely, bedecked with lace and plumes, although his finery was somewhat stained from travel. He was handsome in a bold way, and his restless eyes shifted from side to side, never still an instant.

The host brought wine and food to the rough-hewn table and then stood back in the shadows, like a somber image. His features, now receding into vagueness, now luridly etched in the firelight as it leaped and flickered, were masked in a beard which seemed almost animal-like in thickness. A great nose curved above this beard and two small red eyes stared unblinkingly at his guests.

"Who are you?" suddenly asked the younger man.

"I am the host of the Cleft Skull Tavern," sullenly replied the other. His tone seemed to challenge his questioner to ask further.

"Do you have many guests?" l'Armon pursued.

"Few come twice," the host grunted.

Kane started and glanced up straight into those small red eyes, as if he sought for some hidden meaning in the host's words. The flaming eyes seemed to dilate, then dropped sullenly before the Englishman's cold stare.

"I'm for bed," said Kane abruptly, bringing his meal to a close. "I must take up my journey by daylight."

"And I," added the Frenchman. "Host, show us to our chambers."

Black shadows wavered on the walls as the two followed their silent host down a long, dark hall. The stocky, broad body of their guide seemed to grow and expand in the light of the small candle which he carried, throwing a long, grim shadow behind him.

At a certain door he halted, indicating that they were to sleep there. They entered; the host lit a candle with the one he carried, then lurched back the way he had come.

In the chamber the two men glanced at each other. The only furnishings of the room were a couple of bunks, a chair or two and a heavy table.

"Let us see if there be any way to make fast the door," said Kane.

"I like not the looks of mine host."

"There are racks on door and jamb for a bar," said Gaston, "but no bar."

"We might break up the table and use its pieces for a bar," mused Kane.

"Mon Dieu," said l'Armon, "you are timorous, m'sieu."

Kane scowled. "I like not being murdered in my sleep," he answered gruffly.

"My faith!" the Frenchman laughed. "We are chance met--until I overtook you on the forest road an hour before sunset, we had never seen each other."

"I have seen you somewhere before," answered

Kane, "though I can not now recall where. As for the other, I assume every man is an honest fellow until he shows me he is a rogue; moreover, I am a light sleeper and slumber with a pistol at hand."

The Frenchman laughed again.

"I was wondering how m'sieu could bring himself to sleep in the room with a stranger! Ha! Ha! All right, m'sieu Englishman, let us go forth and take a bar from one of the other rooms."

Taking the candle with them, they went into the corridor. Utter silence reigned and the small candle twinkled redly and evilly in the thick darkness.

"Mine host hath neither guests nor servants," muttered Solomon Kane. "A strange tavern! What is the name, now? These German words come not easily to me--the Cleft Skull? A bloody name, i'faith."

They tried the rooms next to theirs, but no bar rewarded their search. At last they came to the last room at the end of the corridor. They entered. It was furnished like the rest, except that the door was provided with a small barred opening, and fastened from the outside with a heavy bolt, which was secured at one end to the door-jamb. They raised the bolt and looked in.

"There should be an outer window, but there is not," muttered Kane. "Look!"

The floor was stained darkly. The walls and the one bunk were hacked in places, great splinters having been torn away.

"Men have died in here," said Kane, somberly.

"Is yonder not a bar fixed in the wall?"

"Aye, but 'tis made fast," said the Frenchman, tugging at it. "The--"

A section of the wall swung back and Gaston gave a quick exclamation. A small, secret room was revealed, and the two men bent over the grisly thing that lay upon its floor.

"The skeleton of a man!" said Gaston. "And behold, how his bony leg is shackled to the floor! He was imprisoned here and died."

"Nay," said Kane, "the skull is cleft--methinks mine host had a grim reason for the name of his hellish tavern. This man, like us, was no doubt a wanderer who fell into the fiend's hands."

"Likely," said Gaston without interest; he was engaged in idly working the great iron ring from the skeleton's leg bones. Failing in this, he drew his sword and with an exhibition of remarkable strength cut the chain which joined the ring on the leg to a ring set deep in the log floor.

"Why should he shackle a skeleton to the floor?" mused the Frenchman. "Monbleu! 'Tis a waste of good chain. Now, m'sieu," he ironically addressed the white heap of bones, "I have freed you and you may go where you like!"

"Have done!" Kane's voice was deep. "No good will come of mocking the dead."

"The dead should defend themselves," laughed l'Armon. "Somehow, I will slay the man who kills me, though my corpse climb up forty fathoms of ocean to do it."

Kane turned toward the outer door, closing the door of the secret room behind him. He liked not this talk which smacked of demonry and witchcraft; and he was in haste to face the host with the charge of his guilt.

As he turned, with his back to the Frenchman, he felt the touch of cold steel against his neck and knew that a pistol muzzle was pressed close beneath the base of his brain.

"Move not, m'sieu!" The voice was low and silky. "Move not, or I will scatter your few brains over the room."

The Puritan, raging inwardly, stood with his hands in air while l'Armon slipped his pistols and sword from their sheaths.

"Now you can turn," said Gaston, stepping back.

Kane bent a grim eye on the dapper fellow, who stood bareheaded now, hat in one hand, the other hand leveling his long pistol.

"Gaston the Butcher!" said the Englishman somberly. "Fool that I was to trust a Frenchman! You range far, murderer! I remember you now, with that cursed great hat off--I saw you in Calais some years agone."

"Aye--and now you will see me never again. What was that?"

"Rats exploring yon skeleton," said Kane, watching the bandit like a hawk, waiting for a single slight wavering of that black gun muzzle. "The sound was of the rattle of bones."

"Like enough," returned the other. "Now, M'sieu Kane, I know you carry considerable money on your person. I had thought to wait until you slept and then slay you, but the opportunity presented itself and I took it. You trick easily."

"I had little thought that I should fear a man with whom I had broken bread," said Kane, a deep timbre of slow fury sounding in his voice.

The bandit laughed cynically. His eyes narrowed as he began to back slowly toward the outer door. Kane's sinews tensed involuntarily; he gathered himself like a giant wolf about to launch himself in a death leap, but Gaston's hand was like a rock and the pistol never trembled.

"We will have no death plunges after the shot," said Gaston. "Stand still, m'sieu; I have seen men killed by dying men, and I wish to have distance enough between us to preclude that possibility. My faith--I will shoot, you will roar and charge, but you will die before you reach me with your bare hands. And mine host will have another skeleton in his secret niche. That is, if I do not kill him myself. The fool knows me not nor I him, moreover--"

The Frenchman was in the doorway now, sighting along the barrel. The candle, which had been stuck in a niche on the wall, shed a weird and flickering light which did not extend past the doorway. And with the suddenness of death, from the darkness behind Gaston's back, a broad, vague form rose up and a gleaming blade swept down. The Frenchman went to his knees like a butchered ox, his brains spilling from his cleft skull. Above him towered the figure of the host, a wild and terrible spectacle, still holding the hanger with which he had slain the bandit.

"Ho! ho!" he roared. "Back!"

Kane had leaped forward as Gaston fell, but the host thrust into his very face a long pistol which he held in his left hand.

"Back!" he repeated in a tigerish roar, and Kane retreated from the menacing weapon and the insanity in the red eyes.

The Englishman stood silent, his flesh crawling as he sensed a deeper and more hideous threat than the Frenchman had offered. There was something inhuman about this man, who now swayed to and fro like some great forest beast while his mirthless laughter boomed out again.

"Gaston the Butcher!" he shouted, kicking the corpse at his feet. "Ho! ho! My fine brigand will hunt no more! I had heard of this fool who roamed the Black Forest--he wished gold and he found death! Now your gold shall be mine; and more than gold--vengeance!"

"I am no foe of yours," Kane spoke calmly.

"All men are my foes! Look--the marks on my wrists! See--the marks on my ankles! And deep in my back--the kiss of the knout! And deep in my brain, the wounds of the years of the cold, silent cells where I lay as punishment for a crime I never committed!" The voice broke in a hideous, grotesque sob.

Kane made no answer. This man was not the first he had seen whose brain had shattered amid the horrors of the terrible Continental prisons.

"But I escaped!" the scream rose triumphantly. "And here I make war on all men ... What was that?"

Did Kane see a flash of fear in those hideous eyes?

"My sorcerer is rattling his bones!" whispered the host, then laughed wildly. "Dying, he swore his very bones would weave a net of death for me. I shackled his corpse to the floor, and now, deep in the night, I hear his bare skeleton clash and rattle as he seeks to be free, and I laugh, I laugh! Ho! ho! How he yearns to rise and stalk like old King Death along these dark corridors when I sleep, to slay me in my bed!"

Suddenly the insane eyes flared hideously: "You were in that secret room, you and this dead fool! Did he talk to you?"

Kane shuddered in spite of himself. Was it insanity or did he actually hear the faint rattle of bones, as if the skeleton had moved slightly? Kane shrugged his shoulders; rats will even tug at dusty bones.

The host was laughing again. He sidled around Kane, keeping the Englishman always covered, and with his free hand opened the door. All was darkness within, so that Kane could not even see the glimmer of the bones on the floor.

"All men are my foes!" mumbled the host, in the incoherent manner of the insane. "Why should I spare any man? Who lifted a hand to my aid when I lay for years in the vile dungeons of Karlsruhe--and for a deed never proven? Something happened to my brain, then. I became as a wolf--a brother to these of the Black Forest to which I fled when I escaped.

"They have feasted, my brothers, on all who lay in my tavern—all except this one who now clashes his bones, this magician from Russia. Lest he come stalking back through the black shadows when night is over the world, and slay me--for who may slay the dead?--I stripped his bones and shackled him. His sorcery was not powerful enough to save him from me, but all men know that a dead magician is more evil than a living one. Move not, Englishman! Your bones I shall leave in this secret room beside this one, to--"

The maniac was standing partly in the doorway of the secret room, now, his weapon still menacing Kane. Suddenly he seemed to topple backward, and vanished in the darkness; and at the same instant a vagrant gust of wind swept down the outer corridor and slammed the door shut behind him. The candle on the wall flickered and went out. Kane's groping hands, sweeping over the floor, found a pistol, and he straightened, facing the door where the maniac had vanished. He stood in the utter darkness, his blood freezing, while a hideous muffled screaming came from the secret room, intermingled with the dry, grisly rattle of fleshless bones. Then silence fell.

Kane found flint and steel and lighted the candle. Then, holding it in one hand and the pistol in the other, he opened the secret door.

"Great God!" he muttered as cold sweat formed on his body. "This thing is beyond all reason, yet with mine own eyes I see it! Two vows have here been kept, for Gaston the Butcher swore that even in death he would avenge his slaying, and his was the hand which set yon fleshless monster free. And he--"

The host of the Cleft Skull lay lifeless on the floor of the secret room, his bestial face set in lines of terrible fear; and deep in his broken neck were sunk the bare fingerbones of the sorcerer's skeleton.

Sea Curse

And some return by the failing light
And some in the waking dream.
For she hears the heels of the dripping ghosts
That ride the rough roofbeam.

KIPLING

They were the brawlers and braggarts, the loud boasters and hard drinkers of Faring town, John Kulrek and his crony Lie-lip Canool. Many a time have I, a tousle-haired lad, stolen to the tavern door to listen to their curses, their profane arguments and wild sea songs; half fearful and half in admiration of these wild rovers. Aye, all the people of Faring town gazed on them with fear and admiration, for they were not like the rest of the Faring men; they were not content to ply their trade along the coasts and among the shark-teeth shoals. No yawls, no skiffs for them! They fared far, farther than any other man in the village, for they shipped on the great sailing-ships that went out on the white tides to brave the restless grey ocean and make ports in strange lands.

Ah, I mind it was swift times in the little sea-coast village of Faring when John Kulrek came home, with the furtive Lie-lip at his side, swaggering down the gang-plank, in his tarry sea-clothes and the broad leather belt that held his ever-ready dagger; shouting condescending greeting to some favoured acquaintance, kissing some maiden who ventured too near; then up the street, roaring some scarcely decent song of the sea. How the cringers and the idlers, the hangers-on, would swarm about the two desperate heroes, flattering and smirking, guffawing hilariously at each nasty jest. For to the tavern loafers and to some of the weaker among the straightforward villagers, these men with their wild talk and their brutal deeds, their tales of the Seven Seas and the far countries, these men, I say, were valiant knights, nature's noblemen who dared to be men of blood and brawn.

And all feared them, so that when a man was beaten or a woman insulted, the villagers muttered . . . and did nothing. And so when

Moll Farrell's niece was put to shame by John Kulrek, none dared even to put into words what all thought. Moll had never married, and she and the girl lived alone in a little hut down close to the beach, so close that in high tide the waves came almost to the door.

The people of the village accounted old Moll something of a witch, and she was a grim, gaunt old dame who had little to say to anyone. But she minded her own business, and eked out a slim living by gathering clams, and picking up bits of driftwood.

The girl was a pretty, foolish little thing, vain and easily befooled, else she had never yielded to the shark-like blandishments of John Kulrek.

I mind the day was a cold winter day with a sharp breeze out of the east when the old dame came into the village street shrieking that the girl had vanished. All scattered over the beach and back among the bleak inland hills to search for her . . . all save John Kulrek and his cronies who sat in the tavern dicing and toping. All the while beyond the shoals, we heard the never-ceasing droning of the heaving, restless grey monster, and in the dim light of the ghostly dawn Moll Farrell's girl came home.

The tides bore her gently across the wet sands and laid her almost at her own door. Virgin-white she was, and her arms were folded across her still bosom; calm was her face, and the grey tides sighed about her slender limbs. Moll Farrell's eyes were stones, yet she stood above her dead girl and spoke no word till John Kulrek and his crony came reeling down from the tavern, their drinking-jacks still in their hands. Drunk was John Kulrek, and the people gave back for him, murder in their souls; so he came and laughed at Moll Farrell across the body of her girl.

'Zounds!' swore John Kulrek; 'the wench has drowned herself, Lie-lip!'

Lie-lip laughed, with the twist of his thin mouth. He always hated Moll Farrell, for it was she that had given him the name of Lie-lip.

Then John Kulrek lifted his drinking-jack, swaying on his uncertain legs. 'A health to the wench's ghost!' he bellowed, while all stood aghast.

Then Moll Farrell spoke, and the words broke from her in a scream which sent ripples of cold up and down the spines of the throng.

'The curse of the Foul Fiend upon you, John Kulrek!' she screamed. 'The curse of God rest upon your vile soul throughout eternity! May you gaze on sights that shall sear the eyes of you and scorch the soul of you! May you die a bloody death and writhe in hell's flames for a million and a million and yet a million years! I curse you by sea and by land, by earth and by air, by the demons of the swamplands, the fiends of the forest and the goblins of the hills! And you' – her lean finger stabbed at Lie-lip Canool and he started backward, his face paling – 'you shall be the death of John Kulrek and he shall be the death of you! You shall bring John Kulrek to the doors of hell and John Kulrek shall bring you to the gallows-tree! I set the seal of death upon your brow, John Kulrek! You shall live in terror and die in horror far out upon the cold grey sea! But the sea that took the soul of innocence to her bosom shall not take you, but shall fling forth your vile carcass to the sands! Aye, John Kulrek' – and she spoke with such a terrible intensity that the drunken mockery on the man's face changed to one of swinish stupidity – 'the sea roars for the victim it will not keep! There is snow upon the hills, John Kulrek, and ere it melts your corpse will lie at my feet. And I shall spit upon it and be content.'

Kulrek and his crony sailed at dawn for a long voyage, and Moll went back to her hut and her clam-gathering. She seemed to grow leaner and more grim than ever and her eyes smouldered with a light not sane. The days glided by and people whispered among themselves that Moll's days were numbered, for she faded to a ghost of a woman; but she went her way, refusing all aid.

That was a short, cold summer and the snow on the barren inland hills never melted; a thing very unusual, which caused much comment among the villagers. At dusk and at dawn Moll would come up on the beach, gaze up at the snow which glittered on the hills, then out to sea with a fierce intensity in her gaze.

Then the days grew shorter, the nights longer and darker, and the cold grey tides came sweeping along the bleak strands, bearing the rain and sleet of the sharp east breezes.

And upon a bleak day a trading-vessel sailed into the bay and anchored. And all the idlers and the wastrels flocked to the wharfs, for that was the ship upon which John Kulrek and Lie-lip Canool had sailed. Down the gang-plank came Lie-lip, more furtive than ever, but John Kulrek was not there.

To shouted queries, Canool shook his head. 'Kulrek deserted ship at a port of Sumatra,' said he. 'He had a row with the skipper, lads; wanted me to desert, too, but no! I had to see you fine lads again, eh boys?'

Almost cringing was Lie-lip Canool, and suddenly he recoiled as Moll Farrell came through the throng. A moment they stood eying each other; then Moll's grim lips bent in a terrible smile.

'There's blood on your hand, Canool!' she lashed out suddenly – so suddenly that Lie-lip started and rubbed his right hand across his left sleeve.

'Stand aside, witch!' he snarled in sudden anger, striding through the crowd which gave back for him. His admirers followed him to the tavern.

Now, I mind that the next day was even colder; grey fogs came drifting out of the east and veiled the sea and the beaches. There would be no sailing that day, and so all the villagers were in their snug houses or matching tales at the tavern. So it came that Joe, my friend, a lad of my own age, and I, were the ones who saw the first of the strange things that happened.

Being harum-scarum lads of no wisdom, we were sitting in a small rowboat, floating at the end of the wharfs, each shivering and wishing the other would suggest leaving, there being no reason whatever for our being there, save that it was a good place to build air-castles undisturbed.

Suddenly Joe raised his hand. 'Say,' he said, 'd'ye hear? Who can be out on the bay upon a day like this?'

'Nobody. What d'ye hear?'

'Oars. Or I'm a lubber. Listen.'

There was no seeing anything in that fog, and I heard nothing. Yet Joe swore he did, and suddenly his face assumed a strange look.

'Somebody rowing out there, I tell you! The bay is alive with oars from the sound! A score of boats at the least! Ye dolt, can ye not hear?'

Then, as I shook my head, he leaped and began to undo the painter.

'I'm off to see. Name me liar if the bay is not full of boats, all together like a close fleet. Are you with me?'

Yes, I was with him, though I heard nothing. Then out in the greyness we went, and the fog closed behind and before so that we drifted in a vague world of smoke, seeing naught and hearing naught. We were lost in no time, and I cursed Joe for leading us upon a wild goose chase that was like to end with our being swept out to sea. I thought of Moll Farrell's girl and shuddered.

How long we drifted I know not. Minutes faded into hours, hours into centuries. Still Joe swore he heard the oars, now close at hand, now far away, and for hours we followed them, steering our course toward the sound, as the noise grew or receded. This I later thought of, and could not understand.

Then, when my hands were so numb that I could no longer hold the oar, and the forerunning drowsiness of cold and exhaustion was stealing over me, weak white stars broke through the fog which glided suddenly away, fading like a ghost of smoke, and we found ourselves afloat just outside the mouth of the bay. The waters lay smooth as a pond, all dark green and silver in the starlight, and the cold came crisper than ever. I was swinging the boat about, to put back into the bay, when Joe gave a shout, and for the first time I heard the clack of oar-locks. I glanced over my shoulder and my blood went cold.

A great beaked prow loomed above us, a weird, unfamiliar shape against the stars, and as I caught my breath, sheered sharply and swept by us, with a curious swishing I never heard any other craft make. Joe screamed and backed oars frantically, and the boat wallowed out of the way just in time; for though the prow missed us, still otherwise we had died. For from the sides of the ship stood long oars, bank upon bank which swept her along. Though I had never seen such a craft, I knew her for a galley. But what was she doing upon our coasts? They said, the far-farers, that such ships were still in use among the heathens of Barbary; but it was many a long, heaving mile to Barbary, and even so she did not resemble the ships described by those who had sailed far.

We started in pursuit, and this was strange, for though the waters broke about her prow, and she seemed fairly to fly through the waves, yet she was making little speed, and it was no time before we caught up with her. Making our painter fast to a chain far back beyond the reach of the swishing oars, we hailed those on deck. But there came no answer, and at last, conquering our fears, we clambered up the chain and found ourselves upon the strangest deck man has trod for many a long, roaring century.

Joe muttered fearsomely. 'Look, how old it seems! Almost ready to fall to pieces. Why, 'tis fairly rotten!'

There was no one on deck, no one at the long sweep with which the craft was steered. We stole to the hold and looked down the stair. Then and there, if ever men were on the verge of insanity, it was we. For there were rowers there, it is true; they sat upon the rowers' benches and drove the creaking oars through the grey waters. And they that rowed were skeletons!

Shrieking, we plunged across the deck, to fling ourselves into the sea. But at the rail I tripped upon something and fell headlong, and as I lay, I saw a thing which vanquished my fear of the horrors below for an instant. The thing upon which I had tripped was a human body, and in the dim grey light that was beginning to steal across the eastern waves I saw a dagger hilt standing up between his shoulders. Joe was at the rail, urging me to haste, and together we slid down the chain and cut the painter.

Then we stood off into the bay. Straight on kept the grim galley, and we followed, slowly, wondering. She seemed to be heading straight for the beach beside the wharfs, and as we approached, we saw the wharfs thronged with people. They had missed us, no doubt, and now they stood, there in the early dawn light, struck dumb by the apparition which had come up out of the night and the grim ocean.

Straight on swept the galley, her oars a-swish; then ere she reached the shallow water – crash! – a terrific reverberation shook the bay. Before our eyes the grim craft seemed to melt away; then she vanished, and the green waters seethed where she had ridden, but there floated no driftwood there, nor did there ever float any ashore. Aye, something floated ashore, but it was grim driftwood!

We made the landing amid a hum of excited conversation that stopped suddenly. Moll Farrell stood before her hut, limned gauntly against the ghostly dawn, her lean hand pointing sea-ward. And across the sighing wet sands, borne by the grey tide, something came floating; something that the waves dropped at Moll Farrell's feet. And there looked up at us, as we crowded about, a pair of unseeing eyes set in a still, white face. John Kulrek had come home.

Still and grim he lay, rocked by the tide, and as he lurched side-ways, all saw the dagger hilt that stood from his back . . . the dagger all of us had seen a thousand times at the belt of Lie-lip Canool.

'Aye, I killed him!' came Canool's shriek, as he writhed and grov-elled before our gaze. 'At sea on a still night in a drunken brawl I slew him and hurled him overboard! And from the far seas he has followed me' – his voice sank to a hideous whisper – 'because of the curse the sea would not keep his body!'

And the wretch sank down, trembling, the shadow of the gallows already in his eyes.

'Aye!' Strong, deep and exultant was Moll Farrell's voice. 'From the hell of lost craft Satan sent a ship of bygone ages! A ship red with gore and stained with the memory of horrid crimes! None other would bear such a vile carcass! The sea has taken vengeance and has given me mine. See now, how I spit upon the face of John Kulrek.'

And with a ghastly laugh, she pitched forward, the blood starting to her lips. And the sun came up across the restless sea.

The Fearsome Touch of Death

As long as midnight cloaks the earth
With shadows grim and stark,
God save us from the Judas kiss
Of a dead man in the dark.

Old Adam Farrel lay dead in the house wherein he had lived alone for the last twenty years. A silent, churlish recluse, in his life he had known no friends, and only two men had watched his passing.

Dr Stein rose and glanced out the window into the gathering dusk.

'You think you can spend the night here, then?' he asked his companion.

This man, Falred by name, assented.

'Yes, certainly. I guess it's up to me.'

'Rather a useless and primitive custom, sitting up with the dead,' commented the doctor, preparing to depart, 'but I suppose in common decency we will have to bow to precedence. Maybe I can find someone who'll come over here and help you with your vigil.'

Falred shrugged his shoulders. 'I doubt it. Farrel wasn't liked – wasn't known by many people. I scarcely knew him myself, but I don't mind sitting up with the corpse.'

Dr Stein was removing his rubber gloves and Falred watched the process with an interest that almost amounted to fascination. A slight, involuntary shudder shook him at the memory of touching these gloves – slick, cold, clammy things, like the touch of death.

'You may get lonely tonight, if I don't find anyone,' the doctor remarked as he opened the door. 'Not superstitious, are you?'

Falred laughed. 'Scarcely. To tell the truth, from what I hear of Farrel's disposition, I'd rather be watching his corpse than have been his guest in life.'

The door closed and Falred took up his vigil. He seated himself in the only chair the room boasted, glanced casually at the formless, sheeted bulk on the bed opposite him, and began to read by the light of the dim lamp which stood on the rough table.

Outside, the darkness gathered swiftly, and finally Falred laid down his magazine to rest his eyes. He looked again at the shape which had, in life, been the form of Adam Farrel, wondering what quirk in human nature made the sight of a corpse not so unpleasant, but such an object of fear to man. Unthinking ignorance, seeing in dead things a reminder of death to come, he decided lazily, and began idly contemplating what life had held for this grim and crabbed old man, who had neither relatives nor friends, and who had seldom left the house wherein he had died. The usual tales of miser-hoarded wealth had accumulated, but Falred felt so little interest in the whole matter that it was not even necessary for him to overcome any temptation to prey about the house for possible hidden treasure.

He returned to his reading with a shrug. The task was more boresome than he had thought for. After a while he was aware that every time he looked up from his magazine and his eyes fell upon the bed with its grim occupant, he started involuntarily as if he had, for an instant, forgotten the presence of the dead man and was unpleasantly reminded of the fact. The start was slight and instinctive, but he felt almost angered at himself. He realised, for the first time, the utter and deadening silence which enwrapped the house – a silence apparently shared by the night, for no sound came through the window. Adam Farrel lived as far apart from his neighbours as possible, and there was no other house within hearing distance.

Falred shook himself as if to rid his mind of unsavoury speculations, and went back to his reading. A sudden vagrant gust of wind whipped through the window, in which the light in the lamp flickered and went out suddenly. Falred, cursing softly, groped in the darkness for matches, burning his fingers on the lamp chimney. He struck a match, relighted the lamp, and glancing over at the bed, got a horrible mental jolt. Adam Farrel's face stared blindly at him, the dead eyes wide and blank, framed in the gnarled grey features. Even as Falred instinctively shuddered, his reason explained the apparent phenomenon: the sheet that covered the corpse had been carelessly thrown across the face and the sudden puff of wind had disarranged and flung it aside.

Yet there was something grisly about the thing, something fearsomely suggestive – as if, in the cloaking dark, a dead hand had flung aside the sheet, just as if the corpse were about to rise . . .

Falred, an imaginative man, shrugged his shoulders at these ghastly thoughts and crossed the room to replace the sheet. The dead eyes seemed to stare malevolently, with an evilness that transcended the dead man's churlishness in life. The workings of a vivid imagination, Falred knew, and he re-covered the grey face, shrinking as his hand chanced to touch the cold flesh – slick and clammy, the touch of death. He shuddered with the natural revulsion of the living for the dead, and went back to his chair and magazine.

At last, growing sleepy, he lay down upon a couch which, by some strange whim of the original owner, formed part of the room's scant furnishings, and composed himself for slumber. He decided to leave the light burning, telling himself that it was in accordance with the usual custom of leaving lights burning for the dead; for he was not willing to admit to himself that already he was conscious of a dislike for lying in the darkness with the corpse. He dozed, awoke with a start and looked at the sheeted form of the bed. Silence reigned over the house, and outside it was very dark.

The hour was approaching midnight, with its accompanying eerie domination over the human mind. Falred glanced again at the bed where the body lay and found the sight of the sheeted object most repellent. A fantastic idea had birth in his mind, and grew, that beneath the sheet, the mere lifeless body had become a strange, monstrous thing, a hideous, conscious being, that watched him with eyes which burned through the fabric of the cloth. This thought – a mere fantasy, of course – he explained to himself by the legends of vampires, undead ghosts and suchlike – the fearsome attributes with which the living have cloaked the dead for countless ages, since primitive man first recognised in death something horrid and apart from life. Man feared death, thought Falred, and some of this fear of death took hold on the dead so that they, too, were feared. And the sight of the dead engendered grisly thoughts, gave rise to dim fears of hereditary memory, lurking back in the dark corners of the brain.

At any rate, that silent, hidden thing was getting on his nerves. He thought of uncovering the face, on the principle that familiarity breeds contempt. The sight of the features, calm and still in death, would banish, he thought, all such wild conjectures as were haunting him in spite of himself. But the thought of those dead eyes staring in the lamplight was intolerable; so at last he blew out the light and lay down. This fear had been stealing upon him so insidiously and gradually that he had not been aware of its growth.

With the extinguishing of the light, however, and the blotting out of the sight of the corpse, things assumed their true character and proportions, and Falred fell asleep almost instantly, on his lips a faint smile for his previous folly.

He awakened suddenly. How long he had been asleep he did not know. He sat up, his pulse pounding frantically, the cold sweat beading his forehead. He knew instantly where he was, remembered the other occupant of the room. But what had awakened him? A dream – yes, now he remembered – a hideous dream in which the dead man had risen from the bed and stalked stiffly across the room with eyes of fire and a horrid leer frozen on his grey lips. Falred had seemed to lie motionless, helpless; then as the corpse reached out a gnarled and horrible hand, he had awakened.

He strove to pierce the gloom, but the room was all blackness and all without was so dark that no gleam of light came through the window. He reached a shaking hand toward the lamp, then recoiled as if from a hidden serpent. Sitting here in the dark with a fiendish corpse was bad enough, but he dared not light the lamp, for fear that his reason would be snuffed out like a candle at what he might see. Horror, stark and unreasoning, had full possession of his soul; he no longer questioned the instinctive fears that rose in him. All those legends he had heard came back to him and brought a belief in them. Death was a hideous thing, a brain-shattering horror, imbuing life-less men with a horrid malevolence. Adam Farrel in his life had been simply a churlish but harmless man; now he was a terror, a monster, a fiend lurking in the shadows of fear, ready to leap on mankind with talons dipped deep in death and insanity.

Falred sat there, his blood freezing, and fought out his silent battle. Faint glimmerings of reason had begun to touch his fright when a soft, stealthy sound again froze him. He did not recognise it as the whisper of the night wind across the windowsill. His frenzied fancy knew it only as the tread of death and horror. He sprang from the couch, then stood undecided. Escape was in his mind but he was too dazed to even try to formulate a plan of escape. Even his sense of direction was gone. Fear had so stultified his mind that he was not able to think consciously. The blackness spread in long waves about him, and its darkness and void entered into his brain. His motions, such as they were, were instinctive. He seemed shackled with mighty chains and his limbs responded sluggishly, like an imbecile's.

A terrible horror grew up in him and reared its grisly shape, that the dead man was behind him, was stealing upon him from the rear. He no longer thought of lighting the lamp; he no longer thought of anything. Fear filled his whole being; there was room for nothing else.

He backed slowly away in the darkness, hands behind him, in-stinctively feeling the way. With a terrific effort he partly shook the clinging mists of horror from him, and, the cold sweat clammy upon his body, strove to orient himself. He could see nothing, but the bed was across the room, in front of him. He was backing away from it. There was where the dead man was lying, according to all rules of nature; if the thing were, as he felt, behind him, then the old tales were true: death did implant in lifeless bodies an unearthly animation, and dead men did roam the shadows to work their ghastly and evil will upon the sons of men. Then – great God! – what was man but a wailing infant, lost in the night and beset by frightful things from the black abysses and the terrible unknown voids of space and time? These conclusions he did not reach by any reasoning process; they leaped full-grown into his terror-dazed brain. He worked his way slowly backward, groping, clinging to the thought that the dead man must be in front of him.

Then his back-flung hands encountered something – something slick, cold and clammy – like the touch of death. A scream shook the echoes, followed by the crash of a falling body.

The next morning they who came to the house of death found two corpses in the room. Adam Farrel's sheeted body lay motionless upon the bed, and across the room lay the body of Falred, beneath the shelf where Dr Stein had absent-mindedly left his gloves . . . rubber gloves, slick and clammy to the touch of a hand groping in the dark – a hand of one fleeing his own fear – rubber gloves, slick and clammy and cold, like the touch of death.

The Children of the Night

There were, I remember, six of us in Conrad's bizarrely fashioned study, with its queer relics from all over the world and its long rows of books which ranged from the Mandrake Press edition of Boccaccio to a *Missale Romanum*, bound in clasped oak boards and printed in Venice, 1740. Clemants and Professor Kirowan had just engaged in a somewhat testy anthropological argument: Clemants upholding the theory of a separate, distinct Alpine race, while the professor maintained that this so-called race was merely a deviation from an original Aryan stock – possibly the result of an admixture between the southern or Mediterranean races and the Nordic people.

'And how,' asked Clemants, 'do you account for their brachy-cephalicism? The Mediterraneans were as long-headed as the Aryans: would admixture between these dolichocephalic peoples produce a broad-headed intermediate type?'

'Special conditions might bring about a change in an originally long-headed race,' snapped Kirowan. 'Boaz has demonstrated, for instance, that in the case of immigrants to America, skull formations often change in one generation. And Flinders Petrie has shown that the Lombards changed from a long-headed to a round-headed race in a few centuries.'

'But what caused these changes?'

'Much is yet unknown to science,' answered Kirowan, 'and we need not be dogmatic. No one knows, as yet, why people of British and Irish ancestry tend to grow unusually tall in the Darling district of Australia – cornstalks, as they are called – or why people of such descent generally have thinner jaw-structures after a few generations in New England. The universe is full of the unexplainable.'

'And therefore the uninteresting, according to Machen,' laughed Taverel.

Conrad shook his head. 'I must disagree. To me, the unknowable is most tantalisingly fascinating.'

'Which accounts, no doubt, for all the works on witchcraft and demonology I see on your shelves,' said Ketrick, with a wave of his hand toward the rows of books.

And let me speak of Ketrick. Each of the six of us was of the same breed – that is to say, a Briton or an American of British descent. By British, I include all natural inhabitants of the British Isles. We represented various strains of English and Celtic blood, but basically, these strains are the same after all. But Ketrick: to me the man always seemed strangely alien. It was in his eyes that this difference showed externally. They were a sort of amber, almost yellow, and slightly oblique. At times, when one looked at his face from certain angles, they seemed to slant like a Chinaman's.

Others than I had noticed this feature, so unusual in a man of pure Anglo-Saxon descent. The usual myths ascribing his slanted eyes to some pre-natal influence had been mooted about, and I remember Professor Hendrik Brooler once remarked that Ketrick was undoubtedly an atavism, representing a reversion of type to some dim and distant ancestor of Mongolian blood – a sort of freak reversion, since none of his family showed such traces.

But Ketrick comes of the Welsh branch of the Cetrics of Sussex, and his lineage is set down in the *Book of Peers*. There you may read the line of his ancestry, which extends unbroken to the days of Canute. No slightest trace of Mongoloid intermixture appears in the genealogy, and how could there have been such intermixture in old Saxon England? For Ketrick is the modern form of Cedric, and though that branch fled into Wales before the invasion of the Danes, its male heirs consistently married with English families on the border marches, and it remains a pure line of the powerful Sussex Cedrics – almost pure Saxon. As for the man himself, this defect of his eyes, if it can be called a defect, is his only abnormality, except for a slight and occasional lisping of speech. He is highly intellectual and a good companion except for a slight aloofness and a rather callous indifference which may serve to mask an extremely sensitive nature.

Referring to his remark, I said with a laugh: 'Conrad pursues the obscure and mystic as some men pursue romance; his shelves throng with delightful nightmares of every variety.'

Our host nodded. 'You'll find there a number of delectable dishes – Machen, Poe, Blackwood, Maturin . . . look, there's a rare feast – *Horrid Mysteries*, by the Marquis of Grosse – the real eighteenth-century edition.'

Taverel scanned the shelves. 'Weird fiction seems to vie with works on witchcraft, voodoo and dark magic.'

True; historians and chronicles are often dull, tale-weavers never – the masters, I mean. A voodoo sacrifice can be described in such a dull manner as to take all the real fantasy out of it, and leave it merely a sordid murder. I will admit that few writers of fiction touch the true heights of horror – most of their stuff is too concrete, given too much earthly shape and dimensions. But in such tales as Poe's *The Fall of the House of Usher*, Machen's *Black Seal* and Lovecraft's *The Call of Cthulhu* – the three master horror-tales, to my mind – the reader is borne into dark and *outer* realms of imagination.

'But look there,' he continued, 'there, sandwiched between that nightmare of Huysmans' and Walpole's *Castle of Otranto* – Von Junzt's *Nameless Cults*. There's a book to keep you awake at night!'

'I've read it,' said Taverel, 'and I'm convinced the man is mad. His work is like the conversation of a maniac – it runs with startling clarity for awhile, then suddenly merges into vagueness and disconnected ramblings.'

Conrad shook his head. 'Have you ever thought that perhaps it is his very sanity that causes him to write in that fashion? What if he dares not put on paper all he knows? What if his vague suppositions are dark and mysterious hints, keys to the puzzle, to those who know?'

'Bosh!' This from Kirowan. 'Are you intimating that any of the nightmare cults referred to by Von Junzt survive to this day – if they ever existed save in the hag-ridden brain of a lunatic poet and philosopher?'

'Not he alone used hidden meanings,' answered Conrad. 'If you will scan various works of certain great poets you may find double meanings. Men have stumbled on to cosmic secrets in the past and given a hint of them to the world in cryptic words. Do you remember Von Junzt's hints of "a city in the waste"? What do you think of Flecker's lines:

Pass not beneath! Men say there blows in stony deserts still a rose
But with no scarlet to her leaf . . . and from whose heart no perfume flows.

'Men may stumble upon secret things, but Von Junzt dipped deep into forbidden mysteries. He was one of the few men, for instance, who could read the *Necronomicon* in the original Greek translation.'

Taverel shrugged his shoulders, and Professor Kirowan, though he snorted and puffed viciously at his pipe, made no direct reply; for he, as well as Conrad, had delved into the Latin version of the book, and had found there things not even a cold-blooded scientist could answer or refute.

'Well,' he said presently, 'suppose we admit the former existence of cults revolving about such nameless and ghastly gods and entities as Cthulhu, Yog Sothoth, Tsathoggua, Gol-goroth, and the like, I cannot find it in my mind to believe that survivals of such cults lurk in the dark corners of the world today.'

To our surprise Clemants answered. He was a tall, lean man, silent almost to the point of taciturnity, and his fierce struggles with poverty in his youth had lined his face beyond his years. Like many another artist, he lived a distinctly dual literary life, his swashbuckling novels furnishing him a generous income, and his editorial position on *The Cloven Hoof* affording him full artistic expression. *The Cloven Hoof* was a poetry magazine whose bizarre contents had often aroused the shocked interest of the conservative critics.

'You remember Von Junzt makes mention of a so-called Bran cult,' said Clemants, stuffing his pipe-bowl with a peculiarly villain-ous brand of shag tobacco. 'I think I heard you and Taverel dis-cussing it once.'

'As I gather from his hints,' snapped Kirowan, 'Von Junzt includes this particular cult among those still in existence. Absurd.'

Again Clemants shook his head. 'When I was a boy working my way through a certain university, I had for room-mate a lad as poor and ambitious as I. If I told you his name, it would startle you. Though he came of an old Scotch line of Galloway, he was obviously of a non-Aryan type.

'This is in strictest confidence, you understand. But my room-mate talked in his sleep. I began to listen and put his disjointed mumbling together. And in his mutterings I first heard of the ancient cult hinted at by Von Junzt; of the king who rules the Dark Empire, which was a revival of an older, darker empire dating back into the Stone Age; and of the great, nameless cavern where stands the Dark Man – the image of Bran Mak Morn, carved in his likeness by a master-hand while the great king yet lived, and to which each worshipper of Bran makes a pilgrimage once in his or her lifetime. Yes, that cult lives today in the descendants of Bran's people – a silent, unknown current, it flows on in the great ocean of life, waiting for the stone image of the great Bran to breathe and move with sudden life, and come from the great cavern to rebuild their lost empire.'

'And who were the people of that empire?' asked Ketrick.

'Picts,' answered Taverel, 'doubtless the people known later as the wild Picts of Galloway were predominantly Celtic – a mixture of Gaelic, Cymric, aboriginal and possibly Teutonic elements. Whether they took their name from the older race or lent their own name to that race, is a matter yet to be decided. But when Von Junzt speaks of Picts, he refers specifically to the small, dark, garlic-eating peoples of Mediterranean blood who brought the Neolithic culture into Britain. The first settlers of that country, in fact, who gave rise to the tales of earth spirits and goblins.'

'I cannot agree to that last statement,' said Conrad. 'These legends ascribe a deformity and inhumanness of appearance to the characters. There was nothing about the Picts to excite such horror and repulsion in the Aryan peoples. I believe that the Mediterraneans were preceded by a Mongoloid type, very low in the scale of development, whence these tales – '

'Quite true,' broke in Kirowan, 'but I hardly think they preceded the Picts, as you call them, into Britain. We find troll and dwarf legends all over the Continent, and I am inclined to think that both the Mediterranean and Aryan people brought these tales with them from the Continent. They must have been of extremely inhuman aspect, those early Mongoloids.'

'At least,' said Conrad, 'here is a flint mallet a miner found in the Welsh hills and gave to me, which has never been fully explained. It is obviously of no ordinary Neolithic make. See how small it is, compared to most implements of that age; almost like a child's toy; yet it is surprisingly heavy and no doubt a deadly blow could be dealt with it. I fitted the handle to it myself, and you would be surprised to know how difficult it was to carve it into a shape and balance corresponding with the head.'

We looked at the thing. It was well made, polished somewhat like the other remnants of the Neolithic I had seen, yet as Conrad said, it was strangely different. Its small size was oddly disquieting, for it had no appearance of a toy, otherwise. It was as sinister in suggestion as an Aztec sacrificial dagger. Conrad had fashioned the oaken handle with rare skill, and in carving it to fit the head, had managed to give it the same unnatural appearance as the mallet itself had. He had even copied the workmanship of primal times, fixing the head into the cleft of the haft with rawhide.

'My word!' Taverel made a clumsy pass at an imaginary antagonist and nearly shattered a costly Shang vase. 'The balance of the thing is all off-centre; I'd have to readjust all my mechanics of poise and equilibrium to handle it.'

'Let me see it,' Ketrick took the thing and fumbled with it, trying to strike the secret of its proper handling. At length, somewhat irritated, he swung it up and struck a heavy blow at a shield which hung on the wall nearby. I was standing near it; I saw the hellish mallet twist in his hand like a live serpent, and his arm wrenched out of line; I heard a shout of alarmed warning – then darkness came with the impact of the mallet against my head.

Slowly I drifted back to consciousness. First there was dull sensation with blindness and total lack of knowledge as to where I was or what I was; then vague realisation of life and being, and a hard something pressing into my ribs. Then the mists cleared and I came to myself completely.

I lay on my back half-beneath some underbrush and my head throbbed fiercely. Also my hair was caked and clotted with blood, for the scalp had been laid open. But my eyes travelled down my body and limbs, naked but for a deerskin loincloth and sandals of the same material, and found no other wound. That which pressed so uncomfortably into my ribs was my axe, on which I had fallen.

Now an abhorrent babble reached my ears and stung me into clear consciousness. The noise was faintly like language, but not such language as men are accustomed to. It sounded much like the repeated hissing of many great snakes.

I stared. I lay in a great, gloomy forest. The glade was overshadowed, so that even in the daytime it was very dark. Aye – that forest was dark, cold, silent, gigantic and utterly grisly. And I looked into the glade.

I saw a shambles. Five men lay there – at least, what had been five men. Now as I marked the abhorrent mutilations my soul sickened. And about clustered the . . . Things. Humans they were, of a sort, though I did not consider them so. They were short and stocky, with broad heads too large for their scrawny bodies. Their hair was snaky and stringy, their faces broad and square, with flat noses, hideously slanted eyes, a thin gash for a mouth, and pointed ears. They wore the skins of beasts, as did I, but these hides were but crudely dressed. They bore small bows and flint-tipped arrows, flint knives and cudgels. And they conversed in a speech as hideous as themselves, a hissing, reptilian speech that filled me with dread and loathing.

Oh, I hated them as I lay there; my brain flamed with white-hot fury. And now I remembered. We had hunted, we six youths of the

Sword People, and wandered far into the grim forest which our people generally shunned. Weary of the chase, we had paused to rest; to me had been given the first watch, for in those days, no sleep was safe without a sentry. Now shame and revulsion shook my whole being. I had slept – I had betrayed my comrades. And now they lay gashed and mangled – butchered while they slept, by vermin who had never dared to stand before them on equal terms. I, Aryara, had betrayed my trust.

Aye – I remembered. I had slept and in the midst of a dream of the hunt, fire and sparks had exploded in my head and I had plunged into a deeper darkness where there were no dreams. And now the penalty. They who had stolen through the dense forest and smitten me senseless, had not paused to mutilate me. Thinking me dead they had hastened swiftly to their grisly work. Now perhaps they had forgotten me for a time. I had sat somewhat apart from the others, and when struck, had fallen half-under some bushes. But soon they would remember me. I would hunt no more, dance no more in the dances of hunt and love and war, see no more the wattle huts of the Sword People.

But I had no wish to escape back to my people. Should I slink back with my tale of infamy and disgrace? Should I hear the words of scorn my tribe would fling at me, see the girls point their contempt-uous fingers at the youth who slept and betrayed his comrades to the knives of vermin?

Tears stung my eyes, and slow hate heaved up in my bosom, and my brain. I would never bear the sword that marked the warrior. I would never triumph over worthy foes and die gloriously beneath the arrows of the Picts or the axes of the Wolf People or the River People. I would go down to death beneath a nauseous rabble, whom the Picts had long ago driven into forest dens like rats.

And mad rage gripped me and dried my tears, giving in their stead a berserk blaze of wrath. If such reptiles were to bring about my downfall, I would make it a fall long remembered – if such beasts had memories.

Moving cautiously, I shifted until my hand was on the haft of my axe; then I called on Il-marinen and bounded up as a tiger springs. And as a tiger springs I was among my enemies and mashed a flat skull as a man crushes the head of a snake. A sudden wild clamour of fear broke from my victims and for an instant they closed round me, hacking and stabbing. A knife gashed my chest but I gave no heed. A red mist waved before my eyes, and my body and limbs moved in perfect accord with my fighting brain. Snarling, hacking and smiting, I was a tiger among reptiles. In an instant they gave way and fled, leaving me bestriding half a dozen stunted bodies. But I was not satiated.

I was close on the heels of the tallest one, whose head would perhaps come to my shoulder, and who seemed to be their chief. He fled down a sort of runway, squealing like a monstrous lizard, and when I was close at his shoulder, he dived, snake-like, into the bushes. But I was too swift for him, and I dragged him forth and butchered him in a most gory fashion.

And through the bushes I saw the trail he was striving to reach – a path winding in and out among the trees, almost too narrow to allow the traversing of it by a man of normal size. I hacked off my victim's hideous head, and carrying it in my left hand, went up the serpent-path, with my red axe in my right.

Now as I strode swiftly along the path and blood splashed beside my feet at every step from the severed jugular of my foe, I thought of those I hunted. Aye – we held them in so little esteem, we hunted by day in the forest they haunted. What they called themselves, we never knew; for none of our tribe ever learned the accursed hissing sibilances they used as speech; but we called them Children of the Night. And night-things they were indeed, for they slunk in the depths of the dark forests, and in subterraneous dwellings, venturing forth into the hills only when their conquerors slept. It was at night that they did their foul deeds – the quick flight of a flint-tipped arrow to slay cattle, or perhaps a loitering human, the snatching of a child that had wandered from the village.

But it was for more than this we gave them their name; they were, in truth, people of night and darkness and the ancient horror-ridden shadows of bygone ages. For these creatures were very old, and they represented an outworn age. They had once overrun and possessed this land, and they had been driven into hiding and obscurity by the dark, fierce little Picts with whom we contested now, and who hated and loathed them as savagely as did we.

The Picts were different from us in general appearance, being shorter of stature and dark of hair, eyes and skin, whereas we were tall and powerful, with yellow hair and light eyes. But they were cast in the same mould, for all of that. These Children of the Night seemed not human to us, with their deformed dwarfish bodies, yellow skin and hideous faces. Aye, they were reptiles . . . vermin.

And my brain was like to burst with fury when I thought that it was these vermin on whom I was to glut my axe and perish. Bah! There is no glory slaying snakes or dying from their bites. All this rage and fierce disappointment turned on the objects of my hatred, and with the old red mist waving in front of me I swore by all the gods I knew, to wreak such red havoc before I died as to leave a dread memory in the minds of the survivors.

My people would not honour me, in such contempt they held the Children. But those Children that I left alive would remember me and shudder. So I swore, gripping savagely my axe, which was of bronze, set in a cleft of the oaken haft and fastened securely with rawhide.

Now I heard ahead a sibilant, abhorrent murmur, and a vile stench filtered to me through the trees, human, yet less than human. A few moments more and I emerged from the deep shadows into a wide open space. I had never before seen a village of the Children. There was a cluster of earthen domes, with low doorways sunk into the ground; squalid dwelling-places, half-above and half-below the earth. And I knew from the talk of the old warriors that these dwelling-places were connected by underground corridors, so the whole village was like an ant-bed, or a system of snake holes. And I wondered if other tunnels did not run off under the ground and emerge long distances from the villages.

Before the domes clustered a vast group of the creatures, hissing and jabbering at a great rate.

I had quickened my pace, and now as I burst from cover, I was running with the fleetness of my race. A wild clamour went up from the rabble as they saw the avenger, tall, bloodstained and blazing-eyed leap from the forest, and I cried out fiercely, flung the dripping head among them and bounded like a wounded tiger into the thick of them.

Oh, there was no escape for them now! They might have taken to their tunnels but I would have followed, even to the guts of Hell. They knew they must slay me, and they closed around, a hundred strong, to do it.

There was no wild blaze of glory in my brain as there had been against worthy foes. But the old berserk madness of my race was in my blood and the smell of blood and destruction in my nostrils.

I know not how many I slew. I only know that they thronged about me in a writhing, slashing mass, like serpents about a wolf, and I smote until the axe-edge turned and bent and the axe became no more than a bludgeon; and I smashed skulls, split heads, splintered bones, scattered blood and brains in one red sacrifice to Il-marinen, god of the Sword People.

Bleeding from half a hundred wounds, blinded by a slash across the eyes, I felt a flint knife sink deep into my groin and at the same instant a cudgel laid my scalp open. I went to my knees but reeled up again, and saw in a thick red fog a ring of leering, slant-eyed faces. I lashed out as a dying tiger strikes, and the faces broke in red ruin.

And as I sagged, overbalanced by the fury of my stroke, a taloned hand clutched my throat and a flint blade was driven into my ribs and twisted venomously. Beneath a shower of blows I went down again, but the man with the knife was beneath me, and with my left hand I found him and broke his neck before he could writhe away.

Life was waning swiftly; through the hissing and howling of the Children I could hear the voice of Il-marinen. Yet once again I rose stubbornly, through a very whirlwind of cudgels and spears. I could no longer see my foes, even in a red mist. But I could feel their blows and knew they surged about me. I braced my feet, gripped my slippery axe-haft with both hands, and calling once more on Il-marinen I heaved up the axe and struck one last terrific blow. And I must have died on my feet, for there was no sensation of falling; even as I knew, with a last thrill of savagery that slew, even as I felt the splintering of skulls beneath my axe, darkness came with oblivion.

I came suddenly to myself. I was half-reclining in a big armchair and Conrad was pouring water on me. My head ached and a trickle of blood had half-dried on my face. Kirowan, Taverel and Clemants were hovering about, anxiously, while Ketrick stood just in front of me, still holding the mallet, his face schooled to a polite perturbation which his eyes did not show. And at the sight of those cursed eyes a red madness surged up in me.

'There,' Conrad was saying, 'I told you he'd come out of it in a moment; just a light crack. He's taken harder than that. All right now, aren't you, O'Donnel?'

At that I swept them aside, and with a single low snarl of hatred launched myself at Ketrick. Taken utterly by surprise he had no opportunity to defend himself. My hands locked on his throat and we crashed together on the ruins of a divan. The others cried out in amazement and horror and sprang to separate us – or rather, to tear me from my victim, for already Ketrick's slant eyes were beginning to start from their sockets.

'For God's sake, O'Donnel,' exclaimed Conrad, seeking to break my grip, 'what's come over you? Ketrick didn't mean to hit you – let go, you idiot!'

A fierce wrath almost overcame me at these men who were my friends, men of my own tribe, and I swore at them and their blindness, as they finally managed to tear my strangling fingers from Ketrick's throat. He sat up and choked and explored the blue marks my fingers had left, while I raged and cursed, nearly defeating the combined efforts of the four to hold me.

'You fools!' I screamed. 'Let me go! Let me do my duty as a tribesman! You blind fools! I care nothing for the paltry blow he dealt me – he and his dealt stronger blows than that against me, in bygone ages. You fools, he is marked with the brand of the beast – the reptile – the vermin we exterminated centuries ago! I must crush him, stamp him out, rid the clean earth of his accursed pollution!'

So I raved and struggled and Conrad gasped to Ketrick over his shoulder: 'Get out, quick! He's out of his head! His mind is unhinged! Get away from him.'

Now I look out over the ancient dreaming downs and the hills and deep forests beyond and I ponder. Somehow, that blow from that ancient accursed mallet knocked me back into another age and another life. While I was Aryara I had no cognisance of any other life. It was no dream; it was a stray bit of reality wherein I, John O'Donnel, once lived and died, and back into which I was snatched across the voids of time and space by a chance blow. Time and times are but cogwheels, unmatched, grinding on oblivious to one another. Occasionally – oh, very rarely! – the cogs fit; the pieces of the plot snap together momentarily and give men faint glimpses beyond the veil of this everyday blindness we call reality.

I am John O'Donnel and I was Aryara, who dreamed dreams of war-glory and hunt-glory and feast-glory and who died on a red heap of his victims in some lost age. But in what age and where?

The last I can answer for you. Mountains and rivers change their contours; the landscapes alter; but the downs least of all. I look out upon them now and I remember them, not only with John O'Donnel's eyes, but with the eyes of Aryara. They are but little changed. Only the great forest has shrunk and dwindled and in many, many places vanished utterly. But here on these very downs Aryara lived and fought and loved and in yonder forest he died. Kirowan was wrong. The little, fierce, dark Picts were not the first men in the Isles. There were beings before them – aye, the Children of the Night. Legends – why, the Children were not unknown to us when we came into what is now the isle of Britain. We had encountered them before, ages before. Already we had our myths of them. But we found them in Britain. Nor had the Picts totally exterminated them.

Nor had the Picts, as so many believe, preceded us by many centuries. We drove them before us as we came, in that long drift from the East. I, Aryara, knew old men who had marched on that century-long trek; who had been borne in the arms of yellow-haired women over countless miles of forest and plain, and who as youths had walked in the vanguard of the invaders.

As to the age – that I cannot say. But I, Aryara, was surely an Aryan and my people were Aryans – members of one of the thousand unknown and unrecorded drifts that scattered yellow-haired blue-eyed tribes all over the world. The Celts were not the first to come into western Europe. I, Aryara, was of the same blood and appearance as the men who sacked Rome, but mine was a much older strain. Of the language spoke, no echo remains in the waking mind of John O'Donnel, but I knew that Aryara's tongue was to ancient Celtic what ancient Celtic is to modern Gaelic.

Il-marinen! I remember the god I called upon, the ancient, ancient god who worked in metals – in bronze then. For Il-marinen was one of the base gods of the Aryans from whom many gods grew; and he was Wieland and Vulcan in the ages of iron. But to Aryara he was Il-marinen.

And Aryara – he was one of many tribes and many drifts. Not alone did the Sword People come or dwell in Britain. The River People were before us and the Wolf People came later. But they were Aryans like us, light-eyed and tall and blond. We fought them, for the reason that the various drifts of Aryans have always fought each other, just as the Achaeans fought the Dorians, just as the Celts and Germans cut each other's throats; aye, just as the Hellenes and the Persians, who were once one people and of the same drift, split in two different ways on the long trek and centuries later met and flooded Greece and Asia Minor with blood.

Now understand, all this I did not know as Aryara. I, Aryara, knew nothing of all these world-wide drifts of my race. I knew only that my people were conquerors, that a century ago my ancestors had dwelt in the great plains far to the east, plains populous with fierce, yellow-haired, light-eyed people like myself; that my ancestors had come westward in a great drift; and that in that drift, when my tribesmen met tribes of other races, they trampled and destroyed them, and when they met other yellow-haired, light-eyed people, of older or newer drifts, they fought savagely and mercilessly, according to the old, illogical custom of the Aryan people. This Aryara knew, and I, John O'Donnel, who know much more and much less than I, Aryara, knew, have combined the knowledge of these separate selves and have come to conclusions that would startle many noted scientists and historians.

Yet this fact is well known: Aryans deteriorate swiftly in sedentary and peaceful lives. Their proper existence is a nomadic one; when they settle down to an agricultural existence, they pave the way for their downfall; and when they pen themselves with city walls, they seal their doom. Why, I, Aryara, remember the tales of the old men – how the Sons of the Sword, on that long drift, found villages of white-skinned yellow-haired people who had drifted into the west centuries before and had quit the wandering life to dwell among the dark, garlic-eating people and gain their sustenance from the soil. And the old men told how soft and weak they were, and how easily they fell before the bronze blades of the Sword People.

Look – is not the whole history of the Sons of Aryan laid on those lines? Look – how swiftly has Persian followed Mede; Greek, Persian; Roman, Greek; and German, Roman. Aye, and the Norseman followed the Germanic tribes when they had grown flabby from a century or so of peace and idleness, and despoiled the spoils they had taken in the southland.

But let me speak of Ketrick. Ha – the short hairs at the back of my neck bristle at the very mention of his name. A reversion to type – but not to the type of some cleanly Chinaman or Mongol of recent times. The Danes drove his ancestors into the hills of Wales; and there, in what medieval century, and in what foul way did that cursed aboriginal taint creep into the clean Saxon blood of the Celtic line, there to lie dormant so long? The Celtic Welsh never mated with the Children any more than the Picts did. But there must have been survivals – vermin lurking in those grim hills, that had outlasted their time and age. In Aryara's day they were scarcely human. What must a thousand years of retrogression have done to the breed?

What foul shape stole into the Ketrick castle on some forgotten night, or rose out of the dusk to grip some woman of the line, straying in the hills?

The mind shrinks from such an image. But this I know: there must have been survivals of that foul, reptilian epoch when the Ketricks went into Wales. There still may be. But this changeling, this waif of darkness, this horror who bears the noble name of Ketrick, the brand of the serpent is upon him, and until he is destroyed there is no rest for me. Now that I know him for what he is, he pollutes the clean air and leaves the slime of the snake on the green earth. The sound of his lisping, hissing voice fills me with crawling horror and the sight of his eyes inspires me with madness.

And as my ancestors – as I, Aryara, destroyed the scum that writhed beneath our heels, so shall I, John O'Donnel, exterminate the reptilian thing, the monster bred of the snaky taint that slumbered so long unguessed in clean Saxon veins, the vestigial serpent-things left to taunt the Sons of Aryan. They say the blow I received affected my mind; I know it but opened my eyes. Mine ancient enemy walks often on the moors alone, attracted, though he may not know it, by ancestral urgings. And on one of these lonely walks I shall meet him, and when I meet him, I will break his foul neck with my hands, as I, Aryara, broke the necks of foul night-things in the long, long ago.

Then they may take me and break my neck at the end of a rope if they will. I am not blind, if my friends are. And in the sight of the old Aryan god, if not in the blinded eyes of men, I will have kept faith with my tribe.

The Black Stone

They say foul things of Old Times still lurk
In dark forgotten corners of the world,
And Gates still gape to loose, on certain nights,
Shapes pent in Hell

JUSTIN

I read of it first in the strange book of Von Junzt, the German eccentric who lived so curiously and died in such grisly and mysterious fashion. It was my fortune to have access to his *Nameless Cults* in the original edition, the so-called Black Book, published in Dusseldorf in 1839, shortly before a hounding doom overtook the author. Collectors of rare literature were familiar with *Nameless Cults* mainly through the cheap and faulty translation which was pirated in London by Bridewall in 1845, and the carefully expurgated edition put out by the Golden Goblin Press of New York, 1909. But the volume I stumbled upon was one of the unexpurgated German copies, with heavy leather covers and rusty iron hasps. I doubt if there are more than half a dozen such volumes in the entire world today, for the quantity issued was not great, and when the manner of the author's demise was bruited about, many possessors of the book burned their volumes in panic.

Von Junzt spent his entire life (1795–1840) delving into forbidden subjects; he travelled in all parts of the world, gained entrance into innumerable secret societies, and read countless little-known and esoteric books and manuscripts in the original; and in the chapters of the Black Book, which range from startling clarity of exposition to murky ambiguity, there are statements and hints to freeze the blood of a thinking man. Reading what Von Junzt dared put in print arouses uneasy speculations as to what it was that he dared not tell. What dark matters, for instance, were contained in those closely-written pages that formed the unpublished manuscript on which he worked unceasingly for months before his death, and which lay torn and scattered all over the floor of the locked and bolted chamber in which Von Junzt was found dead with the marks of taloned fingers on his throat? It will never be known, for the author's closest friend, the Frenchman Alexis Ladeau, after having spent a whole night piecing the fragments together and reading what was written, burnt them to ashes and cut his own throat with a razor.

But the contents of the published matter are shuddersome enough, even if one accepts the general view that they but represent the ravings of a madman. There among many strange things I found mention of the Black Stone, that curious, sinister monolith that broods among the mountains of Hungary, and about which so many dark legends cluster. Van Junzt did not devote much space to it – the bulk of his grim work concerns cults and objects of dark worship which he maintained existed in his day, and it would seem that the Black Stone represents some order of being lost and forgotten centuries ago. But he spoke of it as one of the keys – a phrase used many times by him, in various relations, and constituting one of the obscurities of his work. And he hinted briefly at curious sights to be seen about the monolith on midsummer's night. He mentioned Otto Dostmann's theory that this monolith was a remnant of the Hunnish invasion and had been erected to commemorate a victory of Attila over the Goths. Von Junzt contradicted this assertion without giving any refutatory facts, merely remarking that to attribute the origin of the Black Stone to the Huns was as logical as assuming that William the Conqueror reared Stonehenge.

This implication of enormous antiquity piqued my interest immensely and after some difficulty I succeeded in locating a rat-eaten and mouldering copy of Dostmann's *Remnants of Lost Empires* (Berlin, 1809, Der Drachenhaus Press). I was disappointed to find that Dostmann referred to the Black Stone even more briefly than had Von Junzt, dismissing it with a few lines as an artefact comparatively modern in contrast with the Greco-Roman ruins of Asia Minor, which were his pet theme. He admitted inability to make out the defaced characters on the monolith but pronounced them unmistakably Mongoloid. However, little as I learned from Dostmann, he did mention the name of the village adjacent to the Black Stone – Stregoicavar – meaning something like Witch-Town.

A close scrutiny of guidebooks and travel articles gave me no further information – Stregoicavar, not on any map that I could find, lay in a wild, little-frequented region, out of the path of casual tourists. But I did find subject for thought in Dornly's *Magyar Folklore*. In his chapter on Dream Myths he mentions the Black Stone and tells of some curious superstitions regarding it – especially the belief that if anyone sleeps in the vicinity of the monolith, that person will be haunted by monstrous nightmares for ever after; and he cited tales of the peasants regarding too-curious people, who ventured to visit the Stone on Midsummer Night and who died raving mad because of something they saw there.

That was all I could gleam from Dornly, but my interest was even more intensely roused as I sensed a distinctly sinister aura about the Stone. The suggestion of dark antiquity, the recurrent hint of unnatural events on Midsummer Night, touched some slumbering instinct in my being, as one senses, rather than hears, the flowing of some dark subterraneous river in the night.

And I suddenly saw a connection between this Stone and a certain weird and fantastic poem written by the mad poet, Justin Geoffrey: *The People of the Monolith*. Inquiries led to the information that Geoffrey had indeed written that poem while travelling in Hungary, and I could not doubt that the Black Stone was the very monolith to which lie referred in his strange verse. Reading his stanzas again, I felt once more the strange dim stirrings of subconscious promptings that I had noticed when first reading of the Stone.

I had been casting about for a place to spend a short vacation and I made up my mind. I went to Stregoicavar. A train of obsolete style carried me from Temesvar to within striking distance, at least, of my objective, and a three days' ride in a bouncing coach brought me to the little village which lay in a fertile valley – high up in the fir-clad mountains.

The journey itself was uneventful, but during the first day we passed the old battlefield of Schomvaal where the brave Polish-Hungarian knight, Count Boris Vladinoff, made his gallant and futile stand against the victorious hosts of Suleiman the magnificent, when the Grand Turk swept over eastern Europe in 1526.

The driver of the coach pointed out to me a great heap of crumbling stones on a hill nearby, under which, he said, the bones of the brave Count lay. I remembered a passage from Larson's Turkish Wars. 'After the skirmish' (in which the Count with his small army had beaten back the Turkish advance-guard) 'the Count was standing beneath the half-ruined walls of the old castle on the hill, giving orders as to the disposition of his forces, when an aide brought to him a small lacquered case which had been taken from the body of the famous Turkish scribe and historian, Selim Bahadur, who had fallen in the fight. The Count took therefrom a roll of parchment and began to read, but he had not read far before he turned very pale and, without saying a word, replaced the parchment in the case and thrust the case into his cloak. At that very instant a hidden Turkish battery suddenly opened fire, and the balls striking the old castle, the Hungarians were horrified to see the halls crash down in ruin, completely covering the brave Count. Without a leader the gallant little army was cut to pieces, and in the warswept years which followed, the bones of the noblemen were never recovered. Today the natives point out a huge and mouldering pile of ruins near Schomvaal beneath which, they say, still rests all that the centuries have left of Count Boris Vladinoff.'

I found the village of Stregoicavar a dreamy, drowsy little village that apparently belied its sinister cognomen – a forgotten back-eddy that Progress had passed by. The quaint houses and the quainter dress and manners of the people were those of an earlier century. They were friendly, mildly curious but not inquisitive, though visitors from the outside world were extremely rare.

'Ten years ago another American came here and stayed a few days in the villa. Aye,' said the owner of the tavern where I had put up, 'a young fellow and queer-acting – mumbled to himself – a poet, I think.'

I knew he must mean Justin Geoffrey.

'Yes, he was a poet,' I answered, 'and he wrote a poem about a bit of scenery near this very village.'

'Indeed.' Mine host's interest was aroused. 'Then, since all great poets are strange in their speech and actions, he must have achieved great fame, for his actions and conversations were the strangest of any man I ever knew.'

'As is usual with artists,' I answered, 'most of his recognition has come since his death.'

'He is dead, then?'

'He died screaming in a madhouse five years ago.'

'Too bad, too bad,' sighed mine host sympathetically. 'Poor lad – he looked too long at the Black Stone.'

My heart gave a leap, but I masked my keen interest and said casually. 'I have heard something of this Black Stone; somewhere near this village, is it not?'

'Nearer than Christian folk wish,' he responded. 'Look!' He drew me to a latticed window and pointed up at the fir-clad slopes of the brooding blue mountains. 'There beyond where you see the bare face of that jutting cliff stands that accursed Stone. Would that it were ground to powder and the powder flung into the Danube to be carried to the deepest ocean! Once men tried to destroy the thing, but each man who laid hammer or maul against it came to an evil end. So now the people shun it.'

'What is there so evil about it?' I asked curiously.

'It is a demon-haunted thing,' he answered uneasily and with the suggestion of a shudder. 'In my childhood I knew a young man who came up from below and laughed at our traditions – in his fool-hardiness he went to the Stone on Midsummer Night and at dawn stumbled into the village again, stricken dumb and mad. Something had shattered his brain and sealed his lips, for until the day of his death, which came soon after, he spoke only to utter terrible blasphemies or to slaver gibberish.

'My own nephew when very small was lost in the mountains and slept in the woods near the Stone, and now in his manhood he is tortured by foul dreams so that at times he makes the night hideous with his screams and wakes with cold sweat upon him.

'But let us talk of something else, Herr; it is not good to dwell upon such things.'

I remarked on the evident age of the tavern and he answered with pride. 'The foundations are more than four hundred years old; the original house was the only one in the village which was not burned to the ground when Suleiman's devil swept through the mountains. Here, in the house that then stood on these same foundations, it is said, the scribe Selim Bahadur had his headquarters while ravaging the country hereabouts.'

I learned then that the present inhabitants of Stregoicavar are not descendants of the people who dwelt there before the Turkish raid of 1526. The present people of Stregoicavar are descended from hardy settlers from the lower valleys who came into the ruined village after the Turk was thrust back.

Mine host did not speak of the extermination of the original inhab-itants with any great resentment and I learned that his ancestors in the lower levels had looked on the mountaineers with even more hatred and aversion than they regarded the Turks. He was rather vague regarding the causes of this feud, but said that the original inhabitants of Stregoicavar had been in the habit of making stealthy raids on the lowlands and stealing girls and children. Moreover, he said that they were not exactly of the same blood as his own people; the sturdy, original Magyar-Slavic stock had mixed and intermarried with a degraded aboriginal race until the breeds had blended, producing an unsavoury amalgamation. Who these aborigines were, he had not the slightest idea, but maintained that they were 'pagans' and had dwelt in the mountains since time immemorial, before the coming of the conquering peoples.

I attached little importance to this tale, seeing in it merely a parallel to the amalgamation of Celtic tribes with Mediterranean aborigines in the Galloway hills, with the resultant mixed race which, as Picts, has such an extensive part in Scotch legendary. Time has a curious foreshortening effect on folklore, and just as tales of the Picts became intertwined with legends of an older Mongoloid race, so that eventually the Picts were ascribed the repulsive appearance of the squat primitives, whose individuality merged, in the telling, into Pictish tales, and was forgotten; so, I felt, the supposed inhuman attributes of the first villagers of Stregoicavar could be traced to older, outworn myths with invading Huns and Mongols.

The morning after my arrival I received directions from mine host, who gave them worriedly, and set out to find the Black Stone. A few hours' tramp up the fir-covered slopes brought me to the face of the rugged, solid stone cliff which jutted boldly from the mountainside. A narrow trail wound up it, and mounting this, I looked out over the peaceful valley of Stregoicavar, which seemed to drowse, guarded on either hand by the great blue mountains. No huts or any sign of human tenancy showed between the cliff whereon I stood and the village. I saw numbers of scattered farms in the valley but all lay on the other side of Stregoicavar, which itself seemed to shrink from the brooding slopes which masked the Black Stone.

The summit of the cliffs proved to be a sort of thickly wooded plateau. I made my way through the dense growth for a short dist-ance and came into a wide glade; and in the centre of the glade reared a gaunt figure of black stone.

It was octagonal in shape, some sixteen feet in height and about a foot and a half thick. It had once evidently been highly polished, but now the surface was thickly dinted as if savage efforts had been made to demolish it; but the hammers had done little more than flake off small bits of stone and mutilate the characters which once had evidently marched up in a spiralling line round and round the shaft to the top. Up to ten feet from the base these characters were almost completely blotted out, so that it was very difficult to trace their direction. Higher up they were plainer, and I managed to squirm part of the way up the shaft and scan them at close range. All were more or less defaced, but I was positive that they symbolised no language now remembered on the face of the earth. I am fairly familiar with all hieroglyphics known to researchers and philologists, and I can say with certainty that those characters were like nothing of which I have ever read or heard. The nearest approach to them that I ever saw were some crude scratches on a gigantic and strangely symmetrical rock in a lost valley of Yucatan. I remember that when I pointed out these marks to the archaeologist who was my companion, he maintained that they either represented natural weathering or the idle scratching of some Indian. To my theory that the rock was really the base of a long-vanished column, he merely laughed, calling my attention to the dimensions of it, which suggested, if it were built with any natural rules of architectural symmetry, a column a thousand feet high. But I was not convinced.

I will not say that the characters on the Black Stone were similar to those on that colossal rock in Yucatan; but one suggested the other. As to the substance of the monolith, again I was baffled. The stone of which it was composed was a dully gleaming black, whose surface, where it was not dinted and roughened, created a curious illusion of semitransparency.

I spent most of the morning there and came away baffled. No connection of the Stone with any other artefact in the world suggested itself to me. It was as if the monolith had been reared by alien hands, in an age distant and apart from human ken.

I returned to the village with my interest in no way abated. Now that I had seen the curious thing, my desire was still more keenly whetted to investigate the matter further and seek to learn by what strange hands and for what strange purpose the Black Stone had been reared in the long ago.

I sought out the tavern keeper's nephew and questioned him in regard to his dreams, but he was vague, though willing to oblige. He did not mind discussing them, but was unable to describe them with any clarity. Though he dreamed the same dreams repeatedly, and though they were hideously vivid at the time, they left no distinct impression on his waking mind. He remembered them only as chaotic nightmares through which huge whirling fires shot lurid tongues of flames and a black drum bellowed incessantly. One thing only: he had seen the Black Stone, not on a mountain slope but set like a spire on a colossal black castle.

As for the rest of the villagers, I found them not inclined to talk about the Stone, with the exception of the schoolmaster, a man of surprising education, who spent much more of his time out in the world than any of the rest.

He was much interested in what I told him of Von Junzt's remarks about the Stone, and warmly agreed with the German author in the alleged age of the monolith. He believed that a coven had once existed in the vicinity and that possibly all of the original villagers had been members of that fertility cult which once threatened to undermine European civilisation and gave rise to the tales of witchcraft. He cited the very name of the village to prove his point; it had not been originally named Stregoicavar, he said; according to legends the builders had called it Xuthltan, which was the aboriginal name of the site on which the village had been built many centuries ago.

This fact roused again an indescribable feeling of uneasiness. The barbarous name did not suggest connection with any Scythic, Slavic or Mongolian race to which an aboriginal people of these mountains would, under natural circumstances, have belonged.

That the Magyars and Slavs of the lower valleys believed the original inhabitants of the village to be members of the witchcraft cult was evident, the schoolmaster said, by the name they gave it, which name continued to be used even after the older settlers had been massacred by the Turks, and the village rebuilt by a cleaner and more wholesome breed.

He did not believe that the members of the cult erected the monolith, but he did believe that they used it as a centre of their activities, and repeating vague legends which had been handed down since before the Turkish invasion, he advanced the theory that the degenerate villagers had used it as a sort of altar on which they offered human sacrifices, using as victims the girls and babies stolen from his own ancestors in the lower valleys.

He discounted the myths of weird events on Midsummer Night, as well as a curious legend of a strange deity which the witch-people of Xuthltan were said to have invoked with chants and wild rituals of flagellation and slaughter.

He had never visited the Stone on Midsummer Night, he said, but he would not fear to do so; whatever had existed or taken place there in the past, had been long engulfed in the mists of time and oblivion. The Black Stone had lost its meaning save as a link to a dead and dusty past.

It was while returning from a visit to this schoolmaster one night about a week after my arrival at Stregoicavar that a sudden recollection

struck me – it was Midsummer Night! The very time that the legends
linked with grisly implications to the Black Stone. I turned away
from the tavern and strode swiftly through the village. Stregoicavar
lay silent; the villagers retired early. I saw no one as I passed rapidly
out of the village and up into the firs which masked the mountain
slopes with whispering darkness. A broad silver moon hung above
the valley, flooding the crags and slopes in a weird light and etching
the shadows blackly. No wind blew through the firs, but a myster-
ious, intangible rustling and whispering was abroad. Surely on such
nights in past centuries, my whimsical imagination told me, naked
witches on magic broomsticks had flown across the valley, pursued
by jeering demoniac familiars.

I came to the cliffs and was somewhat disquieted to note that the
illusive moonlight lent them a subtle appearance I had not noticed
before – in the weird light they appeared less like natural cliffs and
more like the ruins of Cyclopean and Titan-reared battlements
jutting from the mountain-slope.

Shaking off this hallucination with difficulty I came upon the
plateau and hesitated a moment before I plunged into the brooding
darkness of the woods. A sort of breathless tenseness hung over the
shadows, like an unseen monster holding its breath lest it scare away
its prey. I shook off the sensation – a natural one, considering the
eeriness of the place and its evil reputation – and made my way
through the wood, experiencing a most unpleasant sensation that I
was being followed, and halting once, sure that something clammy
and unstable had brushed against my face in the darkness.

I came out into the glade and saw the tall monolith rearing its
gaunt height above the sward. At the edge of the woods on the side
toward the cliffs was a stone which formed a sort of natural seat. I sat
down, reflecting that it was probably while there that the mad poet,
Justin Geoffrey, had written his fantastic *People of the Monolith*. Mine
host thought that it was the Stone which had caused Geoffrey's
insanity, but the seeds of madness had been sown in the poet's brain
long before he ever came to Stregoicavar.

A glance at my watch showed that the hour of midnight was close
at hand. I leaned back, waiting whatever ghostly demonstration might
appear. A thin night wind started up among the branches of the firs,
with an uncanny suggestion of faint, unseen pipes whispering an
eerie and evil tune. The monotony of the sound and my steady
gazing at the monolith produced a sort of self-hypnosis upon me; I
grew drowsy. I fought this feeling, but sleep stole on me in spite of

myself; the monolith seemed to sway and dance, strangely distorted to my gaze, and then I slept.

I opened my eyes and sought to rise, but lay still, as if an icy hand gripped me helpless. Cold terror stole over me; the glade was no longer deserted. It was thronged by a silent crowd of strange people, and my distended eyes took in strange barbaric details of costume which my reason told me were archaic and forgotten even in this backward land. Surely, I thought, these are villagers who have come here to hold some fantastic conclave – but another glance told me that these people were not the folk of Stregoicavar. They were a shorter, more squat race, whose brows were lower, whose faces were broader and duller. Some had Slavic or Magyar features, but those features were degraded as from a mixture of some baser, alien strain I could not classify. Many wore the hides of wild beasts, and their whole appearance, both men and women, was one of sensual brutishness. They terrified and repelled me, but they gave me no heed. They formed in a vast half-circle in front of the monolith and began a sort of chant, flinging their arms in unison and weaving their bodies rhythmically from the waist upward. All eyes were fixed on the top of the Stone which they seemed to be invoking. But the strangest of all was the dimness of their voices; not fifty yards from me hundreds of men and women were unmistakably lifting their voices in a wild chant, yet those voices came to me as a faint indistinguishable murmur as if from across vast leagues of space – or time.

Before the monolith stood a sort of brazier from which a vile, nauseous yellow smoke billowed upward, curling curiously in a swaying spiral around the black shaft, like a vast unstable snake.

On one side of this brazier lay two figures – a young girl, stark naked and bound hand and foot, and an infant, apparently only a few months old. On the other side of the brazier squatted a hideous old hag with a queer sort of black drum on her lap; this drum she beat with slow, light blows of her open palms, but I could not hear the sound.

The rhythm of the swaying bodies grew faster, and into the space between the people and the monolith sprang a naked young woman, her eyes blazing, her long black hair flying loose. Spinning dizzily on her toes, she whirled across the open space and fell prostrate before the Stone, where she lay motionless. The next instant a fantastic figure followed her – a man from whose waist hung a goatskin, and whose features were entirely hidden by a sort of mask made from a huge wolf's head, so that he looked like a monstrous, nightmare being, horribly compounded of elements both human and bestial. In his hand he held a bunch of long fir switches bound together at the larger ends, and the moonlight glinted on a chain of heavy gold looped about his neck.

A smaller chain depending from it suggested a pendant of some sort, but this was missing.

The people tossed their arms violently and seemed to redouble their shouts as this grotesque creature loped across the open space with many a fantastic leap and caper. Coming to the woman who lay before the monolith, he began to lash her with the switches he bore, and she leaped up and spun into the wild steps of the most incredible dance I have ever seen. And her tormentor danced with her, keeping the wild rhythm, matching her every whirl and bound, while incessantly raining cruel blows on her naked body. And at every blow he shouted a single word, over and over, and all the people shouted it back. I could see the working of their lips, and now the faint far-off murmur of their voices merged and blended into one distant shout, repeated over and over with slobbering ecstasy. But what that one word was, I could not make out.

In dizzy whirls spun the wild dancers, while the lookers-on, standing still in their tracks, followed the rhythm of their dance with swaying bodies and weaving arms. Madness grew in the eyes of the capering votaress and was reflected in the eyes of the watchers. Wilder and more extravagant grew the whirling frenzy of that mad dance – it became a bestial and obscene thing, while the old hag howled and battered the drum like a crazy woman, and the switches cracked out a devil's tune.

Blood trickled down the dancer's limbs but she seemed not to feel the lashing save as a stimulus for further enormities of outrageous motion; bounding into the midst of the yellow smoke which now spread out tenuous tentacles to embrace both flying figures, she seemed to merge with that foul fog and veil herself with it. Then emerging into plain view, closely followed by the beast-thing that flogged her, she shot into an indescribable, explosive burst of dynamic mad motion, and on the very crest of that mad wave, she dropped suddenly to the sward, quivering and panting as if completely overcome by her frenzied exertions. The lashing continued with unabated violence and intensity and she began to wriggle toward the monolith on her belly. The priest – or such I will call him – followed, lashing her unprotected body with all the power of his arm as she writhed along, leaving a heavy track of blood on the trampled earth. She reached the monolith, and gasping and panting, flung both arms about it and covered the cold stone with fierce hot kisses, as in frenzied and unholy adoration.

The fantastic priest bounded high in the air, flinging away the red-dabbled switches, and the worshippers, howling and foaming at the mouths, turned on each other with tooth and nail, rending one another's garments and flesh in a blind passion of bestiality. The priest swept up the infant with a long arm, and shouting again that Name, whirled the wailing babe high in the air and dashed its brains out against the monolith, leaving a ghastly stain on the black surface: Cold with horror I saw him rip the tiny body open with his bare brutish fingers and fling handfuls of blood on the shaft, then toss the red and torn shape into the brazier, extinguishing flame and smoke in a crimson rain, while the maddened brutes behind him howled over and over the Name. Then suddenly they all fell prostrate, writhing like snakes, while the priest flung wide his gory hands as in triumph: I opened my mouth to scream my horror and loathing, but only a dry rattle sounded; a huge monstrous toad-like thing squatted on the top of the monolith!

I saw its bloated, repulsive and unstable outline against the moonlight, and set in what would have been the face of a natural creature, its huge, blinking eyes which reflected all the lust, abysmal greed, obscene cruelty and monstrous evil that has stalked the sons of men since their ancestors moved blind and hairless in the tree-tops. In those grisly eyes were mirrored all the unholy things and vile secrets that sleep in the cities under the sea, and that skulk from the light of day in the blackness of primordial caverns. And so that ghastly thing that the unhallowed ritual and sadism and blood had evoked from the silence of the hills, leered and blinked down on its bestial worshippers, who grovelled in abhorrent abasement before it.

Now the beast-masked priest lifted the bound and weakly writhing girl in his brutish hands and held her up toward that horror on the monolith. And as that monstrosity sucked in its breath, lustfully and slobberingly, something snapped in my brain and I fell into a merciful faint.

I opened my eyes on a still white dawn. All the events of the night rushed back on me and I sprang up, then stared about me in amazement. The monolith brooded gaunt and silent above the sward which waved, green and untrampled, in the morning breeze. A few quick strides took me across the glade; here had the dancers leaped and bounded until the ground should have been trampled bare; and here had the votaress wriggled her painful way to the Stone, streaming blood on the earth. But no drop of crimson showed on the uncrushed sward. I looked, shudderingly, at the side of the monolith against which the bestial priest had brained the stolen baby – but no dark stain nor grisly clot showed there.

A dream! It had been a wild nightmare . . . or else . . . I shrugged my shoulders. What vivid clarity for a dream! I returned quietly to the village and entered the inn without being seen. And there I sat meditating over the strange events of the night. More and more was I prone to discard the dream-theory. That what I had seen was illusion and without material substance, was evident. But I believed that I had looked on the mirrored shadow of a deed perpetrated in ghastly actuality in bygone days. But how was I to know? What proof to show that my vision had been a gathering of foul spectres rather than a nightmare originating in my brain?

As if for answer a name flashed into my mind – Selim Bahadur! According to legend this man, who had been a soldier as well as a scribe, had commanded that part of Suleiman's army which had devastated Stregoicavar. It seemed logical enough; and if so, he had gone straight from the blotted-out countryside to the bloody field of Schomvaal, and his doom. I sprang up with a sudden shout – that manuscript which was taken from the Turk's body, and which Count Boris shuddered over – might it not contain some narration of what the conquering Turks found in Stregoicavar? What else could have shaken the iron nerves of the Polish adventurer? And since the bones of the Count had never been recovered, what more certain than that the lacquered case, with its mysterious contents, still lay hidden beneath the ruins that covered Boris Vladinoff? I began packing my bag with fierce haste.

Three days later found me ensconced in a little village a few miles from the old battlefield, and when the moon rose I was working with savage intensity on the great pile of crumbling stone that crowned the hill. It was back-breaking toil – looking back now I cannot see how I accomplished it. I laboured without a pause from moonrise to dawn. As the sun was coming up I tore aside the last tangle of stones and looked on all that was mortal of Count Boris Vladinoff – only a few, pitiful fragments of crumbling bone – and among them, crushed out of all original shape, lay a case whose lacquered surface had kept it from complete decay through the centuries.

I seized it with frenzied eagerness, and back in my tavern chamber I opened the case and found the parchment comparatively intact; and there was something else in the case – a small squat object wrapped in silk. I was wild to plumb the secrets of those yellowed pages, but weariness forbade me. Since leaving Stregoicavar I had hardly slept at all, and the terrific exertions of the previous night combined to overcome me. In spite of myself I was forced to stretch myself on my bed, nor did I awake until sundown.

I snatched a hasty supper, and then in the light of a flickering candle, read the near-Turkish characters that covered the parchment. It was difficult work, for I am not deeply versed in the language and the archaic style of the narrative baffled me. But as I toiled through it a word or a phrase here and there leaped at me and a dimly growing horror shook me in its grip. I bent my energies fiercely to the task, and as the tale grew clearer and took more tangible form my blood chilled in my veins, my hair stood up and my tongue clove to my mouth.

At last when grey dawn was stealing through the latticed window, I laid down the manuscript and took up and unwrapped the thing in the bit of silk. Staring at it with haggard eyes I knew the truth of the matter was clinched, even had it been possible to doubt the veracity of that terrible manuscript.

And I replaced both obscene things in the case, nor did I rest or sleep or eat until that case containing them had been weighted with stones and flung into the deepest current of the Danube which, God grant, carried them back into the Hell from which they came.

It was no dream I dreamed on Midsummer Midnight in the hills above Stregoicavar. Well for Justin Geoffrey that he tarried there only in the sunlight and went his way, for had he gazed upon that ghastly conclave, his mad brain would have snapped before it did. How my own reason held, I do not know.

No . . . it was no dream – I gazed upon a foul rout of votaries long dead, come up from Hell to worship as of old; ghosts that bowed before a ghost. For Hell has long claimed their hideous god.

By what foul alchemy or godless sorcery the Gates of Hell are opened on that one eerie night I do not know, but mine own eyes have seen. And I know I looked on no living thing that night, for the manuscript written in the careful hand of Selim Bahadur narrated at length what he and his raiders found in the valley of Stregoicavar; and I read, set down in detail, the blasphemous obscenities that torture wrung from the lips of screaming worshippers; and I read, too, of the lost, grim black cavern high in the hills where the horri-fied Turks hemmed a monstrous, bloated, wallowing toad-like being and slew it with flame and ancient steel blessed in old times by

Muhammad, and with incantations that were old when Arabia was young. And even staunch old Selim's hand shook as he recorded the cataclysmic, earth-shaking death-howls of the monstrosity, which died not alone; for half-score of his slayers perished with him, in ways that Selim would not or could not describe.

And that squat idol carved of gold and wrapped in silk was an image of himself, and Selim tore it from the golden chain that looped the neck of the slain high priest of the mask.

Well that the Turks swept out that foul valley with torch and clean steel! Such sights as those brooding mountains have looked on belong to the darkness and abysses of lost aeons. No – it is not fear of the toad-thing that makes me shudder in the night. He is made fast in Hell with his nauseous horde, freed only for an hour on the most weird night of the year, as I have seen. And of his worshippers, none remains.

But it is the realisation that such things once crouched beastlike above the souls of men which brings cold sweat to my brow; and I fear to peer again into the leaves of Von Junzt's abomination. For now I understand his repeated phrase of keys! Aye! Keys to Outer Doors – links with an abhorrent past and – who knows? – of abhorrent spheres of the present. And I understand why the tavern-keeper's nightmare-haunted nephew saw in his dream, the Black Stone like a spire on a Cyclopean black castle. If men ever excavate among those mountains they may find incredible things below those masking slopes. For the cave wherein the Turks trapped the thing was not truly a cavern, and I shudder to contemplate the gigantic gulf of aeons which must stretch between this age and the time when the earth shook herself and reared up, like a wave, those blue mountains that, rising, enveloped unthinkable things. May no man ever seek to uproot that ghastly spire men call the Black Stone!

A Key! Aye, it is a Key, symbol of a forgotten horror. That horror has faded into the limbo from which it crawled, loathsomely, in the black dawn of the earth. But what of the other fiendish possibilities hinted at by Von Junzt – what of the monstrous hand which strangled out his life? Since reading what Selim Bahadur wrote, I can no longer doubt anything in the Black Book. Man was not always master of the earth – and is he now? What nameless shapes may even now lurk in the dark places of the world?

Worms of the Earth

<u>Chapter One</u>

"Strike in the nails, soldiers, and let our guest see the reality of our good Roman justice!"

The speaker wrapped his purple cloak closer about his powerful frame and settled back into his official chair, much as he might have settled back in his seat at the Circus Maximus to enjoy the clash of gladiatorial swords. Realization of power colored his every move.

Whetted pride was necessary to Roman satisfaction, and Titus Sulla was justly proud; for he was military governor of Eboracum and answerable only to the emperor of Rome. He was a strongly built man of medium height, with the hawk-like features of the pure-bred Roman. Now a mocking smile curved his full lips, increasing the arrogance of his haughty aspect. Distinctly military in appearance, he wore the golden-scaled corselet and chased breastplate of his rank, with the short stabbing sword at his belt, and he held on his knee the silvered helmet with its plumed crest. Behind him stood a clump of impassive soldiers with shield and spear--blond titans from the Rhineland.

Before him was taking place the scene which

apparently gave him so much real gratification--a scene common enough wherever stretched the far-flung boundaries of Rome. A rude cross lay flat upon the barren earth and on it was bound a man--half-naked, wild of aspect with his corded limbs, glaring eyes and shock of tangled hair. His executioners were Roman soldiers, and with heavy hammers they prepared to pin the victim's hands and feet to the wood with iron spikes.

Only a small group of men watched this ghastly scene, in the dread place of execution beyond the city walls: the governor and his watchful guards; a few young Roman officers; the man to whom Sulla had referred as "guest" and who stood like a bronze image, unspeaking. Beside the gleaming splendor of the Roman, the quiet garb of this man seemed drab, almost somber. He was dark, but he did not resemble the Latins around him. There was about him none of the warm, almost Oriental sensuality of the Mediterranean which colored their features. The blond barbarians behind Sulla's chair were less unlike the man in facial outline than were the Romans. Not his were the full curving red lips, nor the rich waving locks suggestive of the Greek. Nor was his dark complexion the rich olive of the south; rather it was the bleak darkness of the north. The whole aspect of the man vaguely suggested the shadowed mists, the gloom, the cold and the icy winds of the naked northern lands. Even his black eyes were savagely cold, like black fires burning through fathoms of ice.

His height was only medium but there was

something about him which transcended mere physical bulk--a certain fierce innate vitality, comparable only to that of a wolf or a panther. In every line of his supple, compact body, as well as in his coarse straight hair and thin lips, this was evident--in the hawk-like set of the head on the corded neck, in the broad square shoulders, in the deep chest, the lean loins, the narrow feet. Built with the savage economy of a panther, he was an image of dynamic potentialities, pent in with iron self-control.

At his feet crouched one like him in complexion--but there the resemblance ended. This other was a stunted giant, with gnarly limbs, thick body, a low sloping brow and an expression of dull ferocity, now clearly mixed with fear. If the man on the cross resembled, in a tribal way, the man Titus Sulla called guest, he far more resembled the stunted crouching giant.

"Well, Partha Mac Othna," said the governor with studied effrontery, "when you return to your tribe, you will have a tale to tell of the justice of Rome, who rules the south."

"I will have a tale," answered the other in a voice which betrayed no emotion, just as his dark face, schooled to immobility, showed no evidence of the maelstrom in his soul.

"Justice to all under the rule of Rome," said Sulla. "Pax Romana! Reward for virtue, punishment for wrong!" He laughed inwardly at his own black hypocrisy, then continued: "You see, emissary of Pictland, how swiftly Rome punishes the transgressor."

"I see," answered the Pict in a voice which strongly-curbed anger made deep with menace, "that the subject of a foreign king is dealt with as though he were a Roman slave."

"He has been tried and condemned in an unbiased court," retorted Sulla.

"Aye! And the accuser was a Roman, the witnesses Roman, the judge Roman! He committed murder? In a moment of fury he struck down a Roman merchant who cheated, tricked and robbed him, and to injury added insult--aye, and a blow! Is his king but a dog, that Rome crucifies his subjects at will, condemned by Roman courts? Is his king too weak or foolish to do justice, were he informed and formal charges brought against the offender?"

"Well," said Sulla cynically, "you may inform Bran Mak Morn yourself. Rome, my friend, makes no account of her actions to barbarian kings. When savages come among us, let them act with discretion or suffer the consequences."

The Pict shut his iron jaws with a snap that told Sulla further badgering would elicit no reply. The Roman made a gesture to the executioners. One of them seized a spike and placing it against the thick wrist of the victim, smote heavily. The iron point sank deep through the flesh, crunching against the bones. The lips of the man on the cross writhed, though no moan escaped him. As a trapped wolf fights against his cage, the bound victim instinctively wrenched and struggled. The veins swelled in his temples, sweat beaded his low forehead, the muscles in arms and legs writhed and knotted. The hammers fell in inexorable strokes, driving the cruel points deeper and deeper, through wrists and ankles; blood flowed in a black river over the hands that held the spikes, staining the wood of the cross, and the splintering of bones was distinctly heard. Yet the sufferer made no outcry, though his blackened lips writhed back until the gums were visible, and his shaggy head jerked involuntarily from side to side.

The man called Partha Mac Othna stood like an iron image, eyes burning from an inscrutable face, his whole body hard as iron from the tension of his control. At his feet crouched his misshapen servant, hiding his face from the grim sight, his arms locked about his master's knees. Those arms gripped like steel and under his breath the fellow mumbled ceaselessly as if in invocation.

The last stroke fell; the cords were cut from arm and leg, so that the man would hang supported by the nails alone. He had ceased his struggling that only twisted the spikes in his agonizing wounds. His bright black eyes, unglazed, had not left the face of the man called Partha Mac Othna; in them lingered a desperate shadow of hope. Now the soldiers lifted the cross and set the end of it in the hole prepared, stamped the dirt about it to hold it erect. The Pict hung in midair, suspended by the nails in his flesh, but still no sound escaped his lips. His eyes still hung on the somber face of the emissary, but the shadow of hope was fading.

"He'll live for days!" said Sulla cheerfully.

"These Picts are harder than cats to kill! I'll keep a guard of ten soldiers watching night and day to see that no one takes him down before he dies. Ho, there, Valerius, in honor of our esteemed neighbor, King Bran Mak Morn, give him a cup of wine!"

With a laugh the young officer came forward, holding a brimming wine cup, and rising on his toes, lifted it to the parched lips of the sufferer. In the black eyes flared a red wave of unquenchable hatred; writhing his head aside to avoid even touching the cup, he spat full into the young Roman's eyes. With a curse Valerius dashed the cup to the ground, and before any could halt him, wrenched out his sword and sheathed it in the man's body.

Sulla rose with an imperious exclamation of anger; the man called Partha Mac Othna had started violently, but he bit his lip and said nothing. Valerius seemed somewhat surprized at him as he sullenly cleansed his sword. The act had been instinctive, following the insult to Roman pride, the one thing unbearable.

"Give up your sword, young sir!" exclaimed Sulla. "Centurion Publius, place him under arrest. A few days in a cell with stale bread and water will teach you to curb your patrician pride in matters dealing with the will of the empire. What, you young fool, do you not realize that you could not have made the dog a more kindly gift? Who would not rather desire a quick death on the sword than the slow agony on the cross? Take him away. And you, centurion, see that guards remain at the cross so that the body is not cut down until the ravens pick bare the bones. Partha Mac Othna, I go to a banquet at the house of Demetrius--will you not accompany me?"

The emissary shook his head, his eyes fixed on the limp form which sagged on the black-stained cross. He made no reply. Sulla smiled sardonically, then rose and strode away, followed by his secretary who bore the gilded chair ceremoniously, and by the stolid soldiers, with whom walked Valerius, head sunken.

The man called Partha Mac Othna flung a wide fold of his cloak about his shoulder, halted a moment to gaze at the grim cross with its burden, darkly etched against the crimson sky, where the clouds of night were gathering. Then he stalked away, followed by his silent servant.

<u>Chapter Two</u>

In an inner chamber of Eboracum, the man called Partha Mac Othna paced tigerishly to and fro. His sandaled feet made no sound on the marble tiles.

"Grom!" he turned to the gnarled servant. "Well I know why you held my knees so tightly--why you muttered aid of the Moon-Woman—you feared I would lose my self-control and make a mad attempt to succor that poor wretch. By the gods, I believe that was what the dog Roman wished--his iron-cased watchdogs watched me narrowly, I know, and his baiting was harder to bear than ordinarily.

"Gods black and white, dark and light!" He shook his clenched fists above his head in the black gust of his passion. "That I should stand by and see a man of mine butchered on a Roman cross--without justice and with no more trial than that farce! Black gods of R'lyeh, even you would I invoke to the ruin and destruction of those butchers! I swear by the Nameless Ones, men shall die howling for that deed, and Rome shall cry out as a woman in the dark who treads upon an adder!"

"He knew you, master," said Grom.

The other dropped his head and covered his eyes with a gesture of savage pain.

"His eyes will haunt me when I lie dying. Aye, he knew me, and almost until the last, I read in his eyes the hope that I might aid him. Gods and devils, is Rome to butcher my people beneath my very eyes? Then I am not king but dog!"

"Not so loud, in the name of all the gods!" exclaimed Grom in affright. "Did these Romans suspect you were Bran Mak Morn, they would nail you on a cross beside that other."

"They will know it ere long," grimly answered the king. "Too long I have lingered here in the guise of an emissary, spying upon mine enemies. They have thought to play with me, these Romans, masking their contempt and scorn only under polished satire. Rome is courteous to barbarian ambassadors, they give us fine houses to live in, offer us slaves, pander to our lusts with women and gold and wine and games, but all the while they laugh at us; their very courtesy is an insult, and sometimes--as today--their contempt discards all veneer. Bah! I've seen through their baitings--have remained imperturbably serene and swallowed their studied insults. But this--by the fiends of Hell, this is beyond human endurance! My people look to me; if I fail them--if I fail even one--even the lowest of my people, who will aid them? To whom shall they turn? By the gods, I'll answer the gibes of these Roman dogs with black shaft and trenchant steel!"

"And the chief with the plumes?" Grom meant the governor and his gutturals thrummed with the blood-lust. "He dies?" He flicked out a length of steel.

Bran scowled. "Easier said than done. He dies--but how may I reach him? By day his German guards keep at his back; by night they stand at door and window. He has many enemies, Romans as well as barbarians. Many a Briton would gladly slit his throat."

Grom seized Bran's garment, stammering as fierce eagerness broke the bonds of his inarticulate nature.

"Let me go, master! My life is worth nothing. I will cut him down in the midst of his warriors!"

Bran smiled fiercely and clapped his hand on the stunted giant's shoulder with a force that would have felled a lesser man.

"Nay, old war-dog, I have too much need of thee! You shall not throw your life away uselessly. Sulla would read the intent in your eyes, besides, and the javelins of his Teutons would be through you ere you could reach him. Not by the dagger in the dark will we strike this Roman, not by the venom in the cup nor the shaft from the ambush."

The king turned and paced the floor a moment, his head bent in thought. Slowly his eyes grew murky with a thought so fearful he did not speak it aloud to the waiting warrior.

"I have become somewhat familiar with the maze of Roman politics during my stay in this accursed waste of mud and marble," said he. "During a war on the Wall, Titus Sulla, as governor of this province, is supposed to hasten thither with his centuries. But this Sulla does not do; he is no coward, but the bravest avoid certain things--to each man, however bold, his own particular fear. So he sends in his place Caius Camillus, who in times of peace patrols the fens of the west, lest the Britons break over the border. And Sulla takes his place in the Tower of Trajan. Ha!"

He whirled and gripped Grom with steely fingers.

"Grom, take the red stallion and ride north! Let no grass grow under the stallion's hoofs! Ride to Cormac na Connacht and tell him to sweep the frontier with sword and torch! Let his wild Gaels feast their fill of slaughter. After a time I will be with him. But for a time I have affairs in the west."

Grom's black eyes gleamed and he made a passionate gesture with his crooked hand--an instinctive move of savagery. Bran drew a heavy bronze seal from beneath his tunic. "This is my safe-conduct as an emissary to Roman courts," he said grimly. "It will open all gates between this house and Baal-dor. If any official questions you too closely--here!"

Lifting the lid of an iron-bound chest, Bran took out a small, heavy leather bag which he gave into the hands of the warrior.

"When all keys fail at a gate," said he, "try a golden key. Go now!"

There were no ceremonious farewells between the barbarian king and his barbarian vassal. Grom flung up his arm in a gesture of salute; then turning, he hurried out.

Bran stepped to a barred window and gazed out into the moonlit streets.

"Wait until the moon sets," he muttered grimly. "Then I'll take the road to--Hell! But before I go I have a debt to pay."

The stealthy clink of a hoof on the flags reached him.

"With the safe-conduct and gold, not even Rome can hold a Pictish reaver," muttered the king. "Now I'll sleep until the moon sets."

With a snarl at the marble frieze-work and fluted columns, as symbols of Rome, he flung himself down on a couch, from which he had long since impatiently torn the cushions and silk stuffs, as too soft for his hard body. Hate and the black passion of vengeance seethed in him, yet he went instantly to sleep. The first lesson he had learned in his bitter hard life was to snatch sleep any time he could, like a wolf that snatches sleep on the hunting trail. Generally his slumber was as light and dreamless as a panther's, but tonight it was otherwise.

He sank into fleecy gray fathoms of slumber and in a timeless, misty realm of shadows he met the tall, lean, white-bearded figure of old Gonar, the priest of the Moon, high counselor to the king. And Bran stood aghast, for Gonar's face was white as driven snow and he shook as with ague. Well might Bran stand appalled, for in all the years of his life he had never before seen Gonar the Wise show any sign of fear.

"What now, old one?" asked the king. "Goes all well in Baal-dor?"

"All is well in Baal-dor where my body lies sleeping," answered old Gonar. "Across the void I have come to battle with you for your soul. King, are you mad, this thought you have thought in your brain?"

"Gonar," answered Bran somberly, "this day I stood still and watched a man of mine die on the cross of Rome. What his name or his rank, I do not know. I do not care. He might have been a faithful unknown warrior of mine, he might have been an outlaw. I only know that he was mine; the first scents he knew were the scents of the heather; the first light he saw was the sunrise on the Pictish hills. He belonged to me, not to Rome. If punishment was just, then none but me should have dealt it. If he were to be tried, none but me should have been his judge. The same blood flowed in our veins; the same fire maddened our brains; in infancy we listened to the same old tales, and in youth we sang the same old songs. He was bound to my heartstrings, as every man and every woman and every child of Pictland is bound. It was mine to protect him; now it is mine to avenge him."

"But in the name of the gods, Bran," expostulated the wizard, "take your vengeance in another way! Return to the heather--mass your warriors--join with Cormac and his Gaels, and spread a sea of blood and flame the length of the great Wall!"

"All that I will do," grimly answered Bran. "But now--now--I will have a vengeance such as no Roman ever dreamed of! Ha, what do they know of the mysteries of this ancient isle, which sheltered strange life long before Rome rose from the marshes of the Tiber?"

"Bran, there are weapons too foul to use, even against Rome!"

Bran barked short and sharp as a jackal.

"Ha! There are no weapons I would not use against Rome! My back is at the wall. By the blood of the fiends, has Rome fought me fair? Bah! I am a barbarian king with a wolfskin mantle and an iron crown, fighting with my handful of bows and broken pikes against the queen of the world. What have I? The heather hills, the wattle huts, the spears of my shock-headed tribesmen! And I fight Rome--with her armored legions, her broad fertile plains and rich seas-- her mountains and her rivers and her gleaming cities-- her wealth, her steel, her gold, her mastery and her wrath. By steel and fire I will fight her--and by subtlety and treachery--by the thorn in the foot, the adder in the path, the venom in the cup, the dagger in the dark; aye," his voice sank somberly, "and by the worms of the earth!"

"But it is madness!" cried Gonar. "You will perish in the attempt you plan--you will go down to Hell and you will not return! What of your people then?"

"If I can not serve them I had better die," growled the king. "But you can not even reach the beings you seek," cried Gonar. "For untold centuries they have dwelt apart. There is no door by which you can come to them. Long ago they severed the bonds that bound them to the world we know."

"Long ago," answered Bran somberly, "you told me that nothing in the universe was separated from the stream of Life--a saying the truth of which I have often seen evident. No race, no form of life but is close-knit somehow, by some manner, to the rest of Life and the world. Somewhere there is a thin link connecting those I seek to the world I know. Somewhere there is a Door. And somewhere among the bleak fens of the west I will find it."

Stark horror flooded Gonar's eyes and he gave back crying, "Woe! Woe! Woe! to Pictdom! Woe to the unborn kingdom! Woe, black woe to the sons of men! Woe, woe, woe, woe!"

Bran awoke to a shadowed room and the starlight on the window-bars. The moon had sunk from sight though its glow was still faint above the house tops. Memory of his dream shook him and he swore beneath his breath.

Rising, he flung off cloak and mantle, donning a light shirt of black mesh-mail, and girding on sword and dirk. Going again to the iron-bound chest he lifted several compact bags and emptied the clinking contents into the leathern pouch at his girdle. Then wrapping his wide cloak about him, he silently left the house. No servants there were to spy on him--he had impatiently refused the offer of slaves which it was Rome's policy to furnish her barbarian emissaries. Gnarled Grom had attended to all Bran's simple needs.

The stables fronted on the courtyard. A moment's groping in the dark and he placed his hand over a great stallion's nose, checking the nicker of recognition. Working without a light he swiftly bridled and saddled the great brute, and went through the courtyard into a shadowy side street, leading him. The moon was setting, the border of floating shadows widening along the western wall. Silence lay on the marble palaces and mud hovels of Eboracum under the cold stars.

Bran touched the pouch at his girdle, which was heavy with minted gold that bore the stamp of Rome. He had come to Eboracum posing as an emissary of Pictdom, to act the spy. But being a barbarian, he had not been able to play his part in aloof formality and sedate dignity. He retained a crowded memory of wild feasts where wine flowed in fountains; of white-bosomed Roman women, who, sated with civilized lovers, looked with something more than favor on a virile barbarian; of gladiatorial games; and of other games where dice clicked and spun and tall stacks of gold changed hands. He had drunk deeply and gambled recklessly, after the manner of barbarians, and he had had a remarkable run of luck, due possibly to the indifference with which he won or lost. Gold to the Pict was so much dust, flowing through his fingers. In his land there was no need of it. But he had learned its power in the boundaries of civilization.

Almost under the shadow of the northwestern wall he saw ahead of him loom the great watchtower which was connected with and reared above the outer wall. One corner of the castle-like fortress, farthest from the wall, served as a dungeon. Bran left his horse standing in a dark alley, with the reins hanging on the ground, and stole like a prowling wolf into the shadows of the fortress.

The young officer Valerius was awakened from a light, unquiet sleep by a stealthy sound at the barred window. He sat up, cursing softly under his breath as the faint starlight which etched the window-bars fell across the bare stone floor and reminded him of his disgrace. Well, in a few days, he ruminated, he'd be well out of it; Sulla would not be too harsh on a man with such high connections; then let any man or woman gibe at him! Damn that insolent Pict! But wait, he thought suddenly, remembering: what of the sound which had roused him?

"Hsssst!" it was a voice from the window.

Why so much secrecy? It could hardly be a foe-

-yet, why should it be a friend? Valerius rose and crossed his cell, coming close to the window. Outside all was dim in the starlight and he made out but a shadowy form close to the window.

"Who are you?" he leaned close against the bars, straining his eyes into the gloom.

His answer was a snarl of wolfish laughter, a long flicker of steel in the starlight. Valerius reeled away from the window and crashed to the floor, clutching his throat, gurgling horribly as he tried to scream. Blood gushed through his fingers, forming about his twitching body a pool that reflected the dim starlight dully and redly.

Outside Bran glided away like a shadow, without pausing to peer into the cell. In another minute the guards would round the corner on their regular routine. Even now he heard the measured tramp of their iron-clad feet. Before they came in sight he had vanished and they clumped stolidly by the cell-window with no intimation of the corpse that lay on the floor within.

Bran rode to the small gate in the western wall, unchallenged by the sleepy watch. What fear of foreign invasion in Eboracum?--and certain well organized thieves and women-stealers made it profitable for the watchmen not to be too vigilant. But the single guardsman at the western gate--his fellows lay drunk in a nearby brothel - lifted his spear and bawled for Bran to halt and give an account of himself. Silently the Pict reined closer. Masked in the dark cloak, he seemed dim and indistinct to the

Roman, who was only aware of the glitter of his cold eyes in the gloom. But Bran held up his hand against the starlight and the soldier caught the gleam of gold; in the other hand he saw a long sheen of steel. The soldier understood, and he did not hesitate between the choice of a golden bribe or a battle to the death with this unknown rider who was apparently a barbarian of some sort. With a grunt he lowered his spear and swung the gate open. Bran rode through, casting a handful of coins to the Roman. They fell about his feet in a golden shower, clinking against the flags. He bent in greedy haste to retrieve them and Bran Mak Morn rode westward like a flying ghost in the night.

Chapter Three

Into the dim fens of the west came Bran Mak Morn. A cold wind breathed across the gloomy waste and against the gray sky a few herons flapped heavily. The long reeds and marsh-grass waved in broken undulations and out across the desolation of the wastes a few still meres reflected the dull light. Here and there rose curiously regular hillocks above the general levels, and gaunt against the somber sky Bran saw a marching line of upright monoliths--menhirs, reared by what nameless hands?

As a faint blue line to the west lay the foothills that beyond the horizon grew to the wild mountains of Wales where dwelt still wild Celtic tribes--fierce blue-eyed men that knew not the yoke of Rome. A row of well-garrisoned watchtowers held them in check. Even now, far away across the moors, Bran glimpsed the unassailable keep men called the Tower of Trajan.

These barren wastes seemed the dreary accomplishment of desolation, yet human life was not utterly lacking. Bran met the silent men of the fen, reticent, dark of eye and hair, speaking a strange mixed tongue whose long-blended elements had forgotten their pristine separate sources. Bran recognized a certain kinship in these people to himself, but he looked on them with the scorn of a pure-blooded patrician for men of mixed strains.

Not that the common people of Caledonia were altogether pure-blooded; they got their stocky bodies and massive limbs from a primitive Teutonic race which had found its way into the northern tip of the isle even before the Celtic conquest of Britain was completed, and had been absorbed by the Picts. But the chiefs of Bran's folk had kept their blood from foreign taint since the beginnings of time, and he himself was a pure-bred Pict of the Old Race. But these fenmen, overrun repeatedly by British, Gaelic and Roman conquerors, had assimilated blood of each, and in the process almost forgotten their original language and lineage.

For Bran came of a race that was very old, which had spread over western Europe in one vast Dark Empire, before the coming of the Aryans, when the ancestors of the Celts, the Hellenes and the Germans were one primal people, before the days of tribal splitting-off and westward drift.

Only in Caledonia, Bran brooded, had his people resisted the flood of Aryan conquest. He had heard of a Pictish people called Basques, who in the crags of the Pyrenees called themselves an unconquered race; but he knew that they had paid tribute for centuries to the ancestors of the Gaels, before these Celtic conquerors abandoned their mountain-realm and set sail for Ireland. Only the Picts of Caledonia had remained free, and they had been scattered into small feuding tribes--he was the first acknowledged king in five hundred years—the beginning of a new dynasty--no, a revival of an ancient dynasty under a new name. In the very teeth of Rome he dreamed his dreams of empire.

He wandered through the fens, seeking a Door. Of his quest he said nothing to the dark-eyed fenmen. They told him news that drifted from mouth to mouth--a tale of war in the north, the skirl of war-pipe along the winding Wall, of gathering-fires in the heather, of flame and smoke and rapine and the glutting of Gaelic swords in the crimson sea of slaughter. The eagles of the legions were moving northward and the ancient road resounded to the measured tramp of the iron-clad feet. And Bran, in the fens of the west, laughed, well pleased.

In Eboracum, Titus Sulla gave secret word to seek out the Pictish emissary with the Gaelic name who had been under suspicion, and who had vanished the night young Valerius was found dead in his cell with his throat ripped out. Sulla felt that this sudden bursting flame of war on the Wall was connected closely with his execution of a condemned Pictish criminal, and he set his spy system to work, though he felt sure that Partha Mac Othna was by this time far beyond his reach. He prepared to march from Eboracum, but he did not accompany the considerable force of legionaries which he sent north. Sulla was a brave man, but each man has his own dread, and Sulla's was Cormac na Connacht, the black-haired prince of the Gaels, who had sworn to cut out the governor's heart and eat it raw. So Sulla rode with his ever- present bodyguard, westward, where lay the Tower of Trajan with its warlike commander, Caius Camillus, who enjoyed nothing more than taking his superior's place when the red waves of war washed at the foot of the Wall. Devious politics, but the legate of Rome seldom visited this far isle, and what of his wealth and intrigues, Titus Sulla was the highest power in Britain.

And Bran, knowing all this, patiently waited his coming, in the deserted hut in which he had taken up his abode.

One gray evening he strode on foot across the moors, a stark figure, blackly etched against the dim crimson fire of the sunset. He felt the incredible antiquity of the slumbering land, as he walked like the last man on the day after the end of the world. Yet at last he saw a token of human life--a drab hut of wattle and mud, set in the reedy breast of the fen.

A woman greeted him from the open door and Bran's somber eyes narrowed with a dark suspicion. The woman was not old, yet the evil wisdom of ages was in her eyes; her garments were ragged and scanty, her black locks tangled and unkempt, lending her an aspect of wildness well in keeping with her grim surroundings. Her red lips laughed but there was no mirth in her laughter, only a hint of mockery, and under the lips her teeth showed sharp and pointed like fangs.

"Enter, master," said she, "if you do not fear to share the roof of the witch-woman of Dagon-moor!"

Bran entered silently and sat him down on a broken bench while the woman busied herself with the scanty meal cooking over an open fire on the squalid hearth. He studied her lithe, almost serpentine motions, the ears which were almost pointed, the yellow eyes which slanted curiously.

"What do you seek in the fens, my lord?" she asked, turning toward him with a supple twist of her whole body.

"I seek a Door," he answered, chin resting on his fist. "I have a song to sing to the worms of the earth!"

She started upright, a jar falling from her hands to shatter on the hearth.

"This is an ill saying, even spoken in chance," she stammered.

"I speak not by chance but by intent," he answered.

She shook her head. "I know not what you

mean."

"Well you know," he returned. "Aye, you know well! My race is very old--they reigned in Britain before the nations of the Celts and the Hellenes were born out of the womb of peoples. But my people were not first in Britain. By the mottles on your skin, by the slanting of your eyes, by the taint in your veins, I speak with full knowledge and meaning."

Awhile she stood silent, her lips smiling but her face inscrutable.

"Man, are you mad," she asked, "that in your madness you come seeking that from which strong men fled screaming in old times?"

"I seek a vengeance," he answered, "that can be accomplished only by Them I seek."

She shook her head.

"You have listened to a bird singing; you have dreamed empty dreams."

"I have heard a viper hiss," he growled, "and I do not dream. Enough of this weaving of words. I came seeking a link between two worlds; I have found it."

"I need lie to you no more, man of the North," answered the woman. "They you seek still dwell beneath the sleeping hills. They have drawn apart, farther and farther from the world you know."

"But they still steal forth in the night to grip women straying on the moors," said he, his gaze on her slanted eyes. She laughed wickedly.

"What would you of me?"

"That you bring me to Them."

She flung back her head with a scornful laugh. His left hand locked like iron in the breast of her scanty garment and his right closed on his hilt. She laughed in his face.

"Strike and be damned, my northern wolf! Do you think that such life as mine is so sweet that I would cling to it as a babe to the breast?"

His hand fell away.

"You are right. Threats are foolish. I will buy your aid."

"How?" the laughing voice hummed with mockery.

Bran opened his pouch and poured into his cupped palm a stream of gold.

"More wealth than the men of the fen ever dreamed of."

Again she laughed. "What is this rusty metal to me? Save it for some white-breasted Roman woman who will play the traitor for you!"

"Name me a price!" he urged. "The head of an enemy--"

"By the blood in my veins, with its heritage of ancient hate, who is mine enemy but thee?" she laughed and springing, struck catlike. But her dagger splintered on the mail beneath his cloak and he flung her off with a loathsome flit of his wrist which tossed her sprawling across her grass-strewn bunk. Lying there she laughed up at him.

"I will name you a price, then, my wolf, and it may be in days to come you will curse the armor that broke Atla's dagger!" She rose and came close to him, her disquietingly long hands fastened fiercely into his cloak. "I will tell you, Black Bran, king of Caledon! Oh, I knew you when you came into my hut with your black hair and your cold eyes! I will lead you to the doors of Hell if you wish--and the price shall be the kisses of a king!

"What of my blasted and bitter life, I, whom mortal men loathe and fear? I have not known the love of men, the clasp of a strong arm, the sting of human kisses, I, Atla, the were-woman of the moors! What have I known but the lone winds of the fens, the dreary fire of cold sunsets, the whispering of the marsh grasses?--the faces that blink up at me in the waters of the meres, the foot-pad of night--things in the gloom, the glimmer of red eyes, the grisly murmur of nameless beings in the night!

"I am half-human, at least! Have I not known sorrow and yearning and crying wistfulness, and the drear ache of loneliness? Give to me, king--give me your fierce kisses and your hurtful barbarian's embrace. Then in the long drear years to come I shall not utterly eat out my heart in vain envy of the white-bosomed women of men; for I shall have a memory few of them can boast--the kisses of a king! One night of love, oh king, and I will guide you to the gates of Hell!"

Bran eyed her somberly; he reached forth and gripped her arm in his iron fingers. An involuntary shudder shook him at the feel of her sleek skin. He nodded slowly and drawing her close to him, forced his head down to meet her lifted lips.

Chapter Four

The cold gray mists of dawn wrapped King Bran like a clammy cloak. He turned to the woman whose slanted eyes gleamed in the gray gloom.

"Make good your part of the contract," he said roughly. "I sought a link between worlds, and in you I found it. I seek the one thing sacred to Them. It shall be the Key opening the Door that lies unseen between me and Them. Tell me how I can reach it."

"I will," the red lips smiled terribly. "Go to the mound men call Dagon's Barrow. Draw aside the stone that blocks the entrance and go under the dome of the mound. The floor of the chamber is made of seven great stones, six grouped about the seventh. Lift out the center stone--and you will see!"

"Will I find the Black Stone?" he asked.

"Dagon's Barrow is the Door to the Black Stone," she answered, "if you dare follow the Road."

"Will the symbol be well guarded?" He unconsciously loosened his blade in its sheath. The red lips curled mockingly.

"If you meet any on the Road you will die as no mortal man has died for long centuries. The Stone is not guarded, as men guard their treasures. Why should They guard what man has never sought? Perhaps They will be near, perhaps not. It is a chance you must take, if you wish the Stone. Beware, king of Pictdom! Remember it was your folk who, so long ago, cut the thread that bound Them to human life. They were almost human then--they overspread the land and knew the sunlight. Now they have drawn apart. They know not the sunlight and they shun the light of the moon. Even the starlight they hate. Far, far apart have they drawn, who might have been men in time, but for the spears of your ancestors."

The sky was overcast with misty gray, through which the sun shone coldly yellow when Bran came to Dagon's Barrow, a round hillock overgrown with rank grass of a curious fungoid appearance. On the eastern side of the mound showed the entrance of a crudely built stone tunnel which evidently penetrated the barrow. One great stone blocked the entrance to the tomb. Bran laid hold of the sharp edges and exerted all his strength. It held fast. He drew his sword and worked the blade between the blocking stone and the sill. Using the sword as a lever, he worked carefully, and managed to loosen the great stone and wrench it out. A foul charnel house scent flowed out of the aperture and the dim sunlight seemed less to illuminate the cavern- like opening than to be fouled by the rank darkness which clung there.

Sword in hand, ready for he knew not what, Bran groped his way into the tunnel, which was long and narrow, built up of heavy joined stones, and was too low for him to stand erect. Either his eyes became somewhat accustomed to the gloom, or the darkness was, after all, somewhat lightened by the sunlight filtering in through the entrance. At any rate he came into a round low chamber and was able to make out its general dome-like outline. Here, no doubt, in old times, had reposed the bones of him for whom the stones of the tomb had been joined and the earth heaped high above them; but now of those bones no vestige remained on the stone floor. And bending close and straining his eyes, Bran made out the strange, startlingly regular pattern of that floor: six well-cut slabs clustered about a seventh, six-sided stone.

He drove his sword-point into a crack and pried carefully. The edge of the central stone tilted slightly upward. A little work and he lifted it out and leaned it against the curving wall. Straining his eyes downward he saw only the gaping blackness of a dark well, with small, worn steps that led downward and out of sight. He did not hesitate. Though the skin between his shoulders crawled curiously, he swung himself into the abyss and felt the clinging blackness swallow him.

Groping downward, he felt his feet slip and stumble on steps too small for human feet. With one hand pressed hard against the side of the well he steadied himself, fearing a fall into unknown and unlighted depths. The steps were cut into solid rock, yet they were greatly worn away. The farther he progressed, the less like steps they became, mere bumps of worn stone. Then the direction of the shaft changed sharply. It still led down, but at a shallow slant down which he could walk, elbows braced against the hollowed sides, head bent low beneath the curved roof. The steps had ceased altogether and the stone felt slimy to the touch, like a serpent's lair. What beings, Bran wondered, had slithered up and down this slanting shaft, for how many centuries?

The tunnel narrowed until Bran found it rather difficult to shove through. He lay on his back and pushed himself along with his hands, feet first. Still he knew he was sinking deeper and deeper into the very guts of the earth; how far below the surface he was, he dared not contemplate. Then ahead a faint witch-fire gleam tinged the abysmal blackness. He grinned savagely and without mirth. If They he sought came suddenly upon him, how could he fight in that narrow shaft? But he had put the thought of personal fear behind him when he began this hellish quest. He crawled on, thoughtless of all else but his goal.

And he came at last into a vast space where he could stand upright. He could not see the roof of the place, but he got an impression of dizzying vastness. The blackness pressed in on all sides and behind him he could see the entrance to the shaft from which he had just emerged--a black well in the darkness. But in front of him a strange grisly radiance glowed about a grim altar built of human skulls. The source of that light he could not determine, but on the altar lay a sullen night-black object--the Black Stone!

Bran wasted no time in giving thanks that the guardians of the grim relic were nowhere near. He caught up the Stone, and gripping it under his left arm, crawled into the shaft. When a man turns his back on peril its clammy menace looms more grisly than when he advances upon it. So Bran, crawling back up the nighted shaft with his grisly prize, felt the darkness turn on him and slink behind him, grinning with dripping fangs. Clammy sweat beaded his flesh and he hastened to the best of his ability, ears strained for some stealthy sound to betray that fell shapes were at his heels. Strong shudders shook him, despite himself, and the short hair on his neck prickled as if a cold wind blew at his back.

When he reached the first of the tiny steps he felt as if he had attained to the outer boundaries of the mortal world. Up them he went, stumbling and slipping, and with a deep gasp of relief, came out into the tomb, whose spectral grayness seemed like the blaze of noon in comparison to the stygian depths he had just traversed. He replaced the central stone and strode into the light of the outer day, and never was the cold yellow light of the sun more grateful, as it dispelled the shadows of black-winged nightmares of fear and madness that seemed to have ridden him up out of the black deeps. He shoved the great blocking stone back into place, and picking up the cloak he had left at the mouth of the tomb, he wrapped it about the Black Stone and hurried away, a strong revulsion and loathing shaking his soul and lending wings to his strides.

A gray silence brooded over the land. It was desolate as the blind side of the moon, yet Bran felt the potentialities of life--under his feet, in the brown earth--sleeping, but how soon to waken, and in what horrific fashion?

He came through the tall masking reeds to the still deep men called Dagon's Mere. No slightest ripple ruffled the cold blue water to give evidence of the grisly monster legend said dwelt beneath. Bran closely scanned the breathless landscape. He saw no hint of life, human or unhuman. He sought the instincts of his savage soul to know if any unseen eyes fixed their lethal gaze upon him, and found no response. He was alone as if he were the last man alive on earth.

Swiftly he unwrapped the Black Stone, and as it lay in his hands like a solid sullen block of darkness, he did not seek to learn the secret of its material nor scan the cryptic characters carved thereon. Weighing it in his hands and calculating the distance, he flung it far out, so that it fell almost exactly in the middle of the lake. A sullen splash and the waters closed over it. There was a moment of shimmering flashes on the bosom of the lake; then the blue surface stretched placid and unrippled again.

Chapter Five

The were-woman turned swiftly as Bran approached her door. Her slant eyes widened.

"You! And alive! And sane!"

"I have been into Hell and I have returned," he growled. "What is more, I have that which I sought."

"The Black Stone?" she cried. "You really dared steal it? Where is it?"

"No matter; but last night my stallion screamed in his stall and I heard something crunch beneath his thundering hoofs which was not the wall of the stable--and there was blood on his hoofs when I came to see, and blood on the floor of the stall. And I have heard stealthy sounds in the night, and noises beneath my dirt floor, as if worms burrowed deep in the earth. They know I have stolen their Stone. Have you betrayed me?"

She shook her head.

"I keep your secret; they do not need my word to know you. The farther they have retreated from the world of men, the greater have grown their powers in other uncanny ways. Some dawn your hut will stand empty and if men dare investigate they will find nothing - except crumbling bits of earth on the dirt floor."

Bran smiled terribly.

"I have not planned and toiled thus far to fall prey to the talons of vermin. If They strike me down in the night, They will never know what became of their idol--or whatever it be to Them. I would speak with Them."

"Dare you come with me and meet them in the night?" she asked.

"Thunder of all gods!" he snarled. "Who are you to ask me if I dare? Lead me to Them and let me bargain for a vengeance this night. The hour of retribution draws nigh. This day I saw silvered helmets and bright shields gleam across the fens--the new commander has arrived at the Tower of Trajan and Caius Camillus has marched to the Wall."

That night the king went across the dark desolation of the moors with the silent were-woman.

The night was thick and still as if the land lay in ancient slumber. The stars blinked vaguely, mere points of red struggling through the unbreathing gloom. Their gleam was dimmer than the glitter in the eyes of the woman who glided beside the king. Strange thoughts shook Bran, vague, titanic, primeval. Tonight ancestral linkings with these slumbering fens stirred in his soul and troubled him with the phantasmal, eon-veiled shapes of monstrous dreams. The vast age of his race was borne upon him; where now he walked an outlaw and an alien, dark-eyed kings in whose mold he was cast had reigned in old times. The Celtic and Roman invaders were as strangers to this ancient isle beside his people. Yet his race likewise had been invaders, and there was an older race than his—a race whose beginnings lay lost and hidden back beyond the dark oblivion of antiquity.

Ahead of them loomed a low range of hills, which formed the easternmost extremity of those straying chains which far away climbed at last to the mountains of Wales. The woman led the way up what might have been a sheep-path, and halted before a wide black gaping cave.

"A door to those you seek, oh king!" her laughter rang hateful in the gloom. "Dare ye enter?"

His fingers closed in her tangled locks and he shook her viciously.

"Ask me but once more if I dare," he grated, "and your head and shoulders part company! Lead on."

Her laughter was like sweet deadly venom.

They passed into the cave and Bran struck flint and steel. The flicker of the tinder showed him a wide dusty cavern, on the roof of which hung clusters of bats. Lighting a torch, he lifted it and scanned the shadowy recesses, seeing nothing but dust and emptiness.

"Where are They?" he growled.

She beckoned him to the back of the cave and leaned against the rough wall, as if casually. But the king's keen eyes caught the motion of her hand pressing hard against a projecting ledge. He recoiled as a round black well gaped suddenly at his feet. Again her laughter slashed him like a keen silver knife. He held the torch to the opening and again saw small worn steps leading down.

"They do not need those steps," said Atla. "Once they did, before your people drove them into the darkness. But you will need them."

She thrust the torch into a niche above the well; it shed a faint red light into the darkness below. She gestured into the well and Bran loosened his sword and stepped into the shaft. As he went down into the mystery of the darkness, the light was blotted out above him, and he thought for an instant Atla had covered the opening again. Then he realized that she was descending after him.

The descent was not a long one. Abruptly Bran felt his feet on a solid floor. Atla swung down beside him and stood in the dim circle of light that drifted down the shaft. Bran could not see the limits of the place into which he had come.

"Many caves in these hills," said Atla, her voice sounding small and strangely brittle in the vastness, "are but doors to greater caves which lie beneath, even as a man's words and deeds are but small indications of the dark caverns of murky thought lying behind and beneath."

And now Bran was aware of movement in the gloom. The darkness was filled with stealthy noises not like those made by any human foot. Abruptly sparks began to flash and float in the blackness, like flickering fireflies. Closer they came until they girdled him in a wide half-moon. And beyond the ring gleamed other sparks, a solid sea of them, fading away in the gloom until the farthest were mere tiny pin-points of light. And Bran knew they were the slanted eyes of the beings who had come upon him in such numbers that his brain reeled at the contemplation--and at the vastness of the cavern.

Now that he faced his ancient foes, Bran knew no fear. He felt the waves of terrible menace emanating from them, the grisly hate, the inhuman threat to body, mind and soul. More than a member of a less ancient race, he realized the horror of his position, but he did not fear, though he confronted the ultimate Horror of the dreams and legends of his race. His blood raced fiercely but it was with the hot excitement of the hazard, not the drive of terror.

"They know you have the Stone, oh king," said Atla, and though he knew she feared, though he felt her physical efforts to control her trembling limbs, there was no quiver of fright in her voice. "You are in deadly peril; they know your breed of old--oh, they remember the days when their ancestors were men! I can not save you; both of us will die as no human has died for ten centuries. Speak to them, if you will; they can understand your speech, though you may not understand theirs. But it will avail not--you are human--and a Pict."

Bran laughed and the closing ring of fire shrank back at the savagery in his laughter. Drawing his sword with a soul-chilling rasp of steel, he set his back against what he hoped was a solid stone wall. Facing the glittering eyes with his sword gripped in his right hand and his dirk in his left, he laughed as a blood-hungry wolf snarls.

"Aye," he growled, "I am a Pict, a son of those warriors who drove your brutish ancestors before them like chaff before the storm!--who flooded the land with your blood and heaped high your skulls for a sacrifice to the Moon-Woman! You who fled of old before my race, dare ye now snarl at your master? Roll on me like a flood now, if ye dare! Before your viper fangs drink my life I will reap your multitudes like ripened barley--of your severed heads will I build a tower and of your mangled corpses will I rear up a wall! Dogs of the dark, vermin of Hell, worms of the earth, rush in and try my steel! When Death finds me in this dark cavern, your living will howl for the scores of your dead and your Black Stone will be lost to you forever--for only I know where it is hidden and not all the tortures of all the Hells can wring the secret from my lips!"

Then followed a tense silence; Bran faced the fire-lit darkness, tensed like a wolf at bay, waiting the charge; at his side the woman cowered, her eyes ablaze. Then from the silent ring that hovered beyond the dim torchlight rose a vague abhorrent murmur. Bran, prepared as he was for anything, started. Gods, was that the speech of creatures which had once been called men?

Atla straightened, listening intently. From her lips came the same hideous soft sibilances, and Bran, though he had already known the grisly secret of her being, knew that never again could he touch her save with soul-shaken loathing.

She turned to him, a strange smile curving her red lips dimly in the ghostly light.

"They fear you, oh king! By the black secrets of R'lyeh, who are you that Hell itself quails before you? Not your steel, but the stark ferocity of your soul has driven unused fear into their strange minds. They will buy back the Black Stone at any price."

"Good," Bran sheathed his weapons. "They shall promise not to molest you because of your aid of me. And," his voice hummed like the purr of a hunting tiger, "they shall deliver into my hands Titus Sulla, governor of Eboracum, now commanding the Tower of Trajan. This They can do--how, I know not. But I know that in the old days, when my people warred with these Children of the Night, babes disappeared from guarded huts and none saw the stealers come or go. Do They understand?"

Again rose the low frightful sounds and Bran,

who feared not their wrath, shuddered at their voices.

"They understand," said Atla. "Bring the Black Stone to Dagon's Ring tomorrow night when the earth is veiled with the blackness that foreruns the dawn. Lay the Stone on the altar. There They will bring Titus Sulla to you. Trust Them; They have not interfered in human affairs for many centuries, but They will keep their word."

Bran nodded and turning, climbed up the stair with Atla close behind him. At the top he turned and looked down once more. As far as he could see floated a glittering ocean of slanted yellow eyes upturned. But the owners of those eyes kept carefully beyond the dim circle of torchlight and of their bodies he could see nothing. Their low hissing speech floated up to him and he shuddered as his imagination visualized, not a throng of biped creatures, but a swarming, swaying myriad of serpents, gazing up at him with their glittering unwinking eyes.

He swung into the upper cave and Atla thrust the blocking stone back in place. It fitted into the entrance of the well with uncanny precision; Bran was unable to discern any crack in the apparently solid floor of the cavern. Atla made a motion to extinguish the torch, but the king stayed her.

"Keep it so until we are out of the cave," he grunted. "We might tread on an adder in the dark."

Atla's sweetly hateful laughter rose maddeningly in the flickering gloom.

<u>Chapter 6</u>

It was not long before sunset when Bran came again to the reed- grown marge of Dagon's Mere. Casting cloak and sword-belt on the ground, he stripped himself of his short leathern breeches. Then gripping his naked dirk in his teeth, he went into the water with the smooth ease of a diving seal. Swimming strongly, he gained the center of the small lake, and turning, drove himself downward.

The mere was deeper than he had thought. It seemed he would never reach the bottom, and when he did, his groping hands failed to find what he sought. A roaring in his ears warned him and he swam to the surface.

Gulping deep of the refreshing air, he dived again, and again his quest was fruitless. A third time he sought the depth, and this time his groping hands met a familiar object in the silt of the bottom. Grasping it, he swam up to the surface.

The Stone was not particularly bulky, but it was heavy. He swam leisurely, and suddenly was aware of a curious stir in the waters about him which was not caused by his own exertions. Thrusting his face below the surface, he tried to pierce the blue depths with his eyes and thought to see a dim gigantic shadow hovering there.

He swam faster, not frightened, but wary. His feet struck the shallows and he waded up on the shelving shore. Looking back he saw the waters swirl and subside. He shook his head, swearing. He had discounted the ancient legend which made Dagon's Mere the lair of a nameless water-monster, but now he had a feeling as if his escape had been narrow. The time-worn myths of the ancient land were taking form and coming to life before his eyes. What primeval shape lurked below the surface of that treacherous mere, Bran could not guess, but he felt that the fenmen had good reason for shunning the spot, after all.

Bran donned his garments, mounted the black stallion and rode across the fens in the desolate crimson of the sunset's afterglow, with the Black Stone wrapped in his cloak. He rode, not to his hut, but to the west, in the direction of the Tower of Trajan and the Ring of Dagon. As he covered the miles that lay between, the red stars winked out. Midnight passed him in the moonless night and still Bran rode on. His heart was hot for his meeting with Titus Sulla. Atla had gloated over the anticipation of watching the Roman writhe under torture, but no such thought was in the Pict's mind. The governor should have his chance with weapons--with Bran's own sword he should face the Pictish king's dirk, and live or die according to his prowess. And though Sulla was famed throughout the provinces as a swordsman, Bran felt no doubt as to the outcome.

Dagon's Ring lay some distance from the Tower--a sullen circle of tall gaunt stones planted upright, with a rough-hewn stone altar in the center. The Romans looked on these menhirs with aversion; they thought the Druids had reared them; but the

Celts supposed Bran's people, the Picts, had planted them--and Bran well knew what hands reared those grim monoliths in lost ages, though for what reasons, he but dimly guessed.

The king did not ride straight to the Ring. He was consumed with curiosity as to how his grim allies intended carrying out their promise. That They could snatch Titus Sulla from the very midst of his men, he felt sure, and he believed he knew how They would do it. He felt the gnawings of a strange misgiving, as if he had tampered with powers of unknown breadth and depth, and had loosed forces which he could not control. Each time he remembered that reptilian murmur, those slanted eyes of the night before, a cold breath passed over him. They had been abhorrent enough when his people drove Them into the caverns under the hills, ages ago; what had long centuries of retrogression made of them? In their nighted, subterranean life, had They retained any of the attributes of humanity at all?

Some instinct prompted him to ride toward the Tower. He knew he was near; but for the thick darkness he could have plainly seen its stark outline tusking the horizon. Even now he should be able to make it out dimly. An obscure, shuddersome premonition shook him and he spurred the stallion into swift canter.

And suddenly Bran staggered in his saddle as from a physical impact, so stunning was the surprize of what met his gaze. The impregnable Tower of Trajan was no more! Bran's astounded gaze rested on a gigantic pile of ruins--of shattered stone and crumbled granite, from which jutted the jagged and splintered ends of broken beams. At one corner of the tumbled heap one tower rose out of the waste of

crumpled masonry, and it leaned drunkenly as if its foundations had been half-cut away.

Bran dismounted and walked forward, dazed by bewilderment. The moat was filled in places by fallen stones and broken pieces of mortared wall. He crossed over and came among the ruins. Where, he knew, only a few hours before the flags had resounded to the martial tramp of iron-clad feet, and the walls had echoed to the clang of shields and the blast of the loud-throated trumpets, a horrific silence reigned.

Almost under Bran's feet, a broken shape writhed and groaned. The king bent down to the legionary who lay in a sticky red pool of his own blood. A single glance showed the Pict that the man, horribly crushed and shattered, was dying.

Lifting the bloody head, Bran placed his flask to the pulped lips and the Roman instinctively drank deep, gulping through splintered teeth. In the dim starlight Bran saw his glazed eyes roll.

"The walls fell," muttered the dying man. "They crashed down like the skies falling on the day of doom. Ah Jove, the skies rained shards of granite and hailstones of marble!"

"I have felt no earthquake shock," Bran scowled, puzzled.

"It was no earthquake," muttered the Roman. "Before last dawn it began, the faint dim scratching and clawing far below the earth. We of the guard heard it--like rats burrowing, or like worms hollowing out the earth. Titus laughed at us, but all day long we heard it. Then at midnight the Tower quivered and seemed to settle--as if the foundations were being dug away--"

A shudder shook Bran Mak Morn. The worms of the earth! Thousands of vermin digging like moles far below the castle, burrowing away the foundations-- gods, the land must be honeycombed with tunnels and caverns--these creatures were even less human than he had thought--what ghastly shapes of darkness had he invoked to his aid?

"What of Titus Sulla?" he asked, again holding the flask to the legionary's lips; in that moment the dying Roman seemed to him almost like a brother.

"Even as the Tower shuddered we heard a fearful scream from the governor's chamber," muttered the soldier. "We rushed there--as we broke down the door we heard his shrieks--they seemed to recede— into the bowels of the earth! We rushed in; the chamber was empty. His bloodstained sword lay on the floor; in the stone flags of the floor a black hole gaped. Then--the--towers--reeled--the--roof--broke;-- through--a--storm--of--crashing--walls--I--crawled--"

A strong convulsion shook the broken figure.

"Lay me down, friend," whispered the Roman. "I die."

He had ceased to breathe before Bran could comply. The Pict rose, mechanically cleansing his hands. He hastened from the spot, and as he galloped over the darkened fens, the weight of the accursed Black Stone under his cloak was as the weight of a foul nightmare on a mortal breast.

As he approached the Ring, he saw an eery glow within, so that the gaunt stones stood etched like the ribs of a skeleton in which a witch-fire burns. The stallion snorted and reared as Bran tied him to one of the menhirs. Carrying the Stone he strode into the grisly circle and saw Atla standing beside the altar, one hand on her hip, her sinuous body swaying in a serpentine manner. The altar glowed all over with ghastly light and Bran knew someone, probably Atla, had rubbed it with phosphorus from some dank swamp or quagmire.

He strode forward and whipping his cloak from about the Stone, flung the accursed thing on to the altar.

"I have fulfilled my part of the contract," he growled.

"And They, theirs," she retorted. "Look!--They come!"

He wheeled, his hand instinctively dropping to his sword. Outside the Ring the great stallion screamed savagely and reared against his tether. The night wind moaned through the waving grass and an abhorrent soft hissing mingled with it. Between the menhirs flowed a dark tide of shadows, unstable and chaotic. The Ring filled with glittering eyes which hovered beyond the dim illusive circle of illumination cast by the phosphorescent altar. Somewhere in the darkness a human voice tittered and gibbered idiotically. Bran stiffened, the shadows of a horror clawing at his soul.

He strained his eyes, trying to make out the shapes of those who ringed him. But he glimpsed only billowing masses of shadow which heaved and writhed and squirmed with almost fluid consistency.

"Let them make good their bargain!" he exclaimed angrily.

"Then see, oh king!" cried Atla in a voice of piercing mockery.

There was a stir, a seething in the writhing shadows, and from the darkness crept, like a four-legged animal, a human shape that fell down and groveled at Bran's feet and writhed and mowed, and lifting a death's-head, howled like a dying dog. In the ghastly light, Bran, soul-shaken, saw the blank glassy eyes, the bloodless features, the loose, writhing, froth-covered lips of sheer lunacy--gods, was this Titus Sulla, the proud lord of life and death in Eboracum's proud city?

Bran bared his sword.

"I had thought to give this stroke in vengeance," he said somberly. "I give it in mercy--Vale Cosar!"

The steel flashed in the eery light and Sulla's head rolled to the foot of the glowing altar, where it lay staring up at the shadowed sky.

"They harmed him not!" Atla's hateful laugh slashed the sick silence. "It was what he saw and came to know that broke his brain! Like all his heavy-footed race, he knew nothing of the secrets of this ancient land. This night he has been dragged through the deepest pits of Hell, where even you might have blenched!"

"Well for the Romans that they know not the secrets of this accursed land!" Bran roared, maddened, "with its monster-haunted meres, its foul witch-women, and its lost caverns and subterranean realms where spawn in the darkness shapes of Hell!"

"Are they more foul than a mortal who seeks their aid?" cried Atla with a shriek of fearful mirth. "Give them their Black Stone!"

A cataclysmic loathing shook Bran's soul with red fury.

"Aye, take your cursed Stone!" he roared, snatching it from the altar and dashing it among the shadows with such savagery that bones snapped under its impact. A hurried babel of grisly tongues rose and the shadows heaved in turmoil. One segment of the mass detached itself for an instant and Bran cried out in fierce revulsion, though he caught only a fleeting glimpse of the thing, had only a brief impression of a broad strangely flattened head, pendulous writhing lips that bared curved pointed fangs, and a hideously misshapen, dwarfish body that seemed--mottled--all set off by those unwinking reptilian eyes. Gods!--the myths had prepared him for horror in human aspect, horror induced by bestial visage and stunted deformity—but this was the horror of nightmare and the night.

"Go back to Hell and take your idol with you!" he yelled, brandishing his clenched fists to the skies, as the thick shadows receded, flowing back and away from him like the foul waters of some black flood. "Your ancestors were men, though strange and monstrous-- but gods, ye have become in ghastly fact what my people called ye in scorn! Worms of the earth, back into your holes and burrows! Ye foul the air and leave on the clean earth the slime of the serpents ye have become! Gonar was right--there are shapes too foul to use even against Rome!"

He sprang from the Ring as a man flees the touch of a coiling snake, and tore the stallion free. At his elbow Atla was shrieking with fearful laughter, all human attributes dropped from her like a cloak in the night.

"King of Pictland!" she cried, "King of fools! Do you blench at so small a thing? Stay and let me show you real fruits of the pits! Ha! ha! ha! Run, fool, run! But you are stained with the taint--you have called them forth and they will remember! And in their own time they will come to you again!"

He yelled a wordless curse and struck her savagely in the mouth with his open hand. She staggered, blood starting from her lips, but her fiendish laughter only rose higher.

Bran leaped into the saddle, wild for the clean heather and the cold blue hills of the north where he could plunge his sword into clean slaughter and his sickened soul into the red maelstrom of battle, and forget the horror which lurked below the fens of the west. He gave the frantic stallion the rein, and rode through the night like a hunted ghost, until the hellish laughter of the howling were-woman died out in the darkness behind.

The Thing on the Roof

*They lumber through the night
With their elephantine tread;
I shudder in affright
As I cower in my bed.
They lift colossal wings
On the high gable roofs
Which tremble to the trample
Of their mastodonic hoofs.*

JUSTIN GEOFFREY
Out of the Old Land

Let me begin by saying that I was surprised when Tussmann called
on me. We had never been close friends; the man's mercenary in-
stincts repelled me; and since our bitter controversy of three years
before, when he attempted to discredit my *Evidences of Nahua Culture
in Yucatan*, which was the result of years of careful research, our
relations had been anything but cordial. However, I received him
and found his manner hasty and abrupt, but rather abstracted, as if
his dislike for me had been thrust aside in some driving passion that
had hold of him.

His errand was quickly stated. He wished my aid in obtaining a
volume of the first edition of Von Junzt's *Nameless Cults* – the edition
known as the Black Book, not from its colour, but because of its dark
contents. He might almost as well have asked me for the original
Greek translation of the *Necronomicon*. Though since my return from
Yucatan I had devoted practically all my time to my avocation of
book collecting, I had not stumbled on to any hint that the book in
the Düsseldorf edition was still in existence.

A word as to this rare work. Its extreme ambiguity in spots, coupled
with its incredible subject-matter, has caused it long to be regarded
as the ravings of a maniac, and the author was damned with the brand
of insanity. But the fact remains that many of his assertions are
unanswerable, and that he spent the full forty-five years of his life

prying into strange places and discovering secret and abysmal things. Not a great many volumes were printed in the first edition and many of these were burned by their frightened owners when Von Junzt was found strangled in a mysterious manner, in his barred and bolted chamber one night in 1840, six months after he had returned from a mysterious journey to Mongolia.

Five years later a London printer, one Bridewall, pirated the work, and issued a cheap translation for sensational effect, full of grotesque woodcuts, and riddled with misspellings, faulty translations and the usual errors of a cheap and unscholarly printing. This still further discredited the original work, and publishers and public forgot about the book until 1909 when the Golden Goblin Press of New York brought out an edition.

Their production was so carefully expurgated that fully a fourth of the original matter was cut out; the book was handsomely bound and decorated with the exquisite and weirdly imaginative illustrations of Diego Vasquez. The edition was intended for popular consumption but the artistic instinct of the publishers defeated that end, since the cost of issuing the book was so great that they were forced to cite it at a prohibitive price.

I was explaining all this to Tussmann when he interrupted brusquely to say that he was not utterly ignorant in such matters. One of the Golden Goblin books ornamented his library, he said, and it was in it that he found a certain line which aroused his interest. If I could procure him a copy of the original 1839 edition, he would make it worth my while; knowing, he added, that it would be useless to offer me money, he would, instead, in return for my trouble on his behalf, make a full retraction of his former accusations in regard to my Yucatan researches, and offer a complete apology in *The Scientific News*.

I will admit that I was astounded at this, and realised that if the matter meant so much to Tussmann that he was willing to make such concessions, it must indeed be of the utmost importance. I answered that I considered that I had sufficiently refuted his charges in the eyes of the world and had no desire to put him in a humiliating position, but that I would make the utmost efforts to procure him what he wanted.

He thanked me abruptly and took his leave, saying rather vaguely that he hoped to find a complete exposition of something in the Black Book which had evidently been slighted in the later edition.

I set to work, writing letters to friends, colleagues and book dealers all over the world, and soon discovered that I had assumed a task of no small magnitude. Three months elapsed before my efforts were crowned with success, but at last, through the aid of Professor James Clement of Richmond, Virginia, I was able to obtain what I wished.

I notified Tussmann and he came to London by the next train. His eyes burned avidly as he gazed at the thick, dusty volume with its heavy leather covers and rusty iron hasps, and his fingers quivered with eagerness as he thumbed the time-yellowed pages.

And when he cried out fiercely and smashed his clenched fist down on the table I knew that he had found what he hunted.

'Listen!' he commanded, and he read to me a passage that spoke of an old, old temple in a Honduras jungle where a strange god was worshipped by an ancient tribe which became extinct before the coming of the Spaniards. And Tussmann read aloud of the mummy that had been, in life, the last high priest of that vanished people, and which now lay in a chamber hewn in the solid rock of the cliff against which the temple was built. About that mummy's withered neck was a copper chain, and on that chain a great red jewel carved in the form of a toad. This jewel was a key, Von Junzt went on to say, to the treasure of the temple which lay hidden in a subterranean crypt far below the temple's altar.

Tussmann's eyes blazed.

'I have seen that temple! I have stood before the altar. I have seen the sealed-up entrance of the chamber in which, the natives say, lies the mummy of the priest. It is a very curious temple, no more like the ruins of the prehistoric Indians than it is like the buildings of the modern Latin-Americans. The Indians in the vicinity disclaim any former connection with the place; they say that the people who built that temple were a different race from themselves, and were there when their own ancestors came into the country. I believe it to be a remnant of some long-vanished civilisation which began to decay thousands of years before the Spaniards came.

'I would have liked to have broken into the sealed-up chamber, but I had neither the time nor the tools for the task. I was hurrying to the coast, having been wounded by an accidental gunshot in the foot, and I stumbled on to the place purely by chance.

'I have been planning to have another look at it, but circumstances have prevented – now I intend to let nothing stand in my way! By chance I came upon a passage in the Golden Goblin edition of this book, describing the temple. But that was all; the mummy was only briefly mentioned. Interested, I obtained one of Bridewall's translations but ran up against a blank wall of baffling blunders. By some irritating mischance the translator had even mistaken the location of the Temple of the Toad, as Von Junzt calls it, and has it in Guatemala instead of Honduras. The general description is faulty, the jewel is mentioned and the fact that it is a "key". But a key to what, Bridewall's book does not state. I now felt that I was on the track of a real discovery, unless Von Junzt was, as many maintain, a madman. But that the man was actually in Honduras at one time is well attested, and no one could so vividly describe the temple – as he does in the Black Book – unless he had seen it himself. How he learned of the jewel is more than I can say. The Indians who told me of the mummy said nothing of any jewel. I can only believe that Von Junzt found his way into the sealed crypt somehow – the man had uncanny ways of learning hidden things.

'To the best of my knowledge only one other white man has seen the Temple of the Toad besides Von Junzt and myself – the Spanish traveller Juan Gonzales, who made a partial exploration of that country in 1793. He mentioned, briefly, a curious fane that differed from most Indian ruins, and spoke sceptically of a legend current among the natives that there was "something unusual" hidden under the temple. I feel certain that he was referring to the Temple of the Toad.

'Tomorrow I sail for Central America. Keep the book; I have no more use for it. This time I am going fully prepared and I intend to find what is hidden in that temple, if I have to demolish it. It can be nothing less than a great store of gold! The Spaniards missed it, somehow. When they arrived in Central America, the Temple of the Toad was deserted; they were searching for living Indians from whom torture could wring gold, not for mummies of lost peoples. But I mean to have that treasure.'

So saying Tussman took his departure. I sat down and opened the book at the place where he had left off reading, and I sat until midnight, wrapt in Von Junzt's curious, wild and at times utterly vague expoundings. And I found pertaining to the Temple of the Toad certain things which disquieted me so much that the next morning I attempted to get in touch with Tussmann, only to find that he had already sailed.

Several months passed and then I received a letter from Tussmann, asking me to come and spend a few days with him at his estate in Sussex; he also requested me to bring the Black Book with me.

I arrived at Tussmann's rather isolated estate just after nightfall. He lived in almost feudal state, his great ivy-grown house and broad lawns surrounded by high stone walls. As I went up the hedge-bordered way from the gate to the house, I noted that the place had not been well kept in its master's absence. Weeds grew rank among the trees, almost choking out the grass. Among some unkempt bushes over against the outer wall, I heard what appeared to be a horse or an ox blundering and lumbering about. I distinctly heard the clink of its hoof on a stone.

A servant who eyed me suspiciously admitted me and I found Tussmann pacing to and fro in his study like a caged lion. His giant frame was leaner, harder than when I had last seen him; his face was bronzed by a tropic sun. There were more and harsher lines in his strong face and his eyes burned more intensely than ever. A smouldering, baffled anger seemed to underlie his manner.

'Well, Tussmann,' I greeted him, 'what success? Did you find the gold?'

'I found not an ounce of gold,' he growled. 'The whole thing was a hoax – well, not all of it. I broke into the sealed chamber and found the mummy . . . '

'And the jewel?' I exclaimed.

He drew something from his pocket and handed it to me.

I gazed curiously at the thing I held. It was a great jewel, clear and transparent as crystal, but of a sinister crimson, carved, as Von Junzt had declared, in the shape of a toad. I shuddered involuntarily; the image was peculiarly repulsive. I turned my attention to the heavy and curiously wrought copper chain which supported it.

'What are these characters carved on the chain?' I asked curiously.

'I cannot say,' Tussmann replied. 'I had thought perhaps you might know. I find a faint resemblance between them and certain partly defaced hieroglyphics on a monolith known as the Black Stone in the mountains of Hungary. I have been unable to decipher them.'

'Tell me of your trip,' I urged, and over our whisky-and-sodas he began, as if with a strange reluctance.

'I found the temple again with no great difficulty, though it lies in a lonely and little-frequented region. The temple is built against a sheer stone cliff in a deserted valley unknown to maps and explorers. I would not endeavour to make an estimate of its antiquity, but it is built of a sort of unusually hard basalt, such as I have never seen anywhere else, and its extreme weathering suggests incredible age.

'Most of the columns which form its façade are in ruins, thrusting up shattered stumps from worn bases, like the scattered and broken teeth of some grinning hag. The outer walls are crumbling, but the inner walls and the columns which support such of the roof as remains intact, seem good for another thousand years, as well as the walls of the inner chamber.

'The main chamber is a large circular affair with a floor composed of great squares of stone. In the centre stands the altar, merely a huge, round, curiously carved block of the same material. Directly behind the altar, in the solid stone cliff which forms the rear wall of the chamber, is the sealed and hewn-out chamber wherein lay the mummy of the temple's last priest.

'I broke into the crypt with not too much difficulty and found the mummy exactly as is stated in the Black Book. Though it was in a remarkable state of preservation, I was unable to classify it. The withered features and general contour of the skull suggested certain peoples of Lower Egypt, and I feel certain that the priest was a member of a race more akin to the Caucasian than the Indian. Beyond this, I can not make any positive statement.

'But the jewel was there, the chain looped about the dried-up neck.'

From this point Tussmann's narrative became so vague that I had some difficulty in following him and wondered if the tropic sun had affected his mind. He had opened a hidden door in the altar somehow with the jewel – just how, he did not plainly say, and it struck me that he did not clearly understand himself the action of the jewel-key. But the opening of the secret door had had a bad effect on the hardy rogues in his employ. They had refused point-blank to follow him through that gaping black opening which had appeared so mysteriously when the gem was touched to the altar.

Tussmann entered alone with his pistol and electric torch, finding a narrow stone stair that wound down into the bowels of the earth, apparently. He followed this and presently came into a broad corridor, in the blackness of which his tiny beam of light was almost engulfed. As he told this he spoke with strange annoyance of a toad which hopped ahead of him, just beyond the circle of light, all the time he was below ground.

Making his way along dank tunnels and stairways that were wells of solid blackness, he at last came to a heavy door fantastically carved, which he felt must be the crypt wherein was secreted the gold of the ancient worshippers. He pressed the toad-jewel against it at several places and finally the door gaped wide.

'And the treasure?' I broke in eagerly.

He laughed in savage self-mockery.

'There was no gold there, no precious gems – nothing . . . ' – he hesitated – 'nothing that I could bring away.'

Again his tale lapsed into vagueness. I gathered that he had left the temple rather hurriedly without searching any further for the supposed treasure. He had intended bringing the mummy away with him, he said, to present to some museum, but when he came up out of the pits, it could not be found and he believed that his men, in superstitious aversion to having such a companion on their road to the coast, had thrown it into some well or cavern.

'And so,' he concluded, 'I am in England again no richer than when I left.'

'You have the jewel,' I reminded him. 'Surely it is valuable.'

He eyed it without favour, but with a sort of fierce avidness almost obsessional.

'Would you say that it is a ruby?' he asked.

I shook my head. 'I am unable to classify it.'

'And I. But let me see the book.'

He slowly turned the heavy pages, his lips moving as he read. Sometimes he shook his head as if puzzled, and I noticed him dwell long over a certain line.

'This man dipped so deeply into forbidden things,' said he, 'I can not wonder that his fate was so strange and mysterious. He must have had some foreboding of his end – here he warns men not to disturb sleeping things.'

Tussmann seemed lost in thought for some moments.

'Aye, sleeping things,' he muttered, 'that seem dead, but only lie waiting for some blind fool to awake them . . . I should have read further in the Black Book – and I should have shut the door when I left the crypt . . . but I have the key and I'll keep it in spite of Hell.'

He roused himself from his reveries and was about to speak when he stopped short. From somewhere upstairs had come a peculiar sound.

'What was that?' he glared at me. I shook my head and he ran to the door and shouted for a servant. The man entered a few moments later and he was rather pale.

'You were upstairs?' growled Tussmann.

'Yes, sir.'

'Did you hear anything?' asked Tussmann harshly and in a manner almost threatening and accusing.

'I did, sir,' the man answered with a puzzled look on his face.

'What did you hear?' The question was fairly snarled.

'Well, sir,' the man laughed apologetically, 'you'll say I'm a bit off, I fear, but to tell you the truth, sir, it sounded like a horse stamping around on the roof!'

A blaze of absolute madness leaped into Tussmann's eyes.

'You fool!' he screamed. 'Get out of here!' The man shrank back in amazement and Tussmann snatched up the gleaming toad-carved jewel.

'I've been a fool!' he raved. 'I didn't read far enough – and I should have shut the door – but by heaven, the key is mine and I'll keep it in spite of man or devil.'

And with these strange words he turned and fled upstairs. A moment later his door slammed heavily and a servant, knocking timidly, brought forth only a blasphemous order to retire and a luridly worded threat to shoot anyone who tried to obtain entrance into the room.

Had it not been so late I would have left the house, for I was certain that Tussmann was stark mad. As it was, I retired to the room a frightened servant showed me, but I did not go to bed. I opened the pages of the Black Book at the place where Tussmann had been reading.

This much was evident, unless the man was utterly insane: he had stumbled upon something unexpected in the Temple of the Toad. Something unnatural about the opening of the altar door had frightened his men, and in the subterranean crypt Tussmann had found *something* that he had not thought to find. And I believed that he had been followed from Central America, and that the reason for his persecution was the jewel he called the Key.

Seeking some clue in Von Junzt's volume, I read again of the Temple of the Toad, of the strange pre-Indian people who worshipped there, and of the huge, tittering, tentacled, hoofed monstrosity that they worshipped.

Tussmann had said that he had not read far enough when he had first seen the book. Puzzling over this cryptic phrase I came upon the line he had pored over – marked by his thumb nail. It seemed to me to be another of Von Junzt's many ambiguities, for it merely stated that a temple's god was the temple's treasure. Then the dark implication of the hint struck me and cold sweat beaded my forehead.

The Key to the Treasure! And the temple's treasure was the temple's god! And sleeping Things might awaken on the opening of their prison door! I sprang up, unnerved by the intolerable suggestion, and at that moment something crashed in the stillness and the death-scream of a human being burst upon my ears.

In an instant I was out of the room, and as I dashed up the stairs I heard sounds that have made me doubt my sanity ever since. At Tussmann's door I halted, essaying with shaking hand to turn the knob. The door was locked, and as I hesitated I heard from within a hideous high-pitched tittering and then the disgusting squashy sound as if a great, jelly-like bulk was being forced through the window. The sound ceased and I could have sworn I heard a faint swish of gigantic wings. Then silence.

Gathering my shattered nerves, I broke down the door. A foul and overpowering stench billowed out like a yellow mist. Gasping in nausea I entered. The room was in ruins, but nothing was missing except that crimson toad-carved jewel Tussmann called the Key, and that was never found. A foul, unspeakable slime smeared the window-sill, and in the centre of the room lay Tussmann, his head crushed and flattened; and on the red ruin of skull and face, the plain print of an enormous hoof.

The Horror from the Mound

Steve Brill did not believe in ghosts or demons. Juan Lopez did. But neither the caution of the one nor the sturdy scepticism of the other was shield against the horror that fell upon them – the horror forgotten by men for more than three hundred years – a screaming fear monstrously resurrected from the black lost ages.

Yet as Steve Brill sat on his sagging stoop that last evening, his thoughts were as far from uncanny menaces as the thoughts of man can be. His ruminations were bitter but materialistic. He surveyed his farmland and he swore. Brill was tall, rangy and tough as boot-leather – true son of the iron-bodied pioneers who wrenched West Texas from the wilderness. He was browned by the sun and strong as a longhorned steer. His lean legs and the boots on them showed his cowboy instincts, and now he cursed himself that he had ever climbed off the hurricane deck of his crank-eyed mustang and turned to farming. He was no farmer, the young puncher admitted profanely.

Yet his failure had not all been his fault. Plentiful rain in the winter – so rare in West Texas – had given promise of good crops. But as usual, things had happened. A late blizzard had destroyed all the budding fruit. The grain which had looked so promising was ripped to shreds and battered into the ground by terrific hailstorms just as it was turning yellow. A period of intense dryness, followed by another hailstorm, finished the corn.

Then the cotton, which had somehow struggled through, fell before a swarm of grasshoppers which stripped Brill's field almost overnight. So Brill sat and swore that he would not renew his lease – he gave fervent thanks that he did not own the land on which he had wasted his sweat, and that there were still broad rolling ranges to the West where a strong young man could make his living riding and roping.

Now as Brill sat glumly, he was aware of the approaching form of his nearest neighbour, Juan Lopez, a taciturn old Mexican who lived in a hut just out of sight over the hill across the creek, and grubbed for a living. At present he was clearing a strip of land on an adjoining farm, and in returning to his hut he crossed a corner of Brill's pasture.

Brill idly watched him climb through the barbed-wire fence and trudge along the path he had worn in the short dry grass. He had been working at his present job for over a month now, chopping down tough gnarly mesquite trees and digging up their incredibly long roots, and Brill knew that he always followed the same path home. And watching, Brill noted him swerving far aside, seemingly to avoid a low rounded hillock which jutted above the level of the pasture. Lopez went far around this knoll and Brill remembered that the old Mexican always circled it at a distance. And another thing came into Brill's idle mind – Lopez always increased his gait when he was passing the knoll, and he always managed to get by it before sundown – yet Mexican labourers generally worked from the first light of dawn to the last glint of twilight, especially at these grubbing jobs, when they were paid by the acre and not by the day. Brill's curiosity was aroused.

He rose, and sauntering down the slight slope on the crown of which his shack sat, hailed the plodding Mexican.

'Hey, Lopez, wait a minute.'

Lopez halted; looked about, and remained motionless but unenthusiastic as the white man approached.

'Lopez,' said Brill lazily, 'it ain't none of my business, but I just wanted to ask you – how come you always go so far around that old Indian mound?'

'No Babe,' grunted Lopez shortly.

'You're a liar,' responded Brill genially. 'You savvy all right; you speak English as good as me. What's the matter – you think that mound's ha'nted or somethin'!'

Brill could speak Spanish himself and read it, too, but like most Anglo-Saxons he much preferred to speak his own language.

Lopez shrugged his shoulders.

'It is not a good place, no *bueno*,' he muttered, avoiding Brill's eyes. 'Let hidden things rest.'

'I reckon you're scared of ghosts,' Brill bantered. 'Shucks, if that is an Indian mound, them Indians been dead so long their ghosts 'ud be plumb wore out by now.'

Brill knew that the illiterate Mexicans looked with superstitious aversion on the mounds that are found here and there through the south-west – relics of a past and forgotten age, containing the mouldering bones of chiefs and warriors of a lost race.

'Best not to disturb what is hidden in the earth,' grunted Lopez.

'Bosh,' said Brill. 'Me and some boys busted into one of them mounds over in the Palo Pinto country and dug up pieces of a skeleton with some beads and flint arrowheads and the like. I kept some of the teeth a long time till I lost 'em, and I ain't never been ha'nted.'

'Indians?' snorted Lopez unexpectedly. 'Who spoke of Indians? There have been more than Indians in this country. In the old times strange things happened here. I have heard the tales of my people, handed down from generation to generation. And my people were here long before yours, Señor Brill.'

'Yeah, you're right,' admitted Steve. 'First white men in this country was Spaniards, of course. Coronado passed along not very far from here, I hear tell, and Hernando de Estrada's expedition came through here-away back yonder – I dunno how long ago.'

'In 1545,' said Lopez. 'They pitched camp yonder where your corral stands now.'

Brill turned to glance at his rail-fenced corral, inhabited now by his saddlehorse, a pair of workhorses and a scrawny cow.

'How come you know so much about it?' he asked curiously.

'One of my ancestors marched with de Estrada,' answered Lopez. 'A soldier, Porfirio Lopez; he told his son of that expedition, and he told his son, and so down the family line to me, who have no son to whom I can tell the tale.'

'I didn't know you were so well connected,' said Brill. 'Maybe you know somethin' about the gold de Estrada was supposed to have hid around here, somewhere.'

'There was no gold,' growled Lopez. 'De Estrada's soldiers bore only their arms, and they fought their way through hostile country – many left their bones along the trail. Later – many years later – a mule train from Santa Fe was attacked not many miles from here by Comanches and they hid their gold and escaped; so the legends got mixed up. But even their gold is not there now, because gringo buffalo-hunters found it and dug it up.'

Brill nodded abstractedly, hardly heeding. Of all the continent of North America there is no section so haunted by tales of lost or hidden treasure as is the Southwest. Uncounted wealth passed back and forth over the hills and plains of Texas and New Mexico in the old days when Spain owned the gold and silver mines of the New

World and controlled the rich fur trade of the West, and echoes of that wealth linger on in tales of golden caches. Some such vagrant dream, born of failure and pressing poverty, rose in Brill's mind.

Aloud he spoke: 'Well, anyway, I got nothin' else to do and I believe I'll dig into that old mound and see what I can find.'

The effect of that simple statement on Lopez was nothing short of shocking. He recoiled and his swarthy brown face went ashy; his black eyes flared and he threw up his arms in a gesture of intense expostulation.

'Dios, no!' he cried. 'Don't do that, Señor Brill! There is a curse . . . my grandfather told me . . . '

'Told you what?' asked Brill.

Lopez lapsed into sullen silence.

'I cannot speak,' he muttered. 'I am sworn to silence. Only to an eldest son could I open my heart. But believe me when I say better had you cut your throat than break into that accursed mound.'

'Well,' said Brill, impatient of Mexican superstitions, 'if it's so bad, why don't you tell me about it? Gimme a logical reason for not bustin' into it.'

'I cannot speak!' cried the Mexican desperately. 'I know! – but I swore to silence on the Holy Crucifix, just as every man of my family has sworn. It is a thing so dark, it is to risk damnation even to speak of it! Were I to tell you, I would blast the soul from your body. But I have sworn – and I have no son, so my lips are sealed forever.'

'Aw, well,' said Brill sarcastically, 'why don't you write it out?'

Lopez started, stared, and to Steve's surprise, caught at the suggestion.

'I will! *Dios* be thanked the good priest taught me to write when I was a child. My oath said nothing of writing. I only swore not to speak. I will write out the whole thing for you, if you will swear not to speak of it afterward, and to destroy the paper as soon as you have read it.'

'Sure,' said Brill, to humour him, and the old Mexican seemed much relieved.

'*Bueno*! I will go at once and write. Tomorrow as I go to work I will bring you the paper and you will understand why no one must open that accursed mound!'

And Lopez hurried along his homeward path, his stooped shoulders swaying with the effort of his unwonted haste. Steve grinned after him, shrugged his shoulders and turned back toward his own shack. Then he halted, gazing back at the low rounded mound with its grass-grown sides. It must be an Indian tomb, he decided, what with its symmetry and its similarity to other Indian mounds he had seen. He scowled as he tried to figure out the seeming connection between the mysterious knoll and the martial ancestor of Juan Lopez.

Brill gazed after the receding figure of the old Mexican. A shallow valley, cut by a half-dry creek, bordered with trees and underbrush, lay between Brill's pasture and the low sloping hill beyond which lay Lopez's shack. Among the trees along the creek bank the old Mexican was disappearing. And Brill came to a sudden decision.

Hurrying up the slight slope, he took a pick and a shovel from the tool shed built on to the back of his shack. The sun had not yet set and Brill believed he could open the mound deep enough to determine its nature before dark. If not, he could work by lantern light. Steve, like most of his breed, lived mostly by impulse, and his present urge was to tear into that mysterious hillock and find what, if anything, was concealed therein. The thought of treasure came again to his mind, piqued by the evasive attitude of Lopez.

What if, after all, that grassy heap of brown earth hid riches – virgin ore from forgotten mines, or the minted coinage of old Spain? Was it not possible that the musketeers of de Estrada had themselves reared that pile above a treasure they could not bear away, moulding it in the likeness of an Indian mound to fool seekers? Did old Lopez know that? It would not be strange if, knowing of treasure there, the old Mexican refrained from disturbing it. Ridden with grisly superstitious fears, he might well live out a life of barren toil rather than risk the wrath of lurking ghosts or devils – for the Mexicans say that hidden gold is always accursed, and surely there was supposed to be some especial doom resting on this mound. Well, Brill meditated, Latin-Indian devils had no terrors for the Anglo-Saxon, tormented by the demons of drought and storm and crop failure.

Steve set to work with the savage energy characteristic of his breed. The task was no light one; the soil, baked by the fierce sun, was iron-hard, and mixed with rocks and pebbles. Brill sweated profusely and grunted with his efforts, but the fire of the treasure-hunter was on him. He shook the sweat out of his eyes and drove in the pick with mighty strokes that ripped and crumbled the close-packed dirt.

The sun went down, and in the long dreamy summer twilight he worked on, almost oblivious of time or space. He began to be convinced that the mound was a genuine Indian tomb, as he found traces of charcoal in the soil. The ancient people which reared these sepulchres had kept fires burning upon them for days, at some point in the building. All the mounds Steve had ever opened had contained a solid stratum of charcoal a short distance below the surface: But the charcoal traces he found now were scattered about through the soil.

His idea of a Spanish-built treasure trove faded, but he persisted. Who knows? Perhaps that strange folk men now called Mound-Builders had treasure of their own which they laid away with the dead.

Then Steve yelped in exultation as his pick rang on a bit of metal. He snatched it up and held it close to his eyes, straining in the waning light. It was caked and corroded with rust, worn almost paper-thin, but he knew it for what it was – a spur, unmistakably Spanish with its long cruel points. And he halted, completely bewildered. No Spaniard ever reared this mound, with its undeniable marks of aboriginal workmanship. Yet how came that relic of Spanish caballeros hidden deep in the packed soil?

Brill shook his head and set to work again. He knew that in the centre of the mound, if it were indeed an aboriginal tomb, he would find a narrow chamber built of heavy stones, containing the bones of the chief for whom the mound had been reared and the victims sacrificed above it. And in the gathering darkness he felt his pick strike heavily against something granite-like and unyielding. Examination, by sense of feel as well as by sight, proved it to be a solid block of stone, roughly hewn. Doubtless it formed one of the ends of the death-chamber. Useless to try to shatter it. Brill chipped and pecked about it, scraping the dirt and pebbles away from the corners until he felt that wrenching it out would be but a matter of sinking the pick-point underneath and levering it out.

But now he was suddenly aware that darkness had come on. In the young moon objects were dim and shadowy. His mustang nickered in the corral whence came the comfortable crunch of tired beasts' jaws on corn. A whippoorwill called eerily from the dark shadows of the narrow winding creek. Brill straightened reluctantly. Better get a lantern and continue his explorations by its light.

He felt in his pocket with some idea of wrenching out the stone and exploring the cavity by the aid of matches. Then he stiffened. Was it imagination that he heard a faint sinister rustling, which seemed to come from behind the blocking stone? Snakes! Doubtless they had holes somewhere about the base of the mound and there might be a dozen big diamond-backed rattlers coiled up in that cave-like interior waiting for him to put his hand among them.

He shivered slightly at the thought and backed away out of the excavation he had made.

It wouldn't do to go poking about blindly into holes. And for the past few minutes, he realised, he had been aware of a faint foul odour exuding from interstices about the blocking stone – though he admitted that the smell suggested reptiles no more than it did any other menacing scent. It had a charnel-house reek about it – gases formed in the chamber of death, no doubt, and dangerous to the living.

Steve laid down his pick and returned to the house, impatient of the necessary delay. Entering the dark building, he struck a match and located his kerosene lantern hanging on its nail on the wall. Shaking it, he satisfied himself that it was nearly full of coal oil, and lighted it. Then he fared forth again, for his eagerness would not allow him to pause long enough for a bite of food. The mere opening of the mound intrigued him, as it must always intrigue a man of imagination, and the discovery of the Spanish spur had whetted his curiosity.

He hurried from his shack, the swinging lantern casting long distorted shadows ahead of him and behind. He chuckled as he visualised Lopez's thoughts and actions when he learned, on the morrow, that the forbidden mound had been pried into. A good thing he opened it that evening, Brill reflected; Lopez might even have tried to prevent him meddling with it, had he known.

In the dreamy hush of the summer night, Brill reached the mound – lifted his lantern – swore bewilderedly. The lantern revealed his excavations, his tools lying carelessly where he had dropped them – and a black gaping aperture! The great blocking stone lay in the bottom of the excavation he had made, as if thrust carelessly aside. Warily he thrust the lantern forward and peered into the small cave-like chamber, expecting to see he knew not what. Nothing met his eyes except the bare rock sides of a long narrow cell, large enough to receive a man's body, which had apparently been built up of roughly hewn square-cut stones, cunningly and strongly joined together.

'Lopez!' exclaimed Steve furiously. 'The dirty coyote! He's been watchin' me work . . . and when I went after the lantern, he snuck up and pried the rock out and grabbed whatever was in there, I reckon. Blast his greasy hide, I'll fix him!'

Savagely he extinguished the lantern and glared across the shallow, brush-grown valley. And as he looked he stiffened. Over the corner of the hill, on the other side of which the shack of Lopez stood, a shadow moved. The slender moon was setting, the light dim and the play of the shadows baffling. But Steve's eyes were sharpened by the sun and winds of the wastelands, and he knew that it was some two-legged creature that was disappearing over the low shoulder of the mesquite-grown hill.

'Beatin' it to his shack,' snarled Brill. 'He's shore got somethin' or he wouldn't be travellin' at that speed.'

Brill swallowed, wondering why a peculiar trembling had suddenly taken hold of him. What was there unusual about a thieving old greaser running home with his loot? Brill tried to drown the feeling that there was something peculiar about the gait of the dim shadow, which had seemed to move at a sort of slinking lope. There must have been need for swiftness when stocky old Juan Lopez elected to travel at such a strange pace.

'Whatever he found is as much mine as his,' swore Brill, trying to get his mind off the abnormal aspect of the figure's flight. 'I got this land leased and I done all the work diggin'. A curse, heck! No wonder he told me that stuff. Wanted me to leave it alone so he could get it hisself. It's a wonder he ain't dug it up long before this.'

Brill, as he meditated thus, was striding down the gentle slope of the pasture which led down to the creek bed. He passed into the shadows of the trees and dense underbrush and walked across the dry creek bed, noting absently that neither whippoorwill nor hoot-owl called in the darkness. There was a waiting, listening tenseness in the night that he did not like. The shadows in the creek bed seemed too thick, too breathless. He wished he had not blown out the lantern, which he still carried, and was glad he had brought the pick, gripped like a battle-axe in his right hand. He had an impulse to whistle, just to break the silence, then swore and dismissed the thought. Yet he was glad when he clambered up the low opposite bank and emerged into the starlight.

He walked up the slope and onto the hill, and looked down on the mesquite flat wherein stood Lopez's squalid hut. A light showed at the one window.

'Packin' his things for a getaway, I reckon,' grunted Steve. 'Oh, what the – '

He staggered as from a physical impact as a frightful scream knifed the stillness. He wanted to clap his hands over his ears to shut out the horror of that cry, which rose unbearably and then broke in an abhorrent gurgle.

'Good God!' Steve felt the cold sweat spring out upon him. 'Lopez – or somebody – '

Even as he gasped the words he was running down the hill as fast as his long legs could carry him. Some unspeakable horror was taking place in that lonely hut, but he was going to investigate if it meant facing the Devil himself. He tightened his grip on his pick-handle as he ran. Wandering prowlers, murdering old Lopez for the loot he had taken from the mound, Steve thought, and forgot his wrath. It would go hard for anyone he found molesting the old scoundrel, thief though he might be.

He hit the flat, running hard. And then the light in the hut went out and Steve staggered in full flight, bringing up against a mesquite tree with an impact that jolted a grunt out of him and tore his hands on the thorns. Rebounding with a sobbed curse, he rushed for the shack, nerving himself for what he might see – his hair still standing on end at what he had already seen.

Brill tried the one door of the but and found it bolted. He shouted to Lopez and received no answer. Yet utter silence did not reign. From within came a curious muffled worrying sound that ceased as Brill swung his pick crashing against the door. The flimsy portal splintered and Brill leaped into the dark hut, eyes blazing, pick swung high for a desperate onslaught. But no sound ruffled the grisly silence, and in the darkness nothing stirred, though Brill's chaotic imagination peopled the shadowed corners of the hut with shapes of horror.

With a hand damp with perspiration he found a match and struck it. Besides himself only Lopez occupied the hut – old Lopez, stark dead on the dirt floor, arms spread wide like a crucifix, mouth sagging open in a semblance of idiocy, eyes wide and staring with a horror Brill found intolerable. The one window gaped open, showing the method of the slayer's exit – possibly his entrance as well. Brill went to that window and gazed out warily. He saw only the sloping hillside on one hand and the mesquite flat on the other. He started – was that a hint of movement among the stunted shadows of the mesquites and chaparral – or had he but imagined he glimpsed a dim loping figure among the trees?

He turned back, as the match burned down to his fingers. He lit the old coal-oil lamp on the rude table, cursing as he burned his hand. The globe of the lamp was very hot, as if it had been burning for hours.

Reluctantly he turned to the corpse on the floor. Whatever sort of death had come to Lopez, it had been horrible, but Brill, gingerly examining the dead man, found no wound . . . no mark of knife or bludgeon on him. Wait. There was a thin smear of blood on Brill's questing hand. Searching, he found the source . . . three or four tiny punctures in Lopez's throat, from which blood had oozed sluggishly. At first he thought they had been inflicted with a stiletto – a thin round edgeless dagger – then he shook his head. He had seen stiletto wounds – he had the scar of one on his own body. These wounds more resembled the bite of some animal . . . they looked like the marks of pointed fangs.

Yet Brill did not believe they were deep enough to have caused death, nor had much blood flowed from them. A belief, abhorrent with grisly speculations, rose up in the dark corners of his mind – that Lopez had died of fright and that the wounds had been inflicted either simultaneously . . . with his death, or an instant afterward.

And Steve noticed something else; scrawled about on the floor lay a number of dingy leaves of paper, scrawled in the old Mexican's crude hand – he would write of the curse of the mound, he had said. There were the sheets on which he had written, there was the stump of a pencil on the floor, there was the hot lamp globe, all mute witnesses that the old Mexican had been seated at the rough-hewn table writing for hours. Then it was not he who opened the mound chamber and stole the contents . . . but who was it, in God's name? And who or what was it that Brill had glimpsed loping over the shoulder of the hill?

Well, there was but one thing to do – saddle his mustang and ride the ten miles to Coyote Wells, the nearest town, and inform the sheriff of the murder.

Brill gathered up the papers. The last was crumpled in the old man's clutching hand and Brill secured it with some difficulty. Then as he turned to extinguish the light, he hesitated, and cursed himself for the crawling fear that lurked at the back of his mind – fear of the shadowy thing he had seen cross the window just before the light was extinguished in the hut. The long arm of the murderer, he thought, reaching for the lamp to put it out, no doubt. What had there been abnormal or inhuman about that vision, distorted though it must have been in the dim lamplight and shadow? As a man strives to remember the details of a nightmare dream, Steve tried to define in his mind some clear reason that would explain why that flying glimpse had unnerved him to the extent of blundering headlong into a tree, and why the mere vague remembrance of it now caused cold sweat to break out on him.

Cursing himself to keep up his courage, he lighted his lantern, blew out the lamp on the rough table, and resolutely set forth, grasping his pick like a weapon. After all, why should certain seemingly abnormal aspects about a sordid murder upset him? Such crimes were abhorrent, but common enough, especially among Mexicans, who cherished unguessed feuds.

Then as he stepped into the silent star-flecked night he brought up short. From across the creek sounded the sudden soul-shaking scream of a horse in deadly terror . . . then a mad drumming of hoofs that receded in the distance. And Brill swore in rage and dismay. Had a monster cat slain old Lopez? Then why was not the victim marked with the scars of fierce hooked talons? And who extinguished the light in the hut?

As he wondered, Brill was running swiftly toward the dark creek. Not lightly does a cowpuncher regard the stampeding of his stock. As he passed into the darkness of the brush along the dry creek, Brill found his tongue strangely dry. He kept swallowing, and he held the lantern high. It made but faint impression in the gloom, but seemed to accentuate the blackness of the crowding shadows. For some strange reason, the thought entered Brill's chaotic mind that though the land was new to the Anglo-Saxon, it was in reality very old. That broken and desecrated tomb was mute evidence that the land was ancient to man, and suddenly the night and the hills and the shadows bore on Brill with a sense of hideous antiquity. Here had generations of men lived and died before Brill's ancestors ever heard of the land. In the night, in the shadows of this very creek, men had no doubt given up their ghosts in grisly ways. With these reflections Brill hurried through the shadows of the thick trees.

He breathed deeply in relief when he emerged from the trees on his own side. Hurrying up the gentle slope to the railed corral, he held up his lantern, investigating. The corral was empty; not even the placid cow was in sight. And the bars were down. That pointed to human agency, and the affair took on a newly sinister aspect. Someone did not intend that Brill should ride to Coyote Wells that night. It meant that the murderer intended making his getaway and wanted a good start on the law, or else – Brill grinned wryly. Far away across a mesquite flat he believed he could still catch the faint and faraway noise of running horses. What in God's name had given them such a fright? A cold finger of fear played shudderingly on Brill's spine.

Steve headed for the house. He did not enter boldly. He crept clear around the shack, peering shudderingly into the dark windows, listening with painful intensity for some sound to betray the presence of the lurking killer. At last he ventured to open the door and step in. He threw the door back against the wall to find if anyone were hiding behind it, lifted the lantern high and stepped in, heart pounding, pick gripped fiercely, his feelings a mixture of fear and red rage. But no hidden assassin leaped upon him, and a wary exploration of the shack revealed nothing.

With a sigh of relief Brill locked the doors, made fast the windows and lighted his old coal-oil lamp. The thought of old Lopez lying, a glassy-eyed corpse alone in the hut across the creek, made him wince and shiver, but he did not intend to start for town on foot in the night.

He drew from its hiding-place his reliable old Colt .45, spun the blue-steel cylinder, and grinned mirthlessly. Maybe the killer did not intend to leave any witnesses to his crime alive. Well, let him come! He – or they – would find a young cowpuncher with a six-shooter less easy prey than an old unarmed Mexican. And that reminded Brill of the papers he had brought from the hut. Taking care that he was not in line with a window through which a sudden bullet might come, he settled himself to read, with one ear alert for stealthy sounds.

And as he read the crude laborious script, a slow cold horror grew in his soul. It was a tale of fear that the old Mexican had scrawled – a tale handed down from generation – a tale of ancient times.

And Brill read of the wanderings of the caballero Hernando de Estrada and his armoured pikemen, who dared the deserts of the Southwest when all was strange and unknown. There were some forty-odd soldiers, servants, and masters at the beginning, the manuscript ran. There was the captain, de Estrada, and the priest, and young Juan Zavilla, and Don Santiago de Valdez – a mysterious nobleman who had been taken off a helplessly floating ship in the Caribbean Sea – all the others of the crew and passengers had died of plague, he had said, and he had cast their bodies overboard. So de Estrada had taken him aboard the ship that was bearing the expedition from Spain, and de Valdez joined them in their explorations.

Brill read something of their wanderings, told in the crude style of old Lopez, as the old Mexican's ancestors had handed down the tale for over three hundred years. The bare written words dimly reflected the terrific hardships the explorers bad encountered – drought, thirst, floods, the desert sandstorms, the spears of hostile redskins. But it was of another peril that old Lopez told – a grisly lurking horror that fell upon the lonely caravan wandering through the immensity of the wild. Man by man they fell and no man knew the slayer. Fear and black suspicion ate at the heart of the expedition like a canker, and their leader knew not where to turn. This they all knew: among them was a fiend in human form.

Men began to draw apart from each other, to scatter along the line of march, and this mutual suspicion, that sought security in solitude, made it easier for the fiend. The skeleton of the expedition staggered through the wilderness, lost, dazed and helpless, and still the unseen horror hung on their flanks, dragging down the stragglers, preying on drowsing sentries and sleeping men. And on the throat of each was found the wounds of pointed fangs that bled the victim white; so that the living knew with what manner of evil they had to deal. Men reeled through the wild, calling on the saints, or blaspheming in their terror, fighting frenziedly against sleep, until they fell with exhaustion and sleep stole on them with horror and death.

Suspicion centred on a cannibal slave from Calabar. And they put him in chains. But young Juan Zavilla went the way of the rest, and then the priest was taken. But the priest fought off his fiendish assailant and lived long enough to gasp the demon's name to de Estrada. And Brill, shuddering and wide-eyed, read:

. . . and now it was evident to de Estrada that the good priest had spoken the truth, and the slayer was Don Santiago de Valdez, who was a vampire, an undead fiend, subsisting on the blood of the living. And de Estrada called to mind a certain foul nobleman who had lurked, in the mountains of Castile since the days of the Moors, feeding off the blood of helpless victims which lent him a ghastly immortality. This nobleman had been driven forth; none knew where he had fled but it was evident that he and Don Santiago were the same man: He had fled Spain by ship, and de Estrada knew that the people of that ship had died, not by plague as the fiend had represented, but by the fangs of the vampire.

De Estrada and the black man and the few soldiers who still lived went searching for him and found him stretched in bestial sleep in a clump of chaparral; full gorged he was with human blood from his last victim. Now it is well known that a vampire, like a great serpent, when well gorged, falls into a deep sleep and may be taken without peril. But de Estrada was at a loss as to how to dispose of the monster, for how may the dead be slain? For a vampire is a man who has died long ago, yet is quick with a certain foul unlife.

The men urged that the caballero drive a stake through the fiend's heart and cut off his head, uttering the holy words that would crumble the long-dead body into dust, but the priest was dead and de Estrada feared that in the act the monster might waken.

So . . . they took Don Santiago, lifting him softly, and bore him to an old Indian mound near by. This they opened, taking forth the bones they found there, and they placed the vampire within and sealed up the mound. Him grant until Judgment Day.

It is a place accursed, and I wish I had starved elsewhere before I came into this part of the country seeking work – for I have known of the land and the creek and the mound with its terrible secret, ever since childhood; so you see, Señor Brill, why you must not open the mound and wake the fiend . . .

There the manuscript ended with an erratic scratch of the pencil that tore the crumpled leaf.

Brill rose, his heart pounding wildly, his face bloodless, his tongue cleaving to his palate. He gagged and found words.

'That's why the spur was in the mound – one of them Spaniards dropped it while they was diggin' – and I mighta knowed it's been dug into before, the way the charcoal was scattered out – but, good God – '

Aghast he shrank from the black visions – an undead monster stirring in the gloom of his tomb, thrusting from within to push aside the stone loosened by the pick of ignorance – a shadowy shape loping over the hill toward a light that betokened a human prey – a frightful long arm that crossed a dim-lighted window . . .

'It's madness!' he gasped. 'Lopez was plumb loco! They ain't no such things as vampires! If they is, why didn't he get me first, instead of Lopez – unless he was scoutin' around, makin' sure of everything before he pounced? Aw, hell! It's all a pipe-dream – '

The words froze in his throat. At the window a face glared and gibbered soundlessly at him. Two icy eyes pierced his very soul. A shriek burst from his throat and that ghastly visage vanished. But the very air was permeated by the foul scent that had hung about the ancient mound. And now the door creaked . . . bent slowly inward. Brill backed up against the wall, his gun shaking in his hand: It did not occur to him to fire through the door; in his chaotic brain he had but one thought, that only that thin portal of wood separated him from some horror born out of the womb of night and gloom and the black past. His eyes were distended as he saw the door give, as he heard the staples of the bolt groan.

The door burst inward. Brill did not scream. His tongue was frozen to the roof of his mouth. His fear-glazed eyes took in the tall, vulture-like form . . . the icy eyes, the long black fingernails . . . the mouldering garb, hideously ancient . . . the long spurred boot, the slouch hat with its crumbling feather . . . the flowing cloak that was falling to slow shreds. Framed in the black doorway crouched that abhorrent shape out of the past, and Brill's brain reeled. A savage cold radiated from the figure . . . the scent of mouldering clay and charnel-house refuse. And then the undead came at the living like a swooping vulture.

Brill fired point-blank and saw a shred of rotten cloth fly from the Thing's breast. The vampire reeled beneath the impact of the heavy ball, then righted himself and came on with frightful speed. Brill reeled back against the wall with a choking cry, the gun falling from his nerveless hand. The black legends were true, then – human weapons were powerless – for may a man kill one already dead for long centuries, as mortals die?

Then the clawlike hands at his throat roused the young cow-puncher to a frenzy of madness. As his pioneer ancestors fought hand to hand against brain-shattering odds, Steve Brill fought the cold dead crawling thing that sought his life and his soul.

Of that ghastly battle Brill never remembered much. It was a blind chaos in which he screamed beast-like, tore and slugged and hammered, where long black nails like the talons of a panther tore at him, and pointed teeth snapped again and again at his throat. Rolling and tumbling about the room, both half enveloped by the musty folds of that ancient rotting cloak, they smote and tore at each other among the ruins of the shattered furniture, and the fury of the vampire was not more terrible than the fear-crazed desperation of his victim.

They crashed headlong, into the table, knocking it down upon its side, and the coal oil lamp splintered on the floor, spraying the walls with sudden flames. Brill felt the bite of the burning oil that spattered him, but in the red frenzy of the fight he gave no heed. The black talons were tearing at him, the inhuman eyes burning icily into his soul; between his frantic fingers the withered flesh of the monster was hard as dry wood. And wave after wave of blind madness swept over Steve Brill. Like a man battling a nightmare he screamed and smote, while all about them the fire leaped up and caught at the walls and roof.

Through darting jets and licking tongues of flames they reeled and rolled like a demon and a mortal warring on the fire-lanced floors of hell. And in the growing tumult of the flames, Brill gathered himself for one last volcanic burst of frenzied strength. Breaking away and staggering up, gasping and bloody, he lunged blindly at the foul shape and caught it in a grip not even the vampire could break. And whirling his fiendish assailant bodily on high, he dashed him down across the uptilted edge of the fallen table as a man might break a stick of wood across his knee. Something cracked like a snapping branch and the vampire fell from Brill's grasp to writhe in a strange broken posture on the burning floor. Yet it was not dead, for its flaming eyes still burned on Brill with a ghastly hunger, and it strove to crawl toward him with its broken spine, as a dying snake crawls.

Brill, reeling and gasping, shook the blood from his eyes, and staggered blindly through the broken door. And as a man runs from the portals of hell, he ran stumblingly through the mesquite and chaparral until he fell from utter exhaustion. Looking back he saw the flames of the burning house and thanked God that it would burn until the very bones of Don Santiago de Valdez were utterly consumed and destroyed from the knowledge of men.

People of the Dark

I came to Dagon's Cave to kill Richard Brent. I went down the dusky avenues made by the towering trees, and my mood well matched the primitive grimness of the scene.

The approach to Dagon's Cave is always dark, for the mighty branches and thick leaves shut out the sun, and now the sombreness of my own soul made the shadows seem more ominous and gloomy than was natural.

Not far away I heard the slow wash of the waves against the tall cliffs, but the sea itself was out of sight, masked by the dense oak forest. The darkness and the stark gloom of my surroundings gripped my shadowed soul as I passed beneath the ancient branches . . . as I came out into a narrow glade and saw the mouth of the ancient cavern before me. I paused, scanning the cavern's exterior and the dim reaches of the silent oaks.

The man I hated had not come before me! I was in time to carry out my grim intent. For a moment my resolution faltered, then like a wave there surged over me the fragrance of Eleanor Bland, a vision of wavy golden hair and deep grey eyes, changing and mystic as the sea. I clenched my hands until the knuckles showed white, and instinctively touched the wicked snub-nosed revolver whose weight sagged my coat pocket.

But for Richard Brent, I felt certain I had already won this woman, desire for whom made my waking hours a torment and my sleep a torture. Whom did she love? She would not say; I did not believe she knew. Let one of us go away, I thought, and she would turn to the other. And I was going to simplify matters for her . . . and for myself. By chance I had overheard my blonde English rival remark that he intended coming to lonely Dagon's Cave on an idle exploring outing . . . alone.

I am not by nature criminal. I was born and raised in a hard country, and have lived most of my life on the raw edges of the world, where a man took what he wanted, if he could, and mercy was a virtue little known. But it was a torment that racked me day and night that sent me out to take the life of Richard Brent. I have lived hard, and violently, perhaps. When love overtook me, it also was fierce and violent. Perhaps I was not wholly sane, what with my love for Eleanor Bland and my hatred for Richard Brent. Under any other circumstances, I would have been glad to call him friend – a fine, rangy, upstanding young fellow, clear-eyed and strong. But he stood in the way of my desire and he must die.

I stepped into the dimness of the cavern and halted. I had never before visited Dagon's Cave, yet a vague sense of misplaced familiarity troubled me as I gazed on the high arching roof, the even stone walls and the dusty floor. I shrugged my shoulders, unable to place the elusive feeling; doubtless it was evoked by a similarity to caverns in the mountain country of the American Southwest where I was born and spent my childhood.

And yet I knew that I had never seen a cave like this one, whose regular aspect gave rise to myths that it was not a natural cavern, but had been hewn from the solid rock ages ago by the tiny hands of the mysterious Little People, the prehistoric beings of British legend. The whole countryside thereabouts was a haunt for ancient folk lore.

The country folk were predominantly Celtic; here the Saxon invaders had never prevailed, and the legends reached back, in that long-settled countryside, further than anywhere else in England – back beyond the coming of the Saxons, aye, and incredibly beyond that distant age, beyond the coming of the Romans, to those unbelievably ancient days when the native Britons warred with black-haired Irish pirates.

The Little People, of course, had their part in the lore. Legend said that this cavern was one of their last strongholds against the conquering Celts, and hinted at lost tunnels, long fallen in or blocked up, connecting the cave with a network of subterranean corridors which honeycombed the hills. With these chance meditations vying idly in my mind with grimmer speculations, I passed through the outer chamber of the cavern and entered a narrow tunnel which, I knew by former descriptions, connected with a larger room.

It was dark in the tunnel, but not too dark for me to make out the vague, half-defaced outlines of mysterious etchings on the stone walls. I ventured to switch on my electric torch and examine them more closely. Even in their dimness I was repelled by their abnormal and revolting character. Surely no men cast in human mould as we know it, scratched those grotesque obscenities.

The Little People . . . I wondered if those anthropologists were correct in their theory of a squat Mongoloid aboriginal race, so low in the scale of evolution as to be scarcely human, yet possessing a distinct, though repulsive, culture of their own. They had vanished before the invading races, theory said, forming the base of all Aryan legends of trolls, elves, dwarfs and witches. Living in caves from the start, these aborigines had retreated farther and farther into the caverns of the hills before the conquerors, vanishing at last entirely, though folklore fancy pictures their descendants still dwelling in the lost chasms far beneath the hills, loathsome survivors of an outworn age.

I snapped off the torch and passed through the tunnel, to come out into a sort of doorway which seemed entirely too symmetrical to have been the work of nature. I was looking into a vast dim cavern, at a somewhat lower level than the outer chamber, and again I shuddered with a strange alien sense of familiarity. A short flight of steps led down from the tunnel to the floor of the cavern . . . tiny steps, too small for normal human feet, carved into the solid stone. Their edges were greatly worn away, as if by ages of use. I started the descent . . . my foot slipped suddenly. I instinctively knew what was coming – it was all in part with that strange feeling of familiarity – but I could not catch myself. I fell headlong down the steps and struck the stone floor with a crash that blotted out my senses . . .

Slowly, consciousness returned to me, with a throbbing of my head and a sensation of bewilderment. I lifted a hand to my head and found it caked with blood. I had received a blow, or had taken a fall, but so completely had my wits been knocked out of me that my mind was an absolute blank. Where I was, who I was, I did not know. I looked about, blinking in the dim light, and saw that I was in a wide, dusty cavern. I stood at the foot of a short flight of steps which led upward into some kind of tunnel. I ran my hand dazedly through my square-cut black mane, and my eyes wandered over my massive naked limbs and powerful torso. I was clad, I noticed absently, in a sort of loincloth, from the girdle of which swung an empty scabbard, and leathern sandals were on my feet.

Then I saw an object lying at my feet, and stooped and took it up. It was a heavy iron sword, whose broad blade was darkly stained. My fingers fitted instinctively about its hilt with the familiarity of long usage. Then suddenly I remembered and laughed to think that a fall on his head should render me, Conan of the reavers, so completely daft. Aye, it all came back to me now. It had been a raid on the Britons, on whose coasts we continually swooped with torch and sword, from the island called Eireann. That day we of the black-haired Gael had swept suddenly down on a coastal village in our long, low ships and in the hurricane of battle which followed, the Britons had at last given up the stubborn contest and retreated, warriors, women and bairns, into the deep shadows of the oak forests, whither we seldom dared follow.

But I had followed, for there was a girl of my foes whom I desired with a burning passion, a lithe, slim young creature with wavy golden hair and deep grey eyes, changing and mystic as the sea. Her name was Tamera . . . well I knew it, for there was trade between the races as well as war, and I had been in the villages of the Britons as a peaceful visitor, in times of rare truce.

I saw her white half-clad body flickering among the trees as she ran with the swiftness of a doe, and I followed, panting with fierce eagerness. Under the dark shadows of the gnarled oaks she fled, with me in close pursuit, while far away behind us died out the shouts of slaughter and the clashing of swords. Then we ran in silence, save for her quick laboured panting, and I was so close behind her as we emerged into a narrow glade before a sombre-mouthed cavern, that I caught her flying golden tresses with one mighty hand. She sank down with a despairing wail, and even so, a shout echoed her cry and I wheeled quickly to face a rangy young Briton who sprang from among the trees, the light of desperation in his eyes.

'Vertorix!' the girl wailed, her voice breaking in a sob, and fiercer rage welled up in me, for I knew the lad was her lover.

'Run for the forest, Tamera!' he shouted, and leaped at me as a panther leaps, his bronze axe whirling like a flashing wheel about his head. And then sounded the clangour of strife and the hard-drawn panting of combat.

The Briton was as tall as I, but he was lithe where I was massive. The advantage of sheer muscular power was mine, and soon he was on the defensive, striving desperately to parry my heavy strokes with his axe. Hammering on his guard like a smith on an anvil, I pressed him relentlessly, driving him irresistibly before me. His chest heaved, his breath came in laboured gasps, his blood dripped from scalp, chest and thigh where my whistling blade had cut the skin, and all but gone home. As I redoubled my strokes and he bent and swayed beneath them like a sapling in a storm, I heard the girl cry: 'Vertorix! Vertorix! the cave! Into the cave!'

I saw his face pale with a fear greater than that induced by my hacking sword.

'Not there!' he gasped. 'Better a clean death! In Il-marenin's name, girl, run into the forest and save yourself!'

'I will not leave you!' she cried. 'The cave! It is our one chance!'

I saw her flash past us like a flying wisp of white and vanish in the cavern, and with a despairing cry, the youth launched a wild desperate stroke that nigh cleft my skull. As I staggered beneath the blow I had barely parried, he sprang away, leaped into the cavern after the girl and vanished in the gloom.

With a maddened yell that invoked all my grim Gaelic gods, I sprang recklessly after them, not reckoning if the Briton lurked beside the entrance to brain me as I rushed in. But a quick glance showed the chamber empty and a wisp of white disappearing through a dark doorway in the back wall.

I raced across the cavern and came to a sudden halt as an axe licked out of the gloom of the entrance and whistled perilously close to my black-maned head. I gave back suddenly. Now the advantage was with Vertorix, who stood in the narrow mouth of the corridor where I could hardly come at him without exposing myself to the devastating stroke of his axe.

I was near frothing with fury and the sight of a slim white form among the deep shadows behind the warrior drove me into a frenzy. I attacked savagely but warily, thrusting venomously at my foe, and drawing back from his strokes. I wished to draw him out into a wide lunge, avoid it and run him through before he could recover his balance. In the open I could have beat him down by sheer power and heavy blows, but here I could only use the point and that at a disadvantage; I always preferred the edge. But I was stubborn; if I could not come at him with a finishing stroke, neither could he or the girl escape me while I kept him hemmed in the tunnel.

It must have been the realisation of this fact that prompted the girl's action, for she said something to Vertorix about looking for a way leading out, and though he cried out fiercely forbidding her to venture away into the darkness, she turned and ran swiftly down the tunnel to vanish in the dimness. My wrath rose appallingly and I nearly got my head split in my eagerness to bring down my foe before she found a means for their escape.

Then the cavern echoed with a terrible scream and Vertorix cried out like a man death-stricken, his face ashy in the gloom. He whirled, as if he had forgotten me and my sword, and raced down the tunnel like a madman, shrieking Tamera's name. From far away, as if from the bowels of the earth, I seemed to hear her answering cry, mingled with a strange sibilant clamour that electrified me with nameless but instinctive horror. Then silence fell, broken only by Vertorix's frenzied cries, receding farther and farther into the earth.

Recovering myself I sprang into the tunnel and raced after the Briton as recklessly as he had run after the girl. And to give me my due, red-handed reaver though I was, cutting down my rival from behind was less in my mind than discovering what dread thing had Tamera in its clutches.

As I ran along I noted absently that the sides of the tunnel were scrawled with monstrous pictures, and realised suddenly and creepily that this must be the dread Cavern of the Children of the Night, tales of which had crossed the narrow sea to resound horrifically in the ears of the Gaels. Terror of me must have ridden Tamera hard to have driven her into the cavern shunned by her people, where, it was said, lurked the survivors of that grisly race which inhabited the land before the coming of the Picts and Britons, and which had fled before them into the unknown caverns of the hills.

Ahead of me the tunnel opened into a wide chamber, and I saw the white form of Vertorix glimmer momentarily in the semi-darkness and vanish in what appeared to be the entrance of a corridor opposite the mouth of the tunnel I had just traversed. Instantly there sounded a short, fierce shout and the crash of a hard-driven blow, mixed with the hysterical screams of a girl and a medley of serpent-like hissing that made my hair bristle. And at that instant I shot out of the tunnel, running at full speed, and realised too late the floor of the cavern lay several feet below the level of the tunnel. My flying feet missed the tiny steps and I crashed terrifically on the solid stone floor.

Now as I stood in the semi-darkness, rubbing my aching head, all this came back to me, and I stared fearsomely across the vast chamber at that black cryptic corridor into which Tamera and her lover had disappeared, and over which silence lay like a pall. Gripping my sword, I warily crossed the great still cavern and peered into the corridor. Only a denser darkness met my eyes. I entered, striving to pierce the gloom, and as my foot slipped on a wide wet smear on the stone floor, the raw acrid scent of fresh-spilled blood met my nostrils. Someone or something had died there, either the young Briton or his unknown attacker.

I stood there uncertainly, all the supernatural fears that are the heritage of the Gael rising in my primitive soul. I could turn and stride out of these accursed mazes, into the clear sunlight and down to the clean blue sea where my comrades, no doubt, impatiently awaited me after the routing of the Britons. Why should I risk my life among these grisly rat dens? I was eaten with curiosity to know what manner of beings haunted the cavern, and who were called the Children of the Night by the Britons, but it was my love for the yellow-haired girl which drove me down that dark tunnel . . . and love her I did, in my way, and would have been kind to her, had I carried her away to my island haunt.

I walked softly along the corridor, blade ready. What sort of creatures the Children of the Night were, I had no idea, but the tales of the Britons had lent them a distinctly inhuman nature.

The darkness closed around me as I advanced, until I was moving in utter blackness. My groping left hand encountered a strangely carven doorway, and at that instant something hissed like a viper beside me and slashed fiercely at my thigh. I struck back savagely and felt my blind stroke crunch home, and something fell at my feet and died. What thing I had slain in the dark I could not know, but it must have been at least partly human because the shallow gash in my thigh had been made with a blade of some sort, and not by fangs or talons. And I sweated with horror, for the gods know, the hissing voice of the Thing had resembled no human tongue I had ever heard.

And now in the darkness ahead of me I heard the sound repeated, mingled with horrible slitherings, as if numbers of reptilian creatures were approaching. I stepped quickly into the entrance my groping hand had discovered and came near repeating my headlong fall, for instead of letting into another level corridor, the entrance gave on to a flight of dwarfish steps on which I floundered wildly.

Recovering my balance I went on cautiously, groping along the sides of the shaft for support. I seemed to be descending into the very bowels of the earth, but I dared not turn back. Suddenly, far below me, I glimpsed a faint eerie light. I went on, perforce, and came to a spot where the shaft opened into another great vaulted chamber; and I shrank back, aghast.

In the centre of the chamber stood a grim, black altar; it had been rubbed all over with a sort of phosphorus, so that it glowed dully, lending a semi-illumination to the shadowy cavern. Towering behind it on a pedestal of human skulls, lay a cryptic black object, carven with mysterious hieroglyphics. The Black Stone! The ancient, ancient Stone before which, the Britons said, the Children of the Night bowed in gruesome worship, and whose origin was lost in the black mists of a hideously distant past. Once, legend said, it had stood in

that grim circle of monoliths called Stonehenge, before its votaries
had been driven like chaff before the bows of the Picts.

But I gave it but a passing, shuddering glance. Two figures lay,
bound with rawhide thongs, on the glowing black altar. One was
Tamera; the other was Vertorix, bloodstained and dishevelled. His
bronze axe, crusted with clotted blood, lay near the altar. And before
the glowing stone squatted Horror.

Though I had never seen one of those ghoulish aborigines, I knew
this thing for what it was, and shuddered. It was a man of a sort, but
so low in the stage of life that its distorted humanness was more
horrible than its bestiality.

Erect, it could not have been five feet in height. Its body was
scrawny and deformed, its head disproportionately large. Lank snaky
hair fell over a square inhuman face with flabby writhing lips that
bared yellow fangs, flat spreading nostrils and great yellow slant
eyes. I knew the creature must be able to see in the dark as well as a
cat. Centuries of skulking in dim caverns had lent the race terrible
and inhuman attributes. But the most repellent feature was its skin:
scaly, yellow and mottled, like the hide of a serpent. A loincloth
made of a real snake's skin girt its lean loins, and its taloned hands
gripped a short stone-tipped spear and a sinister-looking mallet of
polished flint.

So intently was it gloating over its captives, it evidently had not
heard my stealthy descent. As I hesitated in the shadows of the
shaft, far above me I heard a soft sinister rustling that chilled
the blood in my veins. The Children were creeping down the shaft
behind me, and I was trapped. I saw other entrances opening on
the chamber, and I acted, realising that an alliance with Vertorix
was our only hope. Enemies though we were, we were men, cast
in the same mould, trapped in the lair of these indescribable
monstrosities.

As I stepped from the shaft, the horror beside the altar jerked up
his head and glared full at me. And as he sprang up, I leaped and he
crumpled, blood spurting, as my heavy sword split his reptilian
heart. But even as he died, he gave tongue in an abhorrent shriek
which was echoed far up the shaft. In desperate haste I cut Vert-
orix's bonds and dragged him to his feet. And I turned to Tamera,
who in that dire extremity did not shrink from me, but looked up at
me with pleading, terror-dilated eyes. Vertorix wasted no time in
words, realising chance had made allies of us. He snatched up his
axe as I freed the girl.

'We can't go up the shaft,' he explained swiftly; 'we'll have the whole pack upon us quickly. They caught Tamera as she sought for an exit, and overpowered me by sheer numbers when I followed. They dragged us hither and all but that carrion scattered – bearing word of the sacrifice through all their burrows, I doubt not. Il-marenin alone knows how many of my people, stolen in the night, have died on that altar. We must take our chance in one of these tunnels – all lead to Hell! Follow me!'

Seizing Tamera's hand he ran fleetly into the nearest tunnel and I followed. A glance back into the chamber before a turn in the corridor blotted it from view showed a revolting horde streaming out of the shaft. The tunnel slanted steeply upward, and suddenly ahead of us we saw a bar of grey light. But the next instant our cries of hope changed to curses of bitter disappointment. There was daylight, aye, drifting in through a cleft in the vaulted roof, but far, far above our reach. Behind us the pack gave tongue exultingly. And I halted.

'Save yourselves if you can,' I growled. 'Here I make my stand. They can see in the dark and I cannot. Here at least I can see them. Go!'

But Vertorix halted also. 'Little use to be hunted like rats to our doom. There is no escape. Let us meet our fate like men.'

Tamera cried out, wringing her hands, but she clung to her lover.

'Stand behind me with the girl,' I grunted. 'When I fall, dash out her brains with your axe lest they take her alive again. Then sell your own life as high as you may, for there is none to avenge us.'

His keen eyes met mine squarely.

'We worship different gods, reaver,' he said, 'but all gods love brave men. Mayhap we shall meet again, beyond the Dark.'

'Hail and farewell, Briton!' I growled, and our right hands gripped like steel.

'Hail and farewell, Gael!'

And I wheeled as a hideous horde swept up the tunnel and burst into the dim light, a flying nightmare of streaming snaky hair, foam-flecked lips and glaring eyes. Thundering my war-cry I sprang to meet them and my heavy sword sang and a head spun grinning from its shoulder on an arching fountain of blood. They came upon me like a wave and the fighting madness of my race was upon me. I fought as a maddened beast fights and at every stroke I clove through flesh and bone, and blood spattered in a crimson rain.

Then as they surged in and I went down beneath the sheer weight of their numbers, a fierce yell cut the din and Vertorix's axe sang above me, splattering blood and brains like water. The press slackened and I staggered up, trampling the writhing bodies beneath my feet.

'A stair behind us!' the Briton was screaming. 'Half-hidden in an angle of the wall! It must lead to daylight! Up it, in the name of Ilmarenin!'

So we fell back, fighting our way inch by inch. The vermin fought like blood-hungry devils, clambering over the bodies of the slain to screech and hack. Both of us were streaming blood at every step when we reached the mouth of the shaft, into which Tamera had preceded us.

Screaming like very fiends the Children surged in to drag us down. The shaft was not as light as had been the corridor, and it grew darker as we climbed, but our foes could only come at us from in front. By the gods, we slaughtered them till the stair was littered with mangled corpses and the Children frothed like mad wolves! Then suddenly they abandoned the fray and raced back down the steps.

'What portends this?' gasped Vertorix, shaking the bloody sweat from his eyes.

'Up the shaft, quick!' I panted. 'They mean to mount some other stair and come at us from above!'

So we raced up those accursed steps, slipping and stumbling, and as we fled past a black tunnel that opened into the shaft, far down it we heard a frightful howling. An instant later we emerged from the shaft into a winding corridor, dimly illumined by a vague grey light filtering in from above, and somewhere in the bowels of the earth I seemed to hear the thunder of rushing water. We started down the corridor and as we did so, a heavy weight smashed on my shoulders, knocking me headlong, and a mallet crashed again and again on my head, sending dull red flashes of agony across my brain. With a volcanic wrench I dragged my attacker off and under me, and tore out his throat with my naked fingers. And his fangs met in my arm in his death-bite.

Reeling up, I saw that Tamera and Vertorix had passed out of sight. I had been somewhat behind them, and they had run on, knowing nothing of the fiend which had leaped on my shoulders. Doubtless they thought I was still close on their heels. A dozen steps I took, then halted. The corridor branched and I knew not which way my companions had taken. At blind venture I turned into the left-hand branch, and staggered on in the semi-darkness. I was weak from fatigue and loss of blood, dizzy and sick from the blows I had received. Only the thought of Tamera kept me doggedly on my feet. Now distinctly I heard the sound of an unseen torrent.

That I was not far underground was evident by the dim light which filtered in from somewhere above, and I momentarily expected to come upon another stair. But when I did, I halted in black despair; instead of up, it led down. Somewhere far behind me I heard faintly the howls of the pack, and I went down, plunging into utter darkness. At last I struck a level and went along blindly. I had given up all hope of escape, and only hoped to find Tamera – if she and her lover had not found a way of escape – and die with her. The thunder of rushing water was above my head now, and the tunnel was slimy and dank. Drops of moisture fell on my head and I knew I was passing under the river.

Then I blundered again upon steps cut in the stone, and these led upward. I scrambled up as fast as my stiffening wounds would allow – and I had taken punishment enough to have killed an ordinary man. Up I went and up, and suddenly daylight burst on me through a cleft in the solid rock. I stepped into the blaze of the sun. I was standing on a ledge high above the rushing waters of a river which raced at awesome speed between towering cliffs. The ledge on which I stood was close to the top of the cliff; safety was within arm's length. But I hesitated and such was my love for the golden-haired girl that I was ready to retrace my steps through those black tunnels on the mad hope of finding her. Then I started.

Across the river I saw another cleft in the cliff-wall which fronted me, with a ledge similar to that on which I stood, but longer. In olden times, I doubt not, some sort of primitive bridge connected the two ledges . . . possibly before the tunnel was dug beneath the riverbed. Now as I watched, two figures emerged upon that other ledge – one gashed, dust-stained, limping, gripping a bloodstained axe; the other slim, white and girlish.

Vertorix and Tamera! They had taken the other branch of the corridor at the fork and had evidently followed the windings of the tunnel to emerge as I had done, except that I had taken the left turn and passed clear under the river. And now I saw that they were in a trap. On that side the cliffs rose half a hundred feet higher than on my side of the river, and so sheer a spider could scarce have scaled them. There were only two ways of escape from the ledge: back through the fiend-haunted tunnels, or straight down to the river which raved far beneath.

I saw Vertorix look up the sheer cliffs and then down, and shake his head in despair. Tamara put her arms about his neck, and though I could not hear their voices for the rush of the river, I saw them smile, and then they went together to the edge of the ledge. And out of the cleft swarmed a loathsome mob, as foul reptiles writhe up out of the darkness, and they stood blinking in the sunlight like the night-things they were. I gripped my sword-hilt in the agony of my helplessness until the blood trickled from under my fingernails. Why had not the pack followed me instead of my companions?

The Children hesitated an instant as the two Britons faced them, then with a laugh Vertorix hurled his axe far out into the rushing river, and turning, caught Tamera in a last embrace. Together they sprang far out, and still locked in each other's arms, hurtled downward, struck the madly foaming water that seemed to leap up to meet them, and vanished. And the wild river swept on like a blind, insensate monster, thundering along the echoing cliffs.

A moment I stood frozen, then like a man in a dream I turned, caught the edge of the cliff above me and wearily drew myself up and over, and stood on my feet above the cliffs, hearing like a dim dream the roar of the river far beneath.

I reeled up, dazedly clutching my throbbing head, on which dried blood was clotted. I glared wildly about me. I had clambered the cliffs – no, by the thunder of Crom, I was still in the cavern! I reached for my sword . . .

The mists faded and I stared about dizzily, orienting myself with space and time. I stood at the foot of the steps down which I had fallen. I who had been Conan the reaver, was John O'Brien. Was all that grotesque interlude a dream? Could a mere dream appear so vivid? Even in dreams, we often know we are dreaming, but Conan the reaver had no cognisance of any other existence. More, he remembered his own past life as a living man remembers, though in the waking mind of John O'Brien that memory faded into dust and mist. But the adventures of Conan in the Cavern of the Children stood clear-etched in the mind of John O'Brien.

I glanced across the dim chamber toward the entrance of the tunnel into which Vertorix had followed the girl. But I looked in vain, seeing only the bare blank wall of the cavern. I crossed the chamber, switched on my electric torch – miraculously unbroken in my fall – and felt along the wall.

Ha! I started, as from an electric shock! Exactly where the entrance should have been, my fingers detected a difference in material, a section which was rougher than the rest of the wall. I was convinced that it was of comparatively modern workmanship; the tunnel had been walled up.

I thrust against it, exerting all my strength, and it seemed to me that the section was about to give. I drew back, and taking a deep breath, launched my full weight against it, backed by all the power of my giant muscles. The brittle, decaying wall gave way with a shattering crash and I catapulted through in a shower of stones and falling masonry.

I scrambled up, a sharp cry escaping me. I stood in a tunnel, and I could not mistake the feeling of similarity this time. Here Vertorix had first fallen foul of the Children, as they dragged Tamera away, and here where I now stood the floor had been awash with blood.

I walked down the corridor like a man in a trance. Soon I should come to the doorway on the left . . . aye, there it was, the strangely carven portal, at the mouth of which I had slain the unseen being which reared up in the dark beside me. I shivered momentarily. Could it be possible that remnants of that foul race still lurked hideously in these remote caverns?

I turned into the doorway and my light shone down a long, slanting shaft, with tiny steps cut into the solid stone. Down these had Conan the reaver gone groping and down them went I, John O'Brien, with memories of that other life filling my brain with vague phantasms. No light glimmered ahead of me but I came into the great dim chamber I had known of yore, and I shuddered as I saw the grim black altar etched in the gleam of my torch. Now no bound figures writhed there, no crouching horror gloated before it. Nor did the pyramid of skulls support the Black Stone before which unknown races had bowed before Egypt was born out of time's dawn. Only a littered heap of dust lay strewn where the skulls had upheld the hellish thing. No, that had been no dream: I was John O'Brien, but I had been Conan of the reavers in that other life, and that grim interlude a brief episode of reality which I had relived.

I entered the tunnel down which we had fled, shining a beam of light ahead, and saw the bar of grey light drifting down from above . . . just as in that other, lost age. Here the Briton and I, Conan, had turned at bay. I turned my eyes from the ancient cleft high up in the vaulted roof, and looked for the stair. There it was, half-concealed by an angle in the wall.

I mounted, remembering how hurriedly Vertorix and I had gone up so many ages before, with the horde hissing and frothing at our heels. I found myself tense with dread as I approached the dark, gaping entrance through which the pack had sought to cut us off. I had snapped off the light when I came into the dim-lit corridor below, and now I glanced into the well of blackness which opened on the stair. And with a cry I started back, nearly losing my footing on the worn steps. Sweating in the semi-darkness I switched on the light and directed its beam into the cryptic opening, revolver in hand.

I saw only the bare rounded sides of a small shaftlike tunnel and I laughed nervously. My imagination was running riot; I could have sworn that hideous yellow eyes glared terribly at me from the darkness, and that a crawling something had scuttered away down the tunnel. I was foolish to let these imaginings upset me. The Children had long vanished from these caverns; a nameless and abhorrent race closer to the serpent than the man, they had centuries ago faded back into the oblivion from which they had crawled in the black dawn ages of the Earth.

I came out of the shaft into the winding corridor, which, as I remembered of old, was lighter. Here from the shadows a lurking thing had leaped on my back while my companions ran on, un-knowing. What a brute of a man Conan had been, to keep going after receiving such savage wounds! Aye, in that age all men were iron.

I came to the place where the tunnel forked and as before I took the left-hand branch and came to the shaft that led down. Down this I went, listening for the roar of the river, but not hearing it. Again the darkness shut in about the shaft, so I was forced to have recourse to my electric torch again, lest I lose my footing and plunge to my death. Oh, I, John O'Brien, am not nearly so sure-footed as was I, Conan the reaver; no, nor as tigerishly powerful and quick, either.

I soon struck the dank lower level and felt again the dampness that denoted my position under the riverbed, but still I could not hear the rush of the water. And indeed I knew that whatever mighty river had rushed roaring to the sea in those ancient times, there was no such body of water among the hills today. I halted, flashing my light about. I was in a vast tunnel, not very high of roof, but broad. Other smaller tunnels branched off from it and I wondered at the network which apparently honeycombed the hills.

I cannot describe the grim, gloomy effect of those dark, low-roofed corridors far below the earth. Over all hung an overpowering sense of unspeakable antiquity. Why had the little people carved out these mysterious crypts, and in which black age? Were these caverns their last refuge from the onrushing tides of humanity, or their castles since time immemorial? I shook my head in bewilderment; the bestiality of the Children I had seen, yet somehow they had been able to carve these tunnels and chambers that might balk modern engineers. Even supposing they had but completed a task begun by nature, still it was a stupendous work for a race of dwarfish aborigines.

Then I realised with a start that I was spending more time in these gloomy tunnels than I cared for, and began to hunt for the steps by which Conan had ascended. I found them and, following them up, breathed again deeply in relief as the sudden glow of daylight filled the shaft. I came out upon the ledge, now worn away until it was little more than a bump on the face of the cliff. And I saw the great river, which had roared like a prisoned monster between the sheer walls of its narrow canyon, had dwindled away with the passing aeons until it was no more than a tiny stream, far beneath me, trickling soundlessly among the stones on its way to the sea.

Aye, the surface of the earth changes; the rivers swell or shrink, the mountains heave and topple, the lakes dry up, the continents alter; but under the earth the work of lost, mysterious hands slumbers untouched by the sweep of Time. Their work, aye, but what of the hands that reared that work? Did they, too, lurk beneath the bosoms of the hills?

How long I stood there, lost in dim speculations, I do not know, but suddenly, glancing across at the other ledge, crumbling and weathered, I shrank back into the entrance behind me. Two figures came out upon the ledge and I gasped to see that they were Richard Brent and Eleanor Bland. Now I remembered why I had come to the cavern and my hand instinctively sought the revolver in my pocket. They did not see me. But I could see them, and hear them plainly, too, since no roaring river now thundered between the ledges.

'By gad, Eleanor,' Brent was saying, 'I'm glad you decided to come with me. Who would have guessed there was anything to those old tales about hidden tunnels leading from the cavern? I wonder how that section of wall came to collapse? I thought I heard a crash just as we entered the outer cave. Do you suppose some beggar was in the cavern ahead of us, and broke it in?'

'I don't know,' she answered. 'I remember – oh, I don't know. It almost seems as if I'd been here before, or dreamed I had. I seem to faintly remember, like a far-off nightmare, running, running, running endlessly through these dark corridors with hideous creatures on my heels . . . '

'Was I there?' jokingly asked Brent.

'Yes, and John, too,' she answered. 'But you were not Richard Brent, and John was not John O'Brien. No, and I was not Eleanor Bland, either. Oh, it's so dim and far-off I can't describe it at all. It's hazy and misty and terrible.'

'I understand, a little,' he said unexpectedly. 'Ever since we came to the place where the wall had fallen and revealed the old tunnel, I've had a sense of familiarity with the place. There was horror and danger and battle . . . and love, too.'

He stepped nearer the edge to look down in the gorge, and Eleanor cried out sharply and suddenly, seizing him in a convulsive grasp.

'Don't, Richard, don't! Hold me, oh, hold me tight!'

He caught her in his arms. 'Why, Eleanor, dear, what's the matter?'

'Nothing,' she faltered, but she clung closer to him and I saw she was trembling. 'Just a strange feeling . . . rushing dizziness and fright, just as if I were falling from a great height. Don't go near the edge, Dick; it scares me.'

'I won't, dear,' he answered, drawing her closer to him, and continuing hesitantly: 'Eleanor, there's something I've wanted to ask you for a long time . . . well, I haven't the knack of putting things in an elegant way. I love you, Eleanor; always have. You know that. But if you don't love me, I'll take myself off and won't annoy you any more. Only please tell me one way or another, for I can't stand it any longer. Is it I or the American?'

'You, Dick,' she answered, hiding her face on his shoulder. 'It's always been you, though I didn't know it. I think a great deal of John O'Brien. I didn't know which of you I really loved. But today as we came through those terrible tunnels and climbed those fearful stairs, and just now, when I thought for some strange reason we were falling from the ledge, I realised it was you I loved – that I always loved you, through more lives than this one. Always!'

Their lips met and I saw her golden head cradled on his shoulder. My lips were dry, my heart cold, yet my soul was at peace. They belonged to each other. Aeons ago they lived and loved, and because of that love they suffered and died. And I, Conan, had driven them to that doom.

I saw them turn toward the cleft, their arms about each other, then I heard Tamera – I mean Eleanor – shriek. I saw them both recoil. And out of the cleft a horror came writhing, a loathsome, brain-shattering thing that blinked in the clean sunlight. Aye, I knew it of old – vestige of a forgotten age, it came writhing its horrid shape up out of the darkness of the Earth and the lost past to claim its own.

What three thousand years of retrogression can do to a race hideous in the beginning, I saw, and shuddered. And instinctively I knew that in all the world it was the only one of its kind, a monster that had lived on. God alone knows how many centuries, wallowing in the slime of its dank subterranean lairs. Before the Children had vanished, the race must have lost all human semblance, living as they did the life of the reptile.

This thing was more like a giant serpent than anything else, but it had aborted legs and snaky arms with hooked talons. It crawled on its belly, writhing back mottled lips to bare needle-like fangs, which I felt must drip with venom. It hissed as it reared up its ghastly head on a horribly long neck, while its yellow slanted eyes glittered with all the horror that is spawned in the black lairs under the earth.

I knew those eyes had blazed at me from the dark tunnel opening on the stair. For some reason the creature had fled from me, possibly because it feared my light, and it stood to reason that it was the only one remaining in the caverns, else I had been set upon in the darkness. But for it, the tunnels could be traversed in safety.

Now the reptilian thing writhed toward the humans trapped on the ledge. Brent had thrust Eleanor behind him and stood, face ashy, to guard her as best he could. And I gave thanks silently that I, John O'Brien, could pay the debt I, Conan the reaver, owed these lovers since long ago.

The monster reared up and Brent, with cold courage, sprang to meet it with his naked hands. Taking quick aim, I fired once. The shot echoed like the crack of doom between the towering cliffs, and the Horror, with a hideously human scream, staggered wildly, swayed and pitched headlong, knotting and writhing like a wounded python, to tumble from the sloping ledge and fall plummetlike to the rocks far below.

The Cairn on the Headland

And the next instant this great red loon was shaking me like a dog shaking a rat. 'Where is Meve MacDonnal?' he was screaming. By the saints, it's a grisly thing to hear a madman in a lonely place at midnight screaming the name of a woman dead three hundred years.

THE LONGSHOREMAN'S TALE

'This is the cairn you seek,' I said, laying my hand gingerly on one of the rough stones which composed the strangely symmetrical heap.

An avid interest burned in Ortali's dark eyes. His gaze swept the landscape and came back to rest on the great pile of massive weather-worn boulders.

'What a wild, weird, desolate place!' he said. 'Who would have thought to find such a spot in this vicinity? Except for the smoke rising yonder, one would scarcely dream that beyond that headland lies a great city! Here there is scarcely even a fisherman's hut within sight.'

'The people shun the cairn as they have shunned it for centuries,' I replied.

'Why?'

'You've asked me that before,' I replied impatiently. 'I can only answer that they now avoid by habit what their ancestors avoided through knowledge.'

'Knowledge!' he laughed derisively. 'Superstition!'

I looked at him sombrely with unveiled hate. Two men could scarcely have been of more opposite types. He was slender, self-possessed, unmistakably Latin with his dark eyes and sophisticated air. I am massive, clumsy and bearlike, with cold blue eyes and tousled red hair. We were countrymen in that we were born in the same land; but the homelands of our ancestors were as far apart as South from North.

'Nordic superstition,' he repeated. 'I cannot imagine a Latin people allowing such a mystery as this to go unexplored all these years. The Latins are too practical, too prosaic, if you will. Are you sure of the date of this pile?'

198

'I find no mention of it in any manuscript prior to 1014 A.D.,' I growled, 'and I've read all such manuscripts extant, in the original. MacLiag, King Brian Boru's poet, speaks of the rearing of the cairn immediately after the battle, and there can be little doubt that this is the pile referred to. It is mentioned briefly in the later chronicles of the Four Masters, also in the Book of Leinster, compiled in the late 1150s, and again in the Book of Lecan, compiled by the Mac-Firbis about 1416. All connect it with the battle of Clontarf, without mentioning why it was built.'

'Well, what is the mystery about it?' he queried. 'What more natural than that the defeated Norsemen should rear a cairn above the body of some great chief who had fallen in the battle?'

'In the first place,' I answered, 'there is a mystery concerning the existence of it. The building of cairns above the dead was a Norse, not an Irish, custom. Yet according to the chroniclers, it was not Norsemen who reared this heap. How could they have built it immediately after the battle, in which they had been cut to pieces and driven in headlong flight through the gates of Dublin? Their chieftains lay where they had fallen and the ravens picked their bones. It was Irish hands that heaped these stones.'

'Well, was that so strange?' persisted Ortali. 'In old times the Irish heaped up stones before they went into battle, each man putting a stone in place; after the battle the living removed their stones, leaving in that manner a simple tally of the slain for any who wished to count the remaining stones.'

I shook my head.

'That was in more ancient times; not in the battle of Clontarf. In the first place, there were more than twenty thousand warriors, and four thousand fell here; this cairn is not large enough to have served as a tally of the men killed in battle. And it is too symmetrically built. Hardly a stone has fallen away in all these centuries. No, it was reared to cover something.'

'Nordic superstitions!' the man sneered again.

'Aye, superstitions if you will!' Fired by his scorn, I exclaimed so savagely that he involuntarily stepped back, his hand slipping inside his coat. 'We of North Europe had gods and demons before which the pallid mythologies of the South fade to childishness. At a time when your ancestors were lolling on silken cushions among the crumbling marble pillars of a decaying civilisation, my ancestors were building their own civilisation in hardships and gigantic battles against foes human and inhuman.

'Here on this very plain the Dark Ages came to an end and the light of a new era dawned on the world of hate and anarchy. Here, as even you know, in the year 1014, Brian Boru and his Dalcassian axe-wielders broke the power of the heathen Norsemen forever – those grim anarchistic plunderers who had held back the progress of civilisation for centuries.'

'It was more than a struggle between Gael and Dane for the crown of Ireland. It was a war between the White Christ and Odin, between Christian and pagan. It was the last stand of the heathen . . . of the people of the old, grim ways. For three hundred years the world had writhed beneath the heel of the Viking, and here on Clontarf that scourge was lifted forever.

'Then, as now, the importance of that battle was underestimated by polite Latin and Latinised writers and historians. The polished sophisticates of the civilised cities of the South were not interested in the battles of barbarians in the remote north-western corner of the world – a place and peoples of whose very names they were only vaguely aware. They only knew that suddenly the terrible raids of the sea kings ceased to sweep along their coasts, and in another century the wild age of plunder and slaughter had almost been forgotten – all because a rude, half-civilised people who scantily covered their nakedness with wolf hides rose up against the conquerors.'

'Here was Ragnarok, the fall of the gods! Here in very truth Odin fell, for his religion was given its death-blow. He was last of all the heathen gods to stand before Christianity, and it looked for a time as if his children might prevail and plunge the world back into darkness and savagery. Before Clontarf, legends say, he often appeared on earth to his worshippers, dimly seen in the smoke of the sacrifices where naked human victims died screaming, or riding the wind-torn clouds, his wild locks flying in the gale, or, apparelled like a Norse warrior, dealing thunderous blows in the forefront of nameless battles. But after Clontarf he was seen no more; his worshippers called on him in vain with wild chants and grim sacrifices. They lost faith in him, who had failed them in their wildest hour; his altars crumbled, his priests turned grey and died, and men turned to his conqueror, the White Christ. The reign of blood and iron was forgotten; the age of the red-handed sea kings passed. The rising sun, slowly, dimly, lighted the night of the Dark Ages, and men forgot Odin, who came no more on earth.'

'Aye, laugh if you will! But who knows what shapes of horror have had birth in the darkness, the cold gloom and the whistling black gulfs of the North? In the southern lands the sun shines and flowers bloom; under the soft skies men laugh at demons. But in the North, who can say what elemental spirits of evil dwell in the fierce storms and the darkness? Well may it be that from such fiends of the night men evolved the worship of the grim ones, Odin and Thor, and their terrible kin.'

Ortali was silent for an instant, as if taken aback by my vehemence; then he laughed. 'Well said, my northern philosopher! We will argue these questions another time. I could hardly expect a descendant of Nordic barbarians to escape some trace of the dreams and mysticism of his race. But you cannot expect me to be moved by your imaginings, either. I still believe that this cairn covers no grimmer secret than a Norse chief who fell in the battle – and really your ravings concerning Nordic devils have no bearing on the matter. Will you help me tear into this cairn?'

'No,' I answered shortly.

'A few hours' work will suffice to lay bare whatever it may hide,' he continued as if he had not heard. 'By the way, speaking of superstitions, is there not some wild tale concerning holly connected with this heap?'

'An old legend says that all trees bearing holly were cut down for a league in all directions, for some mysterious reason,' I answered sullenly. 'That's another mystery. Holly was an important part of Norse magic-making. The Four Masters tell of a Norseman – a white-bearded ancient of wild aspect, and apparently a priest of Odin, who was slain by the natives while attempting to lay a branch of holly on the cairn, a year after the battle.'

'Well,' he laughed, 'I have procured a sprig of holly – see? – and shall wear it in my lapel; perhaps it will protect me against your Nordic devils. I feel more certain than ever that the cairn covers a sea king – and they were always laid to rest with all their riches: golden cups and jewel-set sword hilts and silver corselets. I feel that this cairn holds wealth, wealth over which clumsy-footed Irish peasants have been stumbling for centuries, living in want and dying in hunger. Bah! We shall return here at midnight, when we may be fairly certain that we will not be interrupted . . . and you will aid me at the excavations.'

The last sentence was rapped out in a tone that sent a red surge of blood-lust through my brain. Ortali turned and began examining the cairn as he spoke, and almost involuntarily my hand reached out stealthily and closed on a wicked bit of jagged stone that had become detached from one of the boulders. In that instant I was a potential murderer if ever one walked the earth. One blow, quick, silent and savage, and I would be free forever from a slavery bitter as my Celtic ancestors knew beneath the heels of the Vikings.

As if sensing my thoughts, Ortali wheeled to face me. I quickly slipped the stone into my pocket, not knowing whether he noted the action. But he must have seen the red killing instinct burning in my eyes, for again he recoiled and again his hand sought the hidden revolver.

But he only said: 'I've changed my mind. We will not uncover the cairn tonight. Tomorrow night, perhaps. We may be spied upon. Just now I am going back to the hotel.'

I made no reply, but turned my back upon him and stalked moodily away in the direction of the shore. He started up the slope of the headland beyond which lay the city, and when I turned to look at him, he was just crossing the ridge, etched, clearly against the hazy sky. If hate could kill, he would have dropped dead. I saw him in a red-tinged haze, and the pulses in my temples throbbed like hammers.

I turned back toward the shore, and stopped suddenly. Engrossed with my own dark thoughts, I had approached within a few feet of a woman before seeing her. She was tall and strongly made, with a strong stern face, deeply lined and weather-worn as the hills. She was dressed in a manner strange to me, but I thought little of it, knowing the curious styles of clothing worn by certain backward types of our people.

'What would you be doing at the cairn?' she asked in a deep, powerful voice. I looked at her in surprise; she spoke in Gaelic, which was not strange of itself, but the Gaelic she used I had supposed was extinct as a spoken language: it was the Gaelic of scholars, pure, and with a distinctly archaic flavour. A woman from some secluded hill country, I thought, where the people still spoke the unadulterated tongue of their ancestors.

'We were speculating on its mystery,' I answered in the same tongue, hesitantly, however, for though skilled in the more modern form taught in the schools, to match her use of the language was a strain on my knowledge of it. She shook her head slowly.' I like not the dark man who was with you,' she said sombrely. 'Who are you?'

'I'm an American, though born and raised here,' I answered. 'My name is James O'Brien.'

A strange light gleamed in her cold eyes.

'O'Brien . . . You are of my clan. I was born an O'Brien. I married a man of the MacDonnals, but my heart was ever with the folk of my blood.'

'You live hereabouts?' I queried, my mind on her unusual accent.

'Aye, I lived here upon a time,' she answered, 'but I have been far away for a long time. All is changed – changed. I would not have returned, but I was drawn back by a call you would not understand. Tell me, would you open the cairn?'

I started and gazed at her closely, deciding that she had somehow overheard our conversation.

'It is not mine to say,' I answered bitterly. 'Ortali, my companion . . . he will doubtless open it and I am constrained to aid him. Of my own will I would not molest it.'

Her cold eyes bored into my soul.

'Fools rush blind to their doom,' she said sombrely. 'What does this man know of the mysteries of this ancient land? Deeds have been done here whereof the world re-echoed. Yonder, in the long ago, when Tomar's Wood rose dark and rustling against the plain of Contarf, and the Danish walls of Dublin loomed south of the river Liffey, the ravens fed on the slain and the setting sun lighted lakes of crimson. There King Brian, your ancestor and mine, broke the spears of the North. From all lands they came, and from the isles of the sea; they came in gleaming mail and their horned helmets cast long shadows across the land. Their dragon-prows thronged the waves and the sound of their oars was as the beat of a storm.

'On yonder plain the heroes fell like ripe wheat before the reaper. There fell Jarl Sigurd of the Orkneys, and Brodir of Man, last of the sea kings, and all their chiefs. There fell, too, Prince Murrough and his son, Turlogh, and many chieftains of the Gael, and King Brian Boru himself, Erin's mightiest monarch.'

'True!' My imagination was always fired by the epic tales of the land of my birth. 'Blood of mine was spilled here, and, though I have passed the best part of my life in a far land, there are ties of blood to bind my soul to this shore.'

She nodded slowly, and from beneath her robes drew forth something that sparkled dully in the setting sun.

'Take this,' she said. 'As a token of blood tie, I give it to you. I feel the weird of strange and monstrous happenings but this will keep you safe from evil and the people of the night. Beyond reckoning of man, it is holy.'

I took it, wonderingly. It was a crucifix of curiously-worked gold, set with tiny jewels. The workmanship was extremely archaic and unmistakably Celtic. And vaguely within me stirred a memory of a long-lost relic described by forgotten monks in dim manuscripts.

'Great heavens!' I exclaimed. 'This is . . . this must be . . . this can be nothing less than the lost crucifix of Saint Brandon the Blessed!'

'Aye.' She inclined her grim head. 'Saint Brandon's cross, fashioned by the hands of the holy man long ago, before the Norse barbarians made Erin a red hell . . . in the days when a golden peace and holiness ruled the land.'

'But, woman!' I exclaimed wildly. 'I cannot accept this as a gift from you! You cannot know its value! Its intrinsic worth alone is equal to a fortune; as a relic it is priceless – '

'Enough!' Her deep voice struck me suddenly silent. 'Have done with such talk, which is sacrilege. The cross of Saint Brandon is beyond price. It was never stained with gold; only as a free gift has it ever changed hands. I give it to you to shield you against the powers of evil. Say no more.'

'But it has been lost for three hundred years!' I exclaimed. 'How – I – here . . . '

'A holy man gave it to me long ago,' she answered. 'I hid it in my bosom . . . long it lay in my bosom. But now I give it to you; I have come from a far country to give it to you, for there are monstrous happenings in the wind, and it is sword and shield against the people of the night. An ancient evil stirs in its prison, which blind bands of folly may break open; but stronger than any evil is the cross of Saint Brandon, which has gathered power and strength through the long, long ages since that forgotten evil fell to the earth.'

'But who are you?' I exclaimed.

'I am Meve MacDonnal,' she answered.

Then, turning without a word, she strode away in the deepening twilight while I stood bewildered and watched her cross the headland and pass from sight, turning inland as she topped the ridge. Then I, too, shaking myself like a man waking from a dream, went slowly up the slope and across the headland. When I crossed the ridge it was as if I had passed out of one world into another: behind me lay the wilderness and desolation of a weird medieval age; before me pulsed the lights and the roar of modern Dublin. Only one archaic touch was lent to the scene before me: some distance inland loomed the straggling and broken lines of an ancient graveyard, long deserted and grown up in weeds, barely discernible in the dusk. As I looked I saw a tall figure moving ghostily among the crumbling tombs, and I shook my head bewilderedly. Surely Meve MacDonnal was touched with madness, living in the past, like one seeking to stir to flame the ashes of dead yesterday. I set out toward where, in the near distance, began the straggling window-gleams that grew into the swarming ocean of lights that was Dublin.

Back at the suburban hotel where Ortali and I had our rooms, I did not speak to him of the cross the woman had given me. In that, at least, he should not share. I intended keeping it until she requested its return, which I felt sure she would do. Now as I recalled her appearance, the strangeness of her costume returned to me, with one item which had impressed itself on my subconscious mind at the time, but which I had not consciously realised. Meve MacDonnal had been wearing sandals of a type not worn in Ireland for centuries. Well, it was perhaps natural that with her retrospective nature she should imitate the apparel of the past ages which seemed to claim all her thoughts.

I turned the cross reverently in my hands. There was no doubt that it was the very cross for which antiquarians had searched so long in vain, and at last in despair had denied the existence of. The priestly scholar, Michael O'Rourke, in a treatise written about 1690, described the relic at length, chronicled its history exhaustively, and maintained that it was last heard of in the possession of Bishop Liam O'Brien, who, dying in 1955, gave it into the keeping of a kinswoman; but who this woman was, it was never known, and O'Rourke maintained that she kept her possession of the cross a secret, and that it was laid away with her in her tomb.

At another time my elation at discovering the relic would have been extreme, but, at the time, my mind was too filled with hate and smouldering fury. Replacing the cross in my pocket, I fell moodily to reviewing my connections with Ortali, connections which puzzled my friends, but which were simple enough.

Some years before I had been connected with a certain large university in a humble way. One of the professors with whom I worked – a man named Reynolds – was of intolerably overbearing disposition toward those whom he considered his inferiors. I was a poverty-ridden student striving for life in a system which makes the very existence of a scholar precarious. I bore Professor Reynolds' abuse as well as I could, but one day we clashed.

The reason does not matter; it was trivial enough in itself. Because I dared reply to his insults, Reynolds struck me and I knocked him senseless.

That very day he caused my dismissal from the university. Facing not only an abrupt termination of my work and studies, but actual starvation, I was reduced to desperation, and I went to Reynolds' study late that night intending to thrash him within an inch of his life. I found him alone in his study, but the moment I entered, he sprang up and rushed at me like a wild beast, with a dagger he used for a paperweight. I did not strike him; I did not even touch him. As I stepped aside to avoid his rush, a small rug slipped beneath his charging feet: he fell headlong, and, to my horror, in his fall the dagger in his hand was driven into his heart. He died instantly. I was at once aware of my position, I was known to have quarrelled, and even exchanged blows with the man. I had every reason to hate him. If I were found in the study with the dead man, no jury in the world would believe that I had not murdered him. I hurriedly left by the way I had come, thinking that I had been unobserved. But Ortali, the dead man's secretary, had seen me. Returning from a dance, he had observed me entering the premises, and, following me, had seen the whole affair through the window. But this I did not know until later.

The body was found by the professor's housekeeper, and naturally there was a great stir. Suspicion pointed to me, but lack of evidence kept me from being indicted, and this same lack of evidence brought about a verdict of suicide. All this time Ortali had kept quiet. Now he came to me and disclosed what he knew. He knew, of course, that I had not killed Reynolds, but he could prove that I was in the study when the professor met his death, and I knew Ortali was capable of carrying out his threat of swearing that he had seen me murder Reynolds in cold blood. And thus began a systematic blackmail.

I venture to say that a stranger blackmail was never levied. I had no money then; Ortali was gambling on my future, for he was assured of my abilities. He advanced me money, and, by clever wire-pulling, got me an appointment in a large college. Then he sat back to reap the benefits of his scheming, and he reaped full fold of the seed he sowed. In my line I became eminently successful. I soon commanded an enormous salary in my regular work, and I received rich prizes and awards for researches of various difficult natures, and of these Ortali took the lion's share . . . in money at least. I seemed to have the Midas touch. Yet of the wine of my success I tasted only the dregs.

I scarcely had a cent to my name. The money that had flowed through my hands had gone to enrich my slaver, unknown to the world. A man of remarkable gifts, he could have gone to the heights in any line, but for a queer streak in him, which, coupled

with an inordinately avaricious nature, made him a parasite, a blood-
sucking leech.

This trip to Dublin had been in the nature of a vacation for me. I
was worn out with study and labour. But he had somehow heard of
Grimmin's Cairn, as it was called, and, like a vulture that scents
dead flesh, he conceived himself on the track of hidden gold. A
golden wine cup would have been, to him, sufficient reward for the
labour of tearing into the pile, and reason enough for desecrating
or even destroying the ancient landmark. He was a swine whose
only god was gold.

Well, I thought grimly, as I disrobed the bed, all things end, both
good and bad. Such a life as I had lived was unbearable. Ortali had
dangled the gallows before my eyes until it had lost its terrors. I had
staggered beneath the load I carried because of my love for my work.
But all human endurance has its limits. My hands turned to iron as I
thought of Ortali, working beside me at midnight at the lonely cairn.
One stroke, with such a stone as I had caught up that day, and my
agony would be ended. That life and hopes and career and ambition
would be ended as well, could not be helped. Ah, what a sorry, sorry
end to all my high dreams! When a rope and the long drop through
the black trap should cut short an honourable career and a useful life!
And all because of a human vampire who feasted his rotten lust on
my soul, and drove me to murder and ruin.

But I knew my fate was written in the iron books of doom. Sooner
or later I would turn on Ortali and kill him, be the consequences
what they might. And I reached the end of my road. Continual
torture had rendered me, I believe, partly insane. I knew that at
Grimmin's Cairn, when we toiled at midnight, Ortali's life would
end beneath my hands, and my own life be cast away.

Something fell out of my pocket and I picked it up. It was the piece
of sharp stone I had caught up off the cairn. Looking at it moodily, I
wondered what strange hands had touched it in old times, and what
grim secret it helped to hide on the bare headland of Grimmin. I
switched out the light and lay in the darkness, the stone still in my
hand, forgotten, occupied with my own dark broodings. And I glided
gradually into deep slumber.

At first I was aware that I was dreaming, as people often are. All
was dim and vague, and connected in some strange way, I realised,
with the bit of stone still grasped in my sleeping hand. Gigantic,
chaotic scenes and landscapes and events shifted before me, like
clouds that rolled and tumbled before a gale. Slowly these settled

and crystallised into one distinct landscape, familiar and yet wildly strange. I saw a broad bare plain, fringed by the grey sea on one side, and a dark, rustling forest on the other; this plain was cut by a winding river, and beyond this river I saw a city ... such a city as my waking eyes had never seen: bare, stark, massive, with the grim architecture of an earlier, wilder age. On the plain I saw, as in a mist, a mighty battle. Serried ranks rolled backward and forward, steel flashed like a sunlit sea, and men fell like ripe wheat beneath the blades. I saw men in wolfskins, wild and shock-headed, wielding dripping axes, and tall men in horned helmets, and glittering mail, whose eyes were cold and blue as the sea. And I saw myself.

Yes, in my dream I saw and recognised, in a semidetached way, myself. I was tall and rangily powerful; I was shockheaded and naked but for a wolf-hide girt about my loins. I ran among the ranks yelling and smiting with a red axe, and blood ran down my flanks from wounds I scarcely felt. My eyes were cold blue and my shaggy hair and beard were red.

Now for an instant I was cognisant of my dual personality, aware that I was at once the wild man who ran and smote with the gory axe, and the man who slumbered and dreamed across the centuries. But this sensation quickly faded. I was no longer aware of any personality other than that of the barbarian who ran and smote. James O'Brien had no existence; I was Red Cumal, kern of Brian Boru, and my axe was dripping with the blood of my foes.

The roar of conflict was dying away, though here and there struggling clumps of warriors still dotted the plain. Down along the river, half-naked tribesmen, waist-deep in reddening water, tore and slashed with helmeted warriors whose mail could not save them from the stroke of the Dalcassian axe. Across the river a bloody, disorderly horde was staggering through the gates of Dublin.

The sun was sinking low toward the horizon. All day I had fought beside the chiefs. I had seen Jarl Sigurd fall beneath Prince Murrough's sword. I had seen Murrough himself die in the moment of victory, by the hand of a grim mailed giant whose name none knew. I had seen, in the flight of the enemy, Brodir and King Brian fall together at the door of the great king's tent.

Aye, it had been a feasting of ravens, a red flood of slaughter, and I knew that no more would the dragon-prowed fleets sweep from the blue North with torch and destruction. Far and wide the Vikings lay in their glittering mail, as the ripe wheat lies after the reaping. Among them lay thousands of bodies clad in the wolf hides of the tribes, but the dead of the Northern people far outnumbered the dead of Erin. I was weary and sick of the stench of raw blood. I had glutted my soul with slaughter; now I sought plunder. And I found it on the corpse of a richly-clad Norse chief which lay close to the seashore. I tore off the silver-scaled corselet, the horned helmet. They fitted as if made for me, and I swaggered among the dead, calling on my wild comrades to admire my appearance, though the harness felt strange to me, for the Gaels scorned armour and fought half-naked.

In my search for loot I had wandered far out on the plain, away from the river, but still the mail-clad bodies lay thickly strewn, for the bursting of the ranks had scattered fugitives and pursuers all over the countryside, from the dark waving Wood of Tomar to the river and the seashore. And on the seaward slope of Drumna's headland, out of sight of the city and the plain of Clontarf, I came suddenly upon a dying warrior. He was tall and massive, clad in grey mail. He lay partly in the folds of a great dark cloak, and his sword lay broken near his mighty right hand. His horned helmet had fallen from his head and his elf-locks blew in the wind that swept out of the west.

Where one eye should have been was an empty socket, arid the other eye glittered cold and grim as the North Sea, though it was glazing with approach of death. Blood oozed from a rent in his corselet. I approached him warily, a strange cold fear, that I could not understand, gripping me. Axe ready to dash out his brains, I bent over him, and recognised him as the chief who had slain Prince Murrough, and who had mown down the warriors of the Gael like a harvest.. Wherever he had fought, the Norsemen had prevailed, but in all other parts of the field, the Gaels had been irresistible.

And now he spoke to me in Norse and I understood, for had I not toiled as slave among the sea people for long bitter years?

'The Christians have overcome,' he gasped in a voice whose timbre, though low-pitched, sent a curious shiver of fear through me; there was in it an undertone as of icy waves sweeping along a Northern shore, as of freezing winds whispering among the pine trees. 'Doom and shadows stalk on Asgaard and here has fallen Ragnarok. I could not be in all parts of the field at once, and now I am wounded unto death. A spear – a spear with a cross carved in the blade; no other weapon could wound me.'

I realised that the chief, seeing mistily my red beard and the Norse armour I wore, supposed me to be one of his own race. But crawling horror surged darkly in the depths of my soul.

'White Christ, thou hast not yet conquered,' he muttered delir-
iously. 'Lift me up, man, and let me speak to you.'

Now for some reason I complied, and, as I lifted him to a sitting
posture, I shuddered and my flesh crawled at the feel of him, for his
flesh was like ivory . . . smoother and harder than is natural for
human flesh, and colder than even a dying man should be.

'I die as men die;' he muttered. 'Fool, to assume the attributes of
mankind, even though it was to aid the people who deify me. The
gods are immortal, but flesh can perish, even when it clothes a god.
Haste and bring a sprig of the magic plant – even holly – and lay it on
my bosom. Aye, though it be no larger than a dagger point, it will
free me from this fleshy prison I put on when I came to war with men
with their own weapons. And I will shake off this flesh and stalk once
more among the thundering clouds. Woe, then, to all men who bend
not the knee to me! Haste; I will await your coming.'

His lion-like head fell back, and feeling shudderingly under his
corselet, I could distinguish no heartbeat. He was dead, as men die,
but I knew that locked in that semblance of a human body, there but
slumbered the spirit of a fiend of the frost and darkness.

Aye, I knew him: Odin, the Grey Man, the One-eyed, the god of
the North who had taken the form of a warrior to fight for his
people. Assuming the form of a human, he was subject to many of the
limitations of humanity. All men knew this of the gods, who often
walked the earth in the guise of men. Odin, clothed in human semb-
lance, could be wounded by certain weapons, and even slain, but a
touch of the mysterious holly would rouse him in grisly resurrection.
This task he had set me, not knowing me for an enemy; in human
form he could only use human faculties, and these had been impaired
by onstriding death.

My hair stood up and my flesh crawled. I tore from my body the
Norse armour, and fought a wild panic that prompted me to run
blind and screaming with terror across the plain. Nauseated with
fear, I gathered boulders and heaped them for a rude couch, and on
it, shaking with horror, I lifted the body of the Norse god. And as the
sun set and the stars came silently out, I was working with fierce
energy, piling huge rocks above the corpse. Other tribesmen came
up and I told them of what I was sealing up . . . I hoped forever. And
they, shivering with horror, fell to aiding me. No sprig of magic
holly should be laid on Odin's terrible bosom. Beneath these rude
stones the Northern demon should slumber until the thunder of
Judgment Day, forgotten by the world which had once cried out

beneath his iron heel. Yet not wholly forgotten, for, as we laboured, one of my comrades said: 'This shall be no longer Drumna's Headland, but the Headland of the Grey Man.'

That phrase established a connection between my dream-self and my sleeping-self. I started up from sleep exclaiming: 'Grey Man's Headland!'

I looked about dazedly, the furnishings of the room, faintly lighted by the starlight in the windows, seeming strange and unfamiliar until I slowly oriented myself with time and space.

'Grey Man's Headland,' I repeated, 'Grey Man – Graymin – Grimmin – Grimmin's Headland! Great God, the thing under the cairn!'

Shaken, I sprang up, and realised that I still gripped the piece of stone from the cairn. It is well known that inanimate objects retain psychic associations. A round stone from the plain of Jericho has been placed in the land of a hypnotised medium, and she has at once reconstructed in her mind the battle and siege of the city, and the shattering fall of the walls. I did not doubt that this bit of stone had acted as a magnet to drag my modern mind through the mists of the centuries into a life I had known before.

I was more shaken than I can describe, for the whole fantastic affair fitted in too well with certain formless vague sensations concerning the cairn which had already lingered at the back of my mind, to be dismissed as an unusually vivid dream. I felt the need of a glass of wine, and remembered that Ortali always had wine in his room. I hurriedly donned my clothes, opened my door, crossed the corridor and was about to knock at Ortali's door, when I noticed that it was partly open, as if someone had neglected to close it carefully. I entered, switching on a light. The room was empty.

I realised what had occurred. Ortali mistrusted me; he feared to risk himself alone with me in a lonely spot at midnight. He had postponed the visit to the cairn merely to trick me, to give himself a chance to slip away alone.

My hatred for Ortali was for the moment completely submerged by a wild panic of horror at the thought of what the opening of the cairn might result in. For I did not doubt the authenticity of my dream. It was no dream; it was a fragmentary bit of memory, in which I had relived that other life of mine. Grey Man's Headland . . . Grimmin's Headland, and under those rough stones that grisly corpse in its semblance of humanity. I could not hope that, imbued with the imperishable essence of an elemental spirit, that corpse had crumbled to dust in the ages.

Of my race out of the city and across those semi-desolate reaches,
I remember little. The night was a cloak of horror through which
peered red stars like the gloating eyes of uncanny beasts, and my
footfalls echoed hollowly so that repeatedly I thought some monster
loped at my heels.

The straggling lights fell away behind me and I entered the region
of mystery and horror. No wonder that progress had passed to the
right and to the left of this spot, leaving it untouched, a blind back-
eddy given over to goblin-dreams and nightmare memories. Well
that so few suspected its very existence.

Dimly I saw the headland, but fear gripped me and held me aloof.
I had a vague, incoherent idea of finding the ancient woman, Meve
MacDonnal. She was grown old in the mysteries and traditions of
the mysterious land. She could aid me, if indeed the blind fool Ortali
loosed on the world the forgotten demon men once worshipped in
the North.

A figure loomed suddenly in the starlight and I caromed against
him, almost upsetting him. A stammering voice in a thick brogue
protested with the petulance of intoxication. It was a burly long-
shoreman returning to his cottage, no doubt, from some late revel in
a tavern. I seized him and shook him, my eyes glaring wildly in the
starlight.

'I am looking for Meve MacDonnal! Do you know her? Tell me,
you fool! Do you know old Meve MacDonnal?'

It was as if my words sobered him as suddenly as a dash of icy
water in his face. In the starlight I saw his face glimmer whitely and
a catch of fear was at his throat. He sought to cross himself with an
uncertain hand.

'Meve MacDonnal! Are ye mad? What would ye be doin' with her?'

'Tell me!' I shrieked, shaking him savagely. 'Where is Meve Mac-
Donnal?'

'There!' he gasped, pointing with a shaking hand, where dimly in
the night something loomed against the shadows. 'In the name of the
holy saints, begone, by ye madman or devil, and rave an honest man
alone! There, there ye'll find Meve MacDonnal . . . where they laid
her, full three hundred years ago!'

Half heeding his words, I flung him aside with a fierce exclam-
ation, and, as I raced across the weed-grown plain, I heard the
sound of his lumbering flight. Half blind with panic, I came to the
low structure the man had pointed out. And floundering deep in
weeds, my feet sinking into the musty mould, I realised with a shock

that I was in the ancient graveyard on the inland side of Grimmin's Headland, into which I had seen Meve MacDonnal disappear the evening before. I was close by the door of the largest tomb, and with an eerie premonition I leaned close, seeking to make out the deeply carven inscription. And partly by the dim light of the stars and partly by the touch of my tracing fingers, I made out the words and figures, in the half-forgotten Gaelic of three centuries ago:

· MEVE MACDONNAL 1556–1640

With a cry of horror, I recoiled and, snatching out the crucifix she had given me, made to hurl it into the darkness . . . but it was as if an invisible hand caught my wrist. Madness and insanity . . . but I could not doubt: Meve MacDonnal had come to me from the tomb wherein she had rested for three hundred years to give me the ancient, ancient relic entrusted to her so long ago by her priestly kin. The memory of her words came to me, and the memory of Ortali and the Grey Man. From a lesser horror I turned squarely to a greater, and ran swiftly toward the headland which loomed dimly against the stars toward the sea.

As I crossed the ridge I saw, in the starlight, the cairn, and the figure that toiled gnome-like above it. Ortali, with his accustomed, almost superhuman energy, had dislodged many of the boulders; and as I approached, shaking with horrified anticipation, I saw him tear aside the last layer, and I heard his savage cry of triumph that froze me in my tracks some yards behind him, looking down from the slope. An unholy radiance rose from the cairn, and I saw, in the north, the aurora come up suddenly with terrible beauty, paling the starlight. All about the cairn pulsed a weird light, turning the rough stones to a cold shimmering silver, and in this glow I saw Ortali, all heedless, cast aside his pick and lean gloatingly over the aperture he had made – and I saw there the helmeted head, reposing on the couch of stones where I, Red Cumal, had placed it so long ago. I saw the inhuman terror and beauty of that awesome carven face, in which was neither human weakness, pity nor mercy. I saw the soul-freezing glitter of the one eye, which stared wide open in a fearful semblance of life. All up and down the tall mailed figure shimmered and sparkled cold darts and gleams of icy light, like the northern lights that blazed in the shuddering skies. Aye, the Grey Man lay as I had left him more than nine hundred years before, without trace of rust or rot or decay.

And now as Ortali leaned forward to examine his find, a gasping cry broke from his lips . . . for the sprig of holly, worn in his lapel in

213

defiance of 'Nordic superstition', slipped from its place, and in the weird glow I plainly saw it fall upon the mighty mailed breast of the figure, where it blazed suddenly with a brightness too dazzling for human eyes. My cry was echoed by Ortali. The figure moved; the mighty limbs flexed, tumbling the shining stones aside. A new gleam lighted the terrible eye, and a tide of life flooded and animated the carven features.

Out of the cairn he rose, and the northern lights played terribly about him. And the Grey Man changed and altered in horrific transmutation. The human features faded like a fading mask; the armour fell from his body and crumbled to dust as it fell; and the fiendish spirit of ice and frost and darkness that the sons of the North deified as Odin, stood nakedly and terribly, in the stars. About his grisly head played lightnings and the shuddering gleams of the aurora. His towering anthropomorphic form was dark as shadow and gleaming as ice; his horrible crest reared colossally against the vaulting arch of the sky.

Ortali cowered, screaming wordlessly, as the taloned, malformed hands reached for him. In the shadowy, indescribable features of the Thing, there was no tinge of gratitude toward the man who had released it – only a demoniac gloating and a demoniac hate for all the sons of men. I saw the shadowy arms shoot out and strike. I heard Ortali scream once – a single, unbearable screech that broke short at the shrillest pitch. A single instant a blinding blue glare burst about him, lighting his convulsed features and his upward-rolling eyes; then his body was dashed earthward as by an electric shock, so savagely that I distinctly heard the splintering of his bones. But Ortali was dead before he touched the ground – dead, shrivelled and blackened, exactly like a man blasted by a thunderbolt, to which cause, indeed, men later ascribed his death.

The slavering monster that had slain him lumbered now toward me, shadowy, tentacle-like arms outspread, the pale starlight making a luminous pool of his great inhuman eye, his frightful talons dripping with I know not what elemental forces to blast the bodies and souls of men.

But I flinched not, and in that instant I feared him not, neither the horror of his countenance nor the threat of his thunderbolt dooms. For in a blinding white flame had come to me the realisation of why Meve MacDonnal had come from her tomb to bring me the ancient cross which had lain in her bosom for three hundred years, gathering unto itself unseen forces of good and light, which war forever against the shapes of lunacy and shadow.

As I plucked from my garments the ancient cross, I felt the play of gigantic unseen forces in the air about me. I was but a pawn in the game – merely the hand that held the relic of holiness, that was the symbol of the powers opposed forever against the fiends of darkness. As I held it high, from it shot a single shaft of white light, unbearably pure, unbearably white, as if all the awesome forces of Light were combined in the symbol and loosed in one concentrated arrow of wrath against the monster of darkness. And with a hideous shriek the demon reeled back, shrivelling before my eyes. Then, with a great rush of vulture-like wings, he soared into the stars, dwindling among the play of the flaming fires and the lights of the haunted skies, fleeing back into the dark limbo which gave him birth, God only knows how many grisly aeons ago.

Black Talons

Joel Brill slapped shut the book he had been scanning, and gave vent to his dissatisfaction in language more appropriate for the deck of a whaling ship than for the library of the exclusive Corinthian Club. Buckley, seated in an alcove nearby, grinned quietly. Buckley looked more like a college professor than a detective, and perhaps it was less because of a studious nature than a desire to play the part he looked, that caused him to loaf around the library of the Corinthian.

'It must be something unusual to drag you out of your lair at this time of the day,' he remarked. 'This is the first time I ever saw you in the evening. I thought you spent your evenings secluded in your rooms, poring over musty tomes in the interests of that museum you're connected with.'

'I do, ordinarily.' Brill looked as little like a scientist as Buckley looked like a dick. He was squarely built, with thick shoulders and the jaw and fists of a prizefighter; low-browed, with a mane of tousled black hair contrasting with his cold blue eyes.

'You've been shoving your nose into books here since six o'clock,' asserted Buckley.

'I've been trying to get some information for the directors of the museum,' answered Brill. 'Look!' He pointed an accusing finger at the rows of lavishly bound volumes. 'Books till it would sicken a dog – and not a blasted one can tell me the reason for a certain ceremonial dance practised by a certain tribe on the West African Coast.'

'A lot of the members have knocked around a bit,' suggested Buckley. 'Why not ask them?'

'I'm going to.' Brill took down a phone from its hook.

'There's John Galt . . . ' began Buckley.

'Too hard to locate. He flits about like a mosquito with the St Vitus. I'll try Jim Reynolds.' He twirled the dial.

'Thought you'd done some exploring in the tropics yourself,' remarked Buckley.

'Not worthy of the name. I hung around that God-forsaken hell-hole of the West African Coast for a few months until I came down with malaria – Hello!'

A suave voice, too perfectly accented, came along the wire.

'Oh, is that you, Yut Wuen? I want to speak to Mr Reynolds.'

Polite surprise tinged the meticulous tone.

'Why, Mr Reynolds went out in response to your call an hour ago, Mr Brill.'

'What's that?' demanded Brill. 'Went where?'

'Why, surely you remember, Mr Brill.' A faint uneasiness seemed to edge the Chinaman's voice. 'At about nine o'clock you called, and I answered the phone. You said you wished to speak to Mr Reynolds. Mr Reynolds talked to you, then told me to have his car brought around to the side entrance. He said that you had requested him to meet you at the cottage on White Lake shore.'

'Nonsense!' exclaimed Brill. 'This is the first time I've phoned Reynolds for weeks! You've mistaken somebody else for me.'

There was no reply, but a polite stubbornness seemed to flow over the wire. Brill replaced the phone and turned to Buckley, who was leaning forward with aroused interest.

'Something fishy here,' scowled Brill. 'Yut Wuen, Jim's Chinese servant, said *I* called, an hour ago, and Jim went out to meet me. Buckley, you've been here all evening. *Did* I call up anybody? I'm so infernally absent-minded – '

'No, you didn't,' emphatically answered the detective. 'I've been sitting right here close to the phone ever since six o'clock. Nobody's used it. And you haven't left the library during that time. I'm so accustomed to spying on people, I do it unconsciously.'

'Well, say,' said Brill, uneasily, 'suppose you and I drive over to White Lake. If this is a joke, Jim may be over there waiting for me to show up.'

As the city lights fell behind them, and houses gave way to clumps of trees and bushes, velvet black in the star-light, Buckley said: 'Do you think Yut Wuen made a mistake?'

'What else could it be?' answered Brill, irritably.

'Somebody might have been playing a joke, as you suggested. Why should anybody impersonate you to Reynolds?'

'How should I know? But I'm about the only acquaintance he'd bestir himself for, at this time of night. He's reserved, suspicious of people. Hasn't many friends. I happen to be one of the few.'

'Something of a traveller, isn't he?'

'There's no corner of the world with which he isn't familiar.'

'How'd he make his money?' Buckley asked, abruptly.

'I've never asked him. But he has plenty of it.'

The clumps on each side of the road grew denser, and scattered pinpoints of light that marked isolated farm houses faded out behind them. The road tilted gradually as they climbed higher and higher into the wild hill region which, an hour's drive from the city, locked the broad crystalline sheet of silver that men called White Lake. Now ahead of them a glint shivered among the trees, and topping a wooded crest, they saw the lake spread out below them, reflecting the stars in myriad flecks of silver. The road meandered along the curving shore.

'Where's Reynolds' lodge?' inquired Buckley.

Brill pointed. 'See that thick clump of shadows, within a few yards of the water's edge? It's the only cottage on this side of the lake. The others are three or four miles away. None of them occupied, this time of the year. There's a car drawn up in front of the cottage.'

'No light in the shack,' grunted Buckley, pulling up beside the long low roadster that stood before the narrow stoop. The building reared dark and silent before them, blocked against the rippling silver sheen behind it.

'Hey, Jim!' called Brill. 'Jim Reynolds!'

No answer. Only a vague echo shuddering down from the blackly wooded hills.

'Devil of a place at night,' muttered Buckley, peering at the dense shadows that bordered the lake. 'We might be a thousand miles from civilisation.'

Brill slid out of the car. 'Reynolds must be here . . . unless he's gone for a midnight boat ride.'

Their steps echoed loudly and emptily on the tiny stoop. Brill banged the door and shouted. Somewhere back in the woods a night bird lifted a drowsy note. There was no other answer.

Buckley shook the door. It was locked from the inside.

'I don't like this,' he growled. 'Car in front of the cottage . . . door locked on the inside . . . nobody answering it. I believe I'll break the door in – '

'No need.' Brill fumbled in his pocket. 'I'll use my key.'

'How comes it you have a key to Reynolds' shack?' demanded Buckley.

'It was his own idea. I spent some time with him up here last summer, and he insisted on giving me a key, so I could use the cottage any time I wanted to. Turn on your flash, will you? I can't find the lock. All right, I've got it. Hey, Jim! Are you here?'

Buckley's flash played over chairs and card tables, coming to rest on a closed door in the opposite wall. They entered and Buckley heard Brill fumbling about with an arm elevated. A faint click followed and Brill swore.

'The juice is off. There's a line running out from town to supply the cottage owners with electricity, but it must be dead. As long as we're in here, let's go through the house. Reynolds may be sleeping somewhere . . . '

He broke off with a sharp intake of breath. Buckley had opened the door that led to the bedroom. His flash played on the interior . . . on a broken chair, a smashed table . . . a crumpled shape that lay in the midst of a dark widening pool.

'Good God, it's Reynolds!'

Buckley's gun glinted in his hand as he played the flash around the room, sifting the shadows for lurking shapes of menace; it rested on a bolted rear door; rested longer on an open window, the screen of which hung in tatters.

'We've got to have more light,' he grunted. 'Where's the switch? Maybe a fuse has blown.'

'Outside, near that window.' Stumblingly Brill led the way out of the house and around to the window. Buckley flashed his light, grunted.

'The switch has been pulled!' He pushed it back in place, and light flooded the cottage. The light streaming through the windows seemed to emphasise the blackness of the whispering woods around them. Buckley glared into the shadows, seemed to shiver. Brill had not spoken; he shook as with ague.

Back in the house they bent over the man who lay in the middle of the red-splashed floor.

Jim Reynolds had been a stocky, strongly built man of middle age. His skin was brown and weather-beaten, hinting of tropic suns. His features were masked with blood; his head lolled back, disclosing an awful wound beneath his chin.

'His throat's been cut!' stammered Brill. Buckley shook his head.

'Not cut – torn. Good God, it looks like a big cat had ripped him.'

The whole throat had literally been torn out; muscles, arteries, windpipe and the great jugular vein had been severed; the bones of the vertebrae showed beneath.

'He's so bloody I wouldn't have recognised him,' muttered the detective. 'How did you know him so quickly? The instant we saw him, you cried out that it was Reynolds.'

'I recognised his garments and his build,' answered the other. 'But what in God's name killed him?'

Buckley straightened and looked about. 'Where does that door lead to?'

'To the kitchen; but it's locked on this side.'

'And the outer door of the front room was locked on the inside,' muttered Buckley. 'Doesn't take a genius to see how the murderer got in . . . and he – or *it* – went out the same way.'

'What do you mean, *it*?'

'Does that look like the work of a human being?' Buckley pointed to the dead man's mangled throat. Brill winced.

'I've seen boys mauled by the big cats on the West Coast – '

'And whatever tore Reynolds' gullet out, tore that window screen. It wasn't cut with a knife.'

'Do you suppose a panther from the hills . . . ' began Brill.

'A panther smart enough to throw the electric switch before he slid through the window?' scoffed Buckley.

'We don't know the killer threw the switch.'

'Was Reynolds fooling around in the dark, then? No; when I pushed the switch back in place, the light came on in here. That shows it had been on; the button hadn't been pushed back. Whoever killed Reynolds had a reason for wanting to work in the dark. Maybe this was it!' The detective indicated, with a square-shod toe, a stubby chunk of blue steel that lay not far from the body.

'From what I hear about Reynolds, he was quick enough on the trigger.' Buckley slipped on a glove, carefully lifted the revolver, and scanned the chamber. His gaze, roving about the room again, halted at the window, and with a single long stride, he reached it and bent over the sill.

'One shot's been fired from this gun. The bullet's in the window sill. At least, one bullet is, and it's logical to suppose it's the one from the empty chamber of Reynolds' gun. Here's the way I reconstruct the crime: *something* sneaked up to the shack, threw the switch, and came busting through the window. Reynolds shot once in the dark and missed, and then the killer got in his work. I'll take this gun to headquarters; don't expect to find any fingerprints except Reynolds', however. We'll examine the light switch, too, though maybe my dumb pawing erased any fingerprints that might have been there. Say, it's a good thing you have an iron-clad alibi.'

Brill started violently. 'What the Hell do you mean?'

'Why, there's the Chinaman to swear you called Reynolds to his death.'

'Why the devil should I do such a thing?' hotly demanded the scientist.

'Well,' answered Buckley, 'I know you were in the library of the club all evening. That's an unshakable alibi . . . I suppose.'

Brill was tired as he locked the door of his garage and turned toward the house, which rose dark and silent among the trees. He found himself wishing that his sister, with whom he was staying, had not left town for the weekend with her husband and children. Dark empty houses were vaguely repellent to him after the happenings of the night before.

He sighed wearily as he trudged toward the house, under the dense shadows of the trees that lined the driveway. It had been a morbid and harrying day. Tag ends of thoughts and worries flitted through his mind. Uneasily he remembered Buckley's cryptic remark: 'Either Yut Wuen is lying about that telephone call, or . . . ' The detective had left the sentence unfinished, casting a glance at Brill that was as inscrutable as his speech. Nobody believed the Chinaman was deliberately lying. His devotion to his master was well known – a devotion shared by the other servants of the dead man. Police suspicion had failed to connect them in any way with the crime. Apparently none of them had left Reynolds' town house during the day or the night of the murder. Nor had the murder-cottage given up any clues. No tracks had been found on the hard earth, no fingerprints on the gun other than the dead man's, nor any except Buckley's on the light switch. If Buckley had had any luck in trying to trace the mysterious phone call, he had not divulged anything.

Brill remembered, with a twinge of nervousness, the way in which they had looked at him, those inscrutable Orientals. Their features had been immobile, but in their dark eyes had gleamed suspicion and a threat. He had seen it in the eyes of Yut Wuen; of Ali, the Egyptian, a lean, sinewy statue of bronze; of Jugra Singh, the tall, broadshouldered, turbaned Sikh. They had not spoken their thoughts, but their eyes had followed him, hot and burning, like beasts of prey.

Brill turned from the meandering driveway to cut across the lawn. As he passed under the black shadow of the trees, something sudden, clinging and smothering, enveloped his head, and steely arms locked fiercely about him. His reaction was as instinctive and violent as that of a trapped leopard. He exploded into a galvanised burst of frantic action, a bucking heave that tore the stifling cloak from his head, and freed his arms from the arms that pinioned him. But another pair of arms hung like grim Fate to his legs, and figures surged in on him from the darkness. He could not tell the nature of his assailants; they were like denser, moving shadows in the blackness.

Staggering, fighting for balance, he lashed out blindly, felt the jolt of a solid hit shoot up his arm, and saw one of the shadows sway and pitch backward. His other arm was caught in a savage grasp and twisted up behind his back so violently that he felt as if the tendons were being ripped from their roots. Hot breath hissed in his ear, and bending his head forward, he jerked it backward again with all the power of his thick neck muscles. He felt the back of his skull crash into something softer – a man's face. There was a groan, and the crippling grip on his imprisoned arm relaxed. With a desperate wrench he tore away, but the arms that clung to his legs tripped him. He pitched headlong, spreading his arms to break his fall, and even before his fingers touched the ground, something exploded in his brain, showering a suddenly starless night of blackness with red sparks that were engulfed abruptly in formless oblivion.

Joel Brill's first conscious thought was that he was being tossed about in an open boat on a stormy sea. Then as his dazed mind cleared, be realised that he was lying in an automobile which was speeding along an uneven road. His head throbbed; he was bound hand and foot, and blanketed in some kind of a cloak. He could see nothing, could hear nothing but the purr of the racing motor. Bewilderment clouded his mind as be sought for a clue to the identity of the kidnappers. Then a sudden suspicion brought out the cold sweat on his skin.

The car lurched to a halt. Powerful hands lifted him, cloak and all, and he felt himself being carried over a short stretch of level ground, and apparently up a step or so. A key grated in a lock, a door rasped on its hinges. Those carrying him advanced; there was a click, and light shone through the folds of the cloth over Brill's head. He felt himself being lowered onto what felt like a bed. Then the cloth was ripped away, and he blinked in the glare of the light. A cold premon-itory shudder passed over him.

He was lying on the bed in the room in which James Reynolds had died. And about him stood, arms folded, three grim and silent shapes: Yut Wuen, Ali the Egyptian, and Jugra Singh. There was dried blood on the Chinaman's yellow face, and his lip was cut. A dark blue bruise showed on Jugra Singh's jaw.

'The *sahib* awakes,' said the Sikh, in his perfect English.

'What the devil's the idea, Jugra?' demanded Brill, trying to struggle to a sitting posture. 'What do you mean by this? Take these ropes off me – ' His voice trailed away, a shaky resonance of futility as he read the meaning in the hot dark eyes that regarded him.

'In this room our master met his doom,' said Ali.

'*You* called him forth,' said Yut Wuen.

'But I didn't!' raged Brill, jerking wildly at the cords which cut into his flesh. 'Damn it, I knew nothing about it!'

'Your voice came over the wire and our master followed it to his death,' said Jugra Singh.

A panic of helplessness swept over Joel Brill. He felt like a man beating at an insurmountable wall – the wall of inexorable Oriental fatalism, of conviction unchangeable. If even Buckley believed that somehow he, Joel Brill, was connected with Reynolds' death, how was he to convince these immutable Orientals? He fought down an impulse to hysteria.

'The detective, Buckley, was with me all evening,' he said, in a voice unnatural from his efforts at control. 'He has told you that he did not see me touch a phone; nor did I leave his sight. I could not have killed my friend, your master, because while he was being killed, I was either in the library of the Corinthian Club, or driving from there with Buckley.'

'How it was done, we do not know,' answered the Sikh, tranquilly. 'The ways of the *sahibs* are beyond us. But we *know* that somehow, in some manner, you caused our master's death. And we have brought you here to expiate your crime.'

'You mean to murder me?' demanded Brill, his flesh crawling.

'If a *sahib* judge sentenced you, and a *sahib* hangman dropped you through a black trap, white men would call it execution. So it is execution we work upon you, not murder.'

Brill opened his mouth, then closed it, realising the utter futility of argument. The whole affair was like a fantastic nightmare from which he would presently awaken.

Ali came forward with something, the sight of which shook Brill with a nameless foreboding. It was a wire cage, in which a great gaunt rat squealed and bit at the wires. Yut Wuen laid upon a card table a copper bowl, furnished with a slot on each side of the rim, to one of which was made fast a long leather strap. Brill turned suddenly sick.

'These are the tools of execution, *sahib*,' said Jugra Singh, sombrely. 'That bowl shall be laid on your naked belly, the strap drawn about your body and made fast so that the bowl shall not slip. Inside the bowl the rat will be imprisoned. He is ravenous with hunger, wild with fear and rage. For a while he will only run about the bowl, treading on your flesh. But with irons hot from the fire, we shall gradually heat the bowl, until, driven by pain, the rat begins to gnaw his way *out*. He can not gnaw through copper; he can gnaw through flesh . . . through flesh and muscles and intestines and bones, *sahib*.'

Brill wet his lips three times before he found voice to speak.

'You'll hang for this!' he gasped, in a voice he did not himself recognise.

'If it be the will of Allah,' assented Ali calmly. 'This is your fate; what ours is, no man can say. It is the will of Allah that you die with a rat in your bowels. If it is Allah's will, we shall die on the gallows. Only Allah knows.'

Brill made no reply. Some vestige of pride still remained to him. He set his jaw hard, feeling that if he opened his mouth to speak, to reason, to argue, he would collapse into shameful shrieks and entreaties.

Ali set the cage with its grisly occupant on the table beside the copper bowl – without warning the light went out.

In the darkness Brill's heart began to pound suffocatingly. The Orientals stood still, patiently, expecting the light to come on again. But Brill instinctively felt that the stage was set for some drama darker and more hideous than that which menaced him. Silence reigned; somewhere off in the woods a night bird lifted a drowsy note. There was a faint scratching sound, somewhere . . .

'The electric torch,' muttered a ghostly voice which Brill recognised as Jugra Singh's. 'I laid it on the card table. Wait!'.

He heard the Sikh fumbling in the dark; but he was watching the window, a square of dim, star-flecked sky blocked out of blackness. And as Brill watched, he saw something dark and bulky rear up in that square. Etched against the stars he saw a misshapen head, vague monstrous shoulders.

A scream sounded from inside the room, the crash of a wildly thrown missile. On the instant there was a scrambling sound, and the object blotted out the square of starlight, then vanished from it. *It was inside the room.*

Brill, lying frozen in his cords, heard all Hell and bedlam break loose in that dark room. Screams, shouts, strident cries of agony mingled with the smashing of furniture, the impact of blows, and a hideous, worrying, tearing sound that made Brill's flesh crawl. Once the battling pack staggered past the window, but Brill made out only a dim writhing of limbs, the pale glint of steel, and the terrible blaze of a pair of eyes he knew belonged to none of his three captors.

Somewhere a man was moaning horribly, his gasps growing weaker and weaker. There was a last convulsion of movement, the groaning impact of a heavy body; then the starlight in the window was for an instant blotted out again, and silence reigned once more in the cottage on the lake shore; silence broken only by the death gasps in the dark, and the laboured panting of a wounded man.

Brill heard someone stumbling and floundering in the darkness, and it was from this one that the racking panting was emanating. A circle of light flashed on, and in it Brill saw the blood-smeared face of Jugra Singh.

The light wandered erratically away, dancing crazily about the walls. Brill heard the Sikh blundering across the room, moving like a drunken man, or like one wounded unto death. The flash shone full in the scientist's face, blinding him. Fingers tugged awkwardly at his cords, a knife edge was dragged across them, slicing skin as well as hemp.

Jugra Singh sank to the floor. The flash thumped beside him and went out. Brill groped for him, found his shoulder. The cloth was soaked with what Brill knew was blood.

'You spoke truth, *sahib*,' the Sikh whispered. 'How the call came in the likeness of your voice, I do not know. But I know, now, what slew Reynolds, *sahib*. After all these years . . . but they never forget, though the broad sea lies between. Beware! The fiend may return. The gold – the gold was cursed . . . I told Reynolds, *sahib* . . . had he heeded me, he – '

A sudden welling of blood drowned the labouring voice. Under Brill's hand the great body stiffened and twisted in a brief convulsion, then went limp.

Groping on the floor, the scientist failed to find the flashlight. He groped along the wall, found the switch and flooded the cottage with light.

Turning back into the room, a stifled cry escaped his lips.

Jugra Singh lay slumped near the bed; huddled in a corner was Yut Wuen, his yellow hands, palms upturned, limp on the floor at his sides; Ali sprawled face down in the middle of the room. All three were dead. Throats, breasts and bellies were slashed to ribbons; their garments were in strips, and among the rags hung bloody tatters of flesh. Yut Wuen had been disembowelled, and the gaping wounds of the others were like those of sheep after a mountain lion has ranged through the fold.

A blackjack still stuck in Yut Wuen's belt. Ali's dead hand clutched a knife, but it was unstained. Death had struck them before they could use their weapons. But on the floor near Jugra Singh lay a great curved dagger, and it was red to the hilt. Bloody stains led across the floor and up over the window sill. Brill found the flash, snapped it on, and leaned out the window, playing the white beam on the ground outside. Dark, irregular splotches showed, leading off toward the dense woods.

With the flash in one hand and the Sikh's knife in the other, Brill followed those stains. At the edge of the trees he came upon a track, and the short hairs lifted on his scalp. A foot, planted in a pool of blood, had limned its imprint in crimson on the hard loam. And the foot, bare and splay, was that of a human.

That print upset vague theories of a feline or anthropoid killer, stirred nebulous thoughts at the back of his mind – dim and awful race memories of semi-human ghouls, of werewolves who walked like men and slew like beasts.

A low groan brought him to a halt, his flesh crawling. Under the black trees in the silence, that sound was pregnant with grisly probabilities. Gripping the knife firmly, he flashed the beam ahead of him. The thin light wavered, then focused on a black heap that was not part of the forest.

Brill bent over the figure and stood transfixed, transported back across the years and across the world to another wilder, grimmer woodland.

It was a naked black man that lay at his feet, his glassy eyes reflecting the waning light. His legs were short, bowed and gnarled, his arms long, his shoulders abnormally broad, his shaven head set plump between them without visible neck. That head was hideously malformed; the forehead projected almost into a peek, while the back of the skull was unnaturally flattened. White paint banded face, shoulders and breast. But it was at the creature's fingers which Brill looked longest. At first glance they seemed monstrously deformed. Then he saw that those hands were furnished with long curving steel hooks, sharp-pointed, and keen-edged on the concave side. To each finger one of these barbarous weapons was made fast, and those fingers, like the hooks clotted and smeared with blood, twitched exactly as the talons of a leopard twitch.

A light step brought him round. His dimming light played on a tall figure, and Brill mumbled: 'John Galt!' in no great surprise. He was so numbed by bewilderment that the strangeness of the man's presence did not occur to him.

'What in God's name is this?' demanded the tall explorer, taking the light from Brill's hand and directing it on the mangled shape. 'What in Heaven's name is that?'

'A nightmare from Africa!' Brill found his tongue at last, and speech came in a rush. 'An Egbo! A leopard man! I learned of them when I was on the West Coast. He belongs to a native cult which worships the leopard. They take a male infant and subject his head to pressure, to make it deformed; and he is brought up to believe that the spirit of a leopard inhabits his body. He does the bidding of the cult's head, which mainly consists of executing the enemies of the cult. He is, in effect, a human leopard!'

'What's he doing here?' demanded Galt, in seeming incredulity.

'God knows. But he must have been the thing that killed Reynolds. He killed Reynolds' three servants tonight . . . would have killed me, too, I suppose, but Jugra Singh wounded him, and he evidently dragged himself away like a wild beast to die in the jungle – '

Galt seemed curiously uninterested in Brill's stammering narrative.

'Sure he's dead?' he muttered, bending closer to flash the light into the hideous face. The illumination was dim; the battery was swiftly burning out.

As Brill was about to speak, the painted face was briefly convulsed. The glazed eyes gleamed as with a last surge of life. A clawed hand stirred, lifted feebly up toward Galt. A few gutturals seeped through the blubbery lips; the fingers writhed weakly, slipped from the iron talons, which the man lifted, as if trying to hand them to Galt. Then he shuddered, sank back and lay still. He had been stabbed under the heart, and only a beast-like vitality had carried him so far.

Galt straightened and faced Brill, turning the light on him. A beat of silence cut between them, in which the atmosphere was electric with tension.

'You understand the Ekoi dialect?' It was more an assertion than a question.

Brill's heart was pounding, a new bewilderment vying with a rising wrath. 'Yes,' he answered shortly.

'What did that fool say?' softly asked Galt.

Brill set his teeth and stubbornly took the plunge reason cried out against. 'He said,' he replied between his teeth, ' "Master, take my tools to the tribe, and tell them of our vengeance; they will give you what I promised you." '

Even as he ground out the words, his powerful body crouched, his nerves taut for the grapple. But before he could move, the black muzzle of an automatic trained on his belly.

'Too bad you had to understand that deathbed confession, Brill,' said Galt, coolly. 'I don't want to kill you. I've kept blood off *my* hands so far through this affair. Listen, you're a poor man, like most scientists – how'd you consider cutting in on a fortune? Wouldn't that be preferable to getting a slug through your guts and being planted alongside those yellow-bellied stiffs down in Reynolds's shack for them to get the blame?'

'No man wants to die,' answered Brill, his gaze fixed on the light in Galt's hand – the glow which was rapidly turning redder and dimmer.

'Good!' snapped Galt. 'I'll give you the lowdown. Reynolds got his money in the Kameroons – stole gold from the Ekoi, which they had stored in the ju-ju hut; he killed a priest of the Egbo cult in getting away. Jugra Singh was with him. But they didn't get all the gold. And after that the Ekoi took good care to guard it so nobody could steal what was left.

'I knew this fellow, Guja, when I was in Africa. I was after the Ekoi gold then, but I never had a chance to locate it. I met Guja a few months ago, again. He'd been exiled from his tribe for some crime, had wandered to the Coast and been picked up with some more natives who were brought to America for exhibition in the World's Fair.

'Guja was mad to get back to his people, and he spilled the whole story of the gold. Told me that if he could kill Reynolds, his tribe would forgive him. He knew that Reynolds was somewhere in America, but he was helpless as a child to find him. I offered to arrange his meeting with the gold-thief, if Guja would agree to give me some of the gold his tribe hoarded.

'He swore by the skull of the great leopard. I brought him secretly into these hills, and hid him up yonder in a shack the existence of which nobody suspects. It took me a wretched time to teach him just what he was to do. Night after night I went through the thing with him, until he learned the procedure: to watch in the hills until he saw a light flash in Reynolds' shack. Then steal down there, jerk the switch – and kill. These leopard men can see like cats at night.

'I called Reynolds up myself; it wasn't hard to imitate your voice. I used to do impersonations in vaudeville. While Guja was tearing the life out of Reynolds, I was dining at a well-known night club, in full sight of all.

'I came here tonight to smuggle him out of the country. But his blood-lust must have betrayed him. When he saw the light flash on in the cottage again, it must have started a train of associations that led him once more to the cottage, to kill whoever he found there. I saw the tag-end of the business – saw him stagger away from the shack, and then you follow him.

'Now then, I've shot the works. Nobody knows I'm mixed up in this business, but you. Will you keep your mouth shut and take a share of the Ekoi gold?'

The glow went out. In the sudden darkness, Brill, his pent-up feelings exploding at last, yelled: 'Damn you, no! You murdering dog!' and sprang aside. The pistol cracked, an orange jet sliced the darkness, and the bullet fanned Brill's ear as he threw the heavy knife blindly. He heard it rattle futilely through the bushes, and stood frozen with the realisation that he had lost his desperate gamble.

But even as he braced himself against the tearing impact of the bullet he expected, a sudden beam drilled the blackness, illuminating the convulsed features of John Galt.

'Don't move, Galt; I've got the drop on you.'

It was the voice of Buckley. With a snarl, Galt took as desperate a chance as Brill had taken. He wheeled toward the source of the light, snapping down his automatic. But even as he did so, the detective's .45 crashed, and outlined against the brief glare, Galt swayed and fell like a tall tree struck by lightning.

'Dead?' asked the scientist, mechanically.

'Bullet tore through his forearm and smashed his shoulder,' grunted Buckley. 'Just knocked out temporarily. He'll live to decorate the gallows.'

'You – you heard – ?' Brill stuttered.

'Everything. I was just coming around the bend of the lake shore and saw a light in Reynolds' cottage, then your flash bobbing among the trees. I came sneaking through the bushes just in time to hear you give your translation of the dying words. I've been prowling around this lake all night.'

'You suspected Galt all the time?'

The detective grinned wryly.

'I ought to say yes, and establish myself as a super sleuth. But the fact is, I suspected *you* all the time. That's why I came up here to-night – trying to figure out your connection with the murder. That alibi of yours was so iron-clad it looked phoney to me. I had a sneaking suspicion that I'd bumped into a master-mind trying to put over the "perfect crime". I apologise! I've been reading too many detective stories lately!'

'This is the only trail into the swamp, mister.' Steve Harrison's guide pointed a long finger down the narrow path which wound in and out among the live-oaks and cypresses. Harrison shrugged his massive shoulders. The surroundings were not inviting, with the long shadows of the late afternoon sun reaching dusky fingers into the dim recesses among the moss-hung trees.

'You ought to wait till mornin',' opined the guide, a tall lanky man in cowhide boots and sagging overall. 'It's gittin' late, and we don't want to git catched in the swamp after night.'

'I can't wait, Rogers,' answered the detective. 'The man I'm after might get clean away by morning.'

'He'll have to come out by this path,' answered Rogers as they swung along. 'Ain't no other way in or out. If he tries to push through to high ground on the other side, he'll shore fall into a bottomless bog, or git et by a 'gator. There's lots of them. I reckon he ain't much used to swamps?'.

'I don't suppose he ever saw one before. He's city-bred.'

'Then he won't das't leave the beaten path,' confidently predicted Rogers.

'On the other hand, he might, not realising the danger,' grunted Harrison.

'What'd you say he done?' pursued Rogers, directing a jet of tobacco juice at a beetle crawling through the dark loam.

'Knocked an old Chinaman in the head with a meat-cleaver and stole his life-time savings . . . ten thousand dollars, in bills of a thousand each. The old man left a little granddaughter who'll be penniless if this money isn't recovered. That's one reason I want to get this rat before he loses himself in a bog. I want to recover that money, for the kid.'

'And you figure the Chinaman seen goin' down this path a few days ago was him?'

'Couldn't be anybody else,' snapped Harrison. 'We've hounded him half way across the continent, cut him off from the borders and the ports. We were closing in on him when he slipped through, somehow. This was about the only place left for him to hide. I've chased him too far to delay now. If he drowns in the swamp, we'll probably never find him, and the money will be lost, too. The man he murdered was a fine, honest old Chinaman. This fellow, Woon Shang, is bad all the way through.'

'He'll run into some bad folks down here,' ruminated Rogers. 'These came here fifty or sixty years back – refugees from Haiti, or somewhere. You know we ain't far from the coast. They keep to theirselves, and they don't like strangers. *What's that?*'

They were just rounding a bend in the path, and something lay on the ground ahead of them – something black, and dabbled with red, that groaned and moved feebly.

'He's been knifed,' exclaimed Rogers.

It took no expert to deduce that. They bent over him and Rogers voiced profane recognition. 'Why, I know this feller! He ain't no swamp rat. He's Joe Corley. Joe! Joe Corley!'

The wounded man groaned and rolled up his glassy eyes; his skin was ashy with the nearness of approaching death.

'Who stabbed you, Joe?' demanded Rogers.

'De Swamp Cat!' The gasp was scarcely audible. Rogers swore and looked fearfully about him, as if expecting something to spring on them from the trees. 'I wuz tryin' to git outside.'

'What for?' demanded Rogers. 'Didn't you know you'd git jailed if they catched you?'

'Ruther go to de jail-house dan git mixed up . . . in de devilment . . . dey's cookin' up . . . in de swamp.' The voice sank lower as speech grew more difficult.

'What you mean, Joe?' uneasily demanded Rogers.

'Voodoo,' muttered Corley. 'Took dat Chinaman 'stead uh me . . . didn't want me to git away, though . . . then John Bartholomew – uuuugh!'

A trickle of blood started from the corner of his thick lips, he stiffened in brief convulsion and then lay still.

'He's dead!' whispered Rogers, staring down the swamp path with dilated eyes.

'He spoke of a Chinaman,' said Harrison. 'That clinches it that we're on the right trail. Have to leave him here for the time being. Nothing we can do for him now. Let's get going.'

'You aim to go on, after this?' exclaimed Rogers.

'Why not?'

'Mr Harrison,' said Rogers solemnly, 'you offered me a good wage to guide you into this here swamp. But I'm tellin' you fair there ain't enough money to make me go in there now, with night comin' on.'

'But why?' protested Harrison. 'Just because this man got into a fight – '

'It's more 'n just that,' declared Rogers decisively. 'He knowed he'd git jailed on the outside, but he was goin' anyway; that means somethin' had scared the livin' daylights out of him. You heard him say it was the Swamp Cat that got him?'

'Well?'

'Well, the Swamp Cat lives in the swamp. It's been so long since any folks claimed they seen him, I'd begun to believe he was just a myth told to scare people away from the swamp. But this shows he ain't. He killed Joe Corley. He'll kill us if he catches us in the dark. Why, by golly, he may be watchin' us right now!' This thought so disturbed Rogers that he drew a big six-shooter with an enormous length of barrel, and peered about, masticating his quid with a rapidity that showed his mental perturbation.

'Who's the other follow he named, John Bartholomew?' inquired Harrison.

'Don't know. Never heard of him. Come on, let's shove out of here. We'll git some boys and come back after Joe's body.'

'I'm going on,' growled Harrison, rising and dusting his hands.

Rogers stared. 'Man, you're plumb crazy! You'll git lost – '

'Not if I keep to the path.'

'Well, then, the Swamp Cat'll git you, or them 'gators will – '

'I'll take my chance,' answered Harrison brusque ly. 'Woon Shang's somewhere in this swamp. If he manages to get out before I get my hands on him, he may get clean away. I'm going after him.'

'But if you'll wait we'll raise a posse and go after him first thing in the mornin',' urged Rogers.

Harrison did not attempt to explain to the man his almost obsessional preference for working alone. With no further comment he turned and strode off down the narrow path. Rogers yelled after him: 'You're crazy as Hell! If you git as far as Celia Pompoloi's hut, you better stay there tonight! She's the big boss. It's the first cabin you come to. I'm goin' back to town and git a posse, and tomorrow mornin' we'll . . . ' The words became unintelligible among the dense growth as Harrison rounded a turn that shut off the sight of the other man.

As the detective strode along he saw that blood was smeared on the rotting leaves, and there were marks as if something heavy had been dragged over the trail. Joe Corley had obviously crawled for some distance after being attacked. Harrison visualised him dragging himself along on his belly like a crippled snake. The man must have had intense vitality to have gotten so far with a mortal wound in his back. And his fear must have been desperate to so drive him.

Harrison could no longer see the sun, but he knew it was hanging low. The shadows were gathering, and he was plunging deeper and deeper into the swamp. He began to glimpse patches of scummy ooze among the trees, and the path grew more tortuous as it wound to avoid these slimy puddles. Harrison plunged on without pausing. The dense growth might lend concealment to a desperate fugitive, but it was not in the woods, but among the scattered cabins of the swamp dwellers that he expected to find the man he hunted. The city-bred Chinaman, fearful of solitude and unable to fend for himself, would seek the company of men.

The detective wheeled suddenly. About him, in the dusk, the swamp was waking. Insects lifted strident voices, wings of bats or owls beat the air, and bullfrogs boomed from the lily pads. But he had heard a sound that was not of these things. It was a stealthy movement among the trees that marched in solid ranks beside the trail. Harrison drew his .45 and waited. Nothing happened. But in primitive solitudes a man's instincts are whetted. The detective felt that he was being watched by unseen eyes; he could almost sense the intensity of their glare. Was it the Chinaman, after all?

A bush beside the trail moved, without a wind to stir it. Harrison sprang through the curtain of creeper-hung cypresses, gun ready, snarling a command. His feet sank in slimy ooze, he stumbled in rotting vegetation and felt the dangling strands of moss slap against his face. There was nothing behind the bush, but he could have sworn that he saw a shadowy form move and vanish among the trees a short distance away. As he hesitated, he glanced down and saw a distinct mark in the loam. He bent closer; it was the print of a great, bare, splay foot. Moisture was oozing into the depression. A man *had* been standing behind that bush.

With a shrug Harrison stepped back into the trail. That was not the footprint of Woon Shang, and the detective was not looking for anybody else. It was natural that one of the swamp dwellers would spy on a stranger. The detective sent a hail into the gathering darkness, to assure the unseen watcher of his friendly intentions.

There was no reply. Harrison turned and strode on down the trail, not feeling entirely at ease, as he heard, from time to time, a faint snapping of twigs and other sounds that seemed to indicate someone moving along a course paralleling the path. It was not soothing to know that he was being followed by some unseen and possibly hostile being.

It was so dark now that he kept the path more by feel than by sight. About him sounded weird cries of strange birds or animals, and from time to time a deep grunting reverberation that puzzled him until he recognised it as the bellow of a bull alligator. He wondered if the scaly brutes ever crawled up on the trail, and how the fellow that was shadowing him out there in the darkness managed to avoid them. With the thought another twig snapped, much closer to the trail than before. Harrison swore softly, trying to peer into the Stygian gloom under the moss-festooned branches. The fellow was closing in on him with the growing darkness.

There was a sinister implication about the thing that made Harrison's flesh creep a bit. This reptile-haunted swamp-trail was no place for a fight . . . for it seemed probable that the unknown stalker was the killer of Joe Corley. Harrison was meditating on the matter when a light glimmered through the trees ahead of him. Quickening his steps he came abruptly out of the darkness into a grey twilight.

He had reached an expanse of solid ground, where the thinning trees let in the last grey light of the outer dusk. They made a black wall with waving fringes all about a small clearing, and through their boles, on one side, Harrison caught a glimmer of inky water. In the clearing stood a cabin of rough-hewn logs, and through a tiny window shone the light of an oil lamp.

As Harrison emerged from among the growth he glanced back, but saw no movement among the ferns, heard no sound of pursuit. The path, dimly marked on the higher ground, ran past the cabin and vanished in the further gloom. This cabin must be the abode of that Celia Pompoloi Rogers had mentioned. Harrison strode to the sagging stoop and rapped on the handmade door.

Inside there was movement, and the door swung open. Harrison was not prepared for the figure that confronted him. He had expected to see a bare-footed slattern; instead he saw a tall, rangily powerful man, neatly dressed, whose regular features and light skin portrayed his mixed blood.

'Good evening, sir.' The accent hinted of education above the average.

'Name's Harrison,' said the detective abruptly, displaying his badge. 'I'm after a crook that ran in here – a Chinese murderer, named Woon Shang. Know anything about him?'

'Yes, sir,' the man replied promptly. 'That man went past my cabin three days ago.'

'Where is he now?' demanded Harrison.

The other spread his hands in a curiously Latin gesture.

'I can not say. I have little intercourse with the other people who live in the swamp, but it is my belief that he is hiding among them somewhere. I have not seen him pass my cabin going back up the path.'

'Can you guide me to these other cabins?'

'Gladly, sir; by daylight.'

'I'd like to go tonight,' growled Harrison.

'That's impossible, sir,' the other protested. 'It would be most dangerous. You ran a great risk in coming this far alone. The other cabins are further back in the swamp. We do not leave our huts at night; there are many things in the swamp which are dangerous to human beings.'

'The Swamp Cat, for instance?' grunted Harrison.

The man cast him a quick glance of interrogation.

'He killed a man named Joe Corley a few hours ago,' said the detective. 'I found Corley on the trail. And if I'm not mistaken, that same lunatic has been following me for the past half hour.'

The mulatto evinced considerable disquiet and glanced across the clearing into the shadows.

'Come in,' he urged. 'If the Swamp Cat is prowling tonight, no man is safe out of doors. Come in and spend the night with me, and at dawn I will guide you to all the cabins in the swamp.'

Harrison saw no better plan. After all, it was absurd to go blundering about in the night, in an unknown marsh. He realised that he had made a mistake in coming in by himself, in the dusk; but working alone had become a habit with him, and he was tinged with a strong leaven of recklessness. Following a tip he had arrived at the little town on the edge of the swamplands in the mid-afternoon, and plunged on into the woods without hesitation. Now he doubted the wisdom of the move.

'Is this Celia Pompoloi's cabin?' he asked.

'It was,' the mulatto replied. 'She has been dead for three weeks. I live here alone. My name is John Bartholomew.'

Harrison's head snapped up and he eyed the other with new

interest. John Bartholomew; Joe Corley had muttered that name just before he died.

'Did you know Joe Corley?' he demanded.

'Slightly; he came into the swamp to hide from the law. He was a rather low-grade sort of human, though naturally I am sorry to hear of his death.'

'What's a man of your intelligence and education doing in this jungle?' the detective asked bluntly.

Bartholomew smiled rather wryly. 'We can not always choose our environments, Mr Harrison. The waste places of the world provide retreat for others than criminals. Some come to the swamps like your Chinaman, fleeing from the law. Others come to forget bitter disappointments forced upon them by circumstances.'

Harrison glanced about the cabin while Bartholomew was putting a stout bar in place across the door. It had but two rooms, one behind the other, connected by a strongly built door. The slab floor was clean, the room scantily furnished; a table, benches, a bunk built against the wall, all hand-made. There was a fireplace, over which hung primitive cooking utensils, and a cloth-covered cupboard.

'Would you like some fried bacon and corn pone?' asked Bartholomew. 'Or perhaps a cup of coffee? I do not have much to offer you, but – '

'No, thanks, I ate a big meal just before I started into the swamp. Just tell me something about these people.'

'As I said, I have little intercourse with them,' answered Bartholomew. 'They are clannish and suspicious, and keep much to themselves. Their fathers came here from Haiti, following one of the bloody revolutions which have cursed that unfortunate island in the past. They have curious customs. Have you heard of the worship of Voodoo?'

Harrison nodded.

'These people are Voodooists. I know that they have mysterious conclaves back in the swamps. I have heard drums booming in the night, and seen the glow of fires through the trees. I have sometimes felt a little uneasy for my safety at such times. Such people are capable of bloody extremes, when their primitive natures are maddened by the bestial rites of the Voodoo. No one ever comes here unless he is a fugitive from the law. The swamp people carry on their worship without interference.

'Celia Pompoloi, who once occupied this very hut, was a woman of considerable intelligence and some education; she was the one

swamp dweller who ever went "outside", as they call the outer world,
and attended school. Yet, to my actual knowledge, she was the priest-
ess of the cult and presided over their rituals. It is my belief that she
met her fate at last during one of those saturnalias. Her body was
found in the marshes, so badly mangled by the alligators that it was
recognisable only by her garments.'

'What about the Swamp Cat?' asked Harrison.

'A maniac, living like a wild beast in the marshes, only sporadically
violent; but at those times a thing of horror.'

'Would he kill the Chinaman if he had a chance?'

'He would kill anyone when his fit is on him. You said the China-
man was a murderer?'

'Murderer and thief,' grunted Harrison. 'Stole ten grand from the
man he killed.'

Bartholomew looked up as with renewed interest, started to speak,
then evidently changed his mind.

Harrison rose, yawning. 'Think I'll hit the hay,' he announced.

Bartholomew took up the lamp and led his guest into the back
room, which was of the same size as the other, but whose furnishings
consisted only of a bunk and a bench.

'I have but the one lamp, sir,' said Bartholomew. 'I shall leave it
with you.'

'Don't bother,' grunted Harrison, having a secret distrust of oil
lamps, resultant from experiencing an explosion of one in his boy-
hood. 'I'm like a cat in the dark. I don't need it.'

With many apologies for the rough accommodations and wishes
for a good night's sleep, Bartholomew bowed himself out, and the
door closed. Harrison, through force of habit, studied the room. A
little starlight came in through the one small window, which he
noticed was furnished with heavy wooden bars. There was no door
other than the one by which he had entered. He lay down on the
bunk fully dressed, without even removing his shoes, and pondered
rather glumly. He was beset by fears that Woon Shang might escape
him, after all. Suppose the Chinaman slipped out by the way he had
come in? True, local officers were watching at the edge of the
swampland, but Woon Shang might avoid them in the night. And
what if there *was* another way out, known only to the swamp people?
And if Bartholomew was as little acquainted with his neighbours as
he said, what assurance was there that the mulatto would be able to
guide him to the Chinaman's hiding place? These and other doubts
assailed him while he lay and listened to the soft sounds of his host's

retiring, and saw the thin line of light under the door vanish as the lamp was blown out. At last Harrison consigned his doubts to the devil, and fell asleep.

Chapter 2. *Murder tracks*

It was a noise at the windows, a stealthy twisting and wrenching at the bars, that awakened him. He woke quickly, with all his faculties alert, as was his habit. Something bulked in the window, something dark and round, with gleaming spots in it. He realised with a start that it was a human head he saw, with the faint starlight shining on rolling eyes and bared teeth. Without shifting his body, the detective stealthily reached for his gun; lying as he was in the darkness of the bunk, the man watching him could scarcely have seen the movement. But the head vanished, as if warned by some instinct.

Harrison sat up on his bunk, scowling, resisting the natural impulse to rush to the window and look out. That might be exactly what the man outside was wanting. There was something deadly about this business; the fellow had evidently been trying to get in. Was it the same creature that had followed him through the swamp? A sudden thought struck him. What was more likely than that the Chinaman had set a man to watch for a possible pursuer? Harrison cursed himself for not having thought of it before.

He struck a match, cupped it in his hand, and looked at his watch. It was scarcely ten o'clock. The night was still young. He scowled abstractedly at the rough wall behind the bunk, minutely illuminated in the flare of the match, and suddenly his breath hissed between his teeth. The match burned down to his fingers and went out. He struck another and leaned to the wall. Thrust in a chink between the logs was a knife, and its wicked curved blade was grimly smeared and clotted. The implication sent a shiver down Harrison's spine. The blood might be that of an animal . . . but who would butcher a calf or a hog in that room? Why had not the blade been cleansed? It was as if it had been hastily concealed, after striking a murderous blow.

He took it down and looked at it closely. The blood was dried and blackened as if at least many hours had elapsed since it had been let. The weapon was no ordinary butcher's knife . . . Harrison stiffened. *It was a Chinese dagger*. The match went out and Harrison did what the average man would have done. He leaned over the edge of the bunk, the only thing in the room that would conceal an object of any

size, and lifted the cloth that hung to the floor. He did not actually
expect to find the corpse of Woon Shang beneath it. He merely acted
through instinct. Nor did he find a corpse. His hand, groping in the
dark, encountered only the uneven floor and rough logs; then his
fingers felt something else . . . something at once compact and
yielding, wedged between the logs as the knife had been.

He drew it forth; it felt like a flat package of crisp paper, bound
with oiled silk. Cupping a match in his hand, he tore it open. Ten
worn bills met his gaze; on each bill was the numerals of $1,000. He
crushed the match out and sat in the dark, mental pictures tumbling
rapidly across his consciousness.

So John Bartholomew had lied. Doubtless he had taken in the
Chinaman as he had taken in Harrison. The detective visualised a
dim form bending in the darkness above a sleeping figure in that
same bunk . . . a murderous stroke with the victim's own knife.

He growled inarticulately, with the chagrin of the cheated man-
hunter, certain that Woon Shang's body was rotting in some slimy
marsh. At least he had the money. Careless of Bartholomew to hide it
there. But was it? It was only by an accidental chain of circumstances
that he had found it . . .

He stiffened again. Under the door he saw a thin pencil of light.
Had Bartholomew not yet gone to bed? But he remembered the
blowing out of the lamp. Harrison rose and glided noiselessly to the
thick door. When he reached it he heard a low mumble of voices in
the outer room. The speakers moved nearer, stood directly before
the door. He strained his ears and recognised the crisp accents of
John Bartholomew. 'Don't bungle the job,' the mulatto was mutter-
ing. 'Get him before he has a chance to use his gun. He doesn't
suspect anything. I just remember that I left the Chinaman's knife in
the crack over the bunk. But the detective will never see it, in the
dark. He had to come butting in here, this particular night. We can't
let him see what he'd see if he lived through this night.'

'We do de job quick and clean, mastah,' murmured another voice,
with a guttural accent different from any Harrison had ever heard,
and impossible to reproduce.

'All right; we haven't anything to fear from Joe Corley. The Swamp
Cat carried out my instructions.'

'Dat Swamp Cat prowlin' 'round outside right now,' muttered
another man. 'Ah don't like him. Why can't he do dis job?'

'He obeys my orders, but he can't be trusted too far. But we can't
stand here talking like this. The detective will wake up and get

suspicious. Throw open that door and rush him. Knife him in his bunk . . . '

Harrison always believed that the best defence was a strong offensive. There was but one way out of this jam. He took it without hesitation. He hurled a massive shoulder against the door, knocking it open, and sprang into the outer room, gun levelled, and barked: 'Hands up, damn you!'

There were five men in that room: Bartholomew, holding the lamp and shading it with his left hand, and four others, four lean, rangy giants in nondescript garments, with sinister features. Each man of the four had a knife in his hand.

They recoiled with yells of dismay as Harrison crashed upon them. Automatically their hands went up and their knives clattered on the floor.

'Back up against that wall!' snapped Harrison.

They obeyed dumbly, rendered incapable of action by the shock of surprise. Harrison knew that it was John Bartholomew, more than these hulking butchers, that he had to fear.

'Set that lamp on the table,' he snapped. 'Line up there with them – *ha*!'

Bartholomew had stooped to lower the lamp to the table . . . then quick as a cat he threw it crashing to the floor, ducking behind the table with the same motion. Harrison's gun crashed almost simultaneously, but even in the bedlam darkness that followed, the detective knew he had missed. Whirling, he leaped through the outer door. Inside the dark cabin he would have no chance against the knives. As Harrison raced across the clearing he heard Bartholomew's furious voice yelling commands. He rounded the cabin and darted toward the trees on the other side. He had no intention of fleeing until he was run down from behind. He was seeking a place where he could turn at bay and shoot it out with a little advantage on his side. The moon was just coming up above the trees, emphasising rather than illuminating the shadows.

He reached the shadows before they rounded the hut, and glancing back through the bushes, saw them running about the clearing like hunting dogs seek a spoor, howling in primitive blood-lust and disappointment. The growing moonlight glittered on the long knives in their hands.

He drew back further among the trees, finding the ground more solid underfoot than he had expected. Then he came suddenly upon the marshy edge of a stretch of black water. Something grunted and thrashed amidst it, and two green lamps burned suddenly like jewels on the inky water. He recoiled, well knowing what those twin lights were. And as he did so, he bumped full into something that locked fierce arms like an ape about him.

Harrison ducked and heaved, bowing his powerful back like a great cat, and his assailant tumbled over his head and thumped on the ground, still clutching the detective's coat with the grip of a vice. Harrison lunged backward, ripping the garment down the back, wrenching his arms from the sleeves, in his frenzy to free himself.

The man leaped to his feet on the edge of the pool, snarling like a wild beast. Harrison saw a gaunt half naked man with wild strands of hair caked with mud hanging over a contorted mask of a face, the thick loose lips drooling foam. This indeed, he knew, was the dread Swamp Cat.

Still grasping Harrison's torn coat brainlessly in his left hand, his right swept up with a sheen of sharp steel, and even as he sensed the madman's intention, the detective ducked and fired from the hip. The thrown knife hummed by his ear, and with the crash of the shot the Swamp Cat swayed and pitched backward into the black pool. There was a threshing rush, the waters stormed foamily, there was a glimpse of a blunted, reptilian snout, and the trailing body vanished with it.

Harrison stepped back, sickened, and heard behind him the shouting progress of men through the bushes. His hunters had heard the shot. He drew back into the shadows among a cluster of gum trees, and waited, gun in hand. An instant later they rushed out upon the bank of the pool, John Bartholomew and his dusky knife-fighters.

They ranged the bank, gaping, and then Bartholomew laughed and pointed to a blood-stained piece of cloth that floated soggily on the foam-flecked waters.

'The fool's coat! He must have run right into the pool, and the 'gators got him! I can see them tearing at something, over there among the reeds. Hear those bones crack?' Bartholomew's laugh was fiendish to hear.

'Well,' said the mulatto, 'we don't have to worry about him. If they send anybody in after him, we'll just tell them the truth: that he fell into the water and got grabbed by the 'gators, just like Celia Pompoloi.'

'She wuz a awful sight when us foun' huh body,' muttered one of the swamp Negroes.

'We'll never find that much of him,' prophesied Bartholomew.

'Did he say what de Chinaman done?' asked another of the men.

'Just what the Chinaman said; that he'd murdered a man.'

'Wish he'd uh robbed uh bank,' murmured the swamp dweller plaintively. 'Wish he'd uh brung uh lot uh money in wid him.'

'Well, he didn't,' snapped Bartholomew. 'You saw me search him. Now get back to the others and help them watch him. More men may come looking for him tomorrow, but if they do, they're welcome to all of him they can find!' He laughed with sinister meaning, and then added abruptly: 'Hurry and get out of here. I want to be alone. There are spirits to be communed with before the hour arrives, and dread rites that I must perform alone. Go!'

The others bent their heads in a curious gesture of subservience, and trooped away, in the direction of the clearing. He followed leisurely.

Harrison glared after them, turning what he had heard over in his mind. Some of it was gibberish, but certain things were clear. For one thing, the Chinaman was obviously alive, and imprisoned somewhere. Bartholomew had lied about his own relations with the swamp people; one of them he certainly was not, but he was just as certainly a leader among them. Yet he had lied to them about the money. Harrison remembered the mulatto's expression when he had mentioned it to him. The detective believed that Bartholomew had never seen the money; that Woon Shang, suspicious, had hidden it himself before he was attacked.

As long as they believed him dead, he could conduct his investigations without being harried by pursuit. His shirt was of dark material and did not show in the darkness, and the big detective was trained in stealth by adventures in the haunted dives of Oriental quarters where unseen eyes always watched and ears were forever alert.

When he came to the edge of the trees, he saw the four giants trooping down the trail that led deeper into the swamp. They walked in single file, their heads bent forward, stooping from the waist. Bartholomew was just going into the cabin. Harrison started to follow the disappearing forms, then hesitated. Bartholomew was in his power. He could steal up on the cabin, throw his gun on the mulatto and make him tell where Woon Shang was imprisoned – maybe. Even as he ruminated, Bartholomew came out of the cabin and stood peering about with a strange furtiveness. He held a heavy whip in his hand. Presently he glided across the clearing toward the quarter where the detective crouched. He passed within a few yards of Harrison's covert, and the moonlight illumined his features.

Harrison was astounded at the change in his face, at the sinister vitality and evil strength reflected there.

Harrison altered his plans and stole after him, wishing to know on what errand the man went with such secrecy. It was not difficult. Bartholomew looked neither back nor sideways, but wound a tortuous way among inky pools and clusters of rotting vegetation that looked poisonous, even in the moonlight. Presently the detective crouched low; ahead of the mulatto there was a tiny hut, almost hidden among the trees which trailed Spanish moss over it like a grey veil. Bartholomew looked carefully about him, then drew forth a key and manipulated a large padlock on the door. Harrison was convinced that he had been led to the prison of Woon Shang.

Bartholomew disappeared inside, closing the door. A light gleamed through the chinks of the logs. Then came a mumble of voices, too indistinct for Harrison to tell anything about them; that was followed by the sharp, unmistakable crack of a whip on bare flesh, and a shrill cry of pain. Enlightenment came to Harrison. Bartholomew had come secretly to his prisoner – and for what reason but to make him divulge the hiding-place of the money, of which Harrison had spoken? Obviously Bartholomew had no intentions of sharing that money with his mates.

Harrison began to work his way stealthily toward the cabin, fully intending to burst in and put a stop to that lashing. He would cheerfully have shot down Woon Shang himself, had the occasion arisen, but before he reached the hut, the sounds ceased, the light went out and Bartholomew emerged, wiping the perspiration of exertion from his brow. He locked the door, thrust the key in his pocket, and turned away through the trees, trailing his whip in his hand. Harrison, crouching in the shadows, let him go. It was Woon Shang he was after. Bartholomew could be dealt with later.

When the mulatto had disappeared, Harrison rose and strode to the door of the hut. The absence of guards was rather puzzling, after the conversation he had overheard, but be wasted no time on conjecture. The door was secured by a chain made fast to a big hasp driven deep into a log. He thrust his gun barrel through this hasp, and using it as a lever, pried out the hasp with no great difficulty.

Pulling open the door he peered in; it was too dark to see, but be heard somebody's breath coming in jerky hysterical sobs. He struck a match, looked . . . then glared. The prisoner was there, crouching on the dirt floor. But it was not Woon Shang. It was a woman.

She was a mulatto, young, and handsome in her way. She was clad
only in a ragged and scanty chemise, and her hands were bound
behind her. From her wrists a long strand of rawhide ran to a heavy
staple in the wall. She stared wildly at Harrison, her dark eyes reflect-
ing both hope and terror. There were tear stains on her cheeks.

'Who the devil are you?' demanded the detective.

'Celia Pompoloi!' Her voice was rich and musical despite its hyst-
eria. 'Oh, for God's sake let me go! I can't stand it any more. I'll die;
I know I will!'

'I thought you *were* dead,' he grunted.

'John Bartholomew did it!' she exclaimed. 'He persuaded a girl
from "outside" into the swamp, and then he killed her and dressed
her in my clothes, and threw her into the marsh where the alligators
would chew the body till nobody could tell it wasn't me. The people
found it and thought it was Celia Pompoloi. He's kept me here for
three weeks and tortured me every night.'

'Why?' Harrison found and lighted a candle stump stuck on the
wall. Then he stooped and cut the rawhide thongs that bound her
hands. She climbed to her feet, chafing her bruised and swollen
wrists. In her scanty garb the brutality of the floggings she had
received was quite apparent.

'He's a devil!' Her dark eyes flashed murderously; whatever her
wrongs, she obviously was no meek sufferer. 'He came here posing as
a priest of the Great Serpent. He said he was from Haiti, the lying
dog. He's from Santo Domingo, and no more priest than you are. *I*
am the proper priestess of the Serpent, and the people obeyed me.
That's why he put me out of the way. I'll kill him!'

'But why did he lick you?' asked Harrison.

'Because I wouldn't tell him what he wanted to know,' she mutt-
ered sullenly, bending her head and twisting one bare foot behind
the other ankle, school-girl fashion. She did not seem to think of
refusing to answer his questions.

'He came here to steal the jewel, the Heart of the Great Serpent,
which we brought with us from Haiti, long ago. He is no priest. He is
an impostor. He proposed that I give the Heart to him and run away
from my people with him. When I refused, he tied me in this old hut
where none can hear my screams; the swamp people shun it, thinking
it's haunted. He said he'd keep beating me until I told him where the
Heart was hidden, but I wouldn't tell him – not though he stripped
all the flesh from my bones. I alone know that secret, because I am a
priestess of the Serpent, and the guardian of its Heart.'

This was Voodoo stuff with a vengeance; her matter-of-fact manner evinced an unshaken belief in her weird cult.

'Do you know anything about Woon Shang?' he demanded.

'John Bartholomew told me of him in his boastings. He came running from the law and Bartholomew promised to hide him. Then he summoned the swamp men, and they seized the China-man, though he wounded one of them badly with his knife. They made a prisoner of him . . . '

'Why?'

Celia was in that vengeful mood in which a woman recklessly tells everything, and repeats things she would not otherwise mention.

'Bartholomew came saying he was a priest of old time. That's how he caught the fancy of the people. He promised them an *old* sacrifice, of which there has not been one for thirty years. We have offered the white cock and the red cock to the Great Serpent. But Bartholomew promised them the *goat-without-horns*. He did that to get the Heart into his hands, for only then is it taken from its secret hiding place. He thought to get it into his hands and run away before the sacrifice was made. But when I refused to aid him, it upset his plans. Now he can not get the Heart, but he must go through with the sacrifice anyway. The people are becoming impatient. If he fails them, they will kill him.

'He first chose the "outside" man, Joe Corley, who was hiding in the swamp, for the sacrifice; but when the Chinaman came, Barth-olomew decided he would make a better offering. Bartholomew told me tonight that the Chinaman had money, and he was going to make him tell where he hid it, so he would have the money, and the Heart, too, when I finally gave in and told him . . . '

'Wait a minute,' interposed Harrison. 'Let me get this straight. What is it that Bartholomew intends doing with Woon Shang?'

'He will offer him up to the Great Serpent,' she answered, making a conventional gesture of conciliation and adoration as she spoke the dread name.

'A *human* sacrifice?'

'Yes.'

'Well, I'll be damned!' he muttered. 'If I hadn't been raised in the South myself, I'd never believe it. When is this sacrifice to take place?'

'Tonight!'

'Eh, what's that?' He remembered Bartholomew's cryptic in-structions to his henchmen. 'The devil! Where does it happen, and what time?'

'Just before dawn; far back in the swamp.'

'I've got to find Woon Shang and stop it!' he exclaimed. 'Where is he imprisoned?'

'At the place of the sacrifice; many men guard him. You'd never find your way there. You'd drown and get eaten by the 'gators. Besides, if you did get there, the people would tear you to pieces.'

'You lead me there and I'll take care of the people,' he snarled. 'You want revenge on Bartholomew. All right; guide me there and I'll see that you get plenty. I've always worked alone,' he ruminated angrily, 'but the swamp country isn't River Street.'

'I'll do it!' Her eyes blazed and her white teeth gleamed in a mask of passion. 'I'll guide you to the place of the Altar. We'll kill him, the dog!'

'How long will it take us to get there?'

'I could go there in an hour, alone. Guiding you, it will take longer. Much longer, the way we must go. You can't travel the road I would take, alone.'

'I can follow you anywhere you walk,' he grunted, slightly nettled. He glanced at his watch, then extinguished the candle. 'Let's get going. Take the shortest route and don't worry about me. I'll keep up.'

She caught his wrist in a fierce grasp and almost jerked him out of the door, quivering with the eagerness of a hunting hound.

'Wait a minute!' A thought struck him. 'If I go back to the cabin and capture Bartholomew – '

'He will not be there; he is well on his way to the Place of the Altar; better that we beat him there.'

Chapter 3. *Voodoo Lair*

As long as he lived Harrison remembered that race through the swamp, as he followed Celia Pompoloi along pathless ways that seemed impossible. Mire caught at his feet, and sometimes black scummy water lapped about his ankles, but Celia's swift sure feet always found solid ground where none seemed possible, or guided him over bogs that quaked menacingly beneath their weight. She sprang lightly from hummock to hummock, or slid between snaky pools of black slime where unseen monsters grunted and wallowed. Harrison floundered after her, sweating, half nauseated with the miasmic reek of the oozy slime that plastered him; but all the bulldog was roused in him, and he was ready to wade through swamps for a week if the man he hunted was at the other end of the loathsome journey. Dank misty clouds had veiled the sky, through which the moon shone fitfully, and Harrison stumbled like a blind man, depending entirely on his guide, whose dusky half-naked body was all but invisible to him at times in the darkness.

Ahead of them he began to hear a rhythmic throbbing, a barbaric pulsing that grew as they advanced. A red glow flickered through the black trees.

'The flames of the sacrifice!' gasped Celia, quickening her pace. 'Hasten!'

Somewhere in his big, weary body Harrison found enough reserve energy to keep up with her. She seemed to run lightly over bogs that engulfed him to the knees. She possessed the swamp dweller's instinct for safe footing. Ahead of them Harrison saw the shine of something that was not mud, and Celia halted at the verge of a stretch of noisome water.

'The Place of the Altar is surrounded by water on all sides but one,' she hissed. 'We are in the very heart of the swamp, deeper than anyone ever goes except on such occasions as these. There are no cabins near. Follow me! I have a bridge none knows of except myself.'

At a point where the sluggish stream narrowed to some fifty feet, a fallen tree spanned it. Celia ran out upon it, balancing herself upright. She swayed across, a slim ghostly figure in the cloudy light. Harrison straddled the log and hitched himself ignominiously along.

He was too weary to trust *his* equilibrium. His feet dangled a foot or so above the black surface, and Celia, waiting impatiently on the further bank as she peered anxiously at the distant glow, cast him a look over her shoulder and cried a sudden urgent warning.

Harrison jerked up his legs just as something bulky and grisly heaved up out of the water with a great splash and an appalling clash of mighty fangs. Harrison fairly flung himself over the last few feet and landed on the further bank in a more demoralised condition than he would have admitted. A criminal in a dark room with a knife was less nerve-shaking than these ghoulish slayers of the dark waters.

The ground was firmer; they were, as Celia said, on a sort of island in the heart of the marshes. The girl threaded her supple way among the cypresses, panting with the intensity of her emotions. Perspiration soaked her; the hand that held Harrison's wrist was wet and slippery.

A few minutes later, when the glow in the trees had grown to an illuminating glare, she halted and slipped to the damp mould, drawing her companion with her. They looked out upon a scene incredible in its primitive starkness.

There was a clearing, free of underbrush, circled by a black wall of cypress. From its outer edge a sort of natural causeway wandered away into the gloom, and over that low ridge ran a trail, beaten by many feet. The trail ended in the clearing, the ultimate end of the path that Harrison had followed into the swamp. On the other side of the clearing there was a glimpse of dusky water, reflecting the firelight.

In a wide horseshoe formation, their backs to the causeway, sat some fifty men, women and children, resembling Celia Pompoloi in complexion. Harrison had not supposed that so many people inhabited the swamp. Their gaze was fixed on an object in the centre of the opening of the human horseshoe. This was a great block of dark wood that had an unfamiliar appearance, as of an altar, brought from afar. There was an intolerable suggestion about that block, and the misshapen, leering figure that rose behind it – a fantastically carven idol, to whose bestial features the flickering firelight lent life and mobility. Harrison intuitively knew that this monstrosity was never carved in America. The people had brought it with them from Haiti, and surely their ancestors had brought it originally from Africa. There was an aura of the Congo about it, the reek of black squalling jungles, and squirming faceless shapes of a night more primeval than this. Harrison was not superstitious, but he felt gooseflesh rise on his limbs. At the back of his consciousness dim racial memories stirred, conjuring up unstable and monstrous images from the dim mists of the primitive, when men worshipped such gods as these.

Before the idol, near the block, sat an old crone, striking a bowl tom-tom with quick staccato strokes of her open hands; it growled and rumbled and muttered. Their voices were low, but they hummed with a note of hysteria.

Harrison looked in vain for John Bartholomew and Woon Shang. He reached out a hand to get his companion's attention. She did not heed him. Her supple figure was tense and quivering as a taut wire under his hand. A sudden change in the chanting, a wild wolfish baying, brought him about again.

Out of the shadows of the trees behind the idol strode John Bartholomew. He was clad only in a loincloth, and it was as if he had doffed his civilised culture with his clothing. His facial expression, his whole bearing, were changed; he was like an image of barbarism incarnate. Harrison stared at the knotted biceps, the ridged body muscles which the firelight displayed. But something else gripped his whole attention. With John Bartholomew came another, unwillingly, at the sight of whom the crowd gave tongue to another bestial yell.

About Bartholomew's mighty left hand was twisted the pigtail of Woon Shang, whom he dragged after him like a fowl to the chopping block. The Chinaman was stark naked, his yellow body gleaming like old ivory in the fire. His hands were bound behind his back, and he was like a child in the grasp of his executioner. Woon Shang was not a large man; beside the great mulatto he seemed slimmer than ever. His hysterical panting came plainly to Harrison in the silence that fell tensely as the shouting ceased. His straining feet tore at the sod as he struggled against the inexorable advance of his captor. In Bartholomew's right hand shone a great razor-edged crescent of steel. The watchers sucked in their breath loudly; in a single stride they had returned to the jungle whence they had crawled; they were mad for the bloody saturnalia their ancestors had known.

In Bartholomew's face Harrison read stark horror and mad determination. He sensed that the mulatto was not enjoying this ghastly primordial drama into which be had been trapped. He also realised that the man must go through with it, and that he would go through with it. It was more than the jewel heart of the serpent-god for which Bartholomew strove now; it was the continued dominance of these wolfish devil-worshippers on which his life depended.

Harrison rose to one knee, drew and cocked his revolver and sighted along the blue barrel. The distance was not great, but the light was illusive. But he felt he must trust to the chance of sending a slug crashing through John Bartholomew's broad breast. If their priest was shot down, panic might seize them. His finger was crooking about the trigger when something was thrown into the fire. Abruptly the flames died down, throwing everything into deep shallow. As suddenly they flared up again, burning with a weird green radiance. The dusky faces looked like those of drowned corpses in the glow.

In the moment of darkness Bartholomew had reached the block. His victim's head was thrust down upon it, and the mulatto stood like a bronze image, his muscular right arm lifted, poising above his head the broad steel crescent. And then, before could strike the blow that would send Woon Shang's head rolling to the misshapen feet of the grinning idol, before Harrison could jerk the trigger, something froze them all in their places.

Into the weird glow moved a figure, so lithely that it seemed to float in the uncertain light rather than move on earthly feet. In the green glow that lent her features the aspect of death, with perspiration dripping from her draggled garment, Celia Pompoloi looked hideously like the corpse of a drowned woman newly risen from a watery grave.

'Celia!'

It was a scream from a score of gaping mouths. Bedlam followed.

'Celia Pompoloi! Oh Gawd, she done come back from de watah! Done come back from Hell!'

'Yes you dogs!' It was a most unghostly scream from Celia. 'It's Celia Pompoloi, come back from Hell to send John Bartholomew there!'

And like a fury she rushed across the green-lit space, a knife she had found somewhere glittering in her hand. Bartholomew, momentarily paralysed by the appearance of his prisoner, came to life. Releasing Woon Shang he stepped aside and swung the heavy beheading knife with all his power. Harrison saw the great muscles leap up under his glossy skin as he struck. But Celia's spring was that of a swamp panther. It carried her inside the circular sweep of the weighted blade, and her knife flashed as it sank to the hilt under John Bartholomew's heart. With a strangled cry he reeled and fell, dragging her down with him as she strove to wrench her blade free.

Abandoning it she rose, panting, her hair standing on end, her eyes starting from her head, her red lips writhing back in a curl of devilish rage. The people shrieked and gave back from her, still evidently in the grip of the delusion that they looked on one risen from the dead.

'Dogs!' she screamed, an incarnation of fury. 'Fools! Swine! Have you lost your reason, to forget all my teachings, and let this dead dog make of you the beasts your fathers were? Oh – !' Glaring about for a weapon she caught up a blazing fire-brand and rushed at them, striking furiously. Men yelped as the flames bit them, and the sparks showered. Howling, cursing, and screaming they broke and fled, a frenzied mob, streaming out across the causeway, with their maddened priestess at their heels, screaming maledictions and smiting with the splintering faggot. They vanished in the darkness, and their clamour came back faintly.

Harrison rose, shaking his head in wonder, and went stiffly up to the dying fire. Bartholomew was dead, staring glassily up at the moon which was breaking through the scattering clouds. Woon

Shang crouched babbling incoherent Chinese as Harrison hauled him to his feet.

'Woon Shang,' said the detective wearily, 'I arrest you for the murder of Li-keh-tsung. I warn you that anything you say will be used against you.'

That formula seemed to invest the episode with some sanity, in contrast to the fantastic horror of the recent events. The Chinaman made no struggle. He seemed dazed, muttering: 'This will break the heart of my honourable father; he had rather see me dead than dishonoured.'

'You ought to have thought of that before,' said Harrison heavily. Through force of habit he cut Woon Shang's cords and reached for his handcuffs before he realised that they had been lost with his coat.

'Oh, well,' he sighed. 'I don't reckon you'll need them. Let's get going.'

Laying a heavy hand on his captive's naked shoulder, Harrison half guided, half pushed him toward the causeway. The detective was dizzy with fatigue, but combined with it was a muddled determination to get his prisoner out of the swamp and into a jail before he stopped. He felt he had no more to fear from the swamp people, but he wanted to get out of that atmosphere of decay and slime in which he seemed to have been wandering for ages. Woon Shang took note of his condition with furtive sidelong glances, as the stark fear died out of the Chinaman's beady black eyes to be replaced by one of craft.

'I have ten thousand dollars,' he began babbling. 'I will give you all of it if you will let me go . . . '

'Oh, shut up!' groaned Harrison wearily, giving him an exasperated shove. Woon Shang stumbled and went to his knees, his bare shoulder slipping from Harrison's grasp. The detective was stooping, fumbling for him when the Chinaman rose with a chunk of wood in his hand, and smote him savagely on the head. Harrison staggered back, almost falling, and Woon Shang, in a last desperate bid for freedom, dashed, not for the neck of land between which himself and Harrison stood, but straight toward the black water that glimmered beyond the fringe of cypresses. Harrison fired mechanically and without aim, but the fugitive kept straight on and hit the dusky water with a long dive.

Woon Shang's bobbing head was scarcely visible in the shadows of the overhanging ferns. Then a wild shriek cut the night; the water threshed and foamed, there was the glimpse of a writhing, horribly contorted yellow body and of a longer, darker shape, and then the blood-streaked waters closed over Woon Shang forever.

Harrison exhaled gustily and sank down on a rotting log.

'Well,' he said wearily, aloud, 'that winds *that* up. It's better this way. Woon's family had rather he died this way than in the chair, and they're decent folks, in spite of him. If this business had come to trial, I'd have had to tell about Celia shoving a knife into that devil Bartholomew, and I'd hate to see her on trial for killing that rat. This way it can be smoothed over. He had it coming to him. And I've got the money that's coming to old Li-keh-tsung's granddaughter. And it's me for the feather beds and fried steaks of civilisation.'

Names in the Black Book

'Three unsolved murders in a week are not so unusual – for River Street,' grunted Steve Harrison, shifting his muscular bulk restlessly in his chair.

His companion lighted a cigarette, and Harrison observed that her slim hand was none too steady. She was exotically beautiful, a dark, supple figure, with the rich colours of purple Eastern nights and crimson dawns in her dusky hair and red lips. But in her dark eyes Harrison glimpsed the shadow of fear. Only once before had he seen fear in those marvellous eyes, and the memory made him vaguely uneasy.

'It's your business to solve murders,' she said.

'Give me a little time. You can't rush things, when you're dealing with the people of the Oriental quarter.'

'You have less time than you think,' she answered cryptically. 'If you do not listen to me, you'll never solve these killings.'

'I'm listening.'

'But you won't believe. You'll say I'm hysterical – seeing ghosts and shying at shadows.'

'Look here, Joan,' he exclaimed impatiently. 'Come to the point. You called me to your apartment and I came because you said you were in deadly danger. But now you're talking riddles about three men who were killed last week. Spill it plain, won't you?'

'Do you remember Erlik Khan?' she asked abruptly.

Involuntarily his hand sought his face, where a thin scar ran from temple to jaw-rim. 'I'm not likely to forget him,' he said. 'A Mongol who called himself Lord of the Dead. His idea was to combine all the Oriental criminal societies in America in one big organisation, with himself at the head. He might have done it, too, if his own men hadn't turned on him.'

'Erlik Khan has returned,' she said.

'What!' His head jerked up and he glared at her incredulously. 'What are you talking about? I saw him die, and so did you!'

'I saw his hood fall apart as Ali ibn Suleyman struck with his keen-edged scimitar,' she answered. 'I saw him roll to the floor and lie still. And then the house went up in flames, and the roof fell in, and only charred bones were ever found among the ashes. Nevertheless, Erlik Khan has returned.'

Harrison did not reply, but sat waiting for further disclosures, sure they would come in an indirect way. Joan La Tour was half Oriental, and partook of many of the characteristics of her subtle kin.

'How did those three men die?' she asked, though he was aware that she knew as well as he.

'Li-crin, the Chinese merchant, fell from his own roof,' he grunted. 'The people on the street heard him scream and then saw him come hurtling down. Might have been an accident . . . but middle-aged Chinese merchants don't go climbing around on roofs at midnight.

'Ibrahim ibn Achmet, the Syrian curio dealer, was bitten by a cobra. That might have been an accident too, only I know somebody dropped the snake on him through his skylight.

'Jacob Kossova, the exporter, was simply knifed in a back alley. Dirty jobs, all of them, and no apparent motive on the surface. But motives are hidden deep; in River Street. When I find the guilty parties I'll uncover the motives.'

'And these murders suggest nothing to you?' exclaimed the girl, tense with suppressed excitement. 'You do not see the link that connects them? You do not grasp the point they all have in common? Listen – all these men were formerly associated in one way or another with Erlik Khan!'

'Well?' he demanded. 'That doesn't mean that the Khan's spook killed them! We found plenty of bones in the ashes of the house, but there were members of his gang in other parts of the city. His gigantic organisation went to pieces, after his death, for lack of a leader, but the survivors were never uncovered. Some of them might be paying off old grudges.'

'Then why did they wait so long to strike? It's been a year since we saw Erlik Khan die. I tell you, the Lord of the Dead himself, alive or dead, has returned and is striking down these men for one reason or another. Perhaps they refuse to do his bidding once more. Five were marked for death. Three have fallen.'

'How do you know that?' said he.

'Look!' From beneath the cushions of the divan on which she sat she drew something, and rising, came and bent beside him while she unfolded it.

It was a square piece of parchment-like substance, black and glossy. On it were written five names, one below the other, in a bold flowing hand . . . and in crimson, like spilled blood. Through the first three names a crimson bar had been drawn. They were the names of Li-chin, Ibrahim ibn Achmet, and Jacob Kossova. Harrison grunted explosively. The last two names, as yet unmarred, were those of Joan La Tour and Stephen Harrison.

'Where did you get this?' he demanded.

'It was shoved under my door last night, while I slept. If all the doors and windows had not been locked, the police would have found it pinned to my corpse this morning.'

'But still I don't see what connection – '

'It is a page from the Black Book of Erlik Khan!' she cried. 'The book of the dead! I have seen it, when I was a subject of his in the old days. There he kept accounts of his enemies, alive and dead. I saw that book, open, the very day of the night Ali ibn Suleyman killed him – a big book with jade-hinged ebony covers and glossy black parchment pages. Those names were not in it then; they have been written in since Erlik Khan died . . . and that is Erlik Khan's handwriting!'

If Harrison was impressed he failed to show it.

'Does he keep his books in English?'

'No, in a Mongolian script. This is for our benefit. And I know we are hopelessly doomed. Erlik Khan never warned his victims unless he was sure of them.'

'Might be a forgery,' grunted the detective.

'No! No man could imitate Erlik Khan's hand. He wrote those names himself. He has come back from the dead! Hell could not hold a devil as black as he!' Joan was losing some of her poise in her fear and excitement. She ground out the half-consumed cigarette and broke the cover of a fresh carton. She drew forth a slim white cylinder and tossed the package on the table. Harrison took it up and absently extracted one for himself.

'Our names are in the Black Book! It is a sentence of death from which there is no appeal!' She struck a match and was lifting it, when Harrison struck the cigarette from her with a startled oath. She fell back on the divan, bewildered at the violence of his action, and he caught up the package and began gingerly to remove the contents.

'Where'd you get these things?'

'Why, down at the corner drug store, I guess,' she stammered. 'That's where I usually – '

'Not these you didn't,' he grunted. 'These fags have been specially treated. I don't know what it is, but I've seen one puff of the stuff knock a man stone dead. Some kind of a hellish Oriental drug mixed with the tobacco. You were out of your apartment while you were phoning me – '

'I was afraid my wire was tapped,' she answered. 'I went to a public booth down the street.'

'And it's my guess somebody entered your apartment while you were gone and switched cigarettes on you. I only got a faint whiff of the stuff when I started to put that fag in my mouth, but it's unmistakable. Smell it yourself. Don't be afraid. It's deadly only when ignited.'

She obeyed, and turned pale.

'I told you! We were the direct cause of Erlik Khan's overthrow! If you hadn't smelt that drug, we'd both be dead now, as he intended!'

'Well,' he grunted, 'it's a cinch somebody's after you, anyway. I still say it can't be Erlik Khan, because nobody could live after the lick on the head I saw Ali ibn Suleyman hand him, and I don't believe in ghosts. But you've got to be protected until I run down whoever is being so free with his poisoned cigarettes.'

'What about yourself? Your name's in his book, too.'

'Never mind me,' Harrison growled pugnaciously. 'I reckon I can take care of myself.' He looked capable enough, with his cold blue eyes, and the muscles bulging in his coat. He had shoulders like a bull.

'This wing's practically isolated from the rest of the building,' he said, 'and you've got the third floor to yourself?'

'Not only the third floor of the wing,' she answered. 'There's no one else on the third floor anywhere in the building at present.'

'That makes it fine!' he exclaimed irritably. 'Somebody could sneak in and cut your throat without disturbing anyone. That's what they'll try, too, when they realise the cigarettes didn't finish you. You'd better move to a hotel.'

'That wouldn't make any difference,' she answered, trembling. Her nerves obviously were in a bad way. 'Erlik Khan would find me, anywhere. In a hotel, with people coming and going all the time, and the rotten locks they have on the doors, with transoms and fire escapes and everything, it would just be that much easier for him.'

'Well, then, I'll plant a bunch of cops around here.'

'That wouldn't do any good, either. Erlik Khan has killed again and again in spite of the police. They do not understand his ways.'

'That's right,' he muttered, uncomfortably aware of a conviction that to summon men from headquarters would surely be signing those men's death warrants, without accomplishing anything else. It was absurd to suppose that the dead Mongol fiend was behind these murderous attacks, yet . . . Harrison's flesh crawled along his spine at the memory of things that had taken place in River Street – things he had never reported, because he did not wish to be thought either a liar or a madman. The dead do not return . . . but what seems absurd on Thirty-ninth Boulevard takes on a different aspect among the haunted labyrinths of the Oriental quarter.

'Stay with me!' Joan's eyes were dilated, and she caught Harrison's arm with hands that shook violently. 'We can defend these rooms! While one sleeps the other can watch! Do not call the police; their blunders would doom us. You have worked in the quarter for years, and are worth more than the whole police force. The mysterious instincts that are a part of my Eastern heritage are alert to danger. I feel peril for us both, near, creeping closer, gliding around us like serpents in the darkness!'

'But I can't stay here,' he scowled worriedly. 'We can't barricade ourselves and wait for them to starve us out. I've got to hit back – find out who's behind all this. The best defence is a good offence. But I can't leave you here unguarded, either. Damn!' He clenched his big fists and shook his head like a baffled bull in his perplexity.

'There is one man in the city besides yourself I could trust,' she said suddenly. 'One worth more than all the police. With him guarding me I could sleep safely.'

'Who is he?'

'Khoda Khan.'

'That fellow? Why, I thought he'd skipped months ago.'

'No; he's been hiding in Levant Street.'

'But he's a confounded killer himself!'

'No, he isn't; not according to his standards, which means as much to him as yours do to you. He's an Afghan who was raised in a code of blood-feud and vengeance. He's as honourable according to his creed of life as you or I. And he's my friend. He'd die for me.'

'I reckon that means you've been hiding him from the law,' said Harrison with a searching glance which she did not seek to evade. He made no further comment. River Street is not South Park Avenue. Harrison's own methods were not always orthodox, but they generally got results.

'Can you reach him?' he asked abruptly. She nodded.

'All right. Call him and tell him to beat it up here. Tell him he won't be molested by the police, and after the brawl's over, he can go back into hiding. But after that it's open season if I catch him. Use your phone. Wire may be tapped, but we'll have to take the chance. I'll go downstairs and use the booth in the office. Lock the door, and don't open it to anybody until I get back.'

When the bolts clicked behind him, Harrison turned down the corridor toward the stairs. The apartment house boasted no elevator. He watched all sides warily as he went. A peculiarity of architecture had, indeed, practically isolated that wing. The wall opposite Joan's doors was blank. The only way to reach the other suites on that floor was to descend the stair and ascend another on the other side of the building.

As he reached the stair he swore softly; his heel had crunched a small vial on the first step. With some vague suspicion of a planted poison trap he stooped and gingerly investigated the splintered bits and the spilled contents. There was a small pool of colourless liquid which gave off a pungent, musky odour, but there seemed nothing lethal about it.

'Some damned Oriental perfume Joan dropped, I reckon,' he decided. He descended the twisting stair without further delay and was presently in the booth in the office which opened on the street; a sleepy clerk dozed behind the desk.

Harrison got the chief of police on the wire and began abruptly.

'Say, Hoolihan, you remember that Afghan, Khoda Khan, who knifed a Chinaman about three months ago? Yes, that's the one. Well, listen: I'm using him on a job for a while, so tell your men to lay off, if they see him. Pass the word along *pronto*. Yes, I know it's very irregular; so's the job I hold down. In this case it's the choice of using a fugitive from the law, or seeing a law-abiding citizen murdered. Never mind what it's all about. This is my job, and I've got to handle it my own way. All right; thanks.'

He hung up the receiver, thought vigorously for a few minutes, and then dialled another number that was definitely not related to the police station. In place of the chief's booming voice there sounded at the other end of the wire a squeaky whine framed in the argot of the underworld.

'Listen, Johnny,' said Harrison with his customary abruptness, 'you told me you thought you had a lead on the Kossova murder. What about it?'

'It wasn't no lie, boss!' The voice at the other end trembled with excitement. 'I got a tip, and it's big! – *big*! I can't spill it over the phone, and I don't dare stir out. But if you'll meet me at Shan Yang's hop joint, I'll give you the dope. It'll knock you loose from your props, believe me it will!'

'I'll be there in an hour,' promised the detective. He left the booth and glanced briefly out into the street. It was a misty night, as so many River Street nights are. Traffic was only a dim echo from some distant, busier section. Drifting fog dimmed the street lamps, shrouding the forms of occasional passers-by. The stage was set for murder; it only awaited the appearance of the actors in the dark drama.

Harrison mounted the stairs again. They wound up out of the office and up into the third-storey wing without opening upon the second floor at all. The architecture, like much of it in or near the Oriental section, was rather unusual. People of the quarter were notoriously fond of privacy, and even apartment houses were built with this passion in mind. His feet made no sound on the thickly carpeted stairs, though a slight crunching at the top step reminded him of the broken vial again momentarily. He had stepped on the splinters.

He knocked at the locked door, answered Joan's tense challenge and was admitted. He found the girl more self-possessed.

'I talked with Khoda Khan. He's on his way here now. I warned him that the wire might be tapped – that our enemies might know as soon as I called him, and try to stop him on his way here.'

'Good,' grunted the detective. 'While I'm waiting for him I'll have a look at your suite.'

There were four rooms: drawing room in front, with a large bedroom behind it, and behind that two smaller rooms, the maid's bedroom and the bathroom. The maid was not there, because Joan had sent her away at the first intimation of danger threatening. The corridor ran parallel with the suite, and the drawing room, large bedroom and bathroom opened upon it. That made three doors to consider. The drawing room had one big east window, overlooking the street, and one on the south. The big bedroom had one south window, and the maid's room one south and one west window. The bathroom had one window, a small one in the west wall, overlooking a small court bounded by a tangle of alleys and board-fenced backyards.

'Three outside doors and six windows to be watched, and this the top storey,' muttered the detective. 'I still think I ought to get some cops here.' But he spoke without conviction. He was investigating the bathroom when Joan called him cautiously from the drawing room, telling him that she thought she had heard a faint scratching outside the door. Gun in hand he opened the bathroom door and peered out into the corridor. It was empty. No shape of horror stood before the drawing room door. He closed the door, called reassuringly to the girl, and completed his inspection, grunting approval. Joan La Tour was a daughter of the Oriental quarter. Long ago she had provided against secret enemies as far as special locks and bolts could provide. The windows were guarded with heavy iron-braced shutters, and there was no trapdoor, dumb waiter nor skylight anywhere in the suite.

'Looks like you're ready for a siege,' he commented.

'I am. I have canned goods laid away to last for weeks. With Khoda Khan I can hold the fort indefinitely. If things get too hot for you, you'd better come back here yourself . . . if you can. It's safer than the police station – unless they burn the house down.'

A soft rap on the door brought them both around.

'Who is it?' called Joan warily.

'I, Khoda Khan, *sahiba*,' came the answer in a low-pitched, but strong and resonant voice. Joan sighed deeply and unlocked the door. A tall figure bowed with a stately gesture and entered.

Khoda Khan was taller than Harrison, and though he lacked something of the American's sheer bulk, his shoulders were equally broad, and his garments could not conceal the hard lines of his limbs, the tigerish suppleness of his motions. His garb was a curious combination of costume, which is common in River Street. He wore a turban which well set off his hawk nose and black beard, and a long silk coat hung nearly to his knees. His trousers were conventional, but a silk sash girdled his lean waist, and his foot-gear was Turkish slippers.

In any costume it would have been equally evident that there was something wild and untameable about the man. His eyes blazed as no civilised man's ever did, and his sinews were like coiled springs under his coat. Harrison felt much as he would have felt if a panther had padded into the room, for the moment placid but ready at an instant's notice to go flying into flaming-eyed, red-taloned action.

'I thought you'd left the country,' he said.

The Afghan smiled, a glimmer of white amidst the dark tangle of his beard.

'Nay, *sahib*. That son of a dog I knifed did not die.'

'You're lucky he didn't,' commented Harrison. 'If you kill him you'll hang, sure.'

'*Inshallah*,' agreed Khoda Khan cheerfully. 'But it was a matter of izzat – *honour*. The dog fed me swine's flesh. But no matter. The *memsahib* called me and I came.'

'All right. As long as she needs your protection the police won't arrest you. But when the matter's finished, things stand as they were. I'll give you time to hide again, if you wish, and then I'll try to catch you as I have in the past. Or if you want to surrender and stand trial, I'll promise you as much leniency as possible.'

'You speak fairly,' answered Khoda Khan. 'I will protect the *memsahib*, and when our enemies are dead, you and I will begin our feud anew.'

'Do you know anything about these murders?'

'Nay, *sahib*. The *memsahib* called me, saying Mongol dogs threatened her. I came swiftly, over the roofs, lest they seek to ambush me. None molested me. But here is something I found outside the door.'

He opened his hand and exhibited a bit of silk, evidently torn from his sash. On it lay a crushed object that Harrison did not recognise. But Joan recoiled with a low cry.

'God! A black scorpion of Assam!'

'Aye – whose sting is death. I saw it running up and down before the door, seeking entrance. Another man might have stepped upon it without seeing it, but I was on my guard, for I smelled the Flower of Death as I came up the stairs. I saw the thing at the door and crushed it before it could sting me.'

'What do you mean by the Flower of Death?' demanded Harrison.

'It grows in the jungles where these vermin abide. Its scent attracts them as wine draws a drunkard. A trail of the juice had somehow been laid to this door. Had the door been opened before I slew it, it would have darted in and struck whoever happened to be in its way.'

Harrison swore under his breath, remembering the faint scratching noise Joan had heard outside the door.

'I get it now! They put a bottle of that juice on the stairs where it was sure to be stepped on. I did step on it, and broke it, and got the liquid on my shoe. Then I tracked down the stairs, leaving the scent wherever I stepped. Came back upstairs, stepped in the stuff again and tracked it on through the door. Then somebody downstairs turned that scorpion loose – the devil!! That means they've been in this house since I was downstairs! – may be hiding somewhere here now! But somebody had to come into the office to put the scorpion on the trail – I'll ask the clerk – '

'He sleeps like the dead,' said Khoda Khan. 'He did not waken when I entered and mounted the stairs. What matters if the house is full of Mongols? These doors are strong, and I am alert!' From beneath his coat he drew the terrible Khyber knife – a yard long, with an edge like a razor. 'I have slain *men* with this,' he announced, grinning like a bearded mountain devil. 'Pathans, Indians, a Russian or so. These Mongols are dogs on whom the good steel will be shamed.'

'Well,' grunted Harrison. 'I've got an appointment that's overdue now. I feel queer walking out and leaving you two to fight these devils alone. But there'll be no safety for us until I've smashed this gang at its root, and that's what I'm out to do.'

'They'll kill you as you leave the building,' said Joan with conviction.

'Well, I've got to risk it. If you're attacked call the police anyway, and call me, at Shan Yang's joint. I'll come back here some time before dawn. But I'm hoping the tip I expect to get will enable me to hit straight at whoever's after us.'

He went down the hallway with an eerie feeling of being watched, and scanned the stairs as if he expected to see it swarming with black scorpions, and he shied wide of the broken glass on the step. He had an uncomfortable sensation of duty ignored, in spite of himself, though he knew that his two companions did not want the police, and that in dealing with the East it is better to heed the advice of the East.

The clerk still sagged behind his desk. Harrison shook him without avail. The man was not asleep; he was drugged. But his heartbeat was regular, and the detective believed he was in no danger. Anyway, Harrison had no more time to waste. If he kept Johnny Kleck waiting too long, the fellow might become panicky and bolt, to hide in some rat-run for weeks.

He went into the street, where the lamps gleamed luridly through the drifting river mist, half expecting a knife to be thrown at him, or to find a cobra coiled on the seat of his automobile. But he found nothing his suspicion anticipated, even though he lifted the hood and the rumble-seat to see if a bomb had been planted. Satisfying himself at last, he climbed in, and the girl watching him through the slits of a third-storey shutter sighed relievedly to see him roar away unmolested.

Khoda Khan had gone through the rooms, giving approval in his beard of the locks, and having extinguished the lights in the other chambers he returned to the drawing room, where he turned out all lights except one small desk lamp. It shed a pool of light in the centre of the room, leaving the rest in shadowy vagueness.

'Darkness baffles rogues as well as honest men,' he said sagely, 'and I see like a cat in the dark.'

He sat cross-legged near the door that let into the bedroom, which he left partly open. He merged with the shadows so that all of him Joan could make out with any distinctness was his turban and the glimmer of his eyes as he turned his head.

'We will remain in this room, *sahiba*,' he said. 'Having failed with poison and reptile, it is certain that men will next be sent. Lie down on that divan and sleep, if you can. I will keep watch.'

Joan obeyed, but she did not sleep. Her nerves seemed to thrum with tautness. The silence of the house oppressed her, and the few noises of the street made her start.

Khoda Khan sat motionless as a statue, imbued with the savage patience and immobility of the hills that bred him. Grown to manhood on the raw barbaric edge of the world, where survival depended on personal ability, his senses were whetted keener than is possible for civilised men. Even Harrison's trained faculties were blunt in comparison. Khoda Khan could still smell the faint aroma of the Flower of Death, mingled with the acrid odour of the crushed scorpion. He heard and identified every sound in or outside the house – knew which were natural, and which were not.

He heard the sounds on the roof long before his warning hiss brought Joan upright on the divan. The Afghan's eyes glowed like phosphorus in the shadows and his teeth glimmered dimly in a savage grin. Joan looked at him inquiringly. Her civilised ears heard nothing. But he heard and with his ears followed the sounds accurately and located the place where they halted. Joan heard something then, a faint scratching somewhere in the building, but she did not identify it – as Khoda Khan did – as the forcing of the shutters on the bathroom window.

With a quick reassuring gesture to her, Khoda Khan rose and melted like a slinking leopard into the darkness of the bedroom. She took up a blunt-nosed automatic, with no great conviction of reliance upon it, and groped on the table for a bottle of wine, feeling an intense need of stimulants. She was shaking in every limb and cold sweat was gathering on her flesh. She remembered the cigarettes, but the unbroken seal on the bottle reassured her. Even the wisest have their thoughtless moments. It was not until she had begun to drink that the peculiar flavour made her realise that the man who had shifted the cigarettes might just as easily have taken a bottle of wine and left another in its place, a facsimile that included an unbroken seal. She fell back on the divan, gagging.

Khoda Khan wasted no time, because he heard other sounds, out in the hall. His ears told him, as he crouched by the bathroom door, that the shutters had been forced – done almost in silence – and now the window was being jemmied. Then he heard something stealthy and bulky drop into the room. Then it was that he threw open the door and charged in like a typhoon, his long knife held low.

Enough light filtered into the room from outside to limn a powerful, crouching figure, with dim snarling yellow features. The intruder yelped explosively, started a motion – and then the long Khyber knife, driven by an arm nerved to the fury of the Himalayas, ripped him open from groin to breastbone.

Khoda Khan did not pause. He knew there was only one man in the room, but through the open window he saw a thick rope dangling from above. He sprang forward, grasped it with both hands and heaved backward like a bull. The men on the roof holding it released it to keep from being jerked headlong over the edge, and he tumbled backward, sprawling over the corpse, the loose rope in his hands. He yelped exultantly, then sprang up and glided to the door that opened into the corridor. Unless they had another rope, which was unlikely, the men on the roof were temporarily out of the fight.

He flung open the door and ducked deeply. A hatchet cut a great chip out the jamb, and he stabbed upward once, then sprang over a writhing body into the corridor, jerking a big pistol from its hidden scabbard.

The bright light of the corridor did not blind him. He saw a second hatchet-man crouching by the bedroom door, and a man in the silk robes of a mandarin working at the lock of the drawing room door. He was between them and the stairs. As they wheeled toward him he shot the hatchet-man in the belly. An automatic spat in the hand of the mandarin, and Khoda Khan felt the wind of the bullet. The next instant his own gun roared again and the Manchu staggered, the pistol flying from a hand that was suddenly a dripping red pulp. Then he whipped a long knife from his robes with his left hand and came along the corridor like a hurricane, his eyes glaring and his silk garments whipping about him.

Khoda Khan shot him through the head and the mandarin fell so near his feet that the long knife stuck into the floor and quivered a matter of inches from the Afghan's slipper.

But Khoda Khan paused only long enough to pass his knife through the hatchet-man he had shot in the belly – for his fighting ethics were those of the savage Hills – and then he turned and ran back into the bathroom. He fired a shot through the window, though the men on the roof were making [no] further demonstration, and then ran through the bedroom, snapping on lights as he went.

'I have slain the dogs, *sahiba*!' he exclaimed. 'By Allah, they have tasted lead and steel! Others are on the roof but they are helpless for the moment. But men will come to investigate the shots, that being the custom of the *sahibs*, so it is expedient that we decide on our further actions, and the proper lies to tell – Allah!'

Joan La Tour stood bolt upright, clutching the back of the divan. Her face was the colour of marble, and the expression was rigid too, like a mask of horror carved in stone. Her dilated eyes blazed like weird black fire.

'Allah shield us against Shaitan the Damned!' ejaculated Khoda Khan, making a sign with his fingers that antedated Islam by some thousands of years. 'What has happened to you, *sahiba*?'

He moved toward her, to be met by a scream that sent him cowering back, cold sweat starting out on his flesh.

'Keep back!' she cried in a voice he did not recognise. 'You are a demon! You are all demons! I see you! I hear your cloven feet padding in the night! I see your eyes blazing from the shadows! Keep your taloned hands from me! *Aie*!' Foam flecked her lips as she screamed blasphemies in English and Arabic that made Khoda Khan's hair stand stiffly on end.

'*Sahiba*!' he begged, trembling like a leaf. 'I am no demon! I am Khoda Khan! I – ' His outstretched hand touched her, and with an awful shriek she turned and darted for the door, tearing at the bolts. He sprang to stop her, but in her frenzy she was even quicker than he. She whipped the door open, eluded his grasping hand and flew down the corridor, deaf to his anguished yells.

When Harrison left Joan's house, he drove straight to Shan Yang's dive, which, in the heart of River Street, masqueraded as a low-grade drinking joint. It was late. Only a few derelicts huddled about the bar, and he noticed that the barman was a Chinaman that he had never seen before. He stared impassively at Harrison, but jerked a thumb toward the back door, masked by dingy curtains, when the detective asked abruptly: 'Johnny Kleck here?'

Harrison passed through the door, traversed a short dimly-lighted hallway and rapped authoritatively on the door at the other end. In the silence he heard rats scampering. A steel disk in the centre of the door shifted and a slanted black eye glittered in the opening.

'Open the door, Shan Yang,' ordered Harrison impatiently, and the eye was withdrawn, accompanied by the rattling of bolts and chains.

He pushed open the door and entered the room whose illumination was scarcely better than that of the corridor. It was a large, dingy, drab affair, lined with bunks. Fires sputtered in braziers, and Shan Yang was making his way to his accustomed seat behind a low counter near the wall. Harrison spent but a single casual glance on the familiar figure, the well-known dingy silk jacket worked in gilt dragons. Then he strode across the room to a door in the wall opposite the counter to which Shan Yang was making his way. This was an opium joint and Harrison knew it – knew those figures in the bunks were sleeping the sleep of the smoke. Why he had not raided it, as he had raided and destroyed other opium-dens, only Harrison could have said. But law-enforcement on River Street is not the orthodox routine it is on Baskerville Avenue, for instance. Harrison's reasons were those of expediency and necessity. Sometimes certain conventions have to be sacrificed for the sake of more important gains – especially when the law-enforcement of a whole district (and in the Oriental quarter) rests on one's shoulders.

A characteristic smell pervaded the dense atmosphere, in spite of the reek of dope and unwashed bodies – the dank odour of the river, which hangs over the River Street dives or wells up from their floors like the black intangible spirit of the quarter itself. Shan Yang's dive, like many others, was built on the very bank of the river. The back room projected out over the water on rotting piles, at which the black river lapped hungrily.

Harrison opened the door, entered and pushed it to behind him, his lips framing a greeting that was never uttered. He stood dumbly, glaring.

He was in a small dingy room, bare except for a crude table and some chairs. An oil lamp on the table cast a smoky light. And in that light he saw Johnny Kleck. The man stood bolt upright against the far wall, his arms spread like a crucifix, rigid, his eyes glassy and staring, his mean, ratty features twisted in a frozen grin. He did not speak, and Harrison's gaze, travelling down him, halted with a shock. Johnny's feet did not touch the floor by several inches . . .

Harrison's big blue pistol jumped into his hand. Johnny Kleck was dead; that grin was a contortion of horror and agony. He was crucified to the wall by skewer-like dagger blades through his wrists and ankles, his ears spiked to the wall to keep his head upright. But that was not what had killed him. The bosom of Johnny's shirt was charred, and there was a round, blackened hole.

Feeling suddenly sick the detective wheeled, opened the door and stepped back into the larger room. The light seemed dimmer, the smoke thicker than ever. No mumblings came from the bunks; the fires in the braziers burned blue, with weird sputterings. Shan Yang crouched behind the counter. His shoulders moved as if he were tallying beads on an abacus.

'Shan Yang!' the detective's voice grated harshly in the murky silence. 'Who's been in that room tonight besides Johnny Kleck?'

The man behind the counter straightened and looked full at him, and Harrison felt his skin crawl. Above the gilt-worked jacket an unfamiliar face returned his gaze. That was no Shan Yang; it was a man he had never seen – it was a Mongol. He started and stared about him as the men in the bunks rose with supple ease. They were not Chinese; they were Mongols to a man, and their eyes were not clouded by drugs.

With a curse Harrison sprang toward the outer door and with a rush they were on him. His gun crashed and a man staggered in mid-stride. Then the lights went out, the braziers were overturned, and in the Stygian blackness hard bodies caromed against the detective. Long-nailed fingers clawed at his throat, thick arms locked about his waist and legs. Somewhere a sibilant voice was hissing orders.

Harrison's mauling left worked like a piston, crushing flesh and bone; his right wielded the gun barrel like a club. He forged toward the unseen door blindly, dragging his assailants by sheer strength. He seemed to be wading through a solid mass, as if the darkness had turned to bone and muscle about him. A knife licked through his coat, stinging his skin, and then he gasped as a silk cord looped about his neck, shutting off his wind, sinking deeper and deeper into the straining flesh. Blindly he jammed the muzzle against the nearest body and pulled the trigger. At the muffled concussion something fell away from him and the strangling agony lessened. Gasping for breath he groped and tore the cord away – then he was borne down under a rush of heavy bodies and something smashed savagely against his head. The darkness exploded in a shower of sparks that were instantly quenched in Stygian blackness.

The smell of the river was in Steve Harrison's nostrils as he regained his addled senses, river-scent mingled with the odour of stale blood. The blood, he realised, when he had enough sense to realise anything, was clotted on his own scalp. His head swam and he tried to raise a hand to it, thereby discovering that he was bound hand and foot with cords that cut into the flesh. A candle was dazzling his eyes, and for a while he could see nothing else. Then things began to assume their proper proportions, and objects grew out of nothing and became identifiable.

He was lying on a bare floor of new, unpainted wood, in a large square chamber, the walls of which were of stone, without paint or plaster. The ceiling was likewise of stone, with heavy, bare beams, and there was an open trap-door almost directly above him, through which, in spite of the candle, he got a glimpse of stars. Fresh air flowed through that trap, bearing with it the river-smell stronger than ever. The chamber was bare of furniture, the candle stuck in a niche in the wall. Harrison swore, wondering if he was delirious. This was like an experience in a dream, with everything unreal and distorted.

He tried to struggle to a sitting position, but that made his head swim, so that he lay back and swore fervently. He yelled wrathfully, and a face peered down at him through the trap. He cursed the face and it mocked him and was withdrawn. The noise of the door softly opening checked Harrison's profanity and he wriggled around to glare at the intruder.

And he glared in silence, feeling an icy prickling up and down his spine. Once before he had lain bound and helpless, staring up at a tall black-robed figure whose yellow eyes glimmered from the shadow of a dusky hood. But that man was dead; Harrison had seen him cut down by the scimitar of a maddened Druse.

'Erlik Khan!' The words were forced out of him. He licked lips suddenly dry.

'*Aie!*' It was the same ghostly, hollow voice that had chilled him in the old days. 'Erlik Khan, the Lord of the Dead.'

'Are you a man or a ghost?' demanded Harrison.

'I live.'

'But I saw Ali ibn Suleyman kill you!' exclaimed the detective. 'He slashed you across the head with a heavy sword that was sharp as a razor. He was a stronger man than I am. He struck with the full power of his arm. Your hood fell in two pieces – '

'And I fell like a dead man in my own blood,' finished Erlik Khan. 'But the steel cap I wore – as I wear now – under my hood, saved my life as it has more than once. The terrible stroke cracked it across the top and cut my scalp, fracturing my skull and causing concussion of the brain. But I lived, and some of my faithful followers, who escaped the sword of the Druse, carried me down through the subterranean tunnels which led from my house, and so I escaped the burning building. But I lay like a dead man for weeks, and it was not until a very wise man was brought from Mongolia that I recovered my senses, and sanity.

'But now I am ready to take up my work where I left off, though I must rebuild much. Many of my former followers had forgotten my authority. Some required to be taught anew who was master.'

'And you've been teaching them,' grunted Harrison, recovering his pugnacious composure.

'True. Some examples had to be made. One man fell from a roof; a snake bit another, yet another ran into knives in a dark alley. Then there was another matter. Joan La Tour betrayed me in the old days. She knows too many secrets. She had to die. So that she might taste agony in anticipation, I sent her a page from my book of the dead.'

'Your devils killed Kleck,' accused Harrison.

'Of course. All wires leading from the girl's apartment house are tapped. I myself heard your conversation with Kleck. That is why you were not attacked when you left the building. I saw that you were playing into my hands. I sent my men to take possession of Shan Yang's dive. He had no more use for his jacket, presently, so one donned it to deceive you. Kleck had somehow learned of my return; these stool pigeons are clever. But he had time to regret. A man dies hard with a white-hot point of iron bored through his breast.'

Harrison said nothing and presently the Mongol continued.

'I wrote your name in my book because I recognised you as my most dangerous opponent. It was because of you that Ali ibn Suleyman turned against me.

'I am rebuilding my empire again, but more solidly. First I shall consolidate River Street, and create a political machine to rule the city. The men in office now do not suspect my existence. If all were to die, it would not be hard to find others to fill their places . . . men who are not indifferent to the clink of gold.'

'You're mad,' growled Harrison. 'Control a whole city government from a dive in River Street?'

'It has been done,' answered the Mongol tranquilly. 'I will strike like a cobra from the dark. Only the men who obey my agent will live. He will be a figurehead whom men will think the real power, while I remain unseen. You might have been he, if you had a little more intelligence.'

He took a bulky object from under his arm, a thick book with glossy black covers . . . ebony with green jade hinges. He riffled the night-hued pages and Harrison saw they were covered with crimson characters.

'My book of the dead,' said Erlik Khan. 'Many names have been crossed out. Many more have been added since I recovered my sanity. Some of them would interest you; they include names of the mayor, the chief of police, district attorney, a number of aldermen.'

'That lick must have addled your brains permanently,' snarled Harrison. 'Do you think you can substitute a whole city government and get away with it?'

'I can and will. These men will die in various ways, and men of my own choice will succeed them in office. Within a year I will hold this city in the palm of my hand, and there will be none to interfere with me.'

Lying staring up at the bizarre figure, whose features were, as always, shadowed beyond recognition by the hood, Harrison's flesh crawled with the conviction that the Mongol was indeed-mad. His crimson dreams, always ghastly, were too grotesque and incredible for the visions of a wholly sane man. Yet he was dangerous as a maddened cobra. His monstrous plot must ultimately fail, yet he held the lives of many men in his hand. And Harrison lay bound and helpless before him. The detective cursed in fury.

'Always the man of violence,' mocked Erlik Khan, with the suggestion of scorn in his voice. 'Barbarian! who lays his trust in guns and blades, who would check the stride of imperial power with blows of the naked fists! Brainless arm striking blind blows! Well, you have struck your last. Smell the river damp that creeps in through the ceiling? Soon it shall enfold you utterly and your dreams and aspirations will be one with the mist of the river.'

'Where are we?' demanded Harrison.

'On an island below the city, where the marshes begin. Once there were warehouses here, and a factory, but they were abandoned as the city grew in the other direction, and have been crumbling into ruin for twenty years. I purchased the entire island through one of my agents, and am rebuilding to suit my own purposes an old stone mansion which stood here before the factory was built. None notices, because my own henchmen are the workmen, and no one ever comes to this marshy island. The house is invisible from the river, hidden as it is among the tangle of old rotting warehouses. You came here in a motorboat which was anchored beneath the rotting wharves behind Shan Yang's dive. Another boat will presently fetch my men who were sent to dispose of Joan La Tour.'

'They may not find that so easy,' commented the detective.

'Never fear. I know she summoned that hairy wolf, Khoda Khan, to her aid, and it's true that my men failed to slay him before he reached her. But I suppose it was a false sense of trust that caused you to make your appointment with Kleck. I rather expected you to remain with the foolish girl and try to protect her in your way.'

Somewhere below them a gong sounded. Erlik Khan did not start, but there was a surprise in the lift of his head. He closed the black book.

'I have wasted enough time on you,' he said. 'Once before I bade you farewell in one of my dungeons. Then the fanaticism of a crazy Druse saved you. This time there will be no upset of my plans. The only men in this house know no law but my will. I go, but you will not be lonely. Soon one will come to you.'

And with a low, chilling laugh the phantom-like figure moved through the door and disappeared. Outside a lock clicked, and then there was stillness.

The silence was broken suddenly by a muffled scream. It came from somewhere below and was repeated half a dozen times. Harrison shuddered. No one who has ever visited an insane asylum could fail to recognise that sound. It was the shrieking of a mad woman. After these cries the silence seemed even more stifling and menacing.

Harrison swore to quiet his feelings, and again the velvet-capped head leered down at him through the trap.

'Grin, you yellow-bellied ape!' roared Harrison, tugging at his cords until the veins stood out on his temples. 'If I could break these damned ropes I'd knock that grin around where your pigtail ought to be, you – ' The head vanished from the trap and there came a sound like the blow of a butcher's cleaver.

Then another face was poked into the trap – a wild, bearded face, with blazing, bloodshot eyes, and surmounted by a dishevelled turban.

'*Sahib*!' hissed the apparition.

'Khoda Khan!' ejaculated the detective, galvanised. 'What the devil are you doing here?'

'Softly!' muttered the Afghan. 'Let not the accursed ones hear!'

He tossed the loose end of a rope ladder down through the trap and came down in a rush, his bare feet making no sound as he hit the floor. He held his long knife in his teeth, and blood dripped from the point.

Squatting beside the detective he cut him free with reckless slashes that threatened to slice flesh as well as hemp. The Afghan was quivering with half-controlled passion. His teeth gleamed like a wolf's fangs amidst the tangle of his beard.

Harrison sat up, chafing his swollen wrists.

'Where's Joan? Quick, man, where is she?'

'Here! In this accursed den!'

'But – '

'That was she screaming a few minutes ago,' broke in the Afghan, and Harrison's flesh crawled with a vague monstrous premonition.

'But that was a mad woman!' he almost whispered.

'The *sahiba* is mad,' said Khoda Khan sombrely. 'Hearken, *sahib*, and then judge if the fault is altogether mine.

'After you left, the accursed ones let down a man from the roof on a rope. Him I knifed, and I slew three more who sought to force the doors. But when I returned to the *sahiba*, she knew me not. She fled from me into the street, and other devils must have been lurking nearby, because as she ran shrieking along the sidewalk, a big automobile loomed out of the fog and an arm dragged her into the car, from under my very fingers. I saw his accursed face by the light of a street lamp.

'Knowing she were better dead by a bullet than in their hands, I emptied my pistol after the car, but it fled like Shaitan the Damned from the face of Allah, and if I hit anyone in it, I know not. Then as I rent my garments and cursed the day of my birth – for I could not pursue it on foot – Allah willed that another automobile should appear. It was driven by a young man in evening clothes, returning from a revel, no doubt, and being cursed with curiosity he slowed down near the curb to observe my grief.

'So, praising Allah, I sprang in beside him and placing my knife point against his ribs bade him go with speed, and he obeyed in great fear. The car of the damned ones was out of sight, but presently I glimpsed it again, and exhorted the youth to greater speed, so the machine seemed to fly like the steed of the Prophet. So, presently I saw the car halt at the river bank. I made the youth halt likewise, and he sprang out and fled in the other direction in terror.

'I ran through the darkness, hot for the blood of the accursed ones, but before I could reach the bank I saw four Mongols leave the car, carrying the *memsahib* who was bound and gagged, and they entered a motorboat and headed out into the river toward an island which lay on the breast of the water like a dark cloud.

'I cast up and down on the shore like a madman, and was about to leap in and swim, though the distance was great, when I came upon a boat chained to a pile, but one driven by oars. I gave praise to Allah and cut the chain with my knife – see the nick in the edge? – and rowed after the accursed ones with great speed.

'They were far ahead of me, but Allah willed it that their engine should sputter and cease when they had almost reached the island. So I took heart, hearing them cursing in their heathen tongue, and hoped to draw alongside and slay them all before they were aware of me. They saw me not in the darkness, nor heard my oars because of their own noises, but before I could reach-them the accursed engine began again. So they reached a wharf on the marshy shore ahead of me, but they lingered to make the boat fast, so I was not too far behind them as they bore the *memsahib* through the shadows of the crumbling shacks which stood all about.

'Then I was hot to overtake and slay them, but before I could come up with them they had reached the door of a great stone house – this one, *sahib* – set in a tangle of rotting buildings. A steel fence surrounded it, with razor-edged spearheads set along the top, but by Allah! that could not hinder a *lifter* of the Khyber! I went over it without so much as tearing my garments. Inside was a second wall of stone, but it stood in ruins.

'I crouched in the shadows near the house and saw that the windows were heavily barred and the doors strong. Moreover, the lower part of the house is full of armed men. So I climbed a corner of the wall, and it was not easy, but presently I reached the roof which at that part is flat, with a parapet. I expected a watcher, and so there was, but he was too busy taunting his captive to see or hear me until my knife sent him to Hell. Here is his dagger; he bore no gun.'

Harrison mechanically took the wicked, lean-bladed poniard.

'But what caused Joan to go mad?'

'*Sahib*, there was a broken wine bottle on the floor, and a goblet. I had no time to investigate it, but I know that wine must have been poisoned with the juice of the fruit called the black pomegranate. She cannot have drunk much, or she would have died frothing and champing like a mad dog. But only a little will rob one of sanity. It grows in the jungles of Indo-China, and white men say it is a lie. But it is no lie; thrice I have seen men die after having drunk its juice, and more than once I have seen men, and women too, turn mad because of it. I have travelled in that hellish country where it grows.'

'God!' Harrison's foundations were shaken by nausea. Then his big hands clenched into chunks of iron and baleful fire glimmered in his savage blue eyes. The weakness of horror and revulsion was followed by cold fury, dangerous as the blood-hunger of a timber wolf.

'She may be already dead,' he muttered thickly. 'But dead or alive we'll send Erlik Khan to Hell. Try that door.'

It was of heavy teak, braced with bronze straps.

'It is locked,' muttered the Afghan. 'We will burst it.'

He was about to launch his shoulder against it when he stopped short, the long Khyber knife jumping into his fist like a beam of light.

'Someone approaches!' he whispered, and a second later Harrison's duller ears caught a cat-like tread.

Instantly he acted. He shoved the Afghan behind the door and sat down quickly in the centre of the room, wrapped a piece of rope about his ankles and then lay full length, his arms behind and under him. He was lying on the other pieces of severed cord, concealing them, and to the casual glance he resembled a man lying bound hand and foot. The Afghan understood and grinned hugely.

Harrison worked with the celerity of trained mind and muscles that eliminates fumbling delay and bungling. He accomplished his purpose in a matter of seconds and without undue noise. A key grated in the lock as he settled himself, and then the door swung open. A giant Mongol stood limned in the opening. His head was shaven, his square features passionless as the face of a copper idol. In one hand he carried a curiously shaped ebony block, in the other a mace such as was borne by the horsemen of Genghis Khan – a straight-hafted iron bludgeon with a round head covered with steel points, and a knob on the other end to keep the hand from slipping.

He did not see Khoda Khan because when he threw back the door, the Afghan was hidden behind it. Khoda Khan did not stab him as he entered because the Afghan could not see into the outer corridor, and had no way of knowing how many men were following the first.

But the Mongol was alone, and he did not bother to shut the door. He went straight to the man lying on the floor, scowling slightly to see the rope ladder hanging down through the trap, as if it was not usual to leave it that way, but he did not show any suspicion or call to the man on the roof.

He did not examine Harrison's cords. The detective presented the appearance the Mongol had expected, and this fact blunted his faculties as anything taken for granted is likely to do. As he bent down, over his shoulder Harrison saw Khoda Khan glide from behind the door as silently as a panther.

Leaning his mace against his leg, spiked head on the floor, the Mongol grasped Harrison's shirt bosom with one hand, lifted his head and shoulders clear of the floor, while he shoved the block under his head. Like twin striking snakes the detective's hands whipped from behind him and locked on the Mongol's bull throat.

There was no cry; instantly the Mongol's eyes distended and his lips parted in a grin of strangulation. With a terrific heave he reared upright, dragging Harrison with him, but not breaking his hold, and the weight of the big American pulled them both down again. Both hands tore frantically at Harrison's iron wrists; then the giant stiffened convulsively and brief agony reddened his black eyes. Khoda Khan had driven his knife between the Mongol's shoulders so that the point cut through the silk over the man's breastbone.

Harrison caught up the mace, grunting with savage satisfaction. It was a weapon more suited to his temperament than the dagger Khoda Khan had given him. No need to ask its use; if he had been bound and alone when the executioner entered, his brains would now have been clotting its spiked ball and the hollowed ebon block which so nicely accommodated a human head. Erlik Khan's executions varied along the whole gamut from the exquisitely subtle to the crudely bestial.

'The door's open,' said Harrison. 'Let's go!'

There were no keys on the body. Harrison doubted if the key in the door would fit any other in the building, but he locked the door and pocketed the key, hoping that would prevent the body from being soon discovered.

They emerged into a dim-lit corridor which presented the same unfinished appearance as the room they had just left. At the other end stairs wound down into shadowy gloom, and they descended warily, Harrison feeling along the wall to guide his steps. Khoda Khan seemed to see like a cat in the dark; he went down silently and surely. But it was Harrison who discovered the door. His hand, moving along the convex surface, felt the smooth stone give way to wood – a short narrow panel, through which a man could just squeeze. When the wall was covered with tapestry – as he knew it would be when Erlik Khan completed his house – it would be sufficiently hidden for a secret entrance.

Khoda Khan, behind him, was growing impatient at the delay, when somewhere below them both heard a noise simultaneously. It might have been a man ascending the winding stairs and it might not, but Harrison acted instinctively. He pushed and the door opened inward on noiseless oiled springs. A groping foot discovered narrow steps inside. With a whispered word to the Afghan he stepped through and Khoda Khan followed. He pulled the door shut again and they stood in total blackness with a curving wall on either hand. Harrison struck a match and a narrow stair was revealed, winding down.

'This place must be built like a castle,' Harrison muttered, wondering at the thickness of the walls. The match went out and they groped down in darkness too thick for even the Afghan to pierce. And suddenly both halted in their tracks. Harrison estimated that they had reached the level of the second floor, and through the inner wall came the mutter of voices. Harrison groped for another door, or a peep-hole for spying, but he found nothing of the sort. But straining his ear close to the stone, he began to understand what was being said beyond the wall, and a long-drawn hiss between clenched teeth told him that Khoda Khan likewise understood.

The first voice was Erlik Khan's; there was no mistaking that hollow reverberance. It was answered by a piteous, incoherent whimpering that brought sweat suddenly out on Harrison's flesh.

'No,' the Mongol was saying. 'I have come back, not from Hell as your barbarian superstitions suggest, but from a refuge unknown to your stupid police. I was saved from death by the steel cap I always wear beneath my coif. You are at a loss as to how you got here?'

'I don't understand!' It was the voice of Joan La Tour, half-hysterical, but undeniably sane. 'I remember opening a bottle of wine, and as soon as I drank I knew it was drugged. Then everything faded out . . . I don't remember anything except great black walls, and awful shapes skulking in the darkness. I ran through gigantic shadowy halls for a thousand years – '

'They were hallucinations of madness, of the juice of the black pomegranate,' answered Erlik Khan. Khoda Khan was muttering blasphemously in his beard until Harrison admonished him to silence with a fierce dig of his elbow. 'If you had drunk more you would have died like a rabid dog. As it was, you went insane. But I knew the antidote – possessed the drug that restored your sanity.'

'Why?' the girl whimpered bewilderedly.

'Because I did not wish you to die like a candle blown out in the dark, my beautiful white orchid. I wish you to be fully sane so as to taste to the last dregs the shame and agony of death, subtle and prolonged. For the exquisite, an exquisite death. For the coarse-fibered, the death of an ox, such as I have decreed for your friend Harrison.'

'That will be more easily decreed than executed,' she retorted with a flash of spirit.

'It is already accomplished,' the Mongol asserted imperturbably. 'The executioner has gone to him, and by this time Mr Harrison's head resembles a crushed egg.'

'Oh, God!' At the sick grief and pain in that moan Harrison winced and fought a frantic desire to shout out denial and reassurance.

Then she remembered something else to torture her.

'Khoda Khan! What have you done with Khoda Khan?'

The Afghan's fingers clamped like iron on Harrison's arm at the sound of his name.

'When my men brought you away they did not take time to deal with him,' replied the Mongol. 'They had not expected to take you alive, and when fate cast you into their hands, they came away in haste. He matters little. True, he killed four of my best men, but that was merely the deed of a wolf. He has no mentality. He and the detective are much alike – mere masses of brawn, brainless, helpless against intellect like mine. Presently I shall attend to him. His corpse shall be thrown on a dung-heap with a dead pig.'

'Allah!' Harrison felt Khoda Khan trembling with fury. 'Liar! I will feed his yellow guts to the rats!'

Only Harrison's grip on his arm kept the maddened Moslem from attacking the stone wall in an effort to burst through to his enemy. The detective was running his hand over the surface, seeking a door, but only blank stone rewarded him. Erlik Khan had not had time to provide his unfinished house with as many secrets as his rat-runs usually possessed.

They heard the Mongol clap his hands authoritatively, and they sensed the entrance of men into the room. Staccato commands foll-owed in Mongolian, there was a sharp cry of pain or fear, and then

silence followed the soft closing of a door. Though they could not
see, both men knew instinctively that the chamber on the other side
of the wall was empty. Harrison almost strangled with a panic of
helpless rage. He was penned in these infernal walls and Joan La
Tour was being borne away to some abominable doom.

'*Wallah*!' the Afghan was raving. 'They have taken her away to slay
her! Her life and our *izzat* is at stake! By the Prophet's beard and my
feet! I will burn this accursed house! I will slake the fire with Mongol
blood! In Allah's name, *sahib*, let us do something!'

'Come on!' snarled Harrison. 'There must be another door some-
where!'

Recklessly they plunged down the winding stair, and about the
time they had reached the first floor level, Harrison's groping hand
felt a door. Even as he found the catch, it moved under his fingers.
Their noise must have been heard through the wall, for the panel
opened, and a shaven head was poked in, framed in the square of
light. The Mongol blinked in the darkness, and Harrison brought
the mace down on his head, experiencing a vengeful satisfaction as he
felt the skull give way beneath the iron spikes. The man fell face
down in the narrow opening and Harrison sprang over his body into
the outer room before he took time to learn if there were others. But
the chamber was untenanted. It was thickly carpeted, the walls hung
with black velvet tapestries. The doors were of bronze-bound teak,
with gilt-worked arches. Khoda Khan presented an incongruous
contrast, bare-footed, with draggled turban and red-smeared knife.

But Harrison did not pause to philosophise. Ignorant as he was of
the house, one way was as good as another. He chose a door at
random and flung it open, revealing a wide corridor carpeted and
tapestried like the chamber. At the other end, through wide satin
curtains that hung from roof to floor, a file of men was just dis-
appearing – tall, black-silk clad Mongols, heads bent sombrely, like a
train of dusky ghosts. They did not look back.

'Follow them!' snapped Harrison. 'They must be headed for the
execution – '

Khoda Khan was already sweeping down the corridor like a venge-
ful whirlwind. The thick carpet deadened their footfalls, so even
Harrison's big shoes made no noise. There was a distinct feeling of
unreality, running silently down that fantastic hall – it was like a
dream in which natural laws are suspended. Even in that moment
Harrison had time to reflect that this whole night had been like a
nightmare, its violence and bloodshed like an evil dream. Erlik Khan

had loosed the forces of chaos and insanity; murder had gone mad, and its frenzy was imparted to all actions and men caught in its maelstrom,

Khoda Khan would have burst headlong through the curtains – he was already drawing breath for a yell, and lifting his knife – if Harrison had not seized him. The Afghan's sinews were like cords under the detective's hands, and Harrison doubted his own ability to restrain him forcibly, but a vestige of sanity remained to the hillman.

Pushing him back, Harrison gazed between the curtains. There was a great double-valved door there, but it was partly open, and he looked into the room beyond. Khoda Khan's beard was jammed hard against his neck as the Afghan glared over his shoulder.

It was a large chamber, hung like the others with black velvet on which golden dragons writhed. There were thick rugs, and lanterns hanging from the ivory-inlaid ceiling cast a red glow that made for illusion. Black-robed men ranged along the wall might have been shadows but for their glittering eyes.

On a throne-like chair of ebony sat a grim figure, motionless as an image except when its loose robes stirred in the faintly moving air. Harrison felt the short hairs prickle at the back of his neck, just as a dog's hackles rise at the sight of an enemy. Khoda Khan muttered some incoherent blasphemy.

The Mongol's throne was set against a side wall. No one stood near him as he sat in solitary magnificence, like an idol brooding on human doom. In the centre of the room stood what looked uncomfortably like a sacrificial altar – a curiously carved block of stone that might have come out of the heart of the Gobi. On that stone lay Joan La Tour, white as a marble statue, her arms outstretched like a crucifix, her hands and feet extending over the edges of the block. Her dilated eyes stared upward as one lost to hope, aware of doom and eager only for death to put an end to agony. The physical torture had not yet begun, but a gaunt half-naked brute squatted on his haunches at the end of the altar, heating the point of a bronze rod in a dish full of glowing coals.

'Damn!' It was half curse, half sob of fury bursting from Harrison's lips. Then he was hurled aside and Khoda Khan burst into the room like a flying dervish, bristling beard, blazing eyes, knife and all. Erlik Khan came erect with a startled guttural as the Afghan came tearing down the room like a headlong hurricane of destruction. The torturer sprang up just in time to meet the yard-long knife lashing down, and it split his skull down through the teeth.

'*Aie*!' It was a howl from a score of Mongol throats.

'*Allaho akabar*!' yelled Khoda Khan, whirling the red knife about his head. He threw himself on the altar, slashing at Joan's bonds with a frenzy that threatened to dismember the girl.

Then from all sides the black-robed figures swarmed in, not noticing in their confusion that the Afghan had been followed by another grim figure who came with less abandon but with equal ferocity.

They were aware of Harrison only when he dealt a prodigious sweep of his mace, right and left, bowling men over like ten-pins, and reached the altar through the gap made in the bewildered throng. Khoda Khan had freed the girl and he wheeled, spitting like a cat, his bared teeth gleaming and each hair of his beard stiffly on end.

'*Allah*!' he yelled, spat in the faces of the oncoming Mongols, crouched as if to spring into the midst of them, then whirled and rushed headlong at the ebony throne.

The speed and unexpectedness of the move were stunning. With a choked cry Erlik Khan fired and missed at point-blank range – and then the breath burst from Khoda Khan in an ear-splitting yell as his knife plunged into the Mongol's breast and the point sprang a hand's breadth out of his black-clad back.

The impetus of his rush unchecked, Khoda Khan hurtled into the falling figure, crashing it back onto the ebony throne which splintered under the impact of the two heavy bodies. Bounding up, wrenching his dripping knife free, Khoda Khan whirled it high and howled like a wolf.

'*Ya Allah*! Wearer of steel caps! Carry the taste of my knife in your guts to Hell with you!'

There was a long hissing intake of breath as the Mongols stared wide-eyed at the black-robed, red-smeared figure crumpled grotesquely among the ruins of the broken throne; and in the instant that they stood like frozen men, Harrison caught up Joan and ran for the nearest door, bellowing: 'Khoda Khan! This way! Quick!'

With a howl and a whickering of blades the Mongols were at his heels. Fear of steel in his back winged Harrison's big feet, and Khoda Khan ran slantingly across the room to meet him at the door.

'Haste, *sahib*! Down the corridor! I will cover your retreat!'

'No! Take Joan and run!' Harrison literally threw her into the Afghan's arms and wheeled back in the doorway, lifting the mace. He was as berserk in his own way as was Khoda Khan, frantic with the madness that sometimes inspired men in the midst of combat.

The Mongols came on as if they, too, were blood-mad. They jammed the door with square snarling faces and squat silk-clad bodies before he could slam it shut. Knives licked at him, and gripping the mace with both hands he wielded it like a flail, working awful havoc among the shapes that strove in the doorway, wedged by the pressure from behind. The lights, the upturned snarling faces that dissolved in crimson ruin beneath his flailing, all swam in a red mist. He was not aware of his individual identity. He was only a man with a club, transported back fifty thousand years, a hairy-breasted, red-eyed primitive, wholly possessed in the crimson instinct for slaughter.

He felt like howling his incoherent exultation with each swing of his bludgeon that crushed skulls and spattered blood into his face. He did not feel the knives that found him, hardly realising it when the men facing him gave back, daunted at the havoc he was wreaking. He did not close the door then; it was blocked and choked by a ghastly mass of crushed and red-dripping flesh.

He found himself running down the corridor, his breath coming in great gulping gasps, following some dim instinct of preservation or realisation of duty that made itself heard amidst the red dizzy urge to grip his foes and strike, strike, strike, until he was himself engulfed in the crimson waves of death. In such moments the passion to die – die fighting – is almost equal to the will to live.

In a daze, staggering, bumping into walls and caroming off them, he reached the further end of the corridor where Khoda Khan was struggling with a lock. Joan was standing now, though she reeled on her feet, and seemed on the point of collapse. The mob was coming down the long corridor full cry behind them. Drunkenly Harrison thrust Khoda Khan aside and whirling the blood-fouled mace around his head, struck a stupendous blow that shattered the lock, burst the bolts out of their sockets and caved in the heavy panels as if they had been cardboard. The next instant they were through and Khoda Khan slammed the ruins of the door which sagged on its hinges, but some-how held together. There were heavy metal brackets on each jamb, and Khoda Khan found and dropped an iron bar in place just as the mob surged against it.

Through the shattered panels they howled and thrust their knives, but Harrison knew until they hewed away enough wood to enable them to reach in and dislodge it, the bar across the door would hold the splintered barrier in place. Recovering some of his wits, and feeling rather sick, he herded his companions ahead of him with desperate haste. He noticed, briefly, that he was stabbed in the calf, thigh, arm and shoulder. Blood soaked his ribboned shirt and ran down his limbs in streams. The Mongols were hacking at the door, snarling like jackals over carrion.

The apertures were widening, and through then he saw other Mongols running down the corridor with rifles; just as he wondered why they did not shoot through the door, then saw the reason. They were in a chamber which had been converted into a magazine. Cartridge cases were piled high along the wall, and there was at least one box of dynamite. But he looked in vain for rifles or pistols. Evidently they were stored in another part of the building.

Khoda Khan was jerking bolts on an opposite door, but he paused to glare about and yelping *'Allah*!' he pounced on an open case, snatched something out – wheeled, yelled a curse and threw back his arm, but Harrison grabbed his wrist.

'Don't throw that, you idiot! You'll blow us all to Hell! They're afraid to shoot into this room, but they'll have that door down in a second or so, and finish us with their knives. Help Joan!'

It was a hand grenade Khoda Khan had found – the only one in an otherwise empty case, as a glance assured Harrison. The detective threw the door open, slammed it shut behind them as they plunged out into the starlight, Joan reeling, half carried by the Afghan. They seemed to have emerged at the back of the house. They ran across an open space, hunted creatures looking for a refuge. There was a crumbling stone wall, about breast-high to a man, and they ran through a wide gap in it, only to halt, a groan bursting from Harrison's lips. Thirty steps behind the ruined wall rose the steel fence of which Khoda Khan had spoken, a barrier ten feet high, topped with keen points. The door crashed open behind them and a gun spat venomously. They were in a trap. If they tried to climb the fence the Mongols had but to pick them off like monkeys shot off a ladder.

'Down behind the wall!' snarled Harrison, forcing Joan behind an uncrumbled section of the stone barrier. 'We'll make 'em pay for it, before they take us!'

The door was crowded with snarling faces, now leering in triumph. There were rifles in the hands of a dozen. They knew their victims had no firearms, and could not escape, and they themselves could use rifles without fear. Bullets began to splatter on the stone, then with a long-drawn yell Khoda Khan bounded to the top of the wall, ripping out the pin of the hand grenade with his teeth.

'*La illaha illulah; Muhammad rassoul ullah*!' he yelled, and hurled the bomb – not at the group which howled and ducked, but over their heads, into the magazine!

The next instant a rending crash tore the guts out of the night and a blinding blaze of fire ripped the darkness apart. In that glare Harrison had a glimpse of Khoda Khan, etched against the flame, hurtling backward, arms out-thrown . . . then there was utter blackness in which roared the thunder of the fall of the house of Erlik Khan as the shattered walls buckled, the beams splintered, the roof fell in and storey after storey came crashing down on the crumpled foundations.

How long Harrison lay like dead he never knew, blinded, deafened and paralysed; covered by falling debris. His first realisation was that there was something soft under him, something that writhed and whimpered. He had a vague feeling he ought not to hurt this soft something, so he began to shove the broken stones and mortar off him. His arm seemed dead, but eventually he excavated himself and staggered up, looking like a scarecrow in his rags. He groped among the rubble, grasped the girl and pulled her up.

'Joan!' His own voice seemed to come to him from a great distance; he had to shout to make her hear him. Their eardrums had been almost split by the concussion.

'Are you hurt?' He ran his one good hand over her to make sure.

'I don't think so,' she faltered dazedly. 'What – what happened?'

'Khoda Khan's bomb exploded the dynamite. The house fell in on the Mongols. We were sheltered by that wall; that's all that saved us.'

The wall was a shattered heap of broken stone, half covered by rubble – a waste of shattered masonry with broken beams thrust up through the litter, and shards of walls reeling drunkenly. Harrison fingered his broken arm and tried to think, his head swimming.

'Where is Khoda Khan?' cried Joan, seeming finally to shake off her daze.

'I'll look for him.' Harrison dreaded what he expected to find. 'He was blown off the wall like a straw in a wind.'

Stumbling over broken stones and bits of timber, he found the Afghan huddled grotesquely against the steel fence. His fumbling fingers told him of broken bones – but the man was still breathing. Joan came stumbling toward him, to fall beside Khoda Khan and flutter her quick fingers over him, sobbing hysterically.

'If we could get him medical attention he'll live. Listen!' She caught Harrison's arm with galvanised fingers; but he had heard it too – the sputter of a motor that was probably a police launch, coming to investigate the explosion.

Joan was tearing her scanty garments to pieces to staunch the blood that seeped from the Afghan's wounds, when miraculously Khoda Khan's pulped lips moved. Harrison, bending close, caught fragments of words: 'The curse of Allah – swine's flesh – my *izzat*.'

'You needn't worry about your *izzat*,' grunted Harrison, glancing at the ruins which hid the mangled figures that had been Mongolian terrorists. 'After this night's work you'll not go to jail.'

Graveyard Rats

Chapter 1. *The head from the grave*

Saul Wilkinson awoke suddenly, and lay in the darkness with beads of cold sweat on his hands and face. He shuddered at the memory of the dream from which he had awakened.

But horrible dreams were nothing uncommon. Grisly nightmares had haunted his sleep since early childhood. It was another fear that clutched his heart with icy fingers – fear of the sound that had roused him. It had been a furtive step – hands fumbling in the dark.

And now a small scurrying sounded in the room – a rat running back and forth across the floor.

He groped under his pillow with trembling fingers. The house was still, but imagination peopled its darkness with shapes of horror. But it was not all imagination. A faint stir of air told him the door that gave on the broad hallway was open. He knew he had closed that door before he went to bed. And he knew it was not one of his brothers who had come so subtly to his room.

In that fear-tense, hate-haunted household, no man came by night to his brother's room without first making himself known.

This was especially the case since an old feud had claimed the eldest brother four days since – John Wilkinson, shot down in the streets of the little hill-country town by Joel Middleton, who had escaped into the post oak grown hills, swearing still greater vengeance against the Wilkinsons.

All this flashed through Saul's mind as he drew the revolver from under his pillow.

As he slid out of bed, the creak of the springs brought his heart into his throat, and he crouched there for a moment, holding his breath and straining his eyes into the darkness.

Richard was sleeping upstairs, and so was Harrison, the city detective Peter had brought out to hunt down Joel Middleton. Peter's room was on the ground floor, but in another wing. A yell for help might awaken all three, but it would also bring a hail of lead at him, if Joel Middleton were crouching over there in the blackness.

Saul knew this was his fight, and must be fought out alone, in the darkness he had always feared and hated. And all the time sounded that light, scampering patter of tiny feet, racing up and down, up and down . . .

Crouching against the wall, cursing the pounding of his heart, Saul fought to steady his quivering nerves. He was backed against the wall which formed the partition between his room and the hall.

The windows were faint grey squares in the blackness, and he could dimly make out objects of furniture in all except one side of the room. Joel Middleton must be over there, crouching by the old fireplace, which was invisible in the darkness.

But why was he waiting? And why was that accursed rat racing up and down before the fireplace, as if in a frenzy of fear and greed? Just so Saul had seen rats race up and down the floor of the meat-house, frantic to get at flesh suspended out of reach.

Noiselessly, Saul moved along the wall toward the door. If a man was in the room, he would presently be lined between himself and a window. But as he glided along the wall like a night-shirted ghost, no ominous bulk grew out of the darkness. He reached the door and closed it soundlessly, wincing at his nearness to the unrelieved blackness of the hall outside.

But nothing happened. The only sounds were the wild beating of his heart, the loud ticking of the old clock on the mantelpiece, the maddening patter of the unseen rat. Saul clenched his teeth against the shrieking of his tortured nerves. Even in his growing terror he found time to wonder frantically why that rat ran up and down before the fireplace.

The tension became unbearable. The open door proved that Middleton, or someone – or *something* – had come into that room. Why would Middleton come save to kill? But why in God's name had he not struck already? What was he waiting for?

Saul's nerve snapped suddenly. The darkness was strangling him and those pattering rat-feet were red-hot hammers on his crumbling brain. He must have light, even though that light brought hot lead ripping through him.

In stumbling haste he groped to the mantelpiece, fumbling for the lamp. And he cried out – a choked, horrible croak that could not have carried beyond his room. For his hand, groping in the dark on the mantel, had touched the hair on a human scalp!

A furious squeal sounded in the darkness at his feet and a sharp pain pierced his ankle as the rat attacked him, as if he were an intruder seeking to rob it of some coveted object.

But Saul was hardly aware of the rodent as he kicked it away and reeled back, his brain a whirling turmoil. Matches and candles were on the table, and to it he lurched, his hands sweeping the dark and finding what he wanted.

He lighted a candle and turned, gun lifted in a shaking hand. There was no living man in the room except himself. But his distended eyes focused themselves on the mantelpiece . . . and the object on it.

He stood frozen, his brain at first refusing to register what his eyes revealed. Then he croaked inhumanly and the gun crashed on the hearth as it slipped through his numb fingers.

John Wilkinson was dead, with a bullet through his heart. It had been three days since Saul had seen his body nailed into the crude coffin and lowered into the grave in the old Wilkinson family grave-yard. For three days the hard clay soil had baked in the hot sun above the coffined form of John Wilkinson.

Yet from the mantel John Wilkinson's face leered at him . . . white and cold and dead.

It was no nightmare, no dream of madness. There on the mantel-piece rested John Wilkinson's severed head.

And before the fireplace, up and down, up and down, scampered a creature with red eyes, that squeaked and squealed . . . a great grey rat, maddened by its failure to reach the flesh its ghoulish hunger craved.

Saul Wilkinson began to laugh – horrible, soul-shaking shrieks that mingled with the squealing of the grey ghoul. Saul's body rocked to and fro, and the laughter turned to insane weeping, that gave way in turn to hideous screams that echoed through the old house and brought the sleepers out of their sleep.

They were the screams of a madman. The horror of what he had seen had blasted Saul Wilkinson's reason like a blown-out candle flame.

Chapter 2. *Madman's hate*

It was those screams which roused Steve Harrison, sleeping in an upstairs chamber. Before he was fully awake he was on his way down the unlighted stairs, pistol in one hand and flashlight in the other.

Down in the hallway he saw light streaming from under a closed door, and made for it. But another was before him. Just as Harrison reached the landing, he saw a figure rushing across the hall, and flashed his beam on it.

It was Peter Wilkinson, tall and gaunt, with a poker in his hand. He yelled something incoherent, threw open the door and rushed in.

Harrison heard him exclaim: 'Saul! What's the matter? What are you looking at – ' Then a terrible cry: '*My God!*'

The poker clanged on the floor, and then the screams of the maniac rose to a crescendo of fury.

It was at this instant that Harrison reached the door and took in the scene with one startled glance. He saw two men in nightshirts grappling in the candlelight, while from the mantel a cold, dead, white face looked blindly down on them, and a grey rat ran in mad circles about their feet.

Into that scene of horror and madness Harrison propelled his powerful, thick-set body. Peter Wilkinson was in sore straits. He had dropped his poker and now, with blood streaming from a wound in his head, he was vainly striving to tear Saul's lean fingers from his throat.

The glare in Saul's eyes told Harrison the man was mad. Crooking one massive arm about the maniac's neck, he tore him loose from his victim with an exertion of sheer strength that not even the abnormal energy of insanity could resist.

The madman's stringy muscles were like steel wires under the detective's hands, and Saul twisted about in his grasp, his teeth snapping, beastlike, for Harrison's bull-throat. The detective shoved the clawing, frothing fury away from him and smashed a fist to the madman's jaw. Saul crashed to the floor and lay still, eyes glazed and limbs quivering.

Peter reeled back against a table, purple-faced and gagging.

'Get cords, quick!' snapped Harrison, heaving the limp figure off the floor and letting it slump into a great arm-chair. 'Tear that sheet in strips. We've got to tie him up before he comes to. Hell's fire!'

The rat had made a ravening attack on the senseless man's bare feet. Harrison kicked it away, but it squeaked furiously and came charging back with ghoulish persistence. Harrison crushed it under his foot, cutting short its maddened squeal.

Peter, gasping convulsively, thrust into the detective's hands the strips he had torn from the sheet, and Harrison bound the limp limbs with professional efficiency. In the midst of his task he looked up to see Richard, the youngest brother, standing in the doorway, his face like chalk..

'Richard!' choked Peter. 'Look! My God! John's head!'

'I see!' Richard licked his lips. 'But why are you tying up Saul?'

'He's crazy,' snapped Harrison. 'Get me some whiskey, will you?'

As Richard reached for a bottle on a curtained shelf, booted feet hit the porch outside, and a voice yelled: 'Hey, there! Dick! What's wrong?'

'That's our neighbour, Jim Allison,' muttered Peter.

He stepped to the door opposite the one that opened into the hall and turned the key in the ancient lock. That door opened upon a side porch. A tousle-headed man with his pants pulled on over his night-shirt came blundering in.

'What's the matter?' he demanded. 'I heard somebody hollerin', and run over quick as I could. What you doin' to Saul – good God Almighty!'

He had seen the head on the mantel, and his face went ashen.

'Go get the marshal, Jim!' croaked Peter. 'This is Joel Middleton's work!'

Allison hurried out, stumbling as he peered back over his shoulder in morbid fascination.

Harrison had managed to spill some liquor between Saul's livid lips. He handed the bottle to Peter and stepped to the mantel. He touched the grisly object, shivering slightly as he did so. His eyes narrowed suddenly.

'You think Middleton dug up your brother's grave and cut off his head?' he asked.

'Who else?' Peter stared blankly at him.

'Saul's mad. Madmen do strange things. Maybe Saul did this.'

'No! No!' exclaimed Peter, shuddering. 'Saul hasn't left the house all day. John's grave was undisturbed this morning, when I stopped by the old graveyard on my way to the farm. Saul was sane when he went to bed. It was seeing John's head that drove him mad. Joel Middleton has been here, to take this horrible revenge!' He sprang up suddenly, shrilling, 'My God, he may still be hiding in the house somewhere!'

'We'll search it,' snapped Harrison. 'Richard, you stay here with Saul. You might come with me, Peter.'

In the hall outside the detective directed a beam of light on the heavy front door. The key was turned in the massive lock. He turned and strode down the hall, asking: 'Which door is farthest from any sleeping chamber?'

'The back kitchen door!' Peter answered, and led the way. A few moments later they were standing before it. It stood partly open, framing a crack of starlit sky.

'He must have come and gone this way,' muttered Harrison. 'You're sure this door was locked?'

'I locked all outer doors myself,' asserted Peter. 'Look at those scratches on the outer side! And there's the key lying on the floor inside.'

'Old-fashioned lock,' grunted Harrison. 'A man could work the key out with a wire from the outer side and force the lock easily. And this is the logical lock to force, because the noise of breaking it wouldn't likely be heard by anybody in the house.'

He stepped out onto the deep back porch. The broad back yard was without trees or brushes, separated by a barbed-wire fence from a pasture-lot, which ran to a wood-lot thickly grown with post oaks, part of the woods which hemmed in the village of Lost Knob on all sides.

Peter stared toward that woodland, a low, black rampart in the faint starlight, and he shivered.

'He's out there, somewhere!' he whispered. 'I never suspected he'd dare strike at us in our own house. I brought you here to hunt him down. I never thought we'd need you to protect us!'

Without replying, Harrison stepped down into the yard. Peter cringed back from the starlight, and remained crouching at the edge of the porch.

Harrison crossed the narrow pasture and paused at the ancient rail fence which separated it from the woods. They were black as only post oak thickets can be.

No rustle of leaves, no scrape of branches betrayed a lurking presence. If Joel Middleton had been there, he must have already sought refuge in the rugged hills that surrounded Lost Knob.

Harrison turned back toward the house. He had arrived at Lost Knob late the preceding evening. It was now somewhat past midnight. But the grisly news was spreading, even in the dead of night.

The Wilkinson house stood at the western edge of the town, and the Allison house was the only one within a hundred yards of it. But Harrison saw lights springing up in distant windows.

Peter stood on the porch, head out-thrust on his long, buzzard-like neck.

'Find anything?' he called anxiously.

'Tracks wouldn't show on this hard-baked ground,' grunted the detective. 'Just what did you see when you ran into Saul's room?'

'Saul standing before the mantelboard, screaming with his mouth wide open,' answered Peter. 'When I saw – what he saw, I must have cried out and dropped the poker. Then Saul leaped on me like a wild beast.'

'Was his door locked?'

'Closed, but not locked. The lock got broken accidentally a few days ago.'

'One more question: has Middleton ever been in this house before?'

'Not to my knowledge,' replied Peter grimly. 'Our families have hated each other for twenty-five years. Joel's the last of his name.'

Harrison re-entered the house. Allison had returned with the marshal, McVey, a tall, taciturn man who plainly resented the detective's presence. Men were gathering on the side porch and in the yard. They talked in low mutters, except for Jim Allison, who was vociferous in his indignation.

'This finishes Joel Middleton!' he proclaimed loudly. 'Some folks sided with him when he killed John. I wonder what they think now? Diggin' up a dead man and cuttin' his head off! I reckon folks won't wait for no jury to tell 'em what to do with Joel Middleton!'

'Better catch him before you start lynchin' him,' grunted McVey. 'Peter, I'm takin' Saul to the county seat.'

Peter nodded mutely. Saul was recovering consciousness, but the mad glaze of his eyes was unaltered. Harrison spoke: 'Suppose we go to the Wilkinson graveyard and see what we can find? We might be able to track Middleton from there.'

'They brought you in here to do the job they didn't think I was good enough to do,' snarled McVey. 'All right. Go ahead and do it – alone. I'm takin' Saul to the county seat.'

With the aid of his deputies he lifted the bound maniac and strode out. Neither Peter nor Richard offered to accompany him. A tall, gangling man stepped from among his fellows and awkwardly addressed Harrison: 'What the marshal does is his own business, but all of us here are ready to help all we can, if you want to git a posse together and comb the country.'

'Thanks, no.' Harrison was unintentionally abrupt. 'You can help me by all clearing out, right now. I'll work this thing out alone, in my own way, as the marshal suggested.'

The men moved off at once, silent and resentful, and Jim Allison followed them, after a moment's hesitation. When all had gone, Harrison closed the door and turned to Peter.

'Will you take me to the graveyard?'

Peter shuddered. 'Isn't it a terrible risk? Middleton has shown he'll stop at nothing.'

'Why should he?' Richard laughed savagely. His mouth was bitter, his eyes alive with harsh mockery, and lines of suffering were carven deep in his face.

'We never stopped hounding him,' said he. 'John cheated him out of his last bit of land – that's why Middleton killed him. For which you were devoutly thankful!'

'You're talking wild!' exclaimed Peter.

Richard laughed bitterly. 'You old hypocrite! We're all beasts of prey, we Wilkinsons – like this thing!' He kicked the dead rat viciously. 'We all hated each other. You're glad Saul's crazy! You're glad John's dead. Only me left now, and I have a heart disease. Oh, stare if you like! I'm no fool. I've seen you poring over Aaron's lines in *Titus Andronicus*:

> Oft have I digg'd up dead men from their graves,
> And set them upright at their dear friends' doors!

'You're mad yourself!' Peter sprang up, livid.

'Oh, am I?' Richard had lashed himself almost into a frenzy. 'What proof have we that you didn't cut off John's head? You knew Saul was a neurotic, that a shock like that might drive him mad! And you visited the graveyard yesterday!'

Peter's contorted face was a mask of fury. Then, with an effort of iron control, he relaxed and said quietly: 'You are over-wrought, Richard.'

'Saul and John hated you,' snarled Richard. 'I know why. It was because you wouldn't agree to leasing our farm on Wild River to that oil company. But for your stubbornness we might all be wealthy.'

'You know why I wouldn't lease,' snapped Peter. 'Drilling there would ruin the agricultural value of the land – certain profit, not a risky gamble like oil.'

'So you say,' sneered Richard. 'But suppose that's just a smoke screen? Suppose you dream of being the sole, surviving heir, and becoming an oil millionaire all by yourself, with no brothers to share . . . '

Harrison broke in: 'Are we going the chew the rag all night?'

'No!' Peter turned his back on his brother. 'I'll take you to the graveyard. I'd rather face Joel Middleton in the night than listen to the ravings of this lunatic any longer.'

'I'm not going,' snarled Richard. 'Out there in the black night there's too many chances for you to remove the remaining heir. I'll go and stay the rest of the night with Jim Allison.'

He opened the door and vanished in the darkness.

Peter picked up the head and wrapped it in a cloth, shivering lightly as he did so.

'Did you notice how well preserved the face is?' he muttered. 'One would think that after three days – Come on. I'll take it and put it back in the grave where it belongs.'

'I'll kick this dead rat outdoors,' Harrison began, turning – and then stopped short. 'The damned thing's gone!'

Peter Wilkinson paled as his eyes swept the empty floor.

'It was there!' he whispered. 'It was dead. You smashed it! It couldn't come to life and run away.'

'We'll, what about it?' Harrison did not mean to waste time on this minor mystery.

Peter's eyes gleamed wearily in the candlelight.

'It was a graveyard rat!' he whispered. 'I never saw one in an inhabited house, in town, before! The Indians used to tell strange tales about them! They said they were not beasts at all, but evil, cannibal demons, into which entered the spirits of wicked, dead men at whose corpses they gnawed!'

'Hell's fire!' Harrison snorted, blowing out the candle. But his flesh crawled. After all, a dead rat could not crawl away by itself.

Chapter 3. *The feathered shadow*

Clouds had rolled across the stars. The air was hot and stifling. The narrow, rutty road that wound westward into the hills was atrocious. But Peter Wilkinson piloted his ancient Model T Ford skilfully, and the village was quickly lost to sight behind them. They passed no more houses. On each side the dense post oak thickets crowded close to the barbed-wire fences.

Peter broke the silence suddenly: 'How did that rat come into our house? They overrun the woods along the creeks, and swarm in every country graveyard in the hills. But I never saw one in the village before. It must have followed Joel Middleton when he brought the head – '

A lurch and a monotonous bumping brought a curse from Harrison. The car came to a stop with a grind of brakes.

'Flat,' muttered Peter. 'Won't take me long to change tyres. You watch the woods. Joel Middleton might be hiding anywhere.'

That seemed good advice. While Peter wrestled with rusty metal and stubborn rubber, Harrison stood between him and the nearest clump of trees, with his hand on his revolver. The night wind blew fitfully through the leaves, and once he thought he caught the gleam of tiny eyes among the stems.

'That's got it,' announced Peter at last, turning to let down the jack. 'We've wasted enough time.'

'*Listen!*' Harrison started, tensed. Off to the west had sounded a sudden scream of pain or fear. Then there came the impact of racing feet on the hard ground, the crackling of brush, as if someone fled blindly through the bushes within a few hundred yards of the road. In an instant Harrison was over the fence and running toward the sounds.

'Help! Help!' it was the voice of dire terror. 'Almighty God! Help!'

'This way!' yelled Harrison, bursting into an open flat. The unseen fugitive evidently altered his course in response, for the heavy footfalls grew louder, and then there rang out a terrible shriek, and a figure staggered from the bushes on the opposite side of the glade and fell headlong.

The dim starlight showed a vague writhing shape, with a darker figure on its back. Harrison caught the glint of steel, heard the sound of a blow. He threw up his gun and fired at a venture. At the crack of the shot, the darker figure rolled free, leaped up and vanished in the bushes. Harrison ran on, a queer chill crawling along his spine because of what he had seen in the flash of the shot.

He crouched at the edge of the bushes and peered into them. The shadowy figure had come and gone, leaving no trace except the man who lay groaning in the glade.

Harrison bent over him, snapping on his flashlight. He was an old man, a wild, unkempt figure with matted white hair and beard. That beard was stained with red now, and blood oozed from a deep stab in his back.

'Who did this?' demanded Harrison, seeing that it was useless to try to stanch the flow of blood. The old man was dying. 'Joel Middleton?'

'It couldn't have been!' Peter had followed the detective. 'That's old Joash Sullivan, a friend of Joel's. He's half crazy, but I've suspected that he's been keeping in touch with Joel and giving his tips – '

'Joel Middleton,' muttered the old man. 'I'd been to find him, to tell the news about John's head – '

'Where's Joel hiding?' demanded the detective.

Sullivan choked on a flow of blood, spat and shook his head.

'You'll never learn from me!' He directed his eyes on Peter with the eerie glare of the dying. 'Are you taking your brother's head back to his grave, Peter Wilkinson? Be careful you don't find your own grave before this night's done! Evil on all your name! The devil owns your souls and the graveyard rats'll eat your flesh! The ghost of the dead walks the night!'

'What do you mean?' demanded Harrison. 'Who stabbed you?'

'A dead man!' Sullivan was going fast. 'As I come back from meetin' Joel Middleton I met him. Wolf Hunter, the Tonkawa chief your grandpap murdered so long ago, Peter Wilkinson! He chased me and knifed me. I saw him plain, in the starlight – naked in his loinclout and feathers and paint, just as I saw him when I was a child, before your grandpap killed him!

'Wolf Hunter took your brother's head from the grave!' Sullivan's voice was a ghastly whisper. 'He's come back from Hell to fulfil the curse he laid on your grandpa when your grandpap shot him in the back, to get the land his tribe claimed. Beware! His ghost walks the night! The graveyard rats are his servants. The graveyard rats . . . '

Blood burst from his white-bearded lips and he sank back, dead.

Harrison rose sombrely.

'Let him lie. We'll pick up his body as we go back to town. We're going on to the graveyard.'

'Dare we?' Peter's face was white. 'A human I do not fear, not even Joel Middleton, but a ghost . . . '

'Don't be a fool!' snorted Harrison. 'Didn't you say the old man was half crazy?'

'But what if Joel Middleton is hiding somewhere near . . . '

'I'll take care of him!' Harrison had an invincible confidence in his own fighting ability. What he did not tell Peter, as they returned to the car, was that he had had a glimpse of the slayer in the flash of his shot. The memory of that glimpse still had the short hair prickling at the base of his skull.

That figure had been naked but for a loin-cloth and moccasins and a headdress of feathers.

'Who was Wolf Hunter?' he demanded as they drove on.

'A Tonkawa chief,' muttered Peter. 'He befriended my grandfather and was later murdered by him, just as Joash said. They say his bones lie in the old graveyard to this day.'

Peter lapsed into silence, seemingly a prey of morbid broodings.

Some four miles from town the road wound past a dim clearing. That was the Wilkinson graveyard. A rusty barbed-wire fence surrounded a cluster of graves whose white headstones leaned at crazy angles. Weeds grew thick, straggling over the low mounds.

The post oaks crowded close on all sides, and the road wound through them, past the sagging gate. Across the tops of the trees, nearly half a mile to the west, there was visible a shapeless bulk which Harrison knew was the roof of a house.

'The old Wilkinson farmhouse,' Peter answered in reply to his question. 'I was born there, and so were my brothers. Nobody's lived in it since we moved to town, ten years ago.'

Peter's nerves were taut. He glanced fearfully at the black woods around him, and his hands trembled as he lighted a lantern he took from the car. He winced as he picked up the round cloth-wrapped object that lay on the back seat; perhaps he was visualising the cold, white, stony face that cloth concealed.

As he climbed over the low gate and led the way between the weed-grown mounds he muttered: 'We're fools. If Joel Middleton's laying out there in the woods he could pick us both off easy as shooting rabbits.'

Harrison did not reply, and a moment later Peter halted and shone the light on a mound which was bare of weeds. The surface was tumbled and disturbed, and Peter exclaimed: 'Look! I expected to find an open grave. Why do you suppose he took the trouble of filling it again?'

'We'll see,' grunted Harrison. 'Are you game to open that grave?'

'I've seen my brother's head,' answered Peter grimly. 'I think I'm man enough to look on his headless body without fainting. There are tools in the tool-shed in the corner of the fence. I'll get them.'

Returning presently with pick and shovel, he set the lighted lantern on the ground, and the cloth-wrapped head near it. Peter was pale, and sweat stood on his brow in thick drops. The lantern cast their shadows, grotesquely distorted, across the weed-grown graves. The air was oppressive. There was an occasional dull flicker of lightning along the dusky horizons.

'What's that?' Harrison paused, pick lifted. All about them sounded rustlings and scurryings among the weeds. Beyond the circle of lantern light clusters of tiny red beads glittered at him.

'Rats!' Peter hurled a stone and the beads vanished, though the rustlings grew louder. 'They swarm in this graveyard. I believe they'd devour a living man, if they caught him helpless. Begone, you servants of Satan!'

Harrison took the shovel and began scooping out mounds of loose dirt.

'Ought not to be hard work,' he grunted. 'If he dug it out today or early tonight, it'll be loose all the way down . . . '

He stopped short, with his shovel jammed hard against the dirt, and a prickling in the short hairs at the nape of his neck. In the tense silence he heard the graveyard rats running through the grass.

'What's the matter?' A new pallor greyed Peter's face.

'I've hit solid ground,' said Harrison slowly. 'In three days, this clayey soil bakes hard as a brick. But if Middleton or anybody else had opened this grave and refilled it today, the soil would be loose all the way down. It's not. Below the first few inches it's packed and baked hard! The top has been scratched, but the grave has never been opened since it was first filled, three days ago!'

Peter staggered with an inhuman cry.

'Then it's true!' he screamed. 'Wolf Hunter *has* come back! He reached up from Hell and took John's head without opening the grave! He sent his familiar devil into our house in the form of a rat! A ghost-rat that could not be killed! Hands off, curse you!'

For Harrison had caught at him, growling: 'Pull yourself together, Peter!'

But Peter struck his arm aside and tore free. He turned and ran – not toward the car parked outside the graveyard, but toward the opposite fence. He scrambled across the rusty wires with a ripping of cloth and vanished in the woods, heedless of Harrison's shouts.

'Hell!' Harrison pulled up, and swore fervently. Where but in the black-hill country could such things happen? Angrily he picked up the tools and tore into the close-packed clay, baked by a blazing sun into almost iron hardness.

Sweat rolled from him in streams, and he grunted and swore, but persevered with all the power of his massive muscles. He meant to prove or disprove a suspicion growing in his mind – a suspicion that the body of John Wilkinson had never been placed in that grave.

The lightning flashed oftener and closer, and a low mutter of thunder began in the west. An occasional gust of wind made the lantern flicker, and as the mound beside the grave grew higher, and the man digging there sank lower and lower in the earth, the rustling in the grass grew louder and the red beads began to glint in the weeds. Harrison heard the eerie gnashings of tiny teeth all about him, and swore at the memory of grisly legends about the graveyard rats.

The grave was not deep. No Wilkinson would waste much labour on the dead. At last the rude coffin lay uncovered before him. With the point of the pick he pried up one corner of the lid, and held the lantern close. A startled oath escaped his lips. The coffin was not empty. It held a huddled, headless figure.

Harrison climbed out of the grave, his mind racing, fitting together pieces of the puzzle. The stray bits snapped into place, forming a pattern, dim and yet incomplete, but taking shape. He looked for the cloth-wrapped head, and got a frightful shock.

The head was gone!

For an instant Harrison felt cold sweat clammy on his hands. Then he heard a clamorous squeaking, the gnashing of tiny fangs.

He caught up the lantern and shone the light about. In its reflection he saw a white blotch on the grass near a straggling clump of bushes that had invaded the clearing. It was the cloth in which the head had been wrapped. Beyond that a black, squirming mound heaved and tumbled with nauseous life.

With an oath of horror he leaped forward, striking and kicking. The graveyard rats abandoned the head with rasping squeaks, scattering before him like darting black shadows. And Harrison shuddered. It was no face that stared up at him in the lantern light, but a white, grinning skull, to which clung only shreds of gnawed flesh.

While the detective burrowed into John Wilkinson's grave, the graveyard rats had torn the flesh from John Wilkinson's head.

Harrison stooped and picked up the hideous thing, now triply hideous. He wrapped it in the cloth, and as he straightened, something like fright took hold of him.

He was ringed in on all sides by a solid circle of gleaming red sparks that shone from the grass. Held back by their fear, the graveyard rats surrounded him, squealing their hate.

They gave back before him as he turned toward the grave, and he did not see the dark figure that slunk from the bushes behind him. The thunder boomed out, drowning even the squeaking of

the rats, but he heard the swift footfall behind him an instant before
the blow was struck.

He whirled, drawing his gun, and dropping his head, but just as he
whirled, something like a louder clap of thunder exploded in his
head, with a shower of sparks before his eyes.

As he reeled backward he fired blindly, and cried out as the flash
showed him a horrific, half-naked, painted, feathered figure, crouch-
ing with a tomahawk uplifted – the open grave was behind Harrison
as he fell.

Down into the grave he toppled, and his head struck the edge of the
coffin with a sickening impact. His powerful body went limp; and like
darting shadows, from every side raced the graveyard rats, hurling
themselves into the grave in a frenzy of hunger and blood-lust.

Chapter 4. *Rats in Hell*

It seemed to Harrison's stunned brain that he lay in blackness on the
darkened floors of Hell, a blackness lit by darts of flame from the
eternal fires. The triumphant shrieking of demons was in his ears as
they stabbed him with red-hot skewers.

He saw them, now – dancing monstrosities with pointed noses,
twitching ears, red eyes and gleaming teeth – a sharp pain knifed
through his flesh.

And suddenly the mists cleared. He lay, not on the floor of Hell,
but on a coffin in the bottom of a grave; the fires were lightning
flashes from the black sky; and the demons were rats that swarmed
over him, slashing with razor-sharp teeth.

Harrison yelled and heaved convulsively, and at his movement the
rats gave back in alarm. But they did not leave the grave; they massed
solidly along the walls, their eyes glittering redly.

Harrison knew he could have been senseless only a few seconds.
Otherwise, these grey ghouls would have already stripped the living
flesh from his bones . . . as they had ripped the dead flesh from the
head of the man on whose coffin he lay.

Already his body was stinging in a score of places, and his clothing
was damp with his own blood.

Cursing, he started to rise – and a chill of panic shot through him!
Falling, his left arm had been jammed into the partly-open coffin,
and the weight of his body on the lid clamped his hand fast. Harrison
fought down a mad wave of terror.

He would not withdraw his hand unless he could lift his body from the coffin lid . . . and the imprisonment of his hand held him prostrate there.

Trapped!

In a murdered man's grave, his hand locked in the coffin of a headless corpse, with a thousand grey ghoul-rats ready to tear the flesh from his living frame!

As if sensing his helplessness, the rats swarmed upon him. Harrison fought for his life, like a man in a nightmare. He kicked, he yelled, he cursed, he smote them with the heavy six-shooter he still clutched in his hand.

Their fangs tore at him, ripping cloth and flesh, their acrid scent nauseated him; they almost covered him with their squirming, writhing bodies. He beat them back, smashed and crushed them with blows of his six-shooter barrel.

The living cannibals fell on their dead brothers. In desperation he twisted half-over and jammed the muzzle of his gun against the coffin lid.

At the flash of fire and the deafening report, the rats scurried in all directions.

Again and again, he pulled the trigger until the gun was empty. The heavy slugs crashed through the lid, splitting off a great sliver from the edge. Harrison drew his bruised hand from the aperture.

Gagging and shaking, he clambered out of the grave and rose groggily to his feet. Blood was clotted in his hair from the gash the ghostly hatchet had made in his scalp, and blood trickled from a score of tooth-wounds in his flesh. Lightning played constantly, but the lantern was still shining. But it was not on the ground.

It seemed to be suspended in mid-air . . . and then he was aware that it was held in the hand of a man – a tall man in a black slicker, whose eyes burned dangerously under his broad hat-brim. In his other hand a black pistol muzzle menaced the detective's midriff.

'You must be that damn' low-country law Pete Wilkinson brung up here to run me down!' growled this man.

'Then you're Joel Middleton!' grunted Harrison.

'Sure I am!' snarled the outlaw. 'Where's Pete, the old devil?'

'He got scared and ran off.'

'Crazy, like Saul, maybe,' sneered Middleton. 'Well, you tell him I been savin' a slug for his ugly mug a long time. And one for Dick, too.'

'Why did you come here?' demanded Harrison.

'I heard shootin'. I got here just as you was climbin' out of the grave. What's the matter with you? Who was it that broke your head?'

'I don't know his name,' answered Harrison, caressing his aching head.

'Well, it don't make no difference to me. But I want to tell you that I didn't cut John's head off. I killed him because he needed it.' The outlaw swore and spat. 'But I didn't do that other!'

'I know you didn't,' Harrison answered.

'Eh?' The outlaw was obviously startled.

'Do you know which rooms the Wilkinsons sleep in, in their house in town?'

'Naw,' snorted Middleton. 'Never was in their house in my life.'

'I thought not. Whoever put John's head on Saul's mantel knew. The back kitchen door was the only one where the lock could have been forced without waking somebody up. The lock on Saul's door was broken. You couldn't have known those things. It looked like an inside job from the start. The lock was forced to make it look like an outside job.

'Richard spilled some stuff that cinched my belief that it was Peter. I decided to bring him out to the graveyard and see if his nerve would stand up under an accusation across his brother's open coffin. But I hit hard-packed soil and knew the grave hadn't been opened. It gave me a turn and I blurted out what I'd found. But it's simple, after all.

'Peter wanted to get rid of his brothers. When you killed John, that suggested a way to dispose of Saul. John's body stood in its coffin in the Wilkinsons' parlour until it was placed in the grave the next day. No death watch was kept. It was easy for Peter to go into the parlour while his brothers slept, pry up the coffin lid and cut off John's head. He put it on ice somewhere to preserve it. When I touched it I found it was nearly frozen.

'No one knew what had happened, because the coffin was not opened again. John was an atheist, and there was the briefest sort of ceremony. The coffin was not opened for his friends to take a last look, as is the usual custom. Then tonight the head was placed in Saul's room. It drove him raving mad.

'I don't know why Peter waited until tonight, or why he called me into the case. He must be partly insane himself. I don't think he meant to kill me when we drove out here tonight. But when he discovered I knew the grave hadn't been opened tonight, he saw the game was up. I ought to have been smart enough to keep my mouth shut, but I was so sure that Peter had opened the grave to get the head, that when I found it *hadn't* been opened, I spoke involuntarily, without stopping to think of the other alternative. Peter pretended a panic and ran off. Later he sent back his partner to kill me.'

'Who's he?' demanded Middleton.

'How should I know? Some fellow who looks like an Indian!'

'That old yarn about a Tonkawa ghost has went to your brain!' scoffed Middleton.

'I didn't say it was a ghost,' said Harrison, nettled. 'It was real enough to kill your friend Joash Sullivan!'

'What?' yelled Middleton. 'Joash killed? Who done it?'

'The Tonkawa ghost, whoever he is. The body is lying about a mile back, beside the road, amongst the thickets, if you don't believe me.'

Middleton ripped out a terrible oath.

'By God, I'll kill somebody for that! Stay where you are! I ain't goin' to shoot no unarmed man, but if you try to run me down I'll kill you sure as Hell. So keep off my trail. I'm goin', and don't you try to follow me!'

The next instant Middleton had dashed the lantern to the ground where it went out with a clatter of breaking glass.

Harrison blinked in the sudden darkness that followed, and the next lightning flash showed him standing alone in the ancient graveyard.

The outlaw was gone.

Chapter 5. *The Rats Eat*

Cursing, Harrison groped on the ground, lit by the lightning flashes. He found the broken lantern, and he found something else.

Rain drops splashed against his face as he started toward the gate. One instant he stumbled in velvet blackness, the next the tombstones shone white in the dazzling glare. Harrison's head ached frightfully. Only chance and a tough skull had saved his life. The would-be killer must have thought the blow was fatal and fled, taking John Wilkinson's head for what grisly purpose there was no knowing. But the head was gone.

Harrison winced at the thought of the rain filling the open grave, but he had neither the strength nor the inclination to shovel the dirt back in it. To remain in that dark graveyard might well be death. The slayer might return.

Harrison looked back as he climbed the fence. The rain had disturbed the rats; the weeds were alive with scampering, flame-eyed shadows. With a shudder, Harrison made his way to the flivver. He climbed in, found his flashlight and reloaded his revolver.

The rain grew in volume. Soon the rutty road to Lost Knob would be a welter of mud. In his condition he did not feel equal to the task of driving back through the storm over that abominable road. But it could not be long until dawn. The old farmhouse would afford him a refuge until daylight.

The rain came down in sheets, soaking him, dimming the already uncertain lights as he drove along the road, splashing noisily through the mud-puddles. Wind ripped through the post oaks. Once he grunted and batted his eyes. He could have sworn that a flash of lightning had fleetingly revealed a painted, naked, feathered figure gliding among the trees!

The road wound up a thickly wooded eminence, rising close to the bank of a muddy creek. On the summit the old house squatted. Weeds and low bushes straggled from the surrounding woods up to the sagging porch. He parked the car as close to the house as he could get it, and climbed out, struggling with the wind and rain.

He expected to have to blow the lock off the door with his gun, but it opened under his fingers. He stumbled into a musty-smelling room, weirdly lit by the flickering of the lightning through the cracks of the shutters.

His flashlight revealed a rude bunk built against a side wall, a heavy hand-hewn table, a heap of rags in a corner. From this pile of rags black furtive shadows darted in all directions.

Rats! Rats again!

Could he never escape them?

He closed the door and lit the lantern, placing it on the table. The broken chimney caused the flame to dance and flicker, but not enough wind found its way into the room to blow it out. Three doors, leading into the interior of the house, were closed. The floor and walls were pitted with holes gnawed by the rats.

Tiny red eyes glared at him from the apertures.

Harrison sat down on the bunk, flashlight and pistol on his lap. He expected to fight for his life before day broke. Peter Wilkinson was out there in the storm somewhere, with a heart full of murder, and either allied to him or working separately – in either case an enemy to the detective – was that mysterious painted figure.

And that figure was Death, whether living masquerader or Indian ghost. In any event, the shutters would protect him from a shot from the dark, and to get at him his enemies would have to come into the lighted room where he would have an even chance . . . which was all the big detective had ever asked.

To get his mind off the ghoulish red eyes glaring at him from the floor, Harrison brought out the object he had found lying near the broken lantern, where the slayer must have dropped it.

It was a smooth oval of flint, made fast to a handle with rawhide thongs – the Indian tomahawk of an elder generation. And Harrison's eyes narrowed suddenly; there was blood on the flint, and some of it was his own. But on the other point of the oval there was more blood, dark and crusted, with strands of hair lighter than his, clinging to the clotted point.

Joash Sullivan's blood? No. The old man had been knifed. But someone else had died that night. The darkness had hidden another grim deed . . .

Black shadows were stealing across the floor. The rats were coming back . . . ghoulish shapes, creeping from their holes, converging on the heap of rags in the far corner – a tattered carpet, Harrison now saw, rolled in a long compact heap. Why should the rats leap upon that rag? Why should they race up and down along it, squealing and biting at the fabric?

There was something hideously suggestive about its contour . . . a shape that grew more definite and ghastly as he looked.

The rats scattered, squeaking, as Harrison sprang across the room. He tore away the carpet – and looked down on the corpse of Peter Wilkinson.

The back of the head had been crushed. The white face was twisted in a leer of awful terror.

For an instant Harrison's brain reeled with the ghastly possibilities his discovery summoned up. Then he took a firm grasp on himself, fought off the whispering potency of the dark, howling night, the thrashing wet black woods and the abysmal aura of the ancient hills, and recognised the only sane solution of the riddle.

Sombrely he looked down on the dead man. Peter Wilkinson's fright had been genuine, after all. In his blind panic he had reverted to the habits of his boyhood and fled toward his old home . . . and met death instead of security.

Harrison started convulsively as a weird sound smote his ears above the roar of the storm – the wailing horror of an Indian war-whoop. The killer was upon him!

Harrison sprang to a shuttered window, peered through a crack, waiting for a flash of lightning. When it came he fired through the window at a feathered head he saw peering around a tree close to the car.

In the darkness that followed the flash he crouched, waiting – there came another white glare – he grunted explosively but did not fire. The head was still there, and he got a better look at it. The lightning shone weirdly white upon it. ·

It was John Wilkinson's fleshless skull, clad in a feathered head-dress and bound in place – and it was the bait of a trap.

Harrison wheeled and sprang toward the lantern on the table. That grisly ruse had been to draw his attention to the front of the house while the killer slunk upon him through the rear of the building! The rats squealed and scattered. Even as Harrison whirled an inner door began to open. He smashed a heavy slug through the panels, heard a groan and the sound of a falling body, and then, just as he reached a hand to extinguish the lantern, the world crashed over his head.

A blinding burst of lightning, a deafening clap of thunder, and the ancient house staggered from gables to foundations! Blue fire crackled from the ceiling and ran down the walls and over the floor. One livid tongue just flicked the detective's shin in passing.

It was like the impact of a sledgehammer. There was an instant of blindness and numb agony, and Harrison found himself sprawling, half-stunned on the floor. The lantern lay extinguished beside the overturned table, but the room was filled with a lurid light.

He realised that a bolt of lightning had struck the house, and that the upper story was ablaze. He hauled himself to his feet, looking for his gun. It lay halfway across the room, and as he started toward it, the bullet-split door swung open. Harrison stopped dead in his tracks.

Through the door limped a man naked but for a loin-cloth and moccasins on his feet. A revolver in his hand menaced the detective. Blood oozing from a wound in his thigh mingled with the paint with which he had smeared himself.

'So it was you who wanted to be the oil millionaire, Richard!' said Harrison.

The other laughed savagely. 'Aye, and I will be! And no cursed brothers to share with – brothers I always hated, damn them! Don't move! You nearly got me·when you shot through the door. I'm taking no chances with you! Before I send you to Hell, I'll tell you everything.

'As soon as you and Peter started for the graveyard, I realised my mistake in merely scratching the top of the grave – knew you'd hit hard clay and know the grave hadn't been opened. I knew then I'd have to kill you, as well as Peter. I took the rat you mashed when neither of you were looking, so its disappearance would play on Peter's superstitions.

'I rode to the graveyard through the woods, on a fast horse. The Indian disguise was one I thought up long ago. What with that rotten road, and the flat that delayed you, I got to the graveyard before you and Peter did. On the way, though, I dismounted and stopped to kill that old fool Joash Sullivan. I was afraid he might see and recognise me.

'I was watching when you dug into the grave. When Peter got panicky and ran through the woods I chased him, killed him, and brought his body here to the old house. Then I went back after you. I intended bringing your body here, or rather your bones, after the rats finished you, as I thought they would. Then I heard Joel Middleton coming and had to run for it – I don't care to meet that gun-fighting devil anywhere!

'I was going to burn this house with both your bodies in it. People would think, when they found the bones in the ashes, that Middleton killed you both and burnt the house! And now you play right into my hands by coming here! Lightning has struck the house and it's burning! Oh, the gods fight for me tonight!'

A light of unholy madness played in Richard's eyes, but the pistol muzzle was steady, as Harrison stood clenching his great fists helplessly.

'You'll lie here with that fool Peter!' raved Richard. 'With a bullet through your head, until your bones are burnt to such a crisp that nobody can tell how you died! Joel Middleton will be shot down by some posse without a chance to talk. Saul will rave out his days in a madhouse! And I, who will be safely sleeping in my house in town before sun-up, will live out my allotted years in wealth and honour, never suspected – never . . . '

He was sighting along the black barrel, eyes blazing, teeth bared like the fangs of a wolf between painted lips . . . his finger was curling on the trigger.

Harrison crouched tensely, desperately, poising to hurl himself with bare hands at the killer and try to pit his naked strength against hot lead spitting from that black muzzle – then . . .

The door crashed inward behind him and the lurid glare framed a tall figure in a dripping slicker.

An incoherent yell rang to the roof and the gun in the outlaw's hand roared. Again, and again, and yet again it crashed, filling the room with smoke and thunder, and the painted figure jerked to the impact of the tearing lead.

Through the smoke Harrison saw Richard Wilkinson toppling – but he too was firing as he fell. Flames burst through the ceiling, and by their brighter glare Harrison saw a painted figure writhing on the floor, a taller figure wavering in the doorway. Richard was screaming in agony.

Middleton threw his empty gun at Harrison's feet.

'Heard the shootin' and come,' he croaked. 'Reckon that settles the feud for good!' He toppled, and Harrison caught him in his arms, a lifeless weight.

Richard's screams rose to an unbearable pitch. The rats were swarming from their holes. Blood streaming across the floor had dripped into their holes, maddening them. Now they burst forth in a ravening horde that heeded not cries, or movement, or the devouring flames, but only their own fiendish hunger.

In a grey-black wave they swept over the dead man and the dying man. Peter's white face vanished under that wave. Richard's screaming grew thick and muffled. He writhed, half covered by grey, tearing figures who sucked at his gushing blood, tore at his flesh.

Harrison retreated through the door, carrying the dead outlaw. Joel Middleton, outlaw and killer, yet deserved a better fate than was befalling his slayer.

To save that ghoul, Harrison would not have lifted a finger, had it been in his power.

It was not. The graveyard rats had claimed their own. Out in the yard, Harrison let his burden fall limply. Above the roar of the flames still rose those awful, smothered cries.

Through the blazing doorway he had a glimpse of a horror, a gory figure rearing upright, swaying, enveloped by a hundred clinging, tearing shapes. He glimpsed a face that was not a face at all, but a blind, bloody skull-mask. Then the awful scene was blotted out as the flaming roof fell with a thundering, ear-rending crash.

Sparks showered against the sky, the flames rose as the walls fell in, and Harrison staggered away, dragging the dead man, as a storm-wrapped dawn came haggardly over the oak-clad ridges.

Black Wind Blowing

Chapter 1. *'I take this woman!'*

Emmett Glanton jammed on the brakes of his old Model T and skidded to a squealing stop within a few feet of the apparition that had materialised out of the black, gusty night.

'What the Hell do you mean by jumping in front of my car like that?' he yelled wrathfully, recognising the figure that posed grotesquely in the glare of the headlights. It was Joshua, the lumbering halfwit who worked for old John Bruckman; but Joshua in a mood such as Glanton had never seen before. In the white glare of the lights the fellow's broad brutish face was convulsed; foam flecked his lips and his eyes were red as those of a rabid wolf. He brandished his arms and croaked incoherently. Impressed, Glanton opened the door and stepped out of the car. On his feet he was inches taller than Joshua, but his rangy, broad-shouldered frame did not look impressive compared to the stooped, apish bulk of the halfwit.

There was menace in Joshua's mien. Gone was the dull, apathetic expression he usually wore. He bared his teeth and snarled like a wild beast as he rolled toward Glanton.

'Keep away from me, blast you!' Glanton warned. 'What's the matter with you, anyway?'

'You're goin' over there!' mouthed the halfwit, gesturing vaguely southward. 'Old John called you over the phone. I heered him!'

'Yes, he did,' answered Glanton. 'Asked me to come over as quick as I could. Didn't say why. What about it? You want to ride back with me?'

Joshua jumped up and down and battered his hairy breast like an ape with his splay fists. He gnashed his teeth and howled. Glanton's flesh crawled a little. It was black night, with the wind howling under a black sky, whipping the mesquite. And there in that little spot of light that apish figure cavorted and raved like a witch's familiar summoned up from Hell.

'I don't want to ride with you!' bellowed Joshua. 'You ain't goin' there! I'll kill you if you try to go! I'll twist your head off with my hands!' He spread his great fingers and worked them like the hairy legs of great spiders before Glanton's face. Glanton bristled at the threat.

'What are you raving about?' he demanded. 'I don't know why Bruckman called me, but – '

'I know!' howled Joshua, froth flying from his loose, working lips. 'I listened outside the winder! You can't have her! I want her!'

'Want who?' Glanton was bewildered. This was mystery piled on mystery. Black, howling night, and old John Bruckman's voice shrieking over the party line, edged with frenzy, begging and demanding that his neighbour come to him as quickly as his car could get him there; then the wild drive over the wind-lashed road, and now this lunatic prancing in the glare of the headlights and mouthing bloody threats.

Joshua ignored his question. He seemed to have lost what little sense he had ever had. He was acting like a homicidal maniac. And through the rents in his ragged shirt bulged muscles capable of rending the average man limb from limb.

'I never seen one I wanted before!' he screamed. 'But I want her! Old John don't want her! I heered him say so! If you didn't come maybe he'd give her to me! You go on back home or I'll kill you! I'll twist your head off and feed it to the buzzards! You think I'm just a harmless big fool, I bet!'

Grotesquely his bellowing voice rose to a high-pitched squeal.

'Well, if it'll satisfy you,' said Glanton, watching him warily, 'I've always thought you were dangerous. Bruckman's a fool to keep you on the ranch. I've expected you to go clean crazy and kill him some time.'

'I ain't goin' to kill John,' howled Joshua. 'I'm goin' to kill you. You won't be the first, neither. I killed my brother Jake. He beat me once too often. I beat his head to jelly with a rock and dragged the body down the canyon and throwed it into the pool below the rapids!'

A maniacal glee convulsed his face as he screamed his hideous secret to the night, and his eyes looked like nothing this side of Hell.

'So that's what became of Jake! I always wondered why he disappeared and you came to live with old John. Couldn't stay in your shack in that lonely canyon after you killed him, eh?'

A momentary gleam of fear shot the murk of the maniac's eyes.

'He wouldn't stay in the pool,' muttered Joshua. 'He used to come back and scratch at the winder, with his head all bloody. I'd wake up at night and see him lookin' in at me and gaspin' and gurglin' tryin' to talk through the blood in his throat.

'But you won't come back and ha'nt me!' he shrieked suddenly, beginning to sway from side to side like a bull about to charge. 'I'll spike you down with a stake and weight you down with rocks! I'll – ' In the midst of his tirade he lunged suddenly at Glanton.

Glanton knew that if those huge arms ever locked about him his spine would snap like a stick. But he knew, too, that nine times out of ten a maniac will try to reach his victim's throat with his teeth.

Joshua was no exception.

Reverting completely to the beast, he plunged in with his arms groping vaguely, and his jaws thrust out like a wolf's muzzle, slavering teeth bared in the glare of the headlights. Glanton stepped inside those waving arms and smashed his right fist against the out-jutting jaw with all his power. It would have stretched another man senseless. It stopped the halfwit in his tracks, and blood spurted.

Before he could recover his balance Glanton struck again and again, raining terrific blows to face and head, driving Joshua reeling and staggering before him. It was like beating a bull, but the ceaseless smashes kept the maniac off balance, confused and dazed him, kept him on the defensive.

Glanton was beginning to tire, and he wondered desperately what the end would be. The moment his blows began weakening Joshua would shake off his bewilderment and lunge to the attack again . . .

Abruptly they were out of the range of the car lights, and floundering in darkness. In panic lest the maniac should find his throat in the blackness, Glanton swung blindly and desperately, connected glancingly and felt his man fall away from him.

He stumbled himself and went on all fours, almost pitching down the slope that fell away beneath him. Crouching there he heard the sounds of Joshua's thundering fall down the slant. Glanton knew where he was now, knew that a few yards from the road the ground fell away in a steep slope a hundred feet long. It was not hard to navigate by daylight, but by night a man might take a nasty tumble and hurt himself badly on the broken rocks at the bottom. And Joshua, knocked over the edge by Glanton's last wild haymaker, was taking that tumble.

It might have been an animal falling down the slope, from the grunts and howls that welled up from below, but presently, when the rattle of pebbles and the sounds of a heavy rolling body had ceased, there was silence, and Glanton wondered if the lunatic lay senseless or dead at the bottom of the slope.

He called, but there was no answer. Then a sudden shudder shook him. Joshua might be creeping back up the slope in utter silence, this time maybe with a rock in his hand, such a rock as he had used to batter his brother Jake's head into a crimson pulp . . .

Glanton's eyes were getting accustomed to the darkness and he could make out the vague forms of black ridges, boulders and trees. The devil-begotten wind that shrieked through the trees would drown a stealthy footstep. When a man turns his back on peril it assumes an aspect of thousand-fold horror.

When Glanton started back to the car his flesh crawled cold, and at each step he expected to feel a frightful form land on his back, gnashing and tearing. It was with a gasp of relief that he lunged into the car, eased off the hand-brake, and clattered off down the dim road.

He was leaving Joshua behind him, alive or dead, and such was the grim magic of the gusty dark that at the moment he feared Joshua dead no less than Joshua living.

He heaved another sigh of relief when the red spot that was the light of John Bruckman's house began to glow in the black curtain ahead of him. He disliked Bruckman, but the old skinflint was sane at least, and any sane company was welcome after his experience with a brutish maniac in the black heart of this evil night.

A car stood before Bruckman's gate and Glanton recognised it as the one belonging to Lem Richards, justice of the peace in Skurlock, the little village which lay a few miles south of the Bruckman ranch.

Glanton knocked on the door and Bruckman's voice, with a strange, unnatural quaver in it, shouted: 'Who's there? Speak quick, or I'll shoot through the door!'

'It's me, Glanton!' called the ranchman in a hurry. 'You asked me to come, didn't you?'

Chains rattled, a key grated in the lock, and the door swung inward. The black night seemed to flow in after Glanton with the wind that made the lamp flicker and the shadows dance along the walls, and Bruckman moaned and slammed the door in its ebon face. He jammed bolt and chain with trembling hands.

'Your confounded hired hand tried to kill me on the way over,' Glanton began angrily. 'I've told you that lunatic would go bad some day – '

He stopped short. Two other people were in the room. One was
Lem Richards, the justice of the peace, a short, stolid, unimaginative
man who sat before the hearth placidly chewing his quid. The other
was a girl, and at the sight of her a sort of shock passed over Emmett
Glanton, bringing a sudden realisation of his work-hardened hands
and hickory shirt and rusty boots. She was like a breath of perfume
from the world of tinsel and bright lights and evening gowns that
he had almost forgotten in his toil to build up his fortune in this
primitive country.

Her supple young figure was set off to its best advantage by the
neat but costly dress she wore. Her loveliness dazzled Glanton at
first glance; then he looked again and was appalled. For she was
white and cold as a statue of marble, and her dilated eyes stared at
him as though she had just seen a serpent writhe through the door.

'Oh, excuse me!' he said awkwardly, dragging off his battered
Stetson. 'I wouldn't have come busting in here like this if I'd known
there was a lady . . . '

'Never mind that!' snapped John Bruckman. He faced Glanton
across the table, his face limned in the lamp-light. It was a haggard
face, and in the burning eyes Glanton saw fear, murky bestial fear
that made the man repulsive. Bruckman spoke hurriedly, the words
tumbling over each other, and from time to time he glanced at the
big clock on the mantel sullenly ticking off the seconds.

'Glanton, I hold a mortgage on your ranch, and it's due in a few
days. Do you think you can meet your payment?'

Glanton felt like cursing the man. Had he called him over that
windswept road on a night like this to discuss a mortgage? A glance
at the white, tense girl told him something else was behind all this.

'I reckon I can,' he said shortly. 'I'm getting by . . . or would if
you'd stay off my back long enough for me to get a start.'

'I'll do that!' Bruckman's hands were shaking as he fumbled in
his coat. 'Look here! Here's the mortgage!' He tossed a document
on the table. 'And a thousand dollars in cash!' A compact bundle
of banknotes plopped down on the table before Glanton's astoun-
ded eyes. 'It's all yours – mortgage and money – if you'll do one
thing for me!'

'And what's that?'

Bruckman's bony forefinger stabbed at the cringing girl.

'Marry her!'

'What?' Glanton wheeled and stared at her with a new intensity,
and she stared wildly back, in evident fright and bewilderment.

'Marry her?' He ran a hand dazedly across his head, vividly aware of the loneliness of the life he had been leading for the past three years.

'What does the young lady think about it?' he asked.

Bruckman snarled impatiently.

'What does it matter what she thinks? She's my niece, my ward. She'll do as I say. She could do worse than marry you. You're no common ridge-runner. You're a gentleman by birth and breeding – '

'Never mind that,' growled Glanton, waving him aside. He stepped toward the girl.

'Are you willing to marry me?' he asked directly.

She looked full into his eyes for a long moment, with a desperate and pitiful intensity in her gaze. She must have read kindness and honesty there, for suddenly, impulsively, she sprang forward and caught his brown hand in both of hers, crying: 'Yes! Yes! *Please* marry me! Marry me and take me away from *him* . . . ' Her gesture toward John Bruckman was one of fear and loathing, but the old man did not heed. He was staring fearfully at the clock again.

He clapped his hands in a spasm of nervousness.

'Quick! Quick! Lem brought the licence, according to my instructions. He'll marry you now – now! Stand over here by the table and join hands.'

Richards rose heavily and lumbered over to the table, fingering his worn book. All this drama and mystery meant nothing to him, except that another couple were to be married.

And so Emmett Glanton found himself standing holding the quivering hand of a girl he had never seen before, while the justice of the peace mumbled the ritual which made them husband and wife. And only then did he learn the girl's name – Joan Zukor.

'Do you, Emmett, take this woman . . . ' droned the monotonous voice.

Glanton gave his reply mechanically, his fingers involuntarily clenching on the slim fingers they grasped. For, pressed briefly against a window, he had seen a face – a white, blood-streaked mask of murder . . . the face of the halfwit Joshua.

The maniac's eyes burned on Glanton with a mad hate, and on the woman at his side with a sickening flame of desire. Then the face was gone and the window framed only the blackness of the night.

None but Glanton had seen the lunatic. Richards, paid by old John, lumbered stolidly forth and the door shut behind him. Glanton and the girl stood looking at each other speechlessly, in sudden self-consciousness, but old John gave them no pause. He glared at the clock again, which showed ten minutes after eleven, jammed the mortgage and the bank notes into Glanton's hand and pushed him and the girl toward the door. Sweat dripped from his livid face, but a sort of wild triumph mingled with his strange fear.

'Get out! Get off my place! Take your wife and go! I wash my hands of her! I am no longer responsible for her! She's your burden! Go – and go quick!'

Chapter 2. *'Tell them . . . in pity's name'*

In a sort of daze Glanton found himself out on the porch with the girl, and from inside came the sound of drawn bolts and hooked chains.

Angrily he took a step toward the door, then noticed the girl shivering beside him, huddling about her a cloak she had snatched as they were evicted.

'Come on, Joan,' he said awkwardly, taking her arm. 'I think your uncle must be crazy. We'd better go.'

He felt her shudder.

'Yes, let us go quickly.'

Richards, characteristically, had left the yard gate unfastened.

It was flapping and banging in the wind which moaned through the junipers. Glanton groped his way toward the sound, sheltering the cowering girl against the gusts that whipped her cloak about her.

He shivered at the thick-set, cone-shaped outlines of the junipers along the walk. Either of them might be hiding the maniac who had glared through the window. The creature was no longer human; he was a beast of prey, ranging the night.

John Bruckman had given Glanton no chance to warn him of the madman. But Glanton decided he would phone back from his ranch house. They could not loiter there in the darkness, with that skulking fiend abroad.

He half expected to find Joshua crouching in the car, but it was empty, and a feeling of relief flooded him as he turned on the lights and their twin beams lanced the dark. The girl beside him sighed too, though she knew nothing of the death that lurked near them. But she sensed the evil of the night, the menace of the crowding blackness. Even such a dim illumination as this was comforting.

Wordless, Glanton started the car and they began the bumping, jolting ride. He was consumed with curiosity, but hesitated to put the question that itched on his tongue. Presently the girl herself spoke.

'You wonder why my uncle sold me like a slave . . . or an animal!'

'Don't say that!' exclaimed Glanton in quick sympathy. 'You need not – '

'Why *shouldn't* you wonder?' she retorted bitterly. 'I can only say – I don't know. He's my only relative, as far as I know. I've seen him only a few times in my life. Ever since I was a small child I've lived in boarding schools and I always understood he was supplying the money that lodged, dressed and educated me. But he seldom wrote; hardly ever visited me.

'I was in a school in Houston when I received a wire from my uncle ordering me to come to him at once. I came on the train to Skurlock, and arrived about nine tonight. Mr Richards met me at the station. He told me that my uncle had phoned and asked him to drive me out to his ranch. He had the licence with him, though I didn't know it at the time.

'When we got here my uncle told me abruptly that I'd have to marry a young man he had sent for. Naturally, I – I was terrified . . . ' She faltered and then laid a timid hand on his arm. 'I was afraid . . . I didn't know what kind of a man it might be.'

'I'll be a good husband to you, girl,' he said awkwardly, and thrilled with pleasure at the sincerity in her tone as she replied: 'I know it. You have kind eyes and gentle hands. Strong, but gentle.'

They were approaching a place where the road had been straightened by a new track, which, instead of swinging wide around the sloping edge of a steep, thicket-grown knoll, crossed a shallow ravine by a crude bridge and ran close by the knob on the opposite side, where it sheered off in a forty-foot cliff.

As the knoll grew dimly out of the windy darkness ahead of them, a grisly premonition rose in Glanton's breast. Joshua, loping through the mesquite like a lobo wolf, could have reached that knob ahead of them. It was the most logical place along the road for an ambush. A man crouching on the thicket-clad crest of the cliff could hurl a boulder down on a car passing along the new stretch of road . . .

With sudden decision, Glanton wrenched the car into the old track, now a faint trace grown up in broom weeds and prickly pears.

Joan caught at him for support as she was thrown from side to side by the jouncing of the auto. Then as they swung around the slope and came back into the plain road again, behind and above them yammered a fiendish howling – the maddened, primordial shrieking of a baffled beast of prey which realises that his victims have eluded him.

'What's that?' gasped Joan, clutching at Glanton.

'Just a bobcat squalling in the brush on that knob,' he assured her, but it was with convulsive haste that he jammed his foot down on the accelerator and sent the car thundering down the road. Tomorrow, he swore, he'd raise a posse and hunt down that slavering human beast as he would a rabid coyote.

He could imagine the madman loping along the road after them, foam from his bared fangs dripping onto his bare, hairy breast. He was glad the lamp was burning in the parlour of his ranch house. It reached a warm shaft of light to them across the windy reaches of the night.

He did not drive the car into the shed that served as garage. He drove it as close to the porch as he could get it, and opened the car door in the light that streamed from the house, as old Juan Sanchez, his Mexican man-of-all-work, opened the front door.

Glanton was briefly aware of the bareness of his residence. There had been no time to adorn it in his toil to build his spread. But now he must have a front yard with a fence around it and some rose bushes and spineless decorative cacti. Women liked things like that.

'This is my wife, Sanchez,' he said briefly. 'Señora Joan.'

The old Mexican hid his astonishment with a low bow, and said, with the natural courtliness of his race: '*Buenas noches*, señora! Welcome to the *hacienda*.'

In the parlour Glanton said: 'Sit down by the fire and warm yourself, Joan. It's been a cold drive. Sanchez, stir up the fire and throw on some more mesquite chunks. I'm going to call up John Bruckman. There's something he ought to know – '

But even as he reached for the phone the bell jangled discordantly. As he lifted the receiver over the line came John Bruckman's voice, brittle with fear and more than fear – with physical agony.

'Emmett! Emmett Glanton! Tell them – in pity's name tell them that you've married Joan Zukor! Tell them I'm no longer responsible for her!'

'Tell who?' demanded Glanton, all but speechless with amazement.

Joan was on her feet, white-faced; that frantic voice shrieking from the receiver had reached her ears.

'These devils!' squalled the voice of John Bruckman. 'The Black Brothers of – aaagh . . . mercy!'

The voice broke in a loud shriek, and in the brief silence that followed there sounded a low, gurgling, indescribably repellent laugh. And Glanton's hair stood up, for he knew it was not John Bruckman who laughed.

'Hello!' he yelled. 'John! John Bruckman!'

There was no answer. A click told him that the receiver had been hung up at the other end, and a grisly conviction shook him that it had not been John Bruckman's hand who had hung it up.

He turned to the girl, who stood silent and wide-eyed in the middle of the room, as he snatched a gun from its scabbard hanging on the wall.

'I've got to go back to Bruckman's ranch,' he said. 'Something devilish is happening over there, and the old man seems to need help bad.'

She was speechless. Impulsively he took her hands in his and stroked them reassuringly.

'Don't be afraid, kid,' he said. 'Sanchez will take care of you till I get back. And I won't be gone long.'

Chapter 3. *Dead Madness*

As he drew the old Mexican out onto the porch a glance back showed her still standing dumbly in the centre of the room, her hands pressed childishly to her breasts, an image of youthful fright and bewilderment lost in an unfamiliar world of violence and horror.

'I don't know what the Hell's happened over at Bruckman's,' he said swiftly and low-voiced to Sanchez. 'But be careful. Joshua, the halfwit's gone on the rampage. He tried to kill me tonight, and he laid for us at the knob where the new road passes. Probably meant to brain me with a rock and kidnap Joan. Shoot him like a coyote if he shows his head on this ranch while I'm gone.'

'Trust me, *señor!*' Old Sanchez's face was grim as he fondled the worn butt of his old single-action Colt. Men had died before that black muzzle in the wild old days when Sanchez had ridden with Pancho Villa. Sanchez could be depended on. Glanton clapped him on the back, leaped into the Ford and roared away southward.

The road before him was a white crack in a black wall, opening steadily in the glare of the headlights. He drove recklessly, half expecting each moment to see the shambling figure of the maniac spring out of the blackness. Grimly he touched the butt of the pistol thrust into the waistband of his trousers.

Aversion to driving under that gloomy cliff was so strong in Glanton that again he swung aside and followed the dimmer, longer road that wound around the opposite side of the knob.

And as he did so he was aware of another roar, above that of his own racing motor. He caught the reflection of powerful headlights. Some other car was eating up the road, racing northward and taking the shorter cut. As he drove into the open road beyond the knob he looked back and glimpsed a rapidly receding tail-light. A nameless foreboding seized him, urging him to wheel around and race back to his own ranch.

But there was not necessarily anything sinister in a car speeding northward even at that hour. It was probably some ranchman who lived north of Glanton returning home from Skurlock, or some travelling salesman bound for one of the little cow towns still further north, and leaving the paved highways to take a short cut.

There was no light in the window of the Bruckman ranch house as Glanton approached it; only the glow of the fire in the fireplace staining the windows with lurid blood, crimsoning it without illum-inating. There was no sound but the moaning of the ghostly wind through the dark junipers as Glanton went up the walk. But the front door stood open.

Pistol in hand, Glanton peered in. He caught the glimmer of red coals glowing on the hearth. The dry, toneless ticking of the clock made him start nervously.

He called: 'John! John Bruckman!'

No answer, but somewhere a moan rose in the fire-shadowed darkness, a low, whimpering of anguish, thick and gurgling as if through a gag of welling blood. And a steady drip, drip of something wet and sticky on the floor.

Panic clawed at Glanton's spine as he moved toward the smould-ering hearth, instinct drawing him toward the one spot of light in the room. At the moment he did not remember just where stood the table with the oil lamp on it. He must have a moment to gather his wits, to locate it.

He groped for a match, then froze in his tracks. A black hand had materialised out of the shadows, faintly revealed in the light of the glowing embers. It cast something on the coals while Glanton stood transfixed.

Little tongues of red grew to life; the fire rose and the shadows retreated before the widening pool of wavering light. A face grew out of the darkness before Emmett Glanton – a grinning face that was like a carven mask somehow imbued with evil life. White pointed teeth reflected the firelight, eyes red as the eyes of an owl burned at him.

With a choking cry Glanton lifted his gun and fired full at the face. At that range he could not miss. The face vanished with a shattering crash and Glanton was showered with tiny particles that stung his hand.

But a low laugh rang through the room – the laugh he had heard over the phone! Whence it came he could not be sure, but in the flash of intuition that came to him, as it often comes to men in desperate straits, he realised the trick that had been played upon him, and wheeled with a gasp of pure terror. Point blank he fired, with the muzzle jammed against the bulk that was almost on him – the bulk of the fiend that had crept up behind him while he was staring at its reflection in front of him.

There was an agonised grunt and something that swished venom-ously ripped away the front of his shirt. And then the monster was down and floundering in its death throes in the shadows at his feet, and in a panic Glanton fired down at it again and again, until its thrashing ceased and in the deafening silence that followed the booming of the shots he heard only the dry tick-tock of the clock, the drip-drip on the floor and the moaning that rose eerily in the gruesome dark.

His hands were clammy with sweat when he found the oil lamp and lighted it. As the flame sprang up, sending the shadows slinking back to the corners, he glared fearfully at the thing sprawled before the hearth. At least it was a man – a tall, powerful man, naked to the waist, his shoulders and arching chest gigantic, his arms thick with knotting muscles.

Blood oozed from three wounds in that massive torso. He seemed to be stained with some sort of paint from his shaven crown to his fingertips. And the fingers of one hand were frightfully armed, with steel hooks that were hollow nearly to the points and slipped over the fingers, curving and razor sharp, making terrible, tiger-like talons.

The thick lips, drawn back, revealed teeth filed to points, and then Glanton saw that he was not painted all over, after all. In the centre of the breast a circle of white skin showed, and inside that circle there was a strange black symbol; it looked like a blind, black face.

An arrangement of mirrors fastened at right angles to the mantel and to the wall, one shattered by his bullet, revealed the trick by which he meant to take Glanton off guard. He must have made his arrangements, simple and easy enough, when he heard the car driving up. But it was diabolical, betraying a twisted mind.

From where he had been standing, Glanton could not see his own reflection in the mirror on the mantel, but only the reflection of the man behind and to one side of him, like a spectral face floating in the shadows.

What takes long in the telling flashed lightning-like through Glanton's mind as he looked down at the black man; and then he saw something else. He saw old John Bruckman.

The old man lay naked on a table, on his back, arms and legs spread wide, so that his body formed a St Andrew's Cross. Through each hand, nailing it to the wood, and through each ankle, a black spike had been driven.

His tongue had been pulled out of his mouth and a steel skewer was driven through it. A ghastly raw, red patch showed on his breast, where a portion of skin as big as a man's palm had been savagely sliced away. And that piece of skin lay on the table beside him and Glanton gasped at the sight of it. For it bore the same unholy symbol that showed on the breast of the dead man by the hearth. Blood trickled along the table, dripped on the floor.

Nauseated, Glanton drew forth the skewer from John Bruckman's tongue. Bruckman gagged, spat forth a great mouthful of blood and made incoherent sounds.

'Take it easy, John,' said Glanton. 'I'll get some pliers and pull these spikes out – '

'Let them be!' gurgled Bruckman, scarcely intelligible with his butchered tongue. 'They're barbed . . . you'll tear my hands off. I'm dying . . . they hurt me in ways that don't show so plainly. Let me die in as little pain as possible. Sorry . . . would have warned you *he* was waiting for you in the dark . . . but this accursed skewer . . . couldn't even scream. He heard your car and made ready . . . mirrors . . . always carry their paraphernalia with them . . . paraphernalia of illusion . . . deception and murder! Whiskey, quick! On that shelf!'

Though he winced at the sting of the fiery liquid on his mangled tongue, Bruckman's voice grew stronger; and a blaze rose in his bloodshot eyes.

'I'm going to tell you everything,' he panted. 'I'll live that long . . . then you set the law on them . . . blast them off the earth! I've kept the oath until now, even with the threat of death hanging over me, but I thought I could fool them. Curse their black souls, I'll keep their secret no longer! Don't talk or ask questions – listen!'

Strange the tales that dying lips have gasped, but never a stranger tale than that Emmett Glanton heard in the blood-stained room, where a dead black face grinned by a smouldering hearth, and a dying man, spiked to a table, mouthed grisly secrets with a mangled tongue in the smoky light of the guttering lamp, while the black wind moaned and crawled at the rattling windows.

'When I was young, in another land,' panted John Bruckman, 'I was a fool. And I was trapped by my own folly into joining a cult of devil-worshippers – the Black Brothers of Ahriman. Until too late I did not realise what they were . . . nor to what horrors my own terrible oath had bound me. I need not speak of their aims and purposes . . . they were foul beyond conception. Yet they had one characteristic that is so often lacking in many such cults . . . they were sincere – fanatic. They worshipped the fiend Ahriman as zealously as did their heathen ancestors. And they practised human sacrifice. Once each year, on this very night, between midnight and dawn, a young girl was offered up on the burning altar of Ahriman, Lord of Fire. On that glowing altar her body was consumed to ashes and the ashes scattered to the night wind by the black-painted priests.

'I became one of the Black Brothers. On my breast was tattooed indelibly the symbol of Ahriman, which is the symbol of Night – a blind, black face. But at last I sickened of the revolting practices of the cult, and fled from it. I came to America and changed my name. Some of my people were already here – the branch of the family to which Joan belongs.

'With the passing of nineteen years I thought the Black Brothers had forgotten me. I didn't know there were branches in America, in the teeming foreign quarters of the great cities. But I might have known they never forget. And one day I received a cryptic message that shattered my illusions. They had remembered, had traced me, found me – knew all about me. And, in punishment for my desertion, they had chosen my niece, Joan, for the yearly sacrifice.

'That was bad enough, but what nearly drove me mad with terror was knowledge of the custom that attends the sacrifice . . . since time immemorial it's been the habit of the Black Brothers to kill the man nearest the girl chosen for sacrifice . . . father, brother, husband – her "master" according to their ritual. This is partly because of a dim phallic superstition, partly a practical way of eliminating an enemy, for the girl's protector would certainly seek vengeance.

'I knew I couldn't save Joan. She was marked for doom, but I might save myself by shifting responsibility for her to somebody else's shoulders. So I brought her here and married her to you.'

'You swine!' whispered Glanton.

'It did me little good!' gasped Bruckman, his tortured head tossing from side to side. His eyes were glazing and a bloody froth rose to his livid lips. 'They came shortly after you drove away. I was fool enough to let them in . . . told them I was no longer responsible for the chosen maiden. They laughed at me . . . tortured me. I broke away – got to the phone . . . but they had ordered my death, as a renegade brother. They drove away, leaving one of them here to attend to me. You can see he did his work well!'

'Where – where did they go?' Glanton spoke with dry lips, remembering the big automobile roaring northward.

'To your ranch . . . to get Joan . . . I told them where she was – before they started torturing me!'

'You fool! You're telling me this *now*,' Glanton yelled.

But John Bruckman did not hear, for, with a convulsion that spattered foam from his empurpled lips and tore one of the bloody spikes out of the wood, the life went out of him in one great cry.

Chapter 4. *Crackling blue flame*

Like a drunken man, Emmitt Glanton left from that lamp-lit room where a black face on the floor grinned blindly at a blind white face lolling on the table. The black wind ripped at him with mad, invisible fingers as he ran in great leaps to his car.

The drive through the screaming darkness was nightmare, with the black wall splitting before him and closing behind him, horror hounding him like a werewolf on his trail, and the wind howling awful secrets in his ears.

He did not turn aside for the sombre knoll this time, but plunged straight on, thundered over the bridge and rushed past the black cliff. No boulder fell from above. Joshua must have left his ambush long ago.

Three more miles and his heart leaped into his throat and stuck there, a choking chunk of ice. He should be able to see the light in the ranch house window by now – but only the glare of his own headlights knifed the black curtain before him.

Then the ranch house bulked out of the night and on the porch he saw a strange pale spot of radiance glowing. There was no sign of the automobile that had come northward. But he checked his own car suddenly to avoid running over a shape that sprawled in the fenceless yard. It was the mad Joshua, lying face down, one side of his head a mass of blood. He had come only to meet death.

Glanton slid out of the car and ran toward the house, shouting Sanchez's name. His cries died away in the stormy clamour of the wind, and an icy hand gripped his heart.

His dilated eyes were fixed on the pale spot that grew in size and shape as he approached . . . a man's face stared at him – the face of Sanchez, weirdly illuminated. Glanton stole closer, holding his breath. Why should the face of Sanchez glow so in the darkness? Why should he stand so still, unanswering, eyes fixed and glassy? Why should his face be looking down from such a height?

Then Glanton knew. He was looking at Sanchez's severed head, fastened by its long hair to a pillar of the porch. Some sort of phosphorus had been rubbed on the dead face to make that eerie glow.

'Joan!'

It was a cry of agony as Glanton flung himself into the darkened house. Only the wind outside answered him, mocked him. His foot struck something heavy and yielding just inside the door. Sick with horror he found a match and struck it. Near the door lay a headless body, riddled with bullets. It was the body of Sanchez. And but for the corpse the house was empty. The match burned down to Glanton's fingers and he stumbled out of the house.

Out in the yard he fought down hysteria and forced himself to look at the matter rationally. Joshua must have been shot by Sanchez, while trying to sneak up on the house. Then it would have been easy for strangers to catch the old Mexican off-guard. He had not expected an attack from anyone except the halfwit, nor would he have been expecting enemies to come in a motor car. He would have come to the door at a hail from a stopping auto, unsuspectingly showing himself in the lighted doorway. A sudden hail of bullets would have done the rest. And then . . . beads of perspiration broke out on his body. Joan, alone and undefended, with those fiends!

He whirled, gun in hand, as he thought he heard a noise like something moving in the bushes north of the house. It diminished, ceased as he went in that direction. It might have been a steer, or some smaller beast. It might – suddenly he turned and strode toward the car.

The body that had lain there before was gone. Had dead Joshua risen and stalked away in the shadows, and was it he that Glanton had heard stealing northward through the bushes? Glanton did not greatly care. At that moment he was ready to believe any grisliness was possible, and he had no interest in Joshua, dead or alive.

He walked around the house, wiping the sweat from his face with clammy hands. The house stood on a rise. From it he could see the lights of any car fleeing northward, for several miles. He strained his eyes, but saw no distant shaft splitting the dark. The raiders must have already put many miles between them and the scene of their crimes. He must follow – but where? Northward, yes – but a few miles north of his ranch the road split into three forks, each leading eventually into a highway, one of which ran to New Mexico, one to Oklahoma, and one north into the Panhandle.

He twisted his fingers together in an agony of indecision. Then he stiffened. He had seen a light – yet not a distinct shaft like a car light. This was more like a blur in the dark – like the glow of embers not yet extinguished. It seemed to emanate from a spot somewhat east of the road which ran north, and this side of the forks. Night made sight and judgment deceptive, but tracing out that eerie glow was better than sitting in racking inaction.

Fixing the spot in his mind as well as he could, he ran to his car and drove northward. As soon as he had descended the rise on which his house stood he could no longer see the glare, but he drove on until he reached a spot which he believed was the point where the road most closely approached the spot where he had seen the glow. A long wooded ridge stood east of the road at that spot.

He left the car and toiled up the western slope of the ridge, scratching his hands and tearing his clothing on rocks and bushes. And nearly to the crest he heard something that stopped him in his tracks. The wind had dwindled to a fitful moaning, and somewhere ahead of him there rose a weird sound that set his flesh crawling.

Chanting! Beyond that black ridge men were chanting in an evil monotone that brought up shuddersome racial memories, old as time and dim as nightmares, of grim black temples where clouds of foul incense smoke rolled about the feet of bowing worshippers before a blood-stained altar. In a frenzy Glanton charged to the crest, tearing through the thickets by sheer force.

Crouching there he looked down on a scene that wrenched his horrified mind back a thousand years into the black night of the medieval when madness stalked the earth in the guise of men.

At the foot of the ridge, in a wide, natural basin glowed a ring of fire. He saw its apparent source – boulders had been rolled to form a solid circle and these boulders glowed with a blue-white light that was like an icy heat beyond human comprehension. From them rose a glow that hung like an unholy halo above the shallow basin. It was this light he had seen from his ranch. It might have been a glow from the slag-heaps of Hell. And devils were not lacking. He saw them, three of them inside the circle – tall, muscular men, naked, their heads hidden by grinning golden masks made like the faces of beasts.

They stood about a heap of stones which glowed with a dull blue radiance, and on that crude improvised altar lay a slender, unmoving figure.

Glanton almost screamed aloud at the sight. Joan lay there, stark naked, spread-eagled in the form of St Andrew's Cross, her wrists and ankles strapped securely. In that instant Glanton knew what it would mean to him to lose that girl – realised how much she had come to mean to him in the few hours he had known her. His wife! Even at this moment the phrase brought a strange, warm thrill. And now those devils down there were preparing, by some hellish art, to reduce that lovely body into ashes . . .

Madly he hurled himself down the slope, pistol in hand. As he went he heard the chanting cease, and was aware of a strange, yet curiously familiar humming in the air.

Whence it came he could not tell, but it sounded like the pulsing of a giant dynamo. Joan cried out. An edge of pain vibrated through her voice.

The halo over the circle mounted, grew more intensely blue. The rocks glowed with a fiercer light; pale tongues of flame licked up from them. The hue of the altar under the girl was changing. The blue was growing more pronounced, less dull. That the change in its colour was accompanied by painful sensations was evident from Joan's cries and the writhings of her bound body.

Glanton yelled incoherently as his feet hit level ground, and the black men turned quickly toward him. His lips drew back in a wolfish snarl and the old single-action gun went up in a menacing arc as he thumbed back the fanged hammer. He meant to shoot these devils down in their tracks, like so many mad dogs – then his out-thrust left hand touched one of the glowing boulders. Merely touched it, but the contact was like the jolt of a fork of lightning. Glanton was knocked off his feet and rolled, blind and dizzy with brief but stunning agony. As he staggered up, snarling and still gripping his gun, he recognised the truth.

Somehow those boulders had been made conductors of electricity. They were charged with a voltage terrific beyond his understanding. And so was the altar, though as yet the full force had not been turned on.

The rising hum that now filled the air told its own grisly tale. Joan was to die by electricity, not swiftly shocked to death as in an electric chair, but slowly, agonisedly, burned to a crisp – to white ashes to be scattered to the night wind.

With an inhuman yell he threw up his gun and fired. One of the masked men spun on his heels and fell sprawling, but the taller of the remaining two bent quickly and laid a hand on some sort of contraption at his feet.

Instantly the hum grew to a shriek. White fire danced around the ring, blinding and dazzling the man outside. He saw the tall black forms within it vaguely, through a dizzying blue-white curtain of flame.

Shielding his eyes from the glare, panic tugging at his soul, he fired again and again until the hammer fell with an empty snap. He could not hit them. The noise, the glare, bewildered him; everything was thrown out of its proper proportions; vision and perspective were distorted.

He hurled the gun at them and reeled toward the blazing barricade with his bare hands, knowing that to touch it would be death, yet choosing death rather than standing by and watching the girl die. But before he reached it a black shape hurtled past him, out of the darkness. Joshua! Blood clotted his scalp, but his primitive fury, his mad desire for the body on that glowing altar were undimmed.

Like a charging bull he came out of the dark, headlong at the barrier. Running hard and low he bent, gathered his thews and leaped! Only a beast or a madman could have made that leap. He cleared the barrier with a foot to spare; one instant he was etched in mid-air, black against the glare, arms wide and fingers spread like talons, then he hit catlike on his feet within the ring of death.

And as he struck he lunged. The priests were naked and weapon-less. The taller let go the lever he held, sprang aside, stooped and snatched up some object, even as Joshua struck his companion. It might have been a bull that smote and tossed the priest.

Plain above the lessening hum and crackle of blue flame sounded the snap of splintering bones, the shriek of the priest. He was whirled from his feet, a broken, dangling doll, lifted high in apelike arms above the bullet-head and dashed head first to the earth with such fury that the broken corpse rebounded before it lay still. Head down, the killer plunged at the taller priest's throat.

It had been a pistol this man had snatched up, and a raking blast of lead met the charging madman – met him, but did not stop him.

With bullets smacking into his body at close range, Joshua bell-
owed with pain and swayed on his feet, but came on in an irresistible
surge of fury and threw his arms about the body of his foe. He must
have been dying even then, but the blind force of his rush was
enough to carry the priest off his feet. Together they hurtled on – to
crash full against the blazing ring of boulders!

A crack like a clap of thunder, a blinding spray of blue fire, one
awful scream . . . then the reek of burnt flesh filled the air. In the
swiftly dying glare, Emmett Glanton saw two hideous figures crump-
led in a fused, indistinguishable mass against the dulling rocks.

Something had happened to the generator of that terrible power.
The hum had ceased; the demon halo was dying. Already the stones
of the altar had assumed their natural tint. But on it the girl lay limp.

As Glanton crawled over the barrier his heart was in his mouth.
Tenderly he freed her and lifted her, grateful to feel warm, living
flesh under his hands, but setting his teeth against what he might
find . . . but her tender back and limbs showed none of the ghastly
burns he feared.

Obviously no great amount of electricity had been turned into the
altar. He saw wires running in all directions from the amazingly
small, compact, black case-like thing that stood near the altar.

Before he carried Joan out of the ring he smashed the thing with
a heavy rock. The Black Brothers knew secrets that were better
kept from the world at large. Even clean science became hurtful
black magic in their hands. That tiny dynamo, of a type undreamed
of by the world, contained more energy than sane men conceived
of – power to turn naked rocks into live wires. Such a secret could
only be evil.

He whipped off his torn shirt and wrapped the girl in it, as care-
fully he carried her down to the road.

As he went, he thought of Joshua, and the only logical explanation
offered itself. The bullet that had struck the madman had not killed
him, but only creased him and knocked him out. When he came to
himself, he started on the trail of the woman his crazed brain desired,
drawn either by the same glimpse of the distant fire that had drawn
Glanton, or by dark, psychic instinct.

Glanton had almost reached the car when Joan opened her eyes,
stared about her wildly, then clung to him.

'It's all right, kid,' he soothed her. 'You're not hurt. You just
fainted. Everything's all right now. Joshua paid his debt, without
meaning to, poor devil. Look, it's getting daylight. The night's past.'

He meant it in more than its literal sense. 'Take me home, Emmett,' she whimpered, nestling deep into his arms. Then, irrelevantly: 'Kiss me.'

And Emmett Glanton kissed his wife for the first time, just as dawn touched the eastern hills.

The Fire of Asshurbanipal

Yar Am squinted carefully down the blue barrel of his Lee-Enfield, called devoutly on Allah and sent a bullet through the brain of a flying rider.

'Allaho akbar!'

The big Afghan shouted in glee, waving his weapon above his head, 'God is great! By Allah, sahib, I have sent another one of the dogs to Hell!'

His companion peered cautiously over the rim of the sand-pit they had scooped with their hands. He was a lean and wiry American, Steve Clarney by name.

'Good work, old horse,' said this person. 'Four left. Look – they're drawing off.'

The white-robed horsemen were indeed reining away, clustering together just out of accurate rifle-range, as if in council. There had been seven when they had first swooped down on the comrades, but the fire from the two rifles in the sand-pit had been deadly.

'Look, sahib – they abandon the fray!'

Yar Ali stood up boldly and shouted taunts at the departing riders, one of whom whirled and sent a bullet that kicked up sand thirty feet in front of the pit.

'They shoot like the sons of dogs,' said Yar Ali in complacent self-esteem. 'By Allah, did you see that rogue plunge from his saddle as my lead went home? Up, sahib; let us run after them and cut them down!'

Paying no attention to this outrageous proposal – for he knew it was but one of the gestures Afghan nature continually demands . . . Steve rose, dusted off his breeches and gazing after the riders, now white specks far out on the desert, said musingly: 'Those fellows ride as if they had some set purpose in mind – not a bit like men running from a licking.'

'Aye,' agreed Yar Ali promptly and seeing nothing inconsistent with his present attitude and recent bloodthirsty suggestion, 'they ride after more of their kind – they are hawks who give up their prey not quickly. We had best move our position quickly, Steve sahib. They will come back – maybe in a few hours, maybe in a few days – it all depends on how far away lies the oasis of their tribe. But they will be back. We have guns and lives – they want both. And behold.'

The Afghan levered out the empty shell and slipped a single cartridge into the breech of his rifle.

'My last bullet, sahib.'

Steve nodded. 'I've got three left.'

The raiders whom their bullets had knocked from the saddle had been looted by their own comrades. No use searching the bodies which lay in the sand for ammunition. Steve lifted his canteen and shook it. Not much water remained. He knew that Yar Ali had only a little more than he, though the big Afridi, bred in a barren land, had used and needed less water than did the American. As Steve unscrewed the canteen cap and drank very sparingly, he mentally reviewed the chain of events that had led them to their present position.

Wanderers, soldiers of fortune, thrown together by chance and attracted to each other by mutual admiration, he and Yar Ali had wandered from India up through Turkestan and down through Persia, an oddly assorted but highly capable pair. Driven by the restless urge of inherent wanderlust, their avowed purpose – which they swore to and sometimes believed themselves – was the accumulation of some vague and undiscovered treasure, some pot of gold at the foot of some yet unborn rainbow.

Then in ancient Shiraz they had heard of the Fire of Asshurbanipal. From the lips of an ancient Persian trader, who only half believed what he repeated to them, they heard the tale that he in turn had heard from the babbling lips of delirium, in his distant youth. He had been a member of a caravan, fifty years before, which, wandering far on the southern shore of the Persian Gulf trading for pearls, had followed the tale of a rare pearl far into the desert.

The pearl, rumoured found by a diver and stolen by a shaykh of the interior, they did not find, but they did pick up a Turk who was dying of starvation, thirst and a bullet wound in the thigh. As he died in delirium, he babbled a wild tale of a silent dead city of black stone set in the drifting sands of the desert far to the westward, and of a flaming gem clutched in the bony fingers of a skeleton on an ancient throne.

He had not dared bring it away with him, because of an overpowering brooding horror that haunted the place, and thirst had driven him into the desert again, where Bedouins had pursued and wounded him. Yet he had escaped, riding hard until his horse fell under him. He died without telling how he had reached the mythical city in the first place, but the old trader thought he must have come from the northwest – a deserter from the Turkish army, making a desperate attempt to reach the Gulf.

The men of the caravan had made no attempt to plunge still further into the desert in search of the city; for, said the old trader, they believed it to be the ancient, ancient City of Evil spoken of in the *Necronomicon* of the mad Arab Alhazred – the city of the dead on which an ancient curse rested. Legends named it vaguely: the Arabs called it Beled-el-Djinn, the City of Devils, and the Turks, Kara-Shehr, the Black City. And the gem was that ancient and accursed jewel belonging to a king of long ago, whom the Grecians called Sardanapalus and the Semitic peoples Asshurbanipal.

Steve had been fascinated by the tale. Admitting to himself that it was doubtless one of the ten thousand cock-and-bull myths booted about the East, still there was a possibility that he and Yar Ali had stumbled onto a trace of that pot of rainbow gold for which they searched. And Yar Ali had heard hints before of a silent city of the sands; tales had followed the eastbound caravans over the high Persian uplands and across the sands of Turkestan, into the mountain country and beyond – vague tales; whispers of a black city of the djinn, deep in the hazes of a haunted desert.

So, following the trail of the legend, the companions had come from Shiraz to a village on the Arabian shore of the Persian Gulf, and there had heard more from an old man who had been a pearl-driver in his youth. The loquacity of age was on him and he told tales repeated to him by wandering tribesmen who had them in turn from the wild nomads of the deep interior; and again Steve and Yar Ah heard of the still black city with giant beasts carved of stone, and the skeleton sultan who held the blazing gem.

And so, mentally swearing at himself for a fool, Steve had made the plunge, and Yar Ali, secure in the knowledge that all things lay on the lap of Allah, had come with him. Their scanty supply of money had been just sufficient to provide riding-camels and pro-visions for a bold flying invasion of the unknown. Their only chart had been the vague rumours that placed the supposed location of Kara-Shehr.

There had been days of hard travel, pushing the beasts and con-serving water and food. Then, deep in the desert they invaded, they had encountered a blinding sand-wind in which they had lost the camels. After that came long miles of staggering through the sands, battered by a flaming sun, subsisting on rapidly dwindling water from their canteens, and food Yar Ali had in a pouch. No thought of finding the mythical city now. They pushed on blindly, in hope of stumbling upon a spring; they knew that behind them no oases lay within a distance they could hope to cover on foot. It was a desperate chance, but their only one.

Then white-clad hawks had swooped down on them, out of the haze of the skyline, and from a shallow and hastily scooped trench the adventurers had exchanged shots with the wild riders who circled them at top speed. The bullets of the Bedouins had skipped through their makeshift fortifications, knocking dust into their eyes and flicking bits of cloth from their garments, but by good chance neither had been hit.

Their one bit of luck, reflected Clarney, as he cursed himself for a fool. What a mad venture it had been, anyway! To think that two men could so dare the desert and live, much less wrest from its abysmal bosom the secrets of the ages! And that crazy tale of a skeleton hand gripping a flaming jewel in a dead city – bosh! what utter rot! He must have been crazy himself to credit it, the American decided with the clarity of view that suffering and danger bring.

'Well, old horse,' said Steve, lifting his rifle, 'let's get going. It's a toss-up if we die of thirst or get sniped off by the desert-brothers. Anyway, we're doin' no good here.'

'God gives,' agreed Yar Ali cheerfully. 'The sun sinks westward. Soon the coolness of night will be upon us. Perhaps we shall find water yet, sahib. Look, the terrain changes to the south.'

Clarney shaded his eyes against the dying sun. Beyond a level, barren expanse of several miles width, the land did indeed become more broken; aborted hills were in evidence. The American slung his rifle over his arm and sighed.

'Heave ahead; we're food for the buzzards anyhow.'

The sun sank and the moon rose, flooding the desert with weird silver light. Drifted sand glimmered in long ripples, as if a sea had suddenly been frozen into immobility. Steve, parched fiercely by a thirst he dared not fully quench, cursed beneath his breath. The desert was beautiful beneath the moon, with the beauty of a cold marble Lorelei to lure men to destruction. What a mad quest! his weary brain reiterated. the Fire of Asshurbanipal retreated into the mazes of unreality with each dragging step. The desert became not merely a material wasteland, but the grey mists of the lost aeons, in whose depths dreamed sunken things.

Clarney stumbled and swore; was he failing already? Yar Ali swung along with the easy, tireless stride of the mountain man, and Steve set his teeth, nerving himself to greater effort. They were entering the broken country at last, and the going became harder. Shallow gullies and narrow ravines knifed the earth with wavering patterns. Most of them were nearly filled with sand, and there was no trace of water.

'This country was once oasis country,' commented Yar Ali. 'Allah knows how many centuries ago the sand took it, as the sand has taken so many cities in Turkestan.'

They swung on like dead men in a grey land of death.

The moon grew red and sinister as she sank, and shadowy darkness settled over the desert before they had reached a point where they could see what lay beyond the broken belt. Even the big Afghan's feet began to drag, and Steve kept himself erect only by a savage effort of will. At last they toiled up a sort of ridge, on the southern side of which the land sloped downward.

'We rest,' declared Steve. 'There's no water in this hellish country. No use in goin' on for ever. My legs are stiff as gun-barrels. I couldn't take another step to save my neck. Here's a kind of stunted cliff, about as high as a man's shoulder, facing south. We'll sleep in the lee of it.'

'And shall we not keep watch, Steve sahib?'

'We don't,' answered Steve. 'If the Arabs cut our throats while we're asleep, so much the better. We're goners anyhow.'

With which optimistic observation Clarney lay down stiffly in the deep sand. But Yar Ali stood, leaning forward, straining his eyes into the elusive darkness that turned the star-flecked horizons to murky wells of shadow.

'Something lies on the skyline to the south,' he muttered uneasily. 'A hill? I cannot tell, or even be sure that I see anything at all.'

'You're seeing mirages already,' said Steve irritably. 'Lie down and sleep.'

And so saying, Steve slumbered.

The sun in his eyes awoke him. He sat up, yawning, and his first sensation was that of thirst. He lifted his canteen and wet his lips. One drink left. Yar Ali still slept. Steve's eyes wandered over the southern horizon and he started. He kicked the recumbent Afghan.

'Hey, wake up, Ali. I reckon you weren't seeing things after all. There's your hill – and a queer-lookin' one, too.'

The Afridi woke as a wild thing wakes, instantly and completely, his hand leaping to his long knife as he glared about for enemies. His gaze followed Steve's pointing fingers and his eyes widened.

'By Allah and by Allah!' he swore. 'We have come into a land of djinn! That is no hill . . . it is a city of stone in the midst of the sands!'

Steve bounded to his feet like a steel spring released. As he gazed with bated breath, a fierce shout escaped his lips. At his feet the slope of the ridge ran down into a wide and level expanse of sand that stretched away southward. And far away, across those sands, to his straining sight the 'hill' slowly took shape, like a mirage growing from the drifting sands.

He saw great uneven walls, massive battlements; all about crawled the sands like a living, sensate thing, drifted high about the walls, softening the rugged outlines. No wonder that at first glance the whole had appeared like a hill.

'Kara-Shehr!' Clarney exclaimed fiercely. 'Beled-el-Djinn! The city of the dead! It wasn't a pipe-dream after all! We've found it – by Heaven, we've found it! Come on! Let's go!'

Yar Ali shook his head uncertainly and muttered something about evil djinn under his breath, but he followed. The sight of the ruins had swept from Steve his thirst and hunger, and the fatigue that a few hours' sleep had not fully overcome. He trudged on swiftly, oblivious to the rising heat, his eyes gleaming with the lust of the explorer. It was not altogether greed for the fabled gem that had prompted Steve Clarney to risk his life in that grim wilderness; deep in his soul lurked the urge to seek out the hidden places of the world, and that urge had been stirred to the depths by the ancient tales.

Now as they crossed the level wastes that separated the broken land from the city, they saw the shattered walls take clearer form and shape, as if they grew out of the morning sky. The city seemed built of huge blocks of black stone, but how high the walls had been there was no telling because of the sand that drifted high about their base; in many places they had fallen away and the sand hid the fragments entirely.

The sun reached her zenith and thirst intruded itself in spite of zeal and enthusiasm, but Steve fiercely mastered his suffering. His lips were parched and swollen, but he would not take that last drink until he had reached the ruined city. Yar Ali wet his lips from his own canteen and tried to share the remainder with his friend. Steve shook his head and plodded on.

In the ferocious heat of the desert afternoon they reached the ruin, and passing through a wide breach in the crumbling wall, gazed on the dead city. Sand choked the ancient streets and lent fantastic form to huge, fallen and half-hidden columns. So crumbled into decay and so covered with sand was the whole that the explorers could make out little of the original plan of the city; now it was but a waste of drifted sand and crumbling stone over which brooded, like an invisible cloud, an aura of unspeakable antiquity.

But directly in front of them ran a broad avenue, the outline of which not even the ravaging sands and winds of time had been able to efface. On either side of the wide way were ranged huge columns, not unusually tall, even allowing for the sand that hid their bases, but incredibly massive. On the top of each column stood a figure carved from solid stone – great, sombre images, half human, half bestial, partaking of the brooding brutishness of the whole city. Steve cried out in amazement.

'The winged bulls of Nineveh. The bulls with men's heads! By the saints, all the old tales are true! The Assyrians did build this city! The whole tale's true! They must have come here when the Babylonians destroyed Assyria! Why, this scene's a dead ringer for pictures I've seen – reconstructed scenes of old Nineveh! And look!'

He pointed down the broad street to the great building which reared at the other end, a colossal, brooding edifice whose columns and walls of solid black stone blocks defied the winds and sands of time. The drifting, obliterating sea washed about its foundations, overflowing into its doorways, but it would require a thousand years to inundate the whole structure.

'An abode of devils!' muttered Yar Ali, uneasily.

'The temple of Baal!' exclaimed Steve. 'Come on! I was afraid we'd find all the palaces and temples hidden by the sand and have to dig for the gem.'

'Little good it will do us,' muttered Yar Ali. 'Here we die.'

'I reckon so.' Steve unscrewed the cap of his canteen. 'Let's take our last drink. Anyway, we're safe from the Arabs. They'd never dare come here, with their superstitions. We'll drink and then we'll die, I reckon, but first we'll find the jewel. When I pass out, I want to have it in my hand. Maybe a few centuries later some lucky son-of-a-gun will find our skeletons . . . and the gem. Here's to him, whoever he is!'

With which grim jest Clarney drained his canteen and Yar Ali followed suit. They had played their last ace; the rest lay on the lap of Allah.

They strode up the broad way, and Yar Ali glanced nervously to right and left, half expecting to see a horned and fantastic face leering at him from behind a column. Steve him felt the sombre antiquity of the place, and almost found himself fearing a rush of bronze war chariots down the forgotten streets, or to hear the sudden menacing flare of bronze trumpets. The silence in dead cities was so much more intense, he reflected, than that on the open desert.

They came to the portals of the great temple. Rows of immense columns flanked the wide doorway, which was ankle-deep in sand, and from which sagged massive bronze frameworks that had once braced mighty doors, whose polished woodwork had rotted away centuries ago. They passed into a mighty hall of misty twilight whose shadowy stone roof was upheld by columns like the trunks of forest trees. The whole effect of the architecture was one of awesome magnitude and sullen, breathtaking splendour, like a temple built by sombre giants for the abode of dark gods.

Yar Ali walked fearfully, as if he expected to awake sleeping gods, and Steve, without the Afridi's superstitions, yet felt the gloomy majesty of the place lay sombre hands on his soul.

No trace of a footprint showed in the deep dust on the floor; half a century had passed since the affrighted Turk had fled these silent halls. As for the Bedouins, it was easy to see why those superstitious sons of the desert shunned this haunted city – and haunted it was, not by actual ghosts, perhaps, but by the shadows of lost splendours.

As they trod the sands of the hall, which seemed endless, Steve pondered many questions: How did these fugitives from the wrath of frenzied rebels build this city? How did they pass through the country of their foes – for Babylonia lay between Assyria and the Arabian desert. Yet there had been no other place for them to go; westward lay Syria and the sea, and north and east swarmed the 'dangerous Medes', those fierce Aryans whose aid had stiffened the arm of Babylon to smite her foe to the dust.

Possibly, thought Steve, Kara-Shehr – whatever its name had been in those dim days – had been built as an outpost border city before the fall of the Assyrian empire, whither survivals of that overthrow fled. At any rate it was possible that Kara-Shehr had outlasted Nineveh by some centuries – a strange, hermit city, no doubt, cut off from the rest of the world.

Surely, as Yar Ali had said, this was once fertile country, watered by oases; and doubtless in the broken country they had passed over the night before, there had been quarries that furnished the stone for the building of the city.

Then what caused its downfall? Did the encroachment of the sands and the filling up of the springs cause the people to abandon it, or was Kara-Shehr a city of silence before the sands crept over the walls? Did the downfall come from within or without? Did civil war blot out the inhabitants, or were they slaughtered by some powerful foe from the desert? Clarney shook his head in baffled chagrin. The answers to those questions were lost in the maze of forgotten ages.

'Allaho akbar!' They had traversed the great shadowy hall and at its further end they came upon a hideous black stone altar, behind which loomed an ancient god, bestial and horrific. Steve shrugged his shoulders as he recognised the monstrous aspect of the image – aye, Baal, on which black altar in other ages many a screaming, writhing, naked victim had offered up its naked soul. The idol embodied in its utter, abysmal and sullen bestiality the whole soul of this demoniac city. Surely, thought Steve, the builders of Nineveh and Kara-Shehr were cast in another mould from the people of today. Their art and culture were too ponderous, too grimly barren of the lighter aspects of humanity, to be wholly human, as modern man understands humanity.

Their architecture was repellent; of high skill, yet so massive, sullen and brutish in effect as to be almost beyond the comprehension of moderns.

The adventurers passed through a narrow door which opened in the end of the hall close to the idol, and came into a series of wide, dim, dusty chambers connected by column-flanked corridors. Along these they strode in the grey ghostly light, and came at last to a wide stair, whose massive stone steps led upward and vanished in the gloom. Here Yar Ali halted.

'We have dared much, sahib,' he muttered. 'Is it wise to dare more?'

Steve, aquiver with eagerness, yet understood the Afghan's mind. 'You mean we shouldn't go up those stairs?'

'They have an evil look. To what chambers of silence and horror may they lead? When djinn haunt deserted buildings, they lurk in the upper chambers. At any moment a demon may bite off our heads.'

'We're dead men anyhow,' grunted Steve. 'But I tell you – you go on back through the hall and watch while I go upstairs.'

'Watch for a wind on the horizon,' responded the Afghan gloomily, shifting his rifle and loosening his long knife in its scabbard. 'No Bedouin comes here. Lead on, sahib. Thou'rt mad after the manner of all Franks, but I would not leave thee to face the djinn alone.'

So the companions mounted the massive stairs, their feet sinking deep into the accumulated dust of centuries at each step. Up and up they went, to an incredible height, until the depths below merged into a vague gloom.

'We walk blind to our doom, sahib,' muttered Yar Ali. 'Allah il allah . . . and Muhammad is his Prophet! Nevertheless, I feel the presence of slumbering Evil and never again shall I hear the wind blowing up the Khyber Pass.'

Steve made no reply. He did not like the breathless silence that brooded over the ancient temple, nor the grisly grey light that filtered from some hidden source.

Now above them the gloom lightened somewhat and they emerged into a vast circular chamber, greyly illumined by light that filtered in through the high, pierced ceiling. But another radiance lent itself to the illumination. A cry burst from Steve's lips, echoed by Yar Ali.

Standing on the top step of the broad stone stair, they looked directly across the broad chamber, with its dust-covered heavy tile floor and bare black stone walls. From about the centre of the chamber, massive steps led up to a stone daïs, and on this daïs stood a marble throne. About this throne glowed and shimmered an uncanny light, and the awestruck adventurers gasped as they saw its source. On the throne slumped a human skeleton, an almost shapeless mass of mouldering bones. A fleshless hand sagged outstretched upon the broad marble throne-arm, and in its grisly clasp there pulsed and throbbed like a living thing, a great crimson stone.

The Fire of Asshurbanipal! Even after they had found the lost city Steve had not really allowed himself to believe that they would find the gem, or that it even existed in reality. Yet he could not doubt the evidence of his eyes, dazzled by that evil, incredible glow. With a fierce shout he sprang across the chamber and up the steps. Yar Ali was at his heels, but when Steve would have seized the gem, the Afghan laid a hand on his arm.

'Wait!' exclaimed the big Muhammadan. 'Touch it not yet, sahib! A curse lies on ancient things – and surely this is a thing triply accursed! Else why has it lain here untouched in a country of thieves for so many centuries? It is not well to disturb the possessions of the dead.'

'Bosh!' snorted the American. 'Superstitions! The Bedouins were scared by the tales that have come down to 'em from their ancestors. Being desert-dwellers they mistrust cities anyway, and no doubt this one had an evil reputation in its lifetime. And nobody except

Bedouins has seen this place before, except that Turk, who was probably half demented with suffering.

'These bones may be those of the king mentioned in the legend – the dry desert air preserves such things indefinitely – but I doubt it. May be Assyrian – most likely Arab – some beggar that got the gem and then died on that throne for some reason or other.'

The Afghan scarcely heard him. He was gazing in fearful fascination at the great stone, as a hypnotised bird stares into a serpent's eye.

'Look at it, sahib!' he whispered. 'What is it? No such gem as this was ever cut by mortal hands! Look how it throbs and pulses like the heart of a cobra!'

Steve was looking, and he was aware of a strange undefined feeling of uneasiness. Well-versed in the knowledge of precious stones, he had never seen a stone like this. At first glance he had supposed it to be a monster ruby, as told in the legends. Now he was not sure, and he had a nervous feeling that Yar Ali was right, that this was no natural, normal gem. He could not classify the style in which it was cut, and such was the power of its lurid radiance that he found it difficult to gaze at it closely for any length of time. The whole setting was not one calculated to soothe restless nerves. The deep dust on the floor suggested an unwholesome antiquity; the grey light evoked a sense of unreality, and the heavy black walls towered grimly, hinting at hidden things.

'Let's take the stone, and go!' muttered Steve, an unaccustomed panicky dread rising in his bosom.

'Wait!' Yar Ali's eyes were blazing, and he gazed, not at the gem, but at the sullen stone walls. 'We are flies in the lair of the spider! Sahib, as Allah lives, it is more than the ghosts of old fears that lurk over this city of horror! I feel the presence of peril, as I have felt it before – as I felt it in a jungle cavern where a python lurked unseen in the darkness – as I felt it in the temple of Thuggee where the hidden stranglers of Siva crouched to spring upon us – as I feel it now, tenfold!'

Steve's hair prickled. He knew that Yar Ali was a grim veteran, not to be stampeded by silly fear or senseless panic; he well remembered the incidents referred to by the Afghan, as he remembered other occasions upon which Yar Ali's Oriental telepathic instinct had warned him of danger before that danger was seen or heard.

'What is it, Yar Ali?' he whispered.

The Afghan shook his head, his eyes filled with a weird mysterious light as he listened to the dim occult promptings of his subconsciousness.

'I know not; I know it is close to us, and that it is very ancient and very evil. I think – ' Suddenly he halted and wheeled, the eerie light vanishing from his eyes to be replaced by a glare of wolf-like fear and suspicion.

'Hark, sahib!' he snapped. 'Ghosts or dead men mount the stair!'

Steve stiffened as the stealthy pad of soft sandals on stone reached his ear.

'By Judas, Ali!' he rapped; 'something's out there – '

The ancient walls re-echoed to a chorus of wild yells as a horde of savage figures flooded the chamber. For one dazed insane instant Steve believed wildly that they were being attacked by re-embodied warriors of a vanished age; then the spiteful crack of a bullet past his ear and the acrid smell of powder told him that their foes were material enough. Clarney cursed; in their fancied security they had been caught like rats in a trap by the pursuing Arabs.

Even as the American threw up his rifle, Yar Ali fired point-blank from the hip with deadly effect, hurled his empty rifle into the horde and went down the steps like a hurricane, his three-foot Khyber knife shimmering in his hairy hand. Into his gusto for battle went real relief that his foes were human. A bullet ripped the turban from his head, but an Arab went down with a split skull beneath the hillman's first, shearing stroke.

A tall Bedouin clapped his gun-muzzle to the Afghan's side, but before he could pull the trigger, Clarney's bullet scattered his brains. The very number of the attackers hindered their onslaught on the big Afridi, whose tigerish quickness made shooting as dangerous to themselves as to him. The bulk of them swarmed about him, striking with scimitar and rifle-stock while others charged up the steps after Steve. At that range there was no missing; the American simply thrust his rifle muzzle into a bearded face and blasted it into a ghastly ruin. The others came on, screaming like panthers.

And now as he prepared to expend his last cartridge, Clarney saw two things in one flashing instant – a wild warrior who, with froth on his beard and a heavy scimitar uplifted, was almost upon him, and another who knelt on the floor drawing a careful bead on the plunging Yar Ali. Steve made an instant choice and fired over the shoulder of the charging swordsman, killing the rifleman – and voluntarily offering his own life for his friend's; for the scimitar was swinging at his own head. But even as the Arab swung, grunting with the force of the blow, his sandaled foot slipped on the marble steps and the curved blade, veering erratically from its arc, clashed on

Steve's rifle-barrel. In an instant the American clubbed his rifle, and as the Bedouin recovered his balance and again heaved up the scimitar, Clarney struck with all his rangy power, and stock and skull shattered together.

Then a heavy ball smacked into his shoulder, sickening him with the shock.

As he staggered dizzily, a Bedouin whipped a turban-cloth about his feet and jerked viciously. Clarney pitched headlong down the steps, to strike with stunning force. A gun-stock in a brown hand went up to dash out his brains, but an imperious command halted the blow.

'Slay him not, but bind him hand and foot.'

As Steve struggled dazedly against many gripping hands, it seemed to him that somewhere he had heard that imperious voice before.

The American's downfall had occurred in a matter of seconds. Even as Steve's second shot had cracked, Yar Ali had half severed a raider's arm and himself received a numbing blow from a rifle-stock on his left shoulder. His sheepskin coat, worn despite the desert heat, saved his hide from half a dozen slashing knives. A rifle was discharged so close to his face that the powder burnt him fiercely, bringing a bloodthirsty yell from the maddened Afghan. As Yar Ali swung up his dripping blade the rifleman, ashy-faced, lifted his rifle above his head in both hands to parry the downward blow, whereat the Afridi, with a yelp of ferocious exultation, shifted as a jungle cat strikes and plunged his long knife into the Arab's belly. But at that instant a rifle-stock, swung with all the hearty ill-will its wielder could evoke, crashed against the giant's head, laying open the scalp and dashing him to his knees.

With the dogged and silent ferocity of his breed, Yar Ali staggered blindly up again, slashing at foes he could scarcely see, but a storm of blows battered him down again, nor did his attackers cease beating him until he lay still. They would have finished him in short order then, but for another peremptory order from their chief; whereupon they bound the senseless knife-man and flung him down alongside Steve, who was fully conscious and aware of the savage hurt of the bullet in his shoulder.

He glared up at the tall Arab who stood looking down at him.

'Well, sahib,' said this one – and Steve saw he was no Bedouin – 'do you not remember me?'

Steve scowled; a bullet-wound is no aid to concentration.

'You look familiar – by Judas! – you are! Nureddin El Mekru!'

'I am honoured! The sahib remembers!' Nureddin salaamed mockingly. 'And you remember, no doubt, the occasion on which you made me a present of – this!'

The dark eyes shadowed with bitter menace and the shaykh indicated a thin white scar on the angle of his jaw.

'I remember,' snarled Clarney, whom pain and anger did not tend to make docile. 'It was in Somaliland, years ago. You were in the slave-trade then. A wretch escaped from you and took refuge with me. You walked into my camp one night in your high-handed way, started a row and in the ensuing scrap you got a butcher-knife across your face. I wish I'd cut your lousy throat.'

'You had your chance,' answered the Arab. 'Now the tables are turned.'

'I thought your stamping-ground lay west,' growled Clarney; 'Yemen and the Somali country.'

'I quit the slave-trade long ago,' answered the shaykh. 'It is an outworn game. I led a band of thieves in Yemen for a time; then again I was forced to change my location. I came here with a few faithful followers, and by Allah, those wild men nearly slit my throat at first. But I overcame their suspicions, and now I lead more men than have followed me in years.

'They whom you fought off yesterday were my men – scouts I had sent out ahead. My oasis lies far to the west. We have ridden for many days, for I was on my way to this very city. When my scouts rode in and told me of two wanderers, I did not alter my course, for I had business first in Beled-el-Djinn. We rode into the city from the west and saw your tracks in the sand. We followed there, and you were blind buffalo who heard not our coming.'

Steve snarled. 'You wouldn't have caught us so easy, only we thought no Bedouin would dare come into Kara-Shehr.'

Nureddin nodded. 'But I am no Bedouin. I have travelled far and seen many lands and many races, and I have read many books. I know that fear is smoke, that the dead are dead, and that djinn and ghosts and curses are mists that the wind blows away. It was because of the tales of the red stone that I came into this forsaken desert. But it has taken months to persuade my men to ride with me here.

'But I am here! And your presence is a delightful surprise. Doubtless you have guessed why I had you taken alive; I have more elaborate entertainment planned for you and that Pathan swine. Now . . . . I take the Fire of Asshurbanipal and we will go.'

He turned toward the daïs, and one of his men, a bearded one-eyed giant, exclaimed, 'Hold, my lord! Ancient evil reigned here before the days of Muhammad! The djinn howl through these halls when the winds blow, and men have seen ghosts dancing on the walls beneath the moon. No man of mortals has dared this black city for a thousand years – save one, half a century ago, who fled shrieking.

'You have come here from Yemen; you do not know the ancient curse on this foul city, and this evil stone, which pulses like the red heart of Satan! We have followed you here against our judgment, because you have proven yourself a strong man, and have said you hold a charm against all evil beings. You said you but wished to look on this mysterious gem, but now we see it is your intention to take it for yourself. Do not offend the djinn!'

'Nay, Nureddin, do not offend the djinn!' chorused the other Bedouins. The shaykh's own hard-bitten ruffians, standing in a compact group somewhat apart from the Bedouins, said nothing; hardened to crimes and deeds of impiety, they were less affected by the superstitions of the desert men, to whom the dread tale of the accursed city had been repeated for centuries. Steve, even while hating Nureddin with concentrated venom, realised the magnetic power of the man, the innate leadership that had enabled him to overcome thus far the fears and traditions of ages.

'The curse is laid on infidels who invade the city,' answered Nur-eddin, 'not on the Faithful. See, in this chamber have we overcome our kafar foes!'

A white-bearded desert hawk shook his head.

'The curse is more ancient than Muhammad. Evil men reared this black city in the dawn of the Beginnings of Days. They oppressed our ancestors of the black tents, and warred among themselves; aye, the black walls of this foul city were stained with blood, and echoed to the shouts of unholy revel and the whispers of dark intrigues.

'Thus came the stone to the city: there dwelt a magician at the court of Asshurbanipal, and the black wisdom of ages was not denied to him. To gain honour and power for himself, he dared the horrors of a nameless vast cavern in a dark, untravelled land, and from those fiend-haunted depths he brought that blazing gem, which is carved of the frozen flames of Hell! By reason of his fearful power in black magic, he put a spell on the demon which guarded the ancient gem, and so stole away the stone. And the demon slept in the cavern unknowing.

'So this magician – Xuthltan by name – dwelt in the court of the sultan Asshurbanipal and did magic and forecast events by scanning the lurid deeps of the stone, into which no eyes but his could look unblinded. And men called the stone the Fire of Asshurbanipal, in honour of the king.

'But evil came upon the kingdom, and men cried out that it was the curse of the djinn, and the sultan in great fear bade Xuthltan take the gem and cast it into the cavern from which he had taken it, lest worse ill befall them.

'Yet it was not the magician's will to give up the gem wherein he read strange secrets of pre-Adamite days, and he fled to the rebel city of Kara-Shehr, where soon civil war broke out and men strove with one another to possess the gem. Then the king who ruled the city, coveting the stone, seized the magician and put him to death by torture, and in this very room he watched him die; with the gem in his hand the king sat upon the throne . . . even as he has sat upon the throne . . . even as he has sat throughout the centuries . . . even as now he sits!'

The Arab's finger stabbed at the mouldering bones on the marble throne, and the wild desert men blenched; even Nureddin's own scoundrels recoiled, catching their breath, but the shaykh showed no sign of perturbation.

'As Xuthltan died,' continued the old Bedouin, 'he cursed the stone whose magic had not saved him, and he shrieked aloud the fearful words which undid the spell he had put upon the demon in the cavern, and set the monster free. And crying out on the forgotten gods, Cthulhu and Koth and Yog-Sothoth, and all the pre-Adamite dwellers in the black cities under the sea and the caverns of the earth, he called upon them – to take back that which was theirs, and with his dying breath pronounced doom on the false king, and that doom was that the king should sit on his throne holding in his hand the Fire of Asshurbanipal until the thunder of Judgment Day.

'Thereat the great stone cried out as a live thing cries, and the king and his soldiers saw a black cloud spinning up from the floor, and out of the cloud blew a fetid wind, and out of the wind came a grisly shape which stretched forth fearsome paws and laid them on the king, who shrivelled and died at their touch. And the soldiers fled screaming, and all the people of the city ran forth wailing into the desert, where they perished or gained through the wastes to the far oasis towns. Kara-Shehr lay silent and deserted, the haunt of the lizard and the jackal. And when some of the desert people ventured into the city they found the king dead on his throne, clutching the blazing gem, but they dared not lay hand upon it, for they knew the demon lurked near to guard it through all the ages – as he lurks near even as we stand here.'

The warriors shuddered involuntarily and glanced about, and Nureddin said, 'Why did he not come forth when the Franks entered the chamber? Is he deaf, that the sound of the combat has not awakened him?'

'We have not touched the gem,' answered the old Bedouin, 'nor had the Franks molested it. Men have looked on it and lived; but no mortal may touch it and survive.'

Nureddin started to speak, gazed at the stubborn, uneasy faces and realised the futility of argument. His attitude changed abruptly.

'I am master here,' he snapped, dropping a hand to his holster. 'I have not sweated and bled for this gem to be balked at the last by groundless fears! Stand back, all! Let any man cross me at the peril of his head!'

He faced them, his eyes blazing, and they fell back, cowed by the force of his ruthless personality. He strode boldly up the marble steps, and the Arabs caught their breath, recoiling toward the door; Yar Ali, conscious at last, groaned dismally. God! thought Steve, what a barbaric scene! – bound captives on the dust-heaped floor, wild warriors clustered about, gripping their weapons, the raw acrid scent of blood and burnt powder still fouling the air, corpses strewn in a horrid welter of blood, brains and entrails . . . and on the daïs, the hawk-faced shaykh, oblivious to all except the evil crimson glow in the skeleton fingers that rested on the marble throne.

A tense silence gripped all as Nureddin stretched forth his hand slowly, as if hypnotised by the throbbing crimson light. And in Steve's subconsciousness there shuddered a dim echo, as of something vast and loathsome waking suddenly from an age-long slumber. The American's eyes moved instinctively toward the grim Cyclopean walls. The jewel's glow had altered strangely; it burned a deeper, darker red, angry and menacing.

'Heart of all evil,' murmured the shaykh, 'how many princes died for thee in the Beginnings of Happenings? Surely the blood of kings throbs in thee. The sultans and the princesses and the generals who wore thee, they are dust and are forgotten, but thou blazest with majesty undimmed, fire of the world . . . '

Nureddin seized the stone. A shuddery wail broke from the Arabs, cut through by a sharp inhuman cry. To Steve it seemed, horribly, that the great jewel had cried out like a living thing! The stone slipped from the shaykh's hand. Nureddin might have dropped it;

to Steve it looked as though it leaped convulsively, as a live thing might leap. It rolled from the daïs, bounding from step to step, with Nureddin springing after it, cursing as his clutching hand missed it. It struck the floor, veered sharply, and despite the deep dust, rolled like a revolving ball of fire toward the back wall. Nureddin was close upon it – it struck the wall – the shaykh's hand reached for it.

A scream of mortal fear ripped the tense silence. Without warning the solid wall had opened. Out of the black wall that gaped there, a tentacle shot and gripped the shaykh's body as a python girdles its victim, and jerked him headlong into the darkness. And then the wall showed blank and solid once more; only from within sounded a hideous, high-pitched, muffled screaming that chilled the blood of the listeners. Howling wordlessly, the Arabs stampeded, jammed in a battling, screeching mass in the doorway, tore through and raced madly down the wide stairs.

Steve and Yar Ali, lying helplessly, heard the frenzied clamour of their flight fade away into the distance, and gazed in dumb horror at the grim wall. The shrieks had faded into a more horrific silence. Holding their breath, they heard suddenly a sound that froze the blood in their veins – the soft sliding of metal or stone in a groove. At the same time the hidden door began to open, and Steve caught a glimmer in the blackness that might have been the glitter of monstrous eyes. He closed his own eyes; he dared not look upon whatever horror slunk from that hideous black well. He knew that there are strains the human brain cannot stand, and every primitive instinct in his soul cried out to him that this thing was nightmare and lunacy. He sensed that Yar Ali likewise closed his eyes, and the two lay like dead men.

Clarney heard no sound, but he sensed the presence of a horrific evil too grisly for human comprehension – of an Invader from Outer Gulfs and far black reaches of cosmic being. A deadly cold pervaded the chamber, and Steve felt the glare of inhuman eyes sear through his closed lids and freeze his consciousness. If he looked, if he opened his eyes, he knew stark black madness would be his instant lot.

He felt a soul-shakingly foul breath against his face and knew that the monster was bending close above him, but he lay like a man frozen in a nightmare. He clung to one thought: neither he nor Yar Ali had touched the jewel this horror guarded.

Then he no longer smelled the foul odour, the coldness in the air grew appreciably less, and he heard again the secret door slide in its groove. The fiend was returning to its hiding-place. Not all the legions of Hell could have prevented Steve's eyes from opening a trifle. He had only a glimpse as the hidden door slid to – and that one glimpse was enough to drive all consciousness from his brain. Steve Clarney, iron-nerved adventurer, fainted for the only time in his chequered life.

How long he lay there Steve never knew, but it could not have been long, for he was roused by Yar Ali's whisper, 'Lie still, sahib, a little shifting of my body and I can reach thy cords with my teeth.'

Steve felt the Afghan's powerful teeth at work on his bonds, and as he lay with his face jammed into the thick dust, and his wounded shoulder began to throb agonisingly – he had forgotten it until now – he began to gather the wandering threads of his consciousness, and it all came back to him. How much, he wondered dazedly, had been the nightmares of delirium, born from suffering and the thirst that caked his throat? The fight with the Arabs had been real – the bonds and the wounds showed that – but the grisly doom of the shaykh . . . the thing that had crept out of the black entrance in the wall – surely that had been a figment of delirium. Nureddin had fallen into a well or pit of some sort – Steve felt his hands were free and he rose to a sitting posture, fumbling for a pocket-knife the Arabs had overlooked. He did not look up or about the chamber as he slashed the cords that bound his ankles, and then freed Yar Ali, working awkwardly because his left arm was stiff and useless.

'Where are the Bedouins?' he asked, as the Afghan rose, lifting him to his feet.

'Allah, sahib,' whispered Yar Ali, 'are you mad? Have you forgotten? Let us go quickly before the djinn returns!'

'It was a nightmare,' muttered Steve. 'Look . . . the jewel is back on the throne . . . ' His voice died out. Again that red glow throbbed about the ancient throne, reflecting from the mouldering skull; again in the outstretched finger-bones pulsed the Fire of Asshurbanipal. But at the foot of the throne lay another object that had not been there before . . . the severed head of Nureddin el Mekru stared sightlessly up at the grey light filtering through the stone ceiling. The bloodless lips were drawn back from the teeth in a ghastly grin, the staring eyes mirrored an intolerable horror. In the thick dust of the floor three spoors showed one of the shaykhs where he had followed the red jewel as it rolled to the wall, and above it two other sets of tracks, coming to the throne and returning to the wall – vast, shapeless tracks, as of splayed feet, taloned and gigantic, neither human nor animal.

'My God!' choked Steve. 'It was true . . . and the Thing . . . the Thing I saw . . . '

Steve remembered the flight from that chamber as a rushing nightmare, in which he and his companion hurtled headlong down an endless stair that was a grey well of fear, raced blindly through dusty silent chambers, past the glowering idol in the mighty hall and into the blazing light of the desert sun, where they fell slavering, fighting for breath.

Again Steve was roused by the Afridi's voice: 'Sahib, sahib, in the Name of Allah the Compassionate, our luck has turned!'

Steve looked at his companion as a man might look in a trance: The big Afghan's garments were in tatters, and blood-soaked. He was stained with dust and caked with blood, and his voice was a croak. But his eyes were alight with hope and he pointed with a trembling finger.

'In the shade of yon ruined wall!' he croaked, striving to moisten his blackened lips. 'Allah il allah! The horses of the men we killed! With canteens and food-pouches at the saddle-horns! Those dogs fled without halting for the steeds of their comrades!'

New life surged up into Steve's bosom and he rose, staggering.

'Out of here,' he mumbled. 'Out of here, quick!'

Like dying men they stumbled to the horses, tore them loose and climbed fumblingly into the saddles.

'We'll lead the spare mounts,' croaked Steve, and Yar Ali nodded emphatic agreement.

'Belike we shall need them ere we sight the coast.'

Though their tortured nerves screamed for the water that swung in canteens at the saddle-horns, they turned the mounts aside and, swaying in the saddle, rode like flying corpses down the long sandy street of Kara-Shehr, between the ruined palaces and the crumbling columns, crossed the fallen wall and swept out into the desert. Not once did either glance back toward that black pile of ancient horror, nor did either speak until the ruins faded into the hazy distance. Then and only then did they draw rein and ease their thirst.

'Allah il allah!' said Yar Ali piously. 'Those dogs have beaten me until it is as though every bone in my body were broken. Dismount, I beg thee, sahib, and let me probe for that accursed bullet, and dress thy shoulder to the best of my meagre ability.'

While this was going on, Yar Ali spoke, avoiding his friend's eye, 'You said, sahib, you said something about . . . about seeing? What saw ye, in Allah's name?'

A strong shudder shook the American's steely fray 'You didn't look when – when the – the Thing put back the jewel in the skeleton's hand and left Nureddin's head on the daïs?'

'By Allah, not I!' swore Yar Ali. 'My eyes were as closed as if they had been welded together by the molten irons of Satan!'

Steve made no reply until the comrades had once more swung into the saddle and started on their long trek for the coast, which, with spare horses, food, water and weapons, they had a good chance to reach.

'I looked,' the American said sombrely. 'I wish I had not; I know I'll dream about it for the rest of my life. I had only a glance; I couldn't describe it as a man describes an earthly thing. God help me, it wasn't earthly or sane either. Mankind isn't the first owner of the earth; there were Beings here before his coming . . . and now, survivals of hideously ancient epochs. Maybe spheres of alien dimensions press unseen on this material universe today. Sorcerers have called up sleeping devils before now and controlled them with magic. It is not unreasonable to suppose an Assyrian magician could invoke an elemental demon out of the earth to avenge him and guard something that must have come out of Hell in the first place.'

'I'll try to tell you what I glimpsed; then we'll never speak of it again. It was gigantic and black and shadowy; it was a hulking monstrosity that walked upright like a man, but it was like a toad, too, and it was winged and tentacled. I saw only its back; if I'd seen the front of it . . . its face . . . I'd have undoubtedly lost my mind. The old Arab was right; God help us, it was the monster that Xuthltan called up out of the dark blind caverns of the earth to guard the Fire of Asshurbanipal!'

Chapter 1. *The whistler in the dark*

Griswell awoke suddenly, every nerve tingling with a premonition of imminent peril. He stared about wildly, unable at first to remember where he was, or what he was doing there. Moonlight filtered in through the dusty windows, and the great empty room with its lofty ceiling and gaping black fireplace was spectral and unfamiliar. Then as he emerged from the clinging cobwebs of his recent sleep, he remembered where he was and how he came to be there. He twisted his head and stared at his companion, sleeping on the floor near him. John Branner was but a vaguely bulking shape in the darkness that the moon scarcely greyed.

Griswell tried to remember what had awakened him. There was no sound in the house, no sound outside except the mournful hoot of an owl, far away in the piney woods. Now he had captured the illusive memory. It was a dream, a nightmare so filled with dim terror that it had frightened him awake. Recollection flooded back, vividly etching the abominable vision.

Or was it a dream? Certainly it must have been, but it had blended so curiously with recent actual events that it was difficult to know where reality left off and fantasy began.

Dreaming, he had seemed to relive his past few waking hours, in accurate detail. The dream had begun, abruptly, as he and John Branner came in sight of the house where they now lay. They had come rattling and bouncing over the stumpy, uneven old road that led through the pinelands, he and John Branner, wandering far afield from their New England home, in search of vacation pleasure. They had sighted the old house with its balustraded galleries rising amidst a wilderness of weeds and bushes, just as the sun was setting behind it. It dominated their fancy, rearing black and stark and gaunt against the low lurid rampart of sunset, barred by the black pines.

They were tired, sick of bumping and pounding all day over woodland roads. The old deserted house stimulated their imagination with its suggestion of antebellum splendour and ultimate decay. They left the automobile beside the rutty road, and as they went up the winding walk of crumbling bricks, almost lost in the tangle of rank growth, pigeons rose from the balustrades in a fluttering, feathery crowd and swept away with a low thunder of beating wings.

The oaken door sagged on broken hinges. Dust lay thick on the floor of the wide, dim hallway, on the broad steps of the stair that mounted up from the hall. They turned into a door opposite the landing, and entered a large room, empty, dusty, with cobwebs shining thickly in the corners. Dust lay thick over the ashes in the great fireplace.

They discussed gathering wood and building a fire, but decided against it. As the sun sank, darkness came quickly, the thick, black, absolute darkness of the pinelands. They knew that rattlesnakes and copperheads haunted Southern forests, and they did not care to go groping for firewood in the dark. They ate frugally from tins, then rolled in their blankets fully clad before the empty fireplace, and went instantly to sleep.

This, in part, was what Griswell had dreamed. He saw again the gaunt house looming stark against the crimson sunset; saw the flight of the pigeons as he and Branner came up the shattered walk. He saw the dim room in which they presently lay, and he saw the two forms that were himself and his companion, lying wrapped in their blankets on the dusty floor. Then from that point his dream altered subtly, passed out of the realm of the common-place and became tinged with fear. He was looking into a vague, shadowy chamber, lit by the grey light of the moon which streamed in from some obscure source. For there was no window in that room. But in the grey light he saw three silent shapes that hung suspended in a row, and their stillness and their outlines woke chill horror in his soul. There was no sound, no word, but he sensed a Presence of fear and lunacy crouching in a dark corner . . . Abruptly he was back in the dusty, high-ceilinged room, before the great fireplace.

He was lying in his blankets, staring tensely through the dim door and across the shadowy hall, to where a beam of moonlight fell across the balustraded stair, some seven steps up from the landing. And there was something on the stair, a bent, misshapen, shadowy thing that never moved fully into the beam of light. But a dim yellow blur that might have been a face was turned toward him, as if something crouched on the stair, regarding him and his companion. Fright crept chilly through his veins, and it was then that he awoke – if indeed he had been asleep.

He blinked his eyes. The beam of moonlight fell across the stair just as he had dreamed it did; but no figure lurked there. Yet his flesh still crawled from the fear the dream or vision had roused in him; his legs felt as if they had been plunged in ice-water. He made an involuntary movement to awaken his companion, when a sudden sound paralysed him.

It was the sound of whistling on the floor above. Eerie and sweet it rose, not carrying any tune, but piping shrill and melodious. Such a sound in a supposedly deserted house was alarming enough; but it was more than the fear of a physical invader that held Griswell frozen. He could not himself have defined the horror that gripped him. But Branner's blankets rustled, and Griswell saw he was sitting upright. His figure bulked dimly in the soft darkness, the head turned toward the stair as if the man were listening intently. More sweetly and more subtly evil rose that weird whistling.

'John!' whispered Griswell from dry lips. He had meant to shout – to tell Branner that there was somebody upstairs, somebody who could mean them no good; that they must leave the house at once. But his voice died dryly in his throat.

Branner had risen. His boots clumped on the floor as he moved toward the door. He stalked leisurely into the hall and made for the lower landing, merging with the shadows that clustered black about the stair.

Griswell lay incapable of movement, his mind a whirl of bewilderment. Who was that whistling upstairs? Why was Branner going up those stairs? Griswell saw him pass the spot where the moonlight rested, saw his head tilted back as if he were looking at something Griswell could not see, above and beyond the stair. But his face was like that of a sleepwalker. He moved across the bar of moonlight and vanished from Griswell's view, even as the latter tried to shout to him to come back. A ghastly whisper was the only result of his effort.

The whistling sank to a lower note, died out. Griswell heard the stairs creaking under Branner's measured tread. Now he had reached the hallway above, for Griswell heard the clump of his feet moving along it. Suddenly the footfalls halted, and the whole night seemed to hold its breath. Then an awful scream split the stillness, and Griswell started up, echoing the cry.

The strange paralysis that had held him was broken. He took a step toward the door, then checked himself. The footfalls were resumed. Branner was coming back. He was not running. The tread was even more deliberate and measured than before. Now the stairs began to creak again. A groping hand, moving along the balustrade, came into the bar of moonlight; then another, and a ghastly thrill went through Griswell as he saw that the other hand gripped a hatchet – a hatchet which dripped blackly. Was that Branner who was coming down that stair?

Yes! The figure had moved into the bar of moonlight now, and Griswell recognised it. Then he saw Branner's face, and a shriek burst from Griswell's lips. Branner's face was bloodless, corpse-like; gouts of blood dripped darkly down it; his eyes were glassy and set, and blood oozed from the great gash which cleft the crown of his head!

Griswell never remembered exactly how he got out of that accursed house. Afterward he retained a mad, confused impression of smashing his way through a dusty cobwebbed window, of stumbling blindly across the weed-choked lawn, gibbering his frantic horror. He saw the black wall of the pines, and the moon floating in a blood-red mist in which there was neither sanity nor reason.

Some shred of sanity returned to him as he saw the automobile beside the road. In a world gone suddenly mad, that was an object reflecting prosaic reality; but even as he reached for the door, a dry chilling whir sounded in his ears, and he recoiled from the swaying undulating shape that arched up from its scaly coils on the driver's seat and hissed sibilantly at him, darting a forked tongue in the moonlight.

With a sob of horror he turned and fled down the road, as a man runs in a nightmare. He ran without purpose or reason. His numbed brain was incapable of conscious thought. He merely obeyed the blind primitive urge to run – run – run until he fell exhausted.

The black walls of the pines flowed endlessly past him; so he was seized with the illusion that he was getting nowhere. But presently a sound penetrated the fog of his terror . . . the steady, inexorable patter of feet behind him. Turning his head, he saw something loping after him – wolf or dog, he could not tell which, but its eyes glowed like balls of green fire. With a gasp he increased his speed, reeled around a bend in the road, and heard a horse snort; saw it rear and heard its rider curse; saw the gleam of blue steel in the man's lifted hand.

He staggered and fell, catching at the rider's stirrup.

'For God's sake, help me!' he panted. 'The thing! It killed Branner – it's coming after me! Look!'

Twin balls of fire gleamed in the fringe of bushes at the turn of the road. The rider swore again, and on the heels of his profanity came the smashing report of his six-shooter – again and yet again. The fire-sparks vanished, and the rider, jerking his stirrup free from Griswell's grasp, spurred his horse at the bend. Griswell staggered up, shaking in every limb. The rider was out of sight only a moment; then he came galloping back.

'Took to the brush. Timber wolf, I reckon, though I never heard of one chasin' a man before. Do you know what it was?'

Griswell could only shake his head weakly.

The rider, etched in the moonlight, looked down at him, smoking pistol still lifted in his right hand. He was a compactly-built man of medium height, and his broad-brimmed planter's hat and his boots marked him as a native of the country as definitely as Griswell's garb stamped him as a stranger.

'What's all this about, anyway?'

'I don't know,' Griswell answered helplessly. 'My name's Griswell. John Branner – my friend who was travelling with me – we stopped at a deserted house back down the road to spend the night. Something . . . ' at the memory he was choked by a rush of horror. 'My God!' he screamed. 'I must be mad! Something came and looked over the balustrade of the stair – something with a yellow face! I thought I dreamed it, but it must have been real. Then somebody began whistling upstairs, and Branner rose and went up the stairs walking like a man in his sleep, or hypnotised. I heard him scream – or someone screamed; then he came down the stair again with a bloody hatchet in his hand – and my God, sir, he was dead! His head had been split open. I saw brains and clotted blood oozing down his face, and his face was that of a dead man. But he came down the stairs! As God is my witness, John Branner was murdered in that dark upper hallway, and then his dead body came stalking down the stairs with a hatchet in its hand . . . to kill me!'

The rider made no reply; he sat his horse like a statue, outlined against the stars, and Griswell could not read his expression, his face shadowed by his hat-brim.

'You think I'm mad,' he said hopelessly. 'Perhaps I am.'

'I don't know what to think,' answered the rider. 'If it was any

house but the old Blassenville Manor . . . well, we'll see. My name's
Buckner. I'm sheriff of this county. Took a prisoner over to the
county-seat in the next county and was ridin' back late.'

He swung off his horse and stood beside Griswell, shorter than
the lanky New Englander, but much harder knit. There was a
natural manner of decision and certainty about him, and it was
easy to believe that he would be a dangerous man in any sort of
a fight.

'Are you afraid to go back to the house?' he asked, and Griswell
shuddered, but shook his head, the dogged tenacity of Puritan ances-
tors asserting itself.

'The thought of facing that horror again turns me sick.

'But poor Branner . . . ' he choked again. 'We must find his body.
My God!' he cried, unmanned by the abysmal horror of the thing;
'what will we find? If a dead man walks, what – '

'We'll see.' The sheriff caught the reins in the crook of his left
elbow and began filling the empty chambers of his big blue pistol as
they walked along.

As they made the turn Griswell's blood was ice at the thought of
what they might see lumbering up the road with a bloody, grinning
death-mask, but they saw only the house looming spectrally among
the pines, down the road. A strong shudder shook Griswell.

'God, how evil that house looks, against those black pines! It
looked sinister from the very first . . . when we went up the broken
walk and saw those pigeons fly up from the porch . . . '

'Pigeons?' Buckner cast him a quick glance. 'You saw the pigeons?'

'Why, yes! Scores of them perching on the porch railing.'

They strode on for a moment in silence, before Buckner said
abruptly: 'I've lived in this country all my life. I've passed the old
Blassenville place a thousand times, I reckon, at all hours of the day
and night. But I never saw a pigeon anywhere around it, or anywhere
else in these woods.'

'There were scores of them,' repeated Griswell, bewildered.

'I've seen men who swore they'd seen a flock of pigeons perched
along the balusters just at sundown,' said Buckner slowly. 'A tramp
was buildin' a fire in the yard, aimin' to camp there that night. I
passed along there about dark, and he told me about the pigeons. I
came back by there the next mornin'. The ashes of his fire were
there, and his tin cup, and skillet where he'd fried pork, and his
blankets looked like they'd been slept in. Nobody ever saw him
again. That was twelve years ago. They say the pigeons are the souls

of the Blassenvilles, let out of hell at sunset. The red glare in the west is the light from hell, because then the gates of hell are open, and the Blassenvilles fly out.'

'Who were the Blassenvilles?' asked Griswell, shivering.

'They owned all this land here. French-English family. Came here from the West Indies before the Louisiana Purchase. The Civil War ruined them, like it did so many. Some were killed in the war; most of the others died out. Nobody's lived in the Manor since 1890 when Miss Elizabeth Blassenville, the last of the line, fled from the old house one night like it was a plague spot, and never came back to it . . . this your auto?'

They halted beside the car, and Griswell stared morbidly at the grim house. Its dusty panes were empty and blank; but they did not seem blind to him. It seemed to him that ghastly eyes were fixed hungrily on him through those darkened panes. Buckner repeated his question.

'Yes. Be careful. There's a snake on the seat – or there was.'

'Not there now,' grunted Buckner, tying his horse and pulling an electric torch out of the saddle-bag. 'Well, let's have a look.'

He strode up the broken brick walk as matter-of-factly as if he were paying a social call on friends. Griswell followed close at his heels, his heart pounding suffocatingly. A scent of decay and mouldering vegetation blew on the faint wind, and Griswell grew faint with nausea that rose from a frantic abhorrence of these black woods, these ancient plantation houses that hid forgotten secrets of slavery and bloody pride and mysterious intrigues. He had thought of the South as a sunny, lazy land washed by soft breezes laden with spice and warm blossoms. But now he had discovered another, unsuspected side . . . a dark, brooding, fear-haunted side, and the discovery repelled him.

The oaken door sagged as it had before. The blackness of the interior was intensified by the beam of Buckner's light playing on the sill. That beam sliced through the darkness of the hallway and roved up the stair, and Griswell held his breath, clenching his fists. But no shape of lunacy leered down at them. Buckner went in, walking light as a cat, torch in one hand, gun in the other.

As he swung his light into the room across from the stairway, Griswell cried out – and cried out again, almost fainting with the intolerable sickness of what he saw. A trail of blood drops led across the floor, crossing the blankets Branner had occupied, which lay between the door and those in which Griswell had lain.

And Griswell's blankets had a terrible occupant. John Branner lay there, face down, his cleft head revealed in merciless clarity in the steady light. His outstretched hand still gripped the haft of a hatchet, and the blade was embedded deep in the blanket and the floor beneath, just where Griswell's head had lain when he slept there.

A momentary rush of blackness engulfed Griswell. He was not aware that he staggered, or that Buckner caught him. When he could see and hear again, he was violently sick and hung his head against the mantel, retching miserably.

Buckner turned the light full on him, making him blink. Buckner's voice came from behind the blinding radiance, the man himself unseen.

'Griswell, you've told me a yarn that's hard to believe. I saw something chasin' you, but it might have been a timber wolf, or a mad dog.

'If you're holdin' back anything, you better spill it. What you told me won't hold up in any court. You're bound to be accused of killin' your partner. I'll have to arrest you. If you'll give me the straight goods now, it'll make it easier. Now, didn't you kill this fellow, Branner?

'Wasn't it something like this: you quarrelled, he grabbed a hatchet and swung at you, but you dodged and then let him have it?'

Griswell sank down and hid his face in his hands, his head swimming.

'Great God, man, I didn't murder John! Why, we've been friends ever since we were children in school together. I've told you the truth. I don't blame you for not believing me. But God help me, it is the truth!'

The light swung back to the gory head again, and Griswell closed his eyes.

He heard Buckner grunt.

'I believe this hatchet in his hand is the one he was killed with. Blood and brains plastered on the blade, and hairs stickin' to it . . . hairs exactly the same colour as his. This makes it tough for you, Griswell.'

'How so?' the New Englander asked dully.

'Knocks any plea of self-defence in the head. Branner couldn't have swung at you with this hatchet after you split his skull with it. You must have pulled the axe out of his head, stuck it into the floor and clamped his fingers on it to make it look like he'd attacked you.

And it would have been damned clever . . . if you'd used another hatchet.'

'But I didn't kill him,' groaned Griswell. 'I have no intention of pleading self-defence.'

'That's what puzzles me,' Buckner admitted frankly, straightening. 'What murderer would rig up such a crazy story as you've told me, to prove his innocence? Average killer would have told a logical yarn, at least. Hmmm! Blood drops leadin' from the door. The body was dragged – no, couldn't have been dragged. The floor isn't smeared. You must have carried it here, after killin' him in some other place. But in that case, why isn't there any blood on your clothes? Of course you could have changed clothes and washed your hands. But the fellow hasn't been dead long.'

'He walked downstairs and across the room,' said Griswell hopelessly. 'He came to kill me. I knew he was coming to kill me when I saw him lurching down the stair. He struck where I would have been, if I hadn't awakened. That window – I burst out at it. You see it's broken.'

'I see. But if he walked then, why isn't he walkin' now?'

'I don't know! I'm too sick to think straight. I've been fearing that he'd rise up from the floor where he lies and come at me again. When I heard that wolf running up the road after me, I thought it was John chasing me – John, running through the night with his bloody axe and his bloody head, and his death-grin!'

His teeth chattered as he lived that horror over again.

Buckner let his light play across the floor.

'The blood drops lead into the hall. Come on. We'll follow them.'

Griswell cringed. 'They lead upstairs.'

Buckner's eyes were fixed hard on him.

'Are you afraid to go upstairs, with me?'

Griswell's face was grey.

'Yes. But I'm going, with you or without you. The thing that killed poor John may still be hiding up there.'

'Stay behind me,' ordered Buckner. 'If anything jumps us, I'll take care of it. But for your own sake, I warn you that I shoot quicker than a cat jumps, and I don't often miss. If you've got any ideas of layin' me out from behind, forget them.'

'Don't be a fool!' Resentment got the better of his apprehension, and this outburst seemed to reassure Buckner more than any of his protestations of innocence.

'I want to be fair,' he said quietly. 'I haven't indicted and condemned you in my mind already. If only half of what you're tellin' me is the truth, you've been through a hell of an experience, and I don't want to be too hard on you. But you can see how hard it is for me to believe all you've told me.'

Griswell wearily motioned for him to lead the way, unspeaking. They went out into the hall, paused at the landing. A thin string of crimson drops, distinct in the thick dust, led up the steps.

'Man's tracks in the dust,' grunted Buckner. 'Go slow.

'I've got to be sure of what I see, because we're obliteratin' them as we go up. Hmmm! One set goin' up, one comin' down. Same man. Not your tracks. Branner was a bigger man than you are. Blood drops all the way . . . blood on the banisters like a man had laid his bloody hand there . . . a smear of stuff that looks . . . brains. Now what – '

'He walked down the stair, a dead man,' shuddered Griswell. 'Groping with one hand – the other gripping the hatchet that killed him.'

'Or was carried,' muttered the sheriff. 'But if somebody carried him – where are the tracks?'

They came out into the upper hallway, a vast, empty space of dust and shadows where time-crusted windows repelled the moonlight and the ring of Buckner's torch seemed inadequate. Griswell trembled like a leaf. Here, in darkness and horror, John Branner had died.

'Somebody whistled up here,' he muttered. 'John came, as if he were being called.'

Buckner's eyes were blazing strangely in the light.

'The footprints lead down the hall,' he muttered. 'Same as on the stair . . . one set going, one coming. Same prints – Judas!'

Behind him Griswell stifled a cry, for he had seen what prompted Buckner's exclamation. A few feet from the head of the stair Branner's footprints stopped abruptly, then returned, treading almost in the other tracks. And where the trail halted there was a great splash of blood on the dusty floor . . . and other tracks met it – tracks of bare feet, narrow but with splayed toes. They too receded in a second line from the spot.

Buckner bent over them, swearing.

'The tracks meet! And where they meet there's blood and brains on the floor! Branner must have been killed on that spot – with a blow from a hatchet. Bare feet coming out of the darkness to meet shod feet . . . then both turned away again; the shod feet went downstairs, the bare feet went back down the hall.' He directed his light down the hall. The footprints faded into darkness, beyond the reach of the beam. On either hand the closed doors of chambers were cryptic portals of mystery.

'Suppose your crazy tale was true,' Buckner muttered, half to himself. 'These aren't your tracks. They look like a woman's. Suppose somebody did whistle, and Branner went upstairs to investigate. Suppose somebody met him here in the dark and split his head. The signs and tracks would have been, in that case, just as they really are. But if that's so, why isn't Branner lyin' here where he was killed? Could he have lived long enough to take the hatchet away from whoever killed him, and stagger downstairs with it?'

'No, no!' Recollection gagged Griswell. 'I saw him on the stair. He was dead. No man could live a minute after receiving such a wound.'

'I believe it,' muttered Buckner. 'But – it's madness! Or else it's too clever – yet, what sane man would think up and work out such an elaborate and utterly insane plan to escape punishment for murder, when a simple plea of self-defence would have been so much more effective? No court would recognise that story. Well, let's follow these other tracks. They lead down the hall . . . here, what's this?'

With an icy clutch at his soul, Griswell saw the light was beginning to grow dim.

'This battery is new,' muttered Buckner, and for the first time Griswell caught an edge of fear in his voice. 'Come on – out of here quick!'

The light had faded to a faint red glow. The darkness seemed straining into them, creeping with black cat-feet. Buckner retreated, pushing Griswell stumbling behind him as he walked backward, pistol cocked and lifted, down the dark hall. In the growing darkness Griswell heard what sounded like the stealthy opening of a door. And suddenly the blackness about them was vibrant with menace. Griswell knew Buckner sensed it as well as he, for the sheriff's hard body was tense and taut as a stalking panther's.

But without haste he worked his way to the stair and backed down it, Griswell preceding him, and fighting the panic that urged him to scream and burst into mad flight. A ghastly thought brought icy sweat out on his flesh. Suppose the dead man were creeping up the stair behind them in the dark, face frozen in the death-grin, blood-caked hatchet lifted to strike?

This possibility so overpowered him that he was scarcely aware when his feet struck the level of the lower hallway, and he was only then aware that the light had grown brighter as they descended, until it now gleamed with its full power – but when Buckner turned it back up the stairway, it failed to illuminate the darkness that hung like a tangible fog at the head of the stair.

'The damn thing was conjured,' muttered Buckner. 'Nothin' else. It couldn't act like that naturally.'

'Turn the light into the room,' begged Griswell. 'See if John – if John is . . . '

He could not put the ghastly thought into words, but Buckner understood.

He swung the beam around, and Griswell had never dreamed that the sight of the gory body of a murdered man could bring such relief.

'He's still there,' grunted Buckner. 'If he walked after he was killed, he hasn't walked since. But that thing . . . '

Again he turned the light up the stair, and stood chewing his lip and scowling. Three times he half lifted his gun. Griswell read his mind. The sheriff was tempted to plunge back up that stair, take his chance with the unknown. But common sense held him back.

'I wouldn't have a chance in the dark,' he muttered. 'And I've got a hunch the light would go out again.'

He turned and faced Griswell squarely.

'There's no use dodgin' the question. There's somethin' hellish in this house, and I believe I have an inklin' of what it is. I don't believe you killed Branner. Whatever killed him is up there – now. There's a lot about your yarn that don't sound sane; but there's nothin' sane about a flashlight goin' out like this one did. I don't believe that thing upstairs is human. I never met anything I was afraid to tackle in the dark before, but I'm not goin' up there until daylight. It's not long until dawn. We'll wait for it out there on that gallery.'

The stars were already paling when they came out on the broad porch. Buckner seated himself on the balustrade, facing the door, his pistol dangling in his fingers. Griswell sat down near him and leaned back against a crumbling pillar. He shut his eyes, grateful for the faint breeze that seemed to cool his throbbing brain. He experienced a dull sense of unreality. He was a stranger in a strange land, a land that had become suddenly imbued with black horror. The shadow of the noose hovered above him, and in that dark house lay John Branner, with his butchered head . . . like the figments of a dream these facts spun and eddied in his brain until all merged in a grey twilight as sleep came uninvited to his weary soul.

He awoke to a cold white dawn and full memory of the horrors of the night. Mists curled about the stems of the pines, crawled in smoky wisps up the broken walk. Buckner was shaking him.

'Wake up! It's daylight.'

Griswell rose, wincing at the stiffness of his limbs. His face was grey and old.

'I'm ready. Let's go upstairs.'

'I've already been!' Buckner's eyes burned in the early dawn. 'I didn't wake you up. I went as soon as it was light. I found nothin'.'

'The tracks of the bare feet . . . '

'Gone!'

'Gone?'

'Yes, gone! The dust had been disturbed all over the hall, from the point where Branner's tracks ended; swept into corners. No chance of trackin' anything there now. Something obliterated those tracks while we sat here, and I didn't hear a sound. I've gone through the whole house. Not a sign of anything.'

Griswell shuddered at the thought of himself sleeping alone on the porch while Buckner conducted his exploration.

'What shall we do?' he asked listlessly. 'With those tracks gone there goes my only chance of proving my story.'

'We'll take Branner's body into the county-seat,' answered Buckner. 'Let me do the talkin'. If the authorities knew the facts as they appear, they'd insist on you being confined and indicted. I don't believe you killed Branner . . . but neither a district attorney, judge nor jury would believe what you told me, or what happened to us last night. I'm handlin' this thing my own way. I'm not goin' to arrest you until I've exhausted every other possibility.

'Say nothin' about what's happened here, when we get to town. I'll simply tell the district attorney that John Branner was killed by a party or parties unknown, and that I'm workin' on the case.

'Are you game to come back with me to this house and spend the night here, sleepin' in that room as you and Branner slept last night?'

Griswell went white, but answered as stoutly as his ancestors might have expressed their determination to hold their cabins in the teeth of the Pequots: 'I'll do it.'

'Let's go then; help me pack the body out to your auto.'

Griswell's soul revolted at the sight of John Branner's bloodless face in the chill white day, and the feel of his clammy flesh. The grey fog wrapped wispy tentacles about their feet as they carried their grisly burden across the lawn.

Chapter 2. *The snake's brother*

Again the shadows were lengthening over the pinelands, and again two men came bumping along the old road in a car with a New England licence plate.

Buckner was driving. Griswell's nerves were too shattered for him to trust himself at the wheel. He looked gaunt and haggard, and his face was still pallid. The strain of the day spent at the county-seat was added to the horror that still rode his soul like the shadow of a black-winged vulture. He had not slept, had not tasted what he had eaten.

'I told you I'd tell you about the Blassenvilles,' said Buckner. 'They were proud folks, haughty, and pretty damn ruthless when they wanted their way. They didn't treat their slaves as well as the other planters did – got their ideas in the West Indies, I reckon. There was a streak of cruelty in them – especially Miss Celia, the last one of the family to come to these parts. That was long after the slaves had been freed, but she used to whip her mulatto maid just like she was a slave, the old folks say.

'Well, after the Civil War they died off pretty fast, livin' in poverty on the plantation which was allowed to go to ruin. Finally only four girls were left, sisters, livin' in the old house and ekin' out a bare livin', with a few blacks livin' in the old slave huts and workin' the fields on the share. They kept to themselves, bein' proud, and ashamed of their poverty. Folks wouldn't see them for months at a time.

'But folks knew about it when Miss Celia came to live with them. She came from somewhere in the West Indies, where the whole family originally had its roots – a fine, handsome woman, they say, in the early thirties. But she didn't mix with folks any more than the girls did. She brought a mulatto maid with her, and the Blassenville cruelty cropped out in her treatment of this maid. I knew an old man years ago, who swore he saw Miss Celia tie this girl up to a tree, stark naked, and whip her with a horsewhip. Nobody was surprised when she disappeared. Everybody figured she'd run away, of course.

'Well, one day in the spring of 1890 Miss Elizabeth, the youngest girl, came in to town for the first time in maybe a year. She came after supplies. Talked a little more, too, a bit wild. Said Miss Celia had gone, without leaving any word. Said her sisters thought she'd gone back to the West Indies, but she believed her aunt was still in the house. She didn't say what she meant. Just got her supplies and pulled out for the Manor.

'A month went past, and a black came into town and said that Miss Elizabeth was livin' at the Manor alone. Said her three sisters weren't there any more, that they'd left one by one without givin' any word or explanation. She didn't know where they'd gone, and was afraid to stay there alone, but didn't know where else to go. She'd never known anything but the Manor, and had neither relatives nor friends. But she was in mortal terror of something.

'It was a stormy spring night when Miss Elizabeth came tearin' into town on the one horse she owned, nearly dead from fright. She fell from her horse in the square; when she could talk she said she'd found a secret room in the Manor that had been forgotten for a hundred years. And she said that there she found her three sisters, dead, and hangin' by their necks from the ceilin'. She said something chased her and nearly brained her with an axe as she ran out the front door, but somehow she got to the horse and got away. She was nearly crazy with fear, and didn't know what it was that chased her . . . said it looked like a woman with a yellow face.

'About a hundred men rode out there, right away. They searched the house from top to bottom, but they didn't find any secret room, or the remains of the sisters. But they did find a hatchet stickin' in the doorjamb downstairs, with some of Miss Elizabeth's hairs stuck on it, just as she'd said. She wouldn't go back there and show them how to find the secret door; almost went crazy when they suggested it.

'When she was able to travel, the people made up some money and loaned it to her – she was still too proud to accept charity – and she went to California. She never came back, but later it was learned, when she sent back to repay the money they'd loaned her, that she'd married out there.

'Nobody ever bought the house. It stood there just as she'd left it, and as the years passed folks stole all the furnishings out of it. But they came after sunup and left long before sundown.'

'What did the people think about Miss Elizabeth's story?' asked Griswell.

'Well, most folks thought she'd gone a little crazy, livin' in that old house alone. But some people believed that mulatto girl, Joan, didn't run away, after all. They believed she'd hidden in the woods, and glutted her hatred of the Blassenvilles by murderin' Miss Celia and the three girls. They beat up the woods with bloodhounds, but never found a trace of her. If there was a secret room in the house, she might have been hidin' there . . . if there was anything to that theory.'

'She couldn't have been hiding there all these years,' muttered Griswell. 'Anyway, the thing in the house now isn't human.'

Buckner wrenched the wheel around and turned into a dim trace that left the main road and meandered off through the pines.

'Where are you going?'

'There's an old Negro that lives off this way a few miles. I want to talk to him. This old man is nearly a hundred years old. They say he's a voodoo man.'

Griswell shivered at the phrase, staring uneasily at the green forest walls that shut them in. The scent of the pines was mingled with the odours of unfamiliar plants and blossoms. But underlying all was a reek of rot and decay. Again a sick abhorrence of these dark mysterious woodlands almost overpowered him.

'Voodoo!' he muttered. 'I'd forgotten about that . . . I never could think of black magic in connection with the South. To me witchcraft was always associated with old crooked streets in waterfront towns, overhung by gabled roofs that were old when they were hanging witches in Salem; dark musty alleys where black cats and other things might steal at night. Witchcraft always meant the old towns of New England, to me . . . but all this is more terrible than any New England legend . . . these sombre pines, old deserted houses, lost plantations, old tales of madness and horror . . . God, what frightful, ancient terrors there are on this continent fools call "young"!'

'Here's old Jacob's hut,' announced Buckner, bringing the automobile to a halt.

Griswell saw a clearing and a small cabin squatting under the shadows of the huge trees. The pines gave way to oaks and cypresses, bearded with grey trailing moss, and behind the cabin lay the edge of a swamp that ran away under the dimness of the trees, choked with rank vegetation. A thin wisp of blue smoke curled up from the stick-and-mud chimney.

He followed Buckner to the tiny stoop, where the sheriff pushed open the leather-hinged door and strode in. Griswell blinked in the comparative dimness of the interior. A single small window let in a little daylight. An old Negro crouched beside the hearth, watching a pot stew over the open fire. He looked up as they entered, but did not rise. He seemed incredibly old. His face was a mass of wrinkles, and his eyes, dark and vital, were filmed momentarily at times as if his mind wandered.

Buckner motioned Griswell to sit down in a string-bottomed chair, and himself took a rudely-made bench near the hearth, facing the old man.

'Jacob,' he said bluntly, 'the time's come for you to talk. I know you know the secret of Blassenville Manor. I've never questioned you about it, because it wasn't in my line. But a man was murdered there last night, and this man here may hang for it, unless you tell me what haunts that old house of the Blassenvilles.'

The old man's eyes gleamed, then grew misty as if clouds of extreme age drifted across his brittle mind.

'The Blassenvilles,' he murmured, and his voice was mellow and rich, his speech not the patois of the piny woods darky. 'They were proud people, sirs – proud and cruel. Some died in the war, some were killed in duels – the menfolks, sirs. Some died in the Manor . . . the old Manor . . . ' His voice trailed off into unintelligible mumblings.

'What of the Manor?' asked Buckner patiently.

'Miss Celia was the proudest of them all,' the old man muttered. 'The proudest and the cruellest. The black people hated her; Joan most of all. Joan had white blood in her, and she was proud, too. Miss Celia whipped her like a slave.'

'What is the secret of Blassenville Manor?' persisted Buckner.

The film faded from the old man's eyes; they were dark as moon-lit wells.

'What secret, sir? I do not understand.'

'Yes, you do. For years that old house has stood there with its mystery. You know the key to its riddle.'

The old man stirred the stew. He seemed perfectly rational now.

'Sir, life is sweet, even to an old man.'

'You mean somebody would kill you if you told me?'

But the old man was mumbling again, his eyes clouded.

'Not somebody. No human. No human being. The gods of the swamps. My secret is inviolate, guarded by the Big Serpent, the god above all gods. He would send a little brother to kiss me with his cold lips . . . a little brother with a white crescent moon on his head. I sold my soul to the Big Serpent when he made me maker of zuvembies . . . '

Buckner stiffened.

'I heard that word once before,' he said softly, 'from the lips of a dying man, when I was a child. What does it mean?'

Fear filled the eyes of old Jacob.

'What have I said? No – no! I said nothing.'

'Zuvembies,' prompted Buckner.

'Zuvembies,' mechanically repeated the old man, his eyes vacant. 'A zuvembie was once a woman – on the Slave Coast they know of them. The drums that whisper by night in the hills of Haiti tell of them. The makers of zuvembies are honoured of the people of Damballah. It is death to speak of it – it is one of the Snake God's forbidden secrets.'

'You speak of the zuvembies,' said Buckner softly.

'I must not speak of it,' mumbled the old man, and Griswell realised that he was thinking aloud, too far gone in his dotage to be aware that he was speaking at all. 'No man must know that I danced in the Black Ceremony of the voodoo, and was made a maker of zombies and zuvembies. The Big Snake punishes loose tongues with death.'

'A zuvembie is a woman?' prompted Buckner.

'Was a woman. She knew I was a maker of zuvembies . . . she came and stood in my hut and asked for the awful brew.– the brew of ground snake-bones, and the blood of vampire bats, and the dew from a nighthawk's wings, and other elements unnameable. She had danced in the Black Ceremony – she was ripe to become a zuvembie – the Black Brew was all that was needed . . . the other was beautiful . . . I could not refuse her.'

'Who?' demanded Buckner tensely, but the old man's head was sunk on his withered breast, and he did not reply. He seemed to slumber as he sat. Buckner shook him. 'You gave a brew to make a woman a zuvembie . . . what is a zuvembie?'

The old man stirred resentfully and muttered drowsily.

'A zuvembie is no longer human. It knows neither relatives nor friends. It is one with the people of the Black World. It commands the natural demons – owls, bats, snakes and werewolves – and can fetch darkness to blot out a little light. It can be slain by lead or steel, but unless it is slain thus, it lives for ever, and it eats no such food as humans eat. It dwells like a bat in a cave or an old house. Time means naught to the zuvembie; an hour, a day, a year, all is one. It cannot speak human words, nor think as a human thinks, but it can hypno-tise the living by the sound of its voice, and when it slays a man, it can command his lifeless body until the flesh is cold. As long as the blood flows, the corpse is its slave. Its pleasure lies in the slaughter of human beings.'

'And why should one become a zuvembie?' asked Buckner softly.

'Hate,' whispered the old man. 'Hate! Revenge!'

'Was her name Joan?' murmured Buckner.

It was as if the name penetrated the fogs of senility that clouded the voodoo-man's mind. He shook himself and the film faded from his eyes, leaving them hard and gleaming as wet black marble.

'Joan?' he said slowly. 'I have not heard that name for the span of a generation. I seem to have been sleeping, gentlemen; I do not remember – I ask your pardon. Old men fall asleep before the fire, like old dogs. You asked me of Blassenville Manor? Sir, if I were to tell you why I cannot answer you, you would deem it mere superstition.'

As he spoke he was reaching across the hearth for a piece of firewood, groping among the heaps of sticks there. And his voice broke in a scream, as he jerked back his arm convulsively. And a horrible, thrashing, trailing thing came with it. Around the voodoo-man's arm a mottled length of that shape was wrapped, and a wicked wedge-shaped head struck again in silent fury.

The old man fell on the hearth, screaming, upsetting the simmering pot and scattering the embers, and then Buckner caught up a billet of firewood and crushed that flat head. Cursing, he kicked aside the knotting, twisting trunk, glaring briefly at the mangled head. Old Jacob had ceased screaming and writhing; he lay still, staring glassily upward.

'Dead?' whispered Griswell.

'Dead as Judas Iscariot,' snapped Buckner, frowning at the twitching reptile. 'That infernal snake crammed enough poison into his veins to kill a dozen men his age. But I think it was the shock and fright that killed him.'

'What shall we do?' asked Griswell, shivering.

'Leave the body on that bunk. Nothin' can hurt it, if we bolt the door so the wild hogs can't get in, or any cat. We'll carry it into town tomorrow. We've got work to do tonight. Let's get goin'.'

Griswell shrank from touching the corpse, but he helped Buckner lift it on the rude bunk, and then stumbled hastily out of the hut. The sun was hovering above the horizon, visible in dazzling red flame through the black stems of the trees.

They climbed into the car in silence, and went bumping back along the stumpy trail.

'He said the Big Snake would send one of his brothers,' muttered Griswell.

'Nonsense!' snorted Buckner. 'Snakes like warmth, and that swamp is full of them. It crawled in and coiled up among that firewood. Old Jacob disturbed it, and it bit him. Nothin' supernatural about that.'

After a short silence he said, in a different voice, 'That was the first time I ever saw a rattler strike without singin'; and the first time I ever saw a snake with a white crescent moon on its head.'

They were turning in to the main road before either spoke again.

'You think that the mulatto Joan has skulked in the house all these years?' Griswell asked.

'You heard what old Jacob said,' answered Buckner grimly. 'Time means nothin' to a zuvembie.'

As they made the last turn in the road, Griswell braced himself against the sight of Blassenville Manor looming black against the red sunset. When it came into view he bit his lip to keep from shrieking. The suggestion of cryptic horror came back in all its power.

'Look!' he whispered from dry lips as they came to a halt beside the road. Buckner grunted.

From the balustrades of the gallery rose a whirling cloud of pigeons that swept away into the sunset, black against the lurid glare . . .

Chapter 3. *The call of Zuvembie*

Both men sat rigid for a few moments after the pigeons had flown.

'Well, I've seen them at last,' muttered Buckner.

'Only the doomed see them perhaps,' whispered Griswell. 'That tramp saw them . . . '

'Well, we'll see,' returned the Southerner tranquilly, as he climbed out of the car, but Griswell noticed him unconsciously hitch forward his scabbarded gun.

The oaken door sagged on broken hinges. Their feet echoed on the broken brick walk. The blind windows reflected the sunset in sheets of flame. As they came into the broad hall Griswell saw the string of black marks that ran across the floor and into the chamber, marking the path of a dead man.

Buckner had brought blankets out of the automobile. He spread them before the fireplace.

'I'll lie next to the door,' he said. 'You lie where you did last night.'

'Shall we light a fire in the grate?' asked Griswell, dreading the thought of the blackness that would cloak the woods when the brief twilight had died.

'No. You've got a flashlight and so have I. We'll lie here in the dark and see what happens. Can you use that gun I gave you?'

'I suppose so. I never fired a revolver, but I know how it's done.'

'Well, leave the shootin' to me, if possible.' The sheriff seated himself cross-legged on his blankets and emptied the cylinder of his big blue Colt, inspecting each cartridge with a critical eye before he replaced it.

Griswell prowled nervously back and forth, begrudging the slow fading of the light as a miser begrudges the waning of his gold. He leaned with one hand against the mantelpiece, staring down into the dust-covered ashes. The fire that produced those ashes must have been built by Elizabeth Blassenville, more than forty years before. The thought was depressing. Idly he stirred the dusty ashes with his toe. Something came to view among the charred debris – a bit of paper, stained and yellowed. Still idly he bent and drew it out of the ashes. It was a note-book with mouldering cardboard backs.

'What have you found?' asked Buckner, squinting down the gleaming barrel of his gun.

'Nothing but an old note-book. Looks like a diary. The pages are covered with writing . . . but the ink is so faded, and the paper is in such a state of decay that I can't tell much about it. How do you suppose it came in the fireplace, without being burned up?'

'Thrown in long after the fire was out,' surmised Buckner. 'Probably found and tossed in the fireplace by somebody who was in here stealin' furniture. Likely somebody who couldn't read.'

Griswell fluttered the crumbling leaves listlessly, straining his eyes in the fading light over the yellowed scrawls. Then he stiffened.

'Here's an entry that's legible! Listen!' He read: '"I know someone is in the house besides myself. I can hear someone prowling about at night when the sun has set and the pines are black outside. Often in the night I hear it fumbling at my door. Who is it? Is it one of my sisters? Is it Aunt Celia? If it is either of these, why does she steal so subtly about the house? Why does she tug at my door, and glide away when I call to her? Shall I open the door and go out to her? No, no! I dare not! I am afraid. Oh God, what shall I do? I dare not stay here – but where am I to go?"'

'By God!' ejaculated Buckner. 'That must be Elizabeth Blassenville's diary! Go on!'

'I can't make out the rest of the page,' answered Griswell. 'But a few pages further on I can make out some lines.' He read: '"My sisters are dead. I know they are dead. I seem to sense that they died horribly, in fear and agony. But why? Why? If someone murdered Aunt Celia, why should that person murder my poor sisters? Joan – "' He paused, scowling futilely.

'A piece of the page is torn out. Here's another entry under another date – at least I judge it's a date; I can't make it out for sure.

'" – the awful thing that the old Negress hinted at? She named Jacob Blount, and Joan, but she would not speak plainly; perhaps she feared to – " Part of it gone here; then: "No, no! How can it be? She is dead – or gone away. Yet – she was born and raised in the West Indies, and from hints she let fall in the past, I know she delved into the mysteries of the voodoo. I believe she even danced in one of their horrible ceremonies – how could she have been such a beast? And this – this horror. God, can such things be? I know not what to think. If it is she who roams the house at night, who fumbles at my door, who whistles so weirdly and sweetly – no, no, I must be going mad. If I stay here alone I shall die as hideously as my sisters must have died. Of that I am convinced." '

The incoherent chronicle ended as abruptly as it had begun. Griswell was so engrossed in deciphering the scraps that he was not aware that darkness had stolen upon them, hardly aware that Buckner was holding his electric torch for him to read by. Waking from his abstraction he started and darted a quick glance at the black hallway.

'What do you make of it?'

'What I've suspected all the time,' answered Buckner. 'That mulatto maid Joan turned zuvembie to avenge herself on Miss Celia. Probably hated the whole family as much as she did her mistress. She'd taken part in voodoo ceremonies on her native island until she was "ripe", as old Jacob said. All she needed was the Black Brew – he supplied that. She killed Miss Celia and the three older girls, and would have gotten Elizabeth but for chance. She's been lurkin' in this old house all these years, like a snake in a ruin.'

'But why should she murder a stranger?'

'You heard what old Jacob said,' reminded Buckner. 'A zuvembie finds satisfaction in the slaughter of humans. She called Branner up the stair and split his head and stuck the hatchet in his hand, and sent him downstairs to murder you. No court will ever believe that, but if we can produce her body, that will be evidence enough to prove your innocence. My word will be taken, that she murdered Branner. Jacob said a zuvembie could be killed . . . in reporting this affair I don't have to be too accurate in detail.'

'She came and peered over the balustrade of the stair at us,' muttered Griswell. 'But why didn't we find her tracks on the stair?'

'Maybe you dreamed it. Maybe a zuvembie can project her spirit –
hell! why try to rationalise something that's outside the bounds of
rationality? Let's begin our watch.'

'Don't turn out the light!' exclaimed Griswell involuntarily. Then
he added: 'Of course. Turn it out. We must be in the dark as' – he
gagged a bit – 'as Branner and I were.'

But fear like a physical sickness assailed him when the room was
plunged in darkness. He lay trembling and his heart beat so heavily
he felt as if he would suffocate.

'The West Indies must be the plague spot of the world,' muttered
Buckner, a blur on his blankets. 'I've heard of zombies. Never knew
before what a zuvembie was. Evidently some drug concocted by the
voodoo-men to induce madness in women. That doesn't explain
the other things, though: the hypnotic powers, the abnormal long-
evity, the ability to control corpses – no, a zuvembie can't be merely
a mad-woman. It's a monster, something more and less than a
human being, created by the magic that spawns in black swamps
and jungles – well, we'll see.'

His voice ceased, and in the silence Griswell heard the pounding of
his own heart. Outside in the black woods a wolf howled eerily, and
owls hooted. Then silence fell again like a black fog.

Griswell forced himself to lie still on his blankets. Time seemed
at a standstill. He felt as if he were choking. The suspense was
growing unendurable; the effort he made to control his crumbling
nerves bathed his limbs in sweat. He clenched his teeth until his
jaws ached and almost locked, and the nails of his fingers bit deeply
into his palms.

He did not know what he was expecting. The fiend would strike
again – but how? Would it be a horrible, sweet whistling, bare feet
stealing down the creaking steps, or a sudden hatchet-stroke in the
dark? Would it choose him or Buckner? Was Buckner already
dead? He could see nothing in the blackness, but he heard the
man's steady breathing. The Southerner must have nerves of steel.
Or was that Buckner breathing beside him, separated by a narrow
strip of darkness? Had the fiend already struck in silence, and taken
the sheriff's place, there to lie in ghoulish glee until it was ready
to strike? – A thousand hideous fancies assailed Griswell tooth
and claw.

He began to feel that he would go mad if he did not leap to his
feet, screaming, and burst frenziedly out of that accursed house – not
even the fear of the gallows could keep him lying there in the

darkness any longer . . . the rhythm of Buckner's breathing was suddenly broken, and Griswell felt as if a bucket of ice-water had been poured over him. From somewhere above them rose a sound of weird, sweet whistling . . .

Griswell's control snapped, plunging his brain into darkness deeper than the physical blackness which engulfed him. There was a period of absolute blankness, in which a realisation of motion was his first sensation of awakening consciousness. He was running, madly, stumbling over an incredibly rough road. All was darkness about him, and he ran blindly. Vaguely he realised that he must have bolted from the house, and fled for perhaps miles before his overwrought brain began to function. He did not care; dying on the gallows for a murder he never committed did not terrify him half as much as the thought of returning to that house of horror. He was overpowered by the urge to run – run – run as he was running now, blindly, until he reached the end of his endurance. The mist had not yet fully lifted from his brain, but he was aware of a dull wonder that he could not see the stars through the black branches. He wished vaguely that he could see where he was going. He believed he must be climbing a hill, and that was strange, for he knew there were no hills within miles of the Manor. Then above and ahead of him a dim glow began.

He scrambled toward it, over ledge-like projections that were more and more taking on a disquieting symmetry. Then he was horror-stricken to realise that a sound was impacting on his ears – a weird mocking whistle. The sound swept the mists away. Why, what was this? Where was he? Awakening and realisation came like the stunning stroke of a butcher's maul. He was not fleeing along a road, or climbing a hill; he was mounting a stair. He was still in Blassenville Manor! And he was climbing the stair!

An inhuman scream burst from his lips. Above it the mad whistling rose in a ghoulish piping of demoniac triumph. He tried to stop – to turn back – even to fling himself over the balustrade. His shrieking rang unbearably in his own ears. But his will-power was shattered to bits. It did not exist. He had no will. He had dropped his flashlight, and he had forgotten the gun in his pocket. He could not command his own body. His legs, moving stiffly, worked like pieces of mechanism detached from his brain, obeying an outside will. Clumping methodically they carried him shrieking up the stair toward the witch-fire glow shimmering above him.

'Buckner!' he screamed. 'Buckner! Help, for God's sake!'

His voice strangled in his throat. He had reached the upper landing. He was tottering down the hallway. The whistling sank and ceased, but its impulsion still drove him on. He could not see from what source the dim glow came. It seemed to emanate from no central focus. But he saw a vague figure shambling toward him. It looked like a woman, but no human woman ever walked with that skulking gait, and no human woman ever had that face of horror, that leering yellow blur of lunacy – he tried to scream at the sight of that face, at the glint of keen steel in the uplifted claw-like hand . . . but his tongue was frozen.

Then something crashed deafeningly behind him; the shadows were split by a tongue of flame which lit a hideous figure falling backward. Hard on the heels of the report rang an inhuman squawk.

In the darkness that followed the flash Griswell fell to his knees and covered his face with his hands. He did not hear Buckner's voice. The Southerner's hand on his shoulder shook him out of his swoon.

A light in his eyes blinded him. He blinked, shaded his eyes, looked up into Buckner's face, bending at the rim of the circle of light. The sheriff was pale.

'Are you hurt? God, man, are you hurt? There's a butcher's knife there on the floor – '

'I'm not hurt,' mumbled Griswell. 'You fired just in time – the fiend! Where is it? Where did it go?'

'Listen!'

Somewhere in the house there sounded a sickening flopping and flapping as of something that thrashed and struggled in its death convulsions.

'Jacob was right,' said Buckner grimly. 'Lead can kill them. I hit her, all right. Didn't dare use my flashlight, but there was enough light. When that whistlin' started you almost walked over me gettin' out. I knew you were hypnotised, or whatever it is. I followed you up the stairs. I was right behind you, but crouchin' low so she wouldn't see me, and maybe get away again. I almost waited too long before I fired – but the sight of her almost paralysed me. Look!'

He flashed his light down the hall, and now it shone bright and clear. And it shone on an aperture gaping in the wall where no door had showed before.

'The secret panel Miss Elizabeth found!' Buckner snapped. 'Come on!'

He ran across the hallway and Griswell followed him dazedly. The flopping and thrashing came from beyond that mysterious door, and now the sounds had ceased.

The light revealed a narrow, tunnel-like corridor that evidently led through one of the thick walls. Buckner plunged into it without hesitation.

'Maybe it couldn't think like a human,' he muttered, shining his light ahead of him. 'But it had sense enough to erase its tracks last night so we couldn't trail it to that point in the wall and maybe find the secret panel. There's a room ahead – the secret room of the Blassenvilles!'

And Griswell cried out: 'My God! It's the windowless chamber I saw in my dream, with the three bodies hanging – ahhhhh!'

Buckner's light playing about the circular chamber became suddenly motionless. In that wide ring of light three figures appeared, three dried, shrivelled, mummy-like shapes, still clad in the mouldering garments of the last century. Their slippers were clear of the floor as they hung by their withered necks from chains suspended from the ceiling.

'The three Blassenville sisters!' muttered Buckner. 'Miss Elizabeth wasn't crazy, after all.'

'Look!' Griswell could barely make his voice intelligible. 'There – over there in the corner!'

The light moved, halted.

'Was that thing a woman once?' whispered Griswell. 'God, look at that face, even in death. Look at those claw-like hands, with black talons like those of a beast. Yes, it was human, though – even the rags of an old ballroom gown. Why should a mulatto maid wear such a dress, I wonder?'

'This has been her lair for over forty years,' muttered Buckner, brooding over the grinning grisly thing sprawling in the corner. 'This clears you, Griswell – a crazy woman with a hatchet – that's all the authorities need to know. God, what a revenge! – what a foul revenge! Yet what a bestial nature she must have had, in the beginnin', to delve into voodoo as she must have done . . . '

'The mulatto woman?' whispered Griswell, dimly sensing a horror that overshadowed all the rest of the terror.

Buckner shook his head. 'We misunderstood old Jacob's maunderin's, and the things Miss Elizabeth wrote – she must have known, but family pride sealed her lips. Griswell, I understand now; the mulatto woman had her revenge, but not as we'd supposed. She didn't drink the Black Brew old Jacob fixed for her. It was for somebody else, to be given secretly in her food, or coffee, no doubt. Then Joan ran away, leavin' the seeds of the hell she'd sowed to grow.'

'That – that's not the mulatto woman?' whispered Griswell.

'When I saw her out there in the hallway I knew she was no mulatto. And those distorted features still reflect a family likeness. I've seen her portrait, and I can't be mistaken. There lies the creature that was once Celia Blassenville.'

DELENDA EST

'It's no empire, I tell you! It's only a sham. Empire? Pah! Pirates, that's all we are!' It was Hunegais, of course, the ever moody and gloomy, with his braided black locks and drooping moustaches betraying his Slavonic blood. He sighed gustily, and the Falernian wine slopped over the rim of the jade goblet clenched in his brawny hand, to stain his purple, gilt-embroidered tunic. He drank noisily, after the manner of a horse, and returned with melancholy gusto to his original complaint.

'What have we done in Africa? Destroyed the big land-holders and the priests, set ourselves up as landlords. Who works the land? Vandals? Not at all! The same men who worked it under the Romans. We've merely stepped into Roman shoes. We levy taxes and rents, and are forced to defend the land from the accursed Berbers. Our weakness is in our numbers. We can't amalgamate with the people! We'd be absorbed. We can't make allies and subjects out of them; all we can do is maintain a sort of military prestige – we are a small body of aliens sitting in castles and, for the present, enforcing our rule over a big native population – who, it's true, hates us no worse than they hated the Romans, but—'

'Some of that hate could be done away with,' interrupted Athaulf. He was younger than Hunegais, clean-shaven, and not unhandsome; his manners were less primitive. He was a Suevi, whose youth had been spent as a hostage in the East Roman court. 'They are orthodox; if we could bring ourselves to renounce Arianism—'

'*No!*' Hunegais' heavy jaws came together with a snap

eyes flamed with the fanaticism that was, among all the
Teutons, the exclusive possession of his race. 'Never! We
are the masters! It is theirs to submit – not ours. We *know*
the truth of Arian; if the miserable Africans can not realise
their mistake, they must be made to see it – by torch and
sword and rack, if necessary!' Then his eyes dulled again,
and with another gusty sigh from the depths of his belly, he
groped for the wine jug.

'In a hundred years the Vandal kingdom will be a
memory,' he predicted. 'All that holds it together now is the
will of Genseric.' He pronounced it Geiserich.

The individual so named laughed, leaned back in his
carven ebony chair, and stretched out his muscular legs
before him. Those were the legs of a horseman; but their
owner had exchanged the saddle for the deck of a war galley.
Within a generation, he had turned a race of horsemen into
a race of sea-rovers. He was the king of a race whose name
had already become a term for destruction, and he was the
possessor of the finest brain in the known world.

Born on the banks of the Danube and grown to manhood
on that long trek westward, when the drifts of the nations
crushed over the Roman palisades, he had brought to the
crown forged for him in Spain all the wild wisdom the times
could teach, in the feasting of swords and the surge and
crush of races. His wild riders had swept the spears of the
Roman rulers of Spain into oblivion. When the Visigoths
and the Romans joined hands and began to look southward,
it was the intrigues of Genseric which brought Attila's
scarred Huns swarming westward, tusking the flaming
horizons with their myriad lances. Attila was dead now, and
none knew where lay his bones and his treasures, guarded
by the ghosts of five hundred slaughtered slaves; his name
thundered around the world; but in his day he had been but
one of the pawns moved resistlessly by the hand of the
Vandal king.

And when, after Chalons, the Gothic hosts moved down
through the Pyrenees, Genseric had not waited to be crushed
by superior numbers. Men still cursed the name of Boniface,
who called on Genseric to aid him against his rival, Aetius,
and opened the Vandal's road to Africa. His reconciliation
with Rome had been too late; vain as the courage with
which he had sought to undo what he had done. Boniface

galleys of the Vandals were moving northward, the long oars dipping and flashing silver in the starlight, the great vessels heeling and rocking to the lift of the waves.

And in the cabin of the foremost galley, Genseric listened to the conversation of his captains, and smiled gently as he combed his unruly yellow beard with his muscular fingers. There was in his veins no trace of the Scythic blood which set his race somewhat aside from the other Teutons, from the long ago when scattered steppes-riders, drifting westward before the conquering Sarmatians, had come among the people dwelling on the upper reaches of the Elbe. Genseric was pure German; of medium height, with a magnificent sweep of shoulders and chest, and a massive corded neck, his frame promised as much of physical vitality as his wide blue eyes reflected mental vigor.

He was the strongest man in the known world, and he was a pirate – the first of the Teutonic sea-raiders whom men later called Vikings; but his domain of conquest was not the Baltic nor the blue North Sea, but the sunlit shores of the Mediterranean.

'And the will of Genseric,' he laughed, in reply to Hunegais' last remark, 'is that we drink and feast and let tomorrow take care of itself.'

'So you say!' snorted Hunegais, with the freedom that still existed among the barbarians. 'When did you ever let a tomorrow take care of itself? You plot and plot, not for tomorrow alone, but for a thousand tomorrows to come! You need not masquerade with us! We are not Romans to be fooled into thinking *you* are a fool – as Boniface was!'

'Aetius was no fool,' muttered Thrasamund.

'But he's dead, and we are sailing on Rome,' answered Hunegais, with the first sign of satisfaction he had yet evinced. 'Alaric didn't get all the loot, thank God! And I'm glad Attila lost his nerve at the last minute – the more plunder for us.'

'Attila remembered Chalons,' drawled Athaulf. 'There is something about Rome that lives – by the saints, it is strange. Even when the empire seems most ruined – torn, befouled, and tattered – some part of it springs into life again. Stilicho, Theodosius, Aetius – who can tell? Tonight

Hunegais snorted and hammered on the wine-stained board.

'Rome is as dead as the white mare I rode at the taking of Carthage! We have but to stretch out our hands and grasp the plunder of her!'

'There was a great general once who thought as much,' said Thrasamund drowsily. 'A Carthaginian, too, by God! I have forgotten his name. But he beat the Romans at every turn. Cut, slash, that was his way!'

'Well,' remarked Hunegais, 'he must have lost at last, or he would have destroyed Rome.'

'That's so!' ejaculated Thrasamund.

'We are not Carthaginians,' laughed Genseric. 'And who said aught of plundering Rome? Are we not merely sailing to the imperial city in answer to the appeal of the Empress who is beset by jealous foes? And now, get out of here, all of you. I want to sleep.'

The cabin door slammed on the morose predictions of Hunegais, the witty retorts of Athaulf, the mumble of the others. Genseric rose and moved over to the table, to pour himself a last glass of wine. He walked with a limp; a Frankish spear had girded him in the leg long years ago.

He lifted the jeweled goblet to his lips – wheeled with a startled oath. He had not heard the cabin door open, but a man was standing across the table from him.

'By Odin!' Genseric's Arianism was scarcely skin-deep. 'What do you in my cabin?'

The voice was calm, almost placid, after the first startled oath. The king was too shrewd to often evince his real emotions. His hand stealthily closed on the hilt of his sword. A sudden and unexpected stroke—

But the man made no hostile movement. He was a stranger to Genseric, and the Vandal knew he was neither Teuton nor Roman. He was tall, dark, with a stately head, his flowing locks confined by a dark crimson band. A curling, patriarchal beard swept his breast. A dim, misplaced familiarity twitched at the Vandal's mind as he looked.

'I have not come to harm you!' The voice was deep, strong, and resonant. Genseric could tell little of his attire,

'Who are you, and how did you get into my cabin?' he demanded.

'Who I am, it matters not,' returned the other. 'I have been on this ship since you sailed from Carthage. You sailed at night; I came aboard then.'

'I never saw you in Carthage,' muttered Genseric. 'And you are a man who would stand out in a crowd.'

'I dwell in Carthage,' the stranger replied. 'I have dwelt there for many years. I was born there, and my forefathers before me. Carthage is my life!' The last sentence was uttered in a voice so passionate and fierce that Genseric involuntarily stepped back, his eyes narrowing.

'The folk of the city have some cause of complaint against us,' said he. 'But the looting and destruction was not by my orders. Even then it was my intention to make Carthage my capital. If you suffered loss by the sack, why—'

'Not from your wolves,' grimly answered the other. 'Sack of the city? I have seen such a sack as not even you, barbarian, have dreamed of! They call you barbaric. I have seen what civilised Romans can do.'

'Romans have not plundered Carthage in my memory,' muttered Genseric, frowning in some perplexity.

'Poetic justice!' cried the stranger, his hand emerging from his cloak to strike down on the table. Genseric noted that the hand was muscular yet white, the hand of an aristocrat. 'Roman greed and treachery destroyed Carthage, trade rebuilt her in another guise. Now you, barbarian, sail from her harbors to humble her conqueror! Is it any wonder that old dreams silver the cords of your ships and creep amidst the holds, and that forgotten ghosts burst their immemorial tombs to glide upon your decks?'

'Who said anything of humbling Rome?' uneasily demanded Genseric. 'I merely sail to arbitrate a dispute as to succession—'

'Pah!' Again the hand slammed down on the table. 'If you knew what I know, you would sweep that accursed city clean of life before you turn your prows southward again. Even now, those you sail to aid plot your ruin – and a traitor is on board your ship!'

'What do you mean?' Still there was neither excitement nor passion in the Vandal's voice.

'Suppose I gave you proof that your most trusted companion and vassal plots your ruin with those to whose aid you lift your sails?'

'Give me that proof; then ask what you will,' answered Genseric with a touch of grimness.

'Take this in token of faith!' The stranger rang a coin on the table, and caught up a silken girdle which Genseric himself had carelessly thrown down.

'Follow me to the cabin of your counsellor and scribe, the handsomest man among the barbarians—'

'Athaulf?' In spite of himself, Genseric started. 'I trust him beyond all others.'

'Then you are not as wise as I deemed you,' grimly answered the other. 'The traitor within is to be feared more than the foe without. It was not the legions of Rome which conquered *me* – it was the traitors within my gates. Not alone in swords and ships does Rome deal, but with the souls of men. I have come from a far land to save your empire and your life. In return I ask but one thing: drench Rome in blood!'

For an instant the stranger stood transfigured, mighty arm lifted, fist clenched, dark eyes flashing fire. An aura of terrific power emanated from him, awing even the wild Vandal. Then sweeping his purple cloak about him with a kingly gesture, the man stalked to the door and through it, despite Genseric's exclamation and effort to detain him.

Swearing in bewilderment, the king limped to the door, opened it, and glared out on the deck. A lamp burned on the poop. A reek of unwashed bodies came up from the hold where the weary rowers toiled at their oars. The rhythmic clack vied with a dwindling chorus from the ships which followed in a long ghostly line. The moon struck silver from the waves, shone white on the deck. A single warrior stood on guard outside Genseric's door, the moonlight sparkling on his crested golden helmet and Roman corselet. He lifted his javelin in salute.

'Where did he go?' demanded the king.

'Who, my lord?' inquired the warrior stupidly.

'The tall man, dolt,' exclaimed Genseric impatiently. 'The man in the purple cloak who just left my cabin.'

'None has left your cabin since the lord Hugenais and the others went forth, my lord,' replied the Vandal in bewilderment.

'Liar!' Genseric's sword was a ripple of silver in his hand as it slid from its sheath. The warrior paled and shrank back.

'As God is my witness, king,' he swore, 'no such man have I seen this night.'

Genseric glared at him; the Vandal king was a judge of men and he knew this one was not lying. He felt a peculiar twitching of his scalp, and turning without a word, limped hurriedly to Athaulf's cabin. There he hesitated, then threw open the door.

Athaulf lay sprawled across a table in an attitude which needed no second glance to classify. His face was purple, his glassy eyes distended, and his tongue lolled out blackly. About his neck, knotted in such a knot as seamen make, was Genseric's silken girdle. Near one hand lay a quill, near the other, ink and a piece of parchment. Catching it up, Genseric read laboriously.

To her majesty, the empress of Rome:

I, thy faithful servant, have done thy bidding, and am prepared to persuade the barbarian I serve to delay his onset on the imperial city until the aid you expect from Byzantium has arrived. Then I will guide him into the bay I mentioned, where he can be caught as in a vise and destroyed with his whole fleet, and—

The writing ceased with an erratic scrawl. Genseric glared down at him, and again the short hairs lifted on his scalp. There was no sign of the tall stranger, and the Vandal knew he would never be seen again.

'Rome shall pay for this,' he muttered. The mask he wore in public had fallen away; the Vandal's face was that of a hungry wolf. In his glare, in the knotting of his mighty hand, it took no sage to read the doom of Rome. He suddenly remembered that he still clutched in his hand the coin the stranger had dropped on his table. He glanced at it, and his breath hissed between his teeth, as he recognised the characters of an old, forgotten language, the features of a man which he had often seen carved in ancient marble in old Carthage, preserved from Roman hate.

'Hannibal!' muttered Genseric.